THE FOUND DEMON

AMELIA EVERS

For my lucky lovebug, thank you for being my drop of sunshine on a stormy day.

Chapter One

ALYA

Most kids wouldn't pray for the death of their parents, but I do—every day. I pray to my parents, begging for their death. Hoping one day they will listen and die.

They deserve it more than anyone, along with the rest of the gods and goddesses. They all deserve to die for what they have done to the world, for what they did to me. For turning their backs on me and so many others when we needed their help. They sat back and did nothing when flames consumed the lands. They watched the world drown as the ocean rose. They allowed kids to be stolen from families and people to be murdered. They did nothing when wars began time and time again. They savored the death and destruction, getting high off the thrills and screams of the damned.

They loved it.

They loved every second because they knew that with death comes forgiveness, and the all high and mighty gods want to be worshiped. They want to be the controller of people's fate. People will beg and grovel, asking to be forgiven for whatever crimes and horrors they have committed. They pray to the gods to spare them from eternity in the Below. A few lucky souls bowed low enough, kissed the proper boots, said the right words, and were granted reincarnation. Those are the ones I pity most.

You have few memories of your previous life. You crave what your last life lacked, yet you don't know what it is. You spend that life searching for meaning, for a place to belong, and you will never find it because it doesn't exist. There is no happily ever after when you are granted a second chance. There are no do-overs, no magical lever that will make everything how you want. There is only pain and suffering.

They want it that way.

They want you to suffer, so you will once again beg, asking for guidance, for the light at the end of the tunnel, for a better life. But it will never come. They will never answer you. They have never cared and will never care about the puny life of mortals. Mortals are insignificant, worthless, obedient servants whose only purpose is to boost the ego of an immortal being with immense powers.

That is why I pray for my parents' death every day, twice a day if I am feeling generous. I know they hear me. I know they flinch each time my voice travels through them. I know they are part of why I am sitting in this rotting cell with a thief as my only company.

"You're doing it again," his gruff voice snapped my attention to him.

The light from the hall illuminated enough of the cell to know he was glaring at me, annoyed that I was grinding my teeth. I shifted how I sat on the cold, damp stone. My shackles jingled with the movement and rubbed my already raw wrist more. I didn't dare grit my teeth or groan at the pain of it, knowing I would only be lectured or scolded about ruining my teeth.

As the light shifted, so did the shadows on his face, aged skin, and hair near gray. He was all bones, with little muscle. And somehow, after all these years, he's been a prisoner here; his teeth are the only thing that has shown no signs of aging. He was no more than fifty but looked near seventy. Maybe he had a point. Perhaps I shouldn't clamp my jaw hard or grind my teeth every time I think of my parents.

His hands were behind his head as he lay on the thin bed roll. His head shifted to face my gaunt expression and the glare I had mastered after spending time with Lynn. He returned it with a smirk that showed his perfect teeth, and he had sharpened a few of them into deadly points.

After being locked in a cage with the man for what I believe has been three months, I have learned he is more than a thief. I am still unsure what exactly he is and what crime he committed to get sent here.

He turned his head towards the ceiling and watched a water line trickle across it before he sighed harshly. "Will today be the day?"

I remained silent for precisely three minutes, counting each second in my head, making sure the unanswered question would leave him wanting to know more. "Not unless you tell me the real reason you are here."

He clicked his tongue in a way he knew annoyed me. It was condescending. He treats me like a child even though I am thousands of years older than him. Not that he knows it, though. "Like I said, I stole from the King and Queen's chamber and got caught."

His story has always been the same line, over and over again, like he had rehearsed it. "You say that every time, and yet you never tell me what you stole, Benji," I drawled his name, making him cringe. His hatred for his name amused me.

It was always like this: see who could annoy the other person the most. See what happens when one snaps. Most days, we spar verbally, but some days, it turns into a fight, and the guards must separate us. I can feel it in his blows, him holding back for some reason, but so am I. Our bickering and fights keep us alive, reminding us there is a world outside this miserable cell. But it does more than that. It gives us someone to lean on and talk to and reminds us we are not alone. We never will be as long as it's the two of us.

Benji seemed amused with my taunt, enough to cause him to waste the little energy he had to sit up for no reason. He leaned onto his knees and looked across the cell at me, where I sat on the floor. His sunken brown eyes peered into my own in search of an answer I have never given him; a way to tell the lies I have carefully crafted around the truth.

"What I stole does not matter. It is how I stole it that angered them."

I rolled my eyes. "Here we go again. You hired idiots to keep watch while you snuck in from above and landed in a trap. I know your pathetic attempt, along with all the other guards who watch over this cell block. You have told that story a thousand and one times. No one cares!" I snapped the last bit out louder and harsher than I intended.

My words seemed to have affected him somewhat, enough to make him fall harshly onto his back. He held in the whimper from the pain of impact; I had dealt him a harsh blow and cracked a rib when we last fought, and the guards have not tended it to yet. He, in return, had dislocated my arm. It now made a clicking sound every time I rolled my shoulder forward. I don't think I set it correctly, but the guards didn't care enough to have us looked at.

He let out a puff of air. His words came out quickly in a lie. "I stole the King's cloak."

It was my turn to let out a breath of air as I scoffed. "A liar and a thief. You belong with the rats that run about." I shifted again and toyed with the chains so they didn't tug with my movements. "I have dined with *the* Golden Boy King Esen, I saw his plans of genocide, I saw the darkness within him, and yet he never once raised his voice at a servant unless a life depended on it. He had given a broken girl the clothes off his back. He had cared about the injured. Do you expect me to believe that King Calder cherished a cloak so much he threw you in the dungeons for the rest of your miserable life?" My heart ached at thinking of Esen this much. I haven't allowed myself to grieve for his life or Lynn's. I pushed away all thoughts of them and how the plan failed spectacularly, which resulted in their deaths.

Alden was always supposed to die, and now he sits on the throne meant for Esen.

"Yes. That is exactly what I expect you to believe," Benji snipped his words out. I shook my head in disbelief at what I had just heard.

We sat silently for minutes or hours — I am never sure how much time passed. With the guards changing shifts, maids scurried down with food for the prisoners. The small girl passed the singular tray off to the guard assigned to our cell before she hurried back to her cart and continued handing out one tray to each of the twenty guards. Twenty trays for forty prisoners, ensuring we would go hungry and never have enough strength to do much. Fights were rare but were mainly between Benji and me. None dared go against the guards; few tried, and their deaths swiftly followed. I saw it on my first day here. A young man thought he could overpower them. He took two down before the rest surged water into his lungs, and he drowned on dry land.

It had put enough fear in me to know better than to try something without a plan. To not shift and fly away from this place immediately. I had planned it out my first few weeks here, planned the routes, learned the change of guard, and memorized the minutes it took for meals to be distributed. I was going to fly out of here, and then Benji happened.

He angered a guard because he moved too slowly and received a beating. Healers brought some supplies for me to tend to him, and when I did, I learned about him in bits of delirium. He had been brought here when he was entering adulthood and has been alone since. Each cellmate he got never lasted more than a few days. After the fifth person died, he stopped learning their names. He has been alone for thirty years, with only himself to keep his sanity in check. Knowing that pained me like none other.

I understood the pain of being alone all too well. I have done it since my mother cast me out of the family when she took my wings and gifts. I had been alone for so long, and then two demons came into my life and ruined everything. But as Lynn and Esen died, so did a part of Ove, leaving me alone once more. So I had promised myself that the day Benji leaves will be the day I leave too, so he will never be alone again.

I watched the guard turn towards the cell and pull out his key to open the door. "Against the wall," he barked at us. I didn't recognize the voice — he must be new.

Slowly, the two of us stood facing the wall with our hands absorbing the dampness of it. I listened to his footsteps approaching when they stopped. The tray loudly clattered to the ground. I waited for the sound of his feet walking away and the hinges on the door to creak, but his footsteps grew louder as they got closer.

My back tensed at the warmth seeping off of him and onto me. My stomach dropped to the lowest pit of my body when his hand grazed my shoulders and brushed my hair over it. I could smell the alcohol spilling from his mouth as he leaned into me and whispered, "I like a girl with a little bit of meat on her bones. Lose more weight, and then I will have fun with you."

I heard a snarl from beside me as I shut my eyes tight. I am the only woman in this cell block. It's a fear I live with daily, but it has yet to happen. And this new guard was about to unleash my greatest fear.

Benjis' snarl caught the guards' attention. I didn't dare move even after his body was no longer pressed into mine or even after I heard Benjis' body get slammed into the wall. I stood there trying to stop my hands from shaking and find the courage to open my eyes.

"So a rat thinks he can play with a lion?" The guard's voice was haunting, chilling my bones, making me angrily shake. I wanted to pray to my family to ask them to spare Benji, but they wouldn't listen.

I hated this with every second that passed—waiting to see what Benji would say, if he would say anything to protect me. But he didn't, or he couldn't.

I focused on breathing like Esen had taught me, counting the inhales, holding them, and counting the exhales. How much time had passed? How long had I stood there shaking? I could kill him if I knew it didn't mean a certain death for Benji. I had watched Lynn enough to know how to use my shackles to my advantage, to go for the groin or maybe his eyes. Whichever one I could get to first, but I couldn't move because another person's life was on the line, and that was why I shook so horribly.

The warmth and stench of alcohol returned to my body as he once more pressed me into him. A gloved hand grabbed my face, bringing it up towards his own, and he licked the side of my face, dirt and all. I scowled at the act and the feeling of his wet tongue. The sound of pleasure in his throat turned my body to stone.

"The guards say you scream the name of another man in your sleep. You'll be screaming mine by the time I am done with you," he purred into my ears.

And that was what sent Benji into a rage. His roar of anger forced me to open my eyes and see him lunge for the guard, who stepped back, ready for a fight. As drained as he was, he moved swiftly, but the shackles around his ankles slowed him enough for me to reach out and grab onto him.

My arms wrapped around his stomach, and I could feel his intestines shift around my arm. His bones jabbed into me as he fought against my hold, still ready to kill the guard. His voice echoed through the cell out into the hall, carrying a promise, "I will kill you if you touch her again!"

The guard laughed at the sight of me struggling to keep Benji from tearing the man's face off. "I look forward to the day, rat." The guard walked out of the cell and locked us in once more.

I waited until he returned to his post to let go of Benji to ensure the man's face was no longer in our view. "May goddess Aniya curse the air you breathe." Benji spat on the ground towards the cell door.

I flinched hearing her name. It was one that I hadn't heard in a long time.

Goddess Aniya, the true goddess of the seven winds and guide of hearts. She is the one who pushes people to their soulmate. She is the goddess who unleashes winds in all directions. For him to say a curse in a gentle goddess's name was peculiar.

Neither of us said anything more while we ate the stale piece of bread and cold soup that had been given to us to share. We sipped the water sparingly to ensure it lasted until the next mealtime. We said nothing as we curled up with one another on the bedroll to share our warmth.

It wasn't until I was about to drift to sleep when Benji whispered to me, "Who's Eilam?"

Chapter Two

OVE

It was the same every night; the stunning white bird was locked in a bronze cage, desperately trying to find a way out. Her wings harshly collided with the bars with each flap of her wings. With each beating, the cage shuddered but did not break. My voice did nothing to calm her down. It never passed my lips or beak; whichever form I took had no voice. Her chirps were pained and panicked, but it never sounded like they were for her. They were for the small lump of brown fur that was curled up so tightly I couldn't make out what animal it was.

Not even when the water flowed, and the cage submerged into it, drowning both of the animals where her cries for herself.

A cool breeze crossed my face, tickling the hairs on my head enough to wake me up. I let out a shaky breath and sat up in my bed. Looking around the room, I was greeted with a haunting familiarity of the place I once yearned for. The same dark stone walls reflected the many candles spread throughout the room. My bed sat against the wall facing the door with lavish and plush blankets thrown about. My small desk was cluttered with drawings from Lynn that she had done in her youth, but they had since stopped coming.

It is a reminder of what happened three months ago and how we failed, how Lynn failed for the first time in her life, and how she has been punished for it ever since.

Dearil allowed me into the room when she woke up from being unconscious because of Esen ripping all the air out of her lungs. He had left the blade in her chest so she could pull it out on her own, and she had. She pulled out the steel blade I masked as her own, knowing Alden would steal it from his brother and use it against her.

We had planned for it, made sure he knew the blade was the only one that could kill her if stabbed in her heart, and made sure he knew the power of names. We planned every part until Esen took his own life instead of avenging Lynn. We had overestimated his love for her, and we were blind not to make the connection about his prophecy referring to the lighting markings throughout her horns.

We failed.

Lynn failed.

I failed.

I hadn't seen her for a month after that. Then she came to my room, frail and thin. She had no expression when she told me about Dearil's plans for us. We were to wed officially. And every part of that damn ceremony had been a punishment for the both of us. Dearil dressed her like a whore, forced her to walk down the aisle even though she puked as she walked in. He had snarled his rage at her when his eyes landed on the scar between her breasts. She never let the injury heal properly, and it angered him. Once the ceremony started, they brought a blonde mortal girl out. I had felt myself flinch at seeing the similarities she held to Alya. Both had glorious curves that deserved to be worshiped and blonde hair that looked like it flowed with its own wind. But the eyes were different; they were brown instead of a stunning blue.

Dearil had us kill her and stand over her body to solidify the union. As we said our promises to one another, Lynn's lips trembled with her words.

"I will love you until the end."

I had tried to console her after once we were in my room, our room. But she said nothing as she stripped naked and laid there for me to fuck. I hated every second of it, and I know she did too because once we were done, she cried and cried and cried until Trevv took her away.

He took her from me and was fulfilling a promise he had made to her, to take her away from me, from Esen and Alya. He locked her away somewhere even my shadows couldn't find. But once a week, he allowed her to see me. I could tell by the disgust on his face it was not of his choosing but of Dearils.

Every Tuesday, he allowed her to see me so I could get an heir from her and secure my claim to the throne before I even needed to take it. I have grown to cherish Tuesdays, not for the sex, but because I get to see her and know she is alive.

And today is Tuesday.

In a few hours, I can hold her and comfort her as she cries into my chest, arms, or legs, or however she lies for the hour we have together.

As I rub her shoulder, I fake the moans for both of us; my shadows work on her hair, making it tangled. Each week, we do this repeatedly, but not once do we have sex. I won't allow it, no matter how hard she pushes herself onto me. I can't break her more than she already broke herself.

I wait for her patiently, knowing what is to come soon.

***

The gentle knock on my door had me on my feet. Adri led Lynn in as the door opened; she had grown thin. Her hair lacked life, and her eyes no longer shone brightly; she didn't walk purposefully. The Lynn I have known and loved was gone. The woman before me was a ghost of what she had been.

The two stepped into the room, Lynn leaning heavily on Adri, using her as a crutch to make her way over to the bed. She disappeared under the sheets. Not a speck of her or her raggedy gown was to be seen.

My heart shattered seeing her like this. Turning to Adri, she wore a similar pained expression on her human face. Her dark skin made her blue eyes stand out. They had yet to leave Lynn's tiny body. She turned to go when I stopped her.

"I never thanked you for that day. You released the arrow as a warning. Thank you. I am sorry we didn't notice it sooner. I hope Dearil's punishment wasn't too harsh." She said nothing in return. "And thank you for holding back in the fight."

She held onto the door handle and looked back at me. "When you become king, make him suffer like he has made us all suffer."

Adri left before I could tell her I would. I have been planning on ruining his life since the day he first laid hands on Lynn, and I had planned on killing him when he took my mother's life. He will pay, and so will his court.

I waited for the sound of her to disappear into the hall. Once she did, I joined Lynn in the bed and found her curled up as a ball under all the blankets and sheets. She quickly clung to my bad leg, her nails digging into it as she wept.

For the next hour, we did not say one word to each other. My shadows did their job, and I faked my way through it. Every second of that hour was miserable, but I was with her, and that was all that mattered. I could provide a sanctuary for her in her time of need. I will never leave her. I will never hurt her.

Adri came back looking even more solemn than she had when she left. "Adri, I am leaving for a few days for a prisoner exchange with the King." I looked down at Lynn and let out a heartbroken sigh. "Take care of her while I am gone."

I didn't want to leave her, but this was my father's first recognition of me in a royal matter. I can't refuse. And prison exchanges have always sounded entertaining in the stories I have heard from others. With the war going on, there have been several prisoner exchanges, and the advisors of the Courts have dealt with them. But this one is different. They asked for the Kings of the Courts to attend. Dearil thought it would be a good learning experience for me, and my only order is to sit and watch. To never speak unless he allows it.

Lynn's eyes looked up at me, pleading for me not to leave. Or was she pleading not to be taken away again?

"I am afraid I can't do that for you, Prince Ove. The remaining Ghosts are going with you. He has called them all back for this. We are to serve as the royal guard," Adri's smooth voice was calm, but I could hear and see its warning.

Whoever is being traded is astronomical to this war and will probably lead to bloodshed.

I looked back at Lynn. Her eyes were a harsh storm. I could see her calculating something, planning, thinking. She knew something, but that storm quickly faded, and she was gone again.

Adri bowed her head and led Lynn out of the room, shutting the door behind them. Something deep within me awoke, tugging me to chase after them. And I did.

The door flew open, and I saw them walking down the hall. "Lynnora!" They both halted. She looked over her shoulder, waiting for me to catch up, to say something. I went to speak, but no words came out. I didn't know what to say or do. I know sometimes words can offer no comfort, and whatever had broken her had done it so well that no ounce of hope could pull her out. Nothing could save her besides herself, and she didn't want to be saved.

"Take what you want, and don't give a damn," I whispered to myself.

I walked towards her, cupping her face, and pulled it up. "Don't forget where you started. You'll make it one day. I know you will." Placing a kiss on her brow, she leaned into me, her bony arms tightly wrapped around my stomach.

"I'll take it all for you. All of it," she whispered into my chest and let go of me.

I watched the two of them walk away once more. Adri's arm wrapped around Lynn, guiding her as she put her weight on the fourth Ghost, the Ghost of Leevah.

In order of sheer terror, Lynn is the most formidable, followed by Ava, then Adri. But Adri is the fourth eldest Ghost at age twenty-four. She has been a Ghost since she was nineteen and quickly earned the respect she deserved, but she never strives for more. She never competed for Dearil's attention. Instead, she loathed him. It was subtle, but I could pick it out after years of knowing her. She spent most of her time spying on King Elior of the Leevah Court. The sun branded on her neck was a thin white line, similar to most of the citizens of the desert.

She is the only Ghost who has successfully infiltrated their court and lives within it without concern about being discovered. The souls that come through speak highly of her and the generosity she has shown them and their court. Dearil punishes her for each soul who speaks highly of her. I had been unfortunate to be in the room when he heard about the gentle Ghost, and I was the one who dealt some of her punishments on his behalf. Not once has she held it against me; she always looks at me with pity and scowls at the King.

They disappeared around the corner when a man's voice sounded, "Lynn?"

Adri growled, "Leave her alone, bastard."

I wanted to crawl into a hole or have someone defend me like that when Trevv walked around the corner. His soft expression immediately hardened when he saw me. His black eyes had no light, love, or anything good shining. His shoulder-length black hair was pulled back in a bun. His curled horns had pieces missing from fights. The top of one of his pointed ears was completely missing. Before Dearil had summoned him to be his advisor, he was well known among the soldiers, just as any Rahm demon is. Their ability to go to the mortal realm and pass as humans only lasts one hour before they shift back. Dearil uses them on the front lines, makes men think their kind has turned against them, and then once their time is up, they shift back and cause damage.

Even though Lynn is a Maliva because of the genetic mutation, she still has some characteristics of the Rahm. Her horns and ears. Her tail and teeth come from her mother, a Kasts. They, unfortunately, do not have a mortal form and are seen as servants or pets because of their submissive nature.

"Ove," he drawled my name out with disgust.

Pretending to straighten the lapels on my shirt, I drawled his name out. "Trevv. What do you want? I was a little busy fucking your daughter."

He snarled at me, and his shadows grew around me, casting a chill in the air. Allowing my shadows to fight back, I heard their whispers taunting his shadows into him. He scowled at me. "Your father wants you."

I tsked, "Still playing messenger for him, I see."

"Still an insufferable prick?" He questioned me as we met each other halfway in the hall.

Shrugging my shoulders, I brushed past him. "Lynn seems to enjoy suffering in my company." I hated this. I hate using her to get to him, but she is his only weakness.

His weight slammed into me, shoving me against the wall and pinning me to it. "Watch that tongue of yours, boy. Mommy can't save you this time."

His words stung more than I care to admit. She was gone. Dearil had killed her. Shoving the pain deep inside of me, I smirked at him. "I don't need her to save me. Your daughter, however, still needs her daddy to save her. Which one of us will it be, then?" His hand struck my face, leaving a stinging sensation long after his hand fell away. I kept my calm and smirked. "Lynn's favorite word is harder. Maybe that will be my new favorite word, too."

Trevv dropped me and growled, his eyes darkened, begging for a fight. I raised my brow, telling him to strike. He charged at me with a typical Rahm fighting style. Head first to use the horns to ram into the opponent. Quickly stepping to the side, it lowered his head enough to expose his back. Bringing my elbow down on his spine, he let out a howl of pain. He switched his styles to a mortal style, hand to hand.

Stupid fool.

My shadows did all the work. Many of them had once been fighters and were begging to be used. They solidified and struck him over and over. Each time he tried to punch them, they turned back into the air, not taking any damage. He was growing angrier and angrier with each failed blow. He yelled out angrily as he approached me and ran into a solid wall of my shadows. His fists beat on it, searching for a weak spot, his shadows trying to freeze it.

It won't work. Only Dearil has ever successfully gotten through my shadows.

Digging dirt out from under my nails, I looked at him. "It's a shame you are using all this energy to fight me instead of helping your daughter. What would her mother say if she knew you failed your only child?" I knew bringing up Lynn's mother would strike harder than any attack. Her death had broken him.

His hands fell away from my shadows. "You deserve all the pain that is going to come." Trevv walked away, leaving me in the hall.

I kept the solid wall up, separating us a few paces back in case he tried to strike again. The door to Dearil's study came into view, and the guards opened it for us.

The room was dark, but the one fireplace lit the room up, showing the massive desk, bookshelves, and the two individuals who sat at the desk.

Dearil's sharp teeth were hidden, but I could feel them waiting to rip my throat out. The girl sitting across from him turned to face me. Ava had a mischievous smile on her face.

The Demon King waved Trevv off without explanation, and he did not protest as he shut the door behind him. Bowing my head, I took the other open seat. The oversized leather chair was worn in and had a faint smell of something.

He began speaking, "Ava has an interesting theory about why Lynn is not yet with the child." He gestured to her for her to fill me in.

"I believe you are not being satisfied until completion or that your manhood is not working properly."

My eyes went wide with astonishment. I didn't care whose presence I was in or what my outburst would cause; I would not let my *manhood* be insulted by a psychotic bitch. "I can assure you it works just fine, and I am satisfied each time with my wife."

"Ove!" Dearil snapped at me. He leaned back into his chair enough to show me his disheveled clothing. That's what the stench was. He and Ava had entertained one another, and I now sat in the chair they screwed in. She wants everything Lynn has. If she can't get me, then my father would do.

The King continued, "You have yet to get any of your other whores pregnant, so I am wondering if you are the issue and not Lynn as I had originally thought. If that is the case, our lineage must continue another way."

I grabbed onto the edge of the seat, my nails digging into it. "And how do you propose we do that if I am what you claim?" There was not a chance in Below that I am infertile. I thought I would be after my burning, but the healer assured me I wasn't.

"You divorce her, and I make her my wife. I should have done so from the start."

No.

The cruel king smiled at me. I did nothing to hide the shock or horror I now felt. "You have three months to sire an heir. After that, I will do it and label him as king."

No.

I looked at Ava, who was smiling with pleasure. This was her plan to get me away from Lynn so she could take me for herself.

I can't allow any of this to happen. I have to protect Lynn.

CHAPTER THREE

LYNNORA

I was numb that day and still am, but that day was the day I accepted the feeling. Dearil had dressed me in sheer fabric, all parts of my body to be seen by those who attended our wedding. Nothing was left to the imagination. The doors to the ballroom had opened, and that was when things fell apart.

I had forced myself to hold my head high even after puking, but it pained me because everywhere I looked, I saw Esen. My guilt grew and quickly multiplied, cascading through me like an avalanche. I had done this to myself; I had killed the one person who ever saw the good in me. Even after the demon king had forced me into something I didn't want to become, Esen still saw me for me.

I could feel how wide my eyes were with panic as they looked between each guest and only saw Esen. All of them were waiting for me to walk down the aisle. I remember Ove standing on the dais at the altar with a weak smile, one he forced to be there. The hush between the few guests as they waited for me to walk, to do something, was unnerving.

But I couldn't.

I was frozen as the avalanche inside me coursed through my veins. I forced myself down that aisle to my patient groom, and as the vows were being said, I saw Esen's face again.

Even now, as I look at Ove, all I see is the man I killed because I was wrong. Esen was not what I thought he was, and I paid the price for it.

I killed the Golden Boy, King Esen.

I killed him.

I did it.

I failed.

And I lost everything.

Chapter Four

OVE

They had sent the invitation out to all nine kings. Whoever was being traded must be important. Dearil did not clue me in who it was or what court they belonged to. A part of me wonders if he knows.

My wings tucked in tightly, my talons holding firm on the tip of the mast as the ship gently swayed with the waves. We were playing our role nicely; we arrived two days early out of the Below and secured ourselves a ship, hanging the black flag with a silver bone on its mast. We anchored off the island coast to wait for a day before returning to where we started.

The Isle of Blessed is the gateway into the Below, but no one knows its secret besides the gods and demons. We had planned for it; we arrived early so none would see the eight of us come through, and we planned to sail South for a day before returning here once we were done. Our ancestors have always sailed South to ensure the illusion of us leaving.

Below me were shouts of the men as they were readying to lower the anchor and preparing the rowboats to take us to the island. Its shores are too shallow and filled with a reef that will destroy any ship that tries to go through it.

The dark sky was slowly turning blue and orange, masking the stars that had been shining brightly. The new light illuminated the water and the small island that was not far out, and I could see the single building. Nine spiral pillars held its domed roof up. Looking around the island, I saw two ships lowering boats—one from the North bearing a green banner with a leaf. My eyes floated down to the six Ghosts. Looking over at them, I found Iris with her poison daggers strapped to her side; she was assigned to Ter and King Ellev.

The boat closest to us bore the banner of Leevah Court. Adri was already looking at it and trying to see who was aboard. Even I needed help to make out who was on there or getting onto the small row boat meant to carry them inland.

Scanning the ocean again, the rest of the ships appeared as the sun's rays exposed them. One by one, I surveyed them, assessing who would be a threat, questioning if the Ghosts would willingly reveal who they were if it meant protecting us. Ivy, the other half of Iris, belonged to King Calder of the Auk Court. Kay and her sword assassinate and spy in the Dahr Court. Natalia hides in the shadows of Fahir's flames. Her sisters call her the Silent Reaper. And then there is Ava, with her unhealthy obsession with King Myor of the Sparan Court. She thinks that since Lynn made Esen fall in love with her, she will do the same with her King.

Seven out of nine kings had shown. I didn't expect Daxon to show. He doesn't care for anyone other than himself. But I had expected Alden to show.

Water splashed below us. The boat holding Dearil and the six Ghosts were rowing to the island. Leave it to my father to forget me. Pushing off the mast, I soared to the boat and landed on its ledge. My father gave me a look of disapproval. Making room on the bench, I shifted back.

The unexpected weight rocked the boat, forcing me to fall into Ava's lap. She grinned broadly down at me. Before I could push myself off her, Adri was already pulling me up and scowling at the girl. I nodded my thanks to her and once more faced my father.

"Hoods and masks up," he ordered the girls. They all obeyed. He had dressed them for his pleasure. They wore a floor-length skirt that only had fabric covering their asses and a thin strip down the front. All six had identical black boots that went past their knees. They each wore a different top that only covered their breasts. They clasped a hood around their throats, supporting a mask covering their mouth and noses.

Their muscles were showing with each movement of the boat. Was that why he dressed them like this? To intimidate the Kings and their men. To tell them if they pick a fight, it will be against women who will win. Whatever the reason may be, I'm not too fond of it. I don't trust him with the Ghosts. He uses them for whatever purpose and doesn't ask for their permission. Then again, I do things without asking permission.

"Why isn't Lynn here?" She was his right-hand soldier, his favorite Ghost. Before he sent her to Arymn, she went wherever he went.

I could see the look in his black eyes, contemplating telling me. "She is far too valuable to bring here."

I didn't say anything in return. The boat continued to push through the gentle waves as we got closer to the island. Ivy and Iris stopped rowing, and the boat hit the sand. Natalia and Kay lept gracefully, pulling the boat further onto the sand and out of the water. The six Ghosts stood in a semi-circle, surveying the land as King Dearil and I exited the boat. They quickly fell into a complete circle around us as we approached the single building.

He cut me a glare as if to say; *you know your orders, and you don't need to speak aside from introductions.*

I nodded my understanding and stayed silent as we entered the building I was all too familiar with.

There were no walls. Instead, it was nine spiral pillars holding up the dome roof. At the base of each pillar was a throne made of sandstone. Each throne had the emblem of the King it sat. In the middle of the room held the portal to the Below, but all others see it as a table showing the world's stars.

I have always disliked this place; the gods built it, and with it, they cast magic that prohibited the use of magic. They wanted to ensure that kings could not be killed in a meeting. Each time I go through here, I can feel my gifts dampen as they crawl into a space inside me to recoil from the magic of the gods.

Two Kings were already on their thrones, with their advisors standing beside them and their guards behind them. I looked over at King Kaj of Ter. His slim frame and pale skin were not what took me by surprise. The emerald green eyes looked like they knew all the world's secrets.

I bowed. "King Kaj, it is a pleasure to meet you," I spoke in the language of the Kings. Only high-ranked members of the court know it. The Ghosts have yet to be included in learning it. Dearil does not deem them worthy enough, but I must know it since I will one day be King.

Kaj remained in his seat and looked me over. "Prince Ove, I presume?"

"Yes, Your Majesty."

Voices filled the room. Bowing my head again, the room quickly filled with kings, advisors, guards, and either queens or mistresses. With each one, I said my hellos and introduced myself. I remembered my schooling of each king and challenged myself to know who was who without looking at the branding on their neck.

King Calder of Auk Court had brown hair and a beard. His ivory skin looks permanently wet. Hakan from Fahir Court has reddish eyes from all the smoke in his domain. His short gray beard stands out against his tan skin, and he is also the oldest at fifty-three.

King Myor has similarities to Esen, both blonde and fit, but Myor's brown eyes look like lighting is coursing through them. King Kek of Dahr is the second eldest at age fifty but looks the oldest and most frail. And then there is King Elior of Leevah with his eternal youth. His gold eyes shine brightly no matter how the light is being cast on them. He wore tan pants and an oversized tan shirt that showed his sculpted chest. His dark skin was stunning, with no mark other than a scar down his neck. His beard was twisted into braids, as was his hair.

Conversation flowed effortlessly between allies but hardened by the enemy. King Calder, Kaj, and Elior conversed while others did the same. Advisors all talked to one another, but there was no Trevv, and it was a relief not to have to worry about him today as well.

Sticking with the Ghosts, I surveyed each king carefully. Watching how they interacted with those around them, who were hostile to whom, what was being said, and by whom. If Lynn is away from here to do her job, I will do my best and fill her in if she asks.

There has been no sign of a prisoner, no inclination as to who called for the meeting. Others were realizing it as well.

"Why am I here?" Myor snapped at his advisor, who stammered in search of a response.

"Calder, did you call for us? Rumor has it you have an important prisoner in your deepest dungeon." Hakan questioned the Auk King, who shrugged his shoulder and did not reply.

I have heard about his prison. Once you go in, the only way out is in a coffin. You never leave it.

Kaj and Elior were mumbling, too quiet for me to hear. I looked at Iris to see if she could or knew, but she kept her eyes locked on Dearil as he approached the two Kings and clamped his hands onto their shoulders.

"Come now, let us sit and discuss." Dearil's calm demeanor was fooling no one. They all know he is the sadist among them. He is a monster in disguise.

None wanting to argue with him, they all took their thrones. Staying in my spot beside my father, the Kings all looked at me, carefully examining me and trying to figure out what type of man I am and what type of King I would become. I was watching them, too, seeing who would be a threat. So far, only Myor seems to be itching for a fight. The rest are sensible enough to know that the way to settle any disagreements from today will be on the battlefield.

There has been so much bloodshed in the three months since it started. Dearil hadn't wasted a moment. The second our feet entered the Below with word that Esen was dead, the battles began. He had men already stationed throughout Nevano and was waiting for the time to strike. Our failure granted it.

Dearil began the questioning, "Why are we here, Calder?"

King Calder took offense by not being addressed with his title and for being accused of something. "I did not summon you imbeciles."

"So you do not have a blonde-haired beauty in your keep?" Hakan asked disappointingly.

My stomach churned, Alya. Last I knew of her, Alden tried to make her his mistress even though he had yet to wed. I felt guilty leaving her behind, but I had no choice. Lynn and I needed to keep up the appearance of her death, and Alya had unfortunately not listened when we told her to leave.

Her broken voice still haunts me, the cries for Lynn and Esen. She suffered like the rest of us did, but worse. She still believes Lynn is dead. Could that be her that Hakan is talking about? No, she is brilliant. She wouldn't allow herself to get caught, and we ensured that there was no proof of tying her to Esen's death. She was an innocent bystander.

Accusations kept getting thrown about to the point I shut them out and sunk into the bottomless black pit within myself. My thoughts on Alya and if she was suffering because of us. If we had unknowingly done this to her. How would we get her out? If she would forgive us for it, for all of it.

A feminine snicker sounded behind me, followed by a hiss. Something that was said was entertaining one of the Ghosts, no doubt Ava. And one elder was putting her in her place.

Looking around the room again, the Kings were all still arguing, sides being established. But Elior kept staring at me. No, he stared at my hand and the thin white line on my finger. The only scar I genuinely liked was because a small bird nipped my finger. Something so simple and humane had left a scar on a demon. It was astounding, and I cherished it.

Elior spoke to the Kings despite his eyes still on my hand. "If none of you summoned us, I am leaving before *this* becomes another war among Kings."

He rose when footsteps sounded behind us. All eyes looked at the man walking into the pavilion. King Alden of Arymn Court.

His green eyes landed on me, and he sneered. His men were carrying a box, but there was no sign of an advisor or Alya. Only Vince, the general and spymaster. Had he been promoted? Vince looked at me with pity but continued to his spot beside Alden's throne.

"What is the meaning of this, Alden? Call us here and then show up late!" Calder snapped at the new King. Calders' lack of announcing Alden's new title was not because of being in an alliance with him but because he did not respect Alden or see him as King. We could all hear the disdain in his voice.

Alden did not answer; instead, he stared at Dearil and me. His men set the box down close to us when he spoke. "I called you all here today to return a demon to its master."

Shock and curiosity spread through me like wildfire. Demons do not get taken as prisoners of war. Their time limit in bodies is too short, so if they get caught, the body dies, and they return to the Below. Those capable of being in mortal form for prolonged periods are all accounted for.

Alden made a mistake.

"What is it you want in exchange for this prisoner?" Dearil questioned the King. All others had fallen silent, patiently waiting to see who was inside the box and what the Demon King would exchange for it.

Alden smirked at me and tilted his head. "I want Lynnora Fenwald dead."

"Consider it done if the one inside the box is useful to me." Dearil did not hesitate to answer back. He did nothing to negotiate. He will kill Lynn for a demon he doesn't know.

I looked at my father silently, begging him not to agree to these terms. He has said she is far too important. He ignored my plea.

Alden waved his hand, and his men opened the box, tipping it onto its side as a man spilled out.

Holy gods, no.

How?

How is he whole?

How is he alive?

His chest rose steadily as if he was in a deep slumber. A forked tongue hung out of his mouth, and two large fangs were displayed. Even from here, I could smell the poison that was coating them.

The last Serpence demon is Esen. With each death, his skin is shed and made anew. His blonde hair has turned golden brown, filled with dirt, and caked in blood. His muscles were still well-defined. They had shackled his wrists and ankles.

Alden smirked. "If you do not want him, then Mjor will be pleased to take him and punish him for what he had planned."

Dearil motioned for the Ghosts to collect him and take him.

No.

If he takes him, he will kill him and then hold up his end of the bargain and kill Lynn. Something deep and primal stirred within me as their hands reached for his body. And then he was gone.

I couldn't see him. I couldn't smell the poison on his fangs. He was gone.

A gasp traveled through the kings and their people, and they looked around to see where he had vanished. None showed any inclination where Esen's body went.

Dearil shrugged his shoulders. "I suppose the deal is off, then." He rose and walked away with the Ghosts. "Ove, stay behind in case he shows up. Kill him if he does."

I nodded my understanding and stayed where he had left me. My eyes focused on the spot he vanished from. How could a grown man disappear like that? He was unconscious; he had no control over his body.

Conversations flowed, minutes passed, then hours, and he had yet to reappear. Kings and their guards slowly left. Most of Dearil's alliance left the minute he was gone. Alden and Elior were all that was left.

Alden rose from his throne and patted my shoulder. "Ayla sends her regards." He paused and chuckled to himself. "I'm sure that's what she would want me to say if she was still with me." A hiss sounded behind me, one that I was familiar with. Adri was with me, at least.

With those words, he confirmed what I had been fearing at this meeting. Alya was in Auk's prison.

Elior looked me over and gestured for me to sit on my father's throne. Not wanting to be rude, I did so. The moment my back touched the chair, Esen's body lay before me exactly where we had all last seen it.

My eyes were wide with horror and amazement, expecting Adri to make a move to take the body. Instead, she went and stood beside King Elior. Removing her mask and hood, she planted a kiss on his cheek.

He smiled widely up at her, taking her hand and patting it. I was too stunned to speak. Words had failed me before, but never like this. Three monumental things occurred in thirty seconds. I didn't know where to start.

CHAPTER FIVE

ALYA

In the days since Benji asked me about telling him who Eilam was, I never told him, but I thought about it. What that man did for me, who I am. I thought about all of it—every second of every day. We were locked in a cell with nothing to discuss, yet talking was the only thing that kept us from going insane.

Each night was the same, too. The new guard, whom Benji and I have started calling Lion, came in to deliver dinner, and with each meal, he grabbed onto a part of me, licked my face, and left.

Benji kept his anger in check. There had been no more outbursts from him, and I endured every miserable second of it. We had discussed telling the captain of the guard, but we knew he wouldn't listen. We are prisoners; we are nobody to them. So I slept every night in fear that Lion would come in and do as he pleased.

Benji's frail body brought me comfort as I clung to him each night, afraid that if I let go of him, one of us would vanish. He held onto me tightly and then would pray to his favorite goddess, Aniya, to look over us through the night. I never told him she was not listening and would do nothing for us. I didn't want to take away the shred of hope he still clung to.

The guards changed, and Lion left us in peace; our usual day guard brought our breakfast. Benji and I sat around the tray, savoring the bread and thinly sliced meat. I looked at Benji and found the words to the question I had been festering on.

"Benji, why does seeing the Lion act like that with me anger you so much?"

He paused and let out a shaky breath before answering. "Aside from the fact that what he is doing is wrong and foul, it is personal for me. — I had an elder sister once, and I was there the day she was murdered. She told me to hide in the closet and not to watch. I hid, but I watched. I still can't get her screams out of my mind. The man who killed her decided he wanted more from her." Benji nervously rubbed his hands together. "He raped her, then he killed her. The worst part is, he still wanted more from her, so he raped her again, and again, long after her body went cold."

Tears fell down his face. "I-" I released a heartbroken sigh and moved to him, pulling him into my arms. "I'm sorry you had to see that and that she had to endure that. I promise to fight and kill the bastard if he takes it further than he has."

"You shouldn't kill him. I will do it for you."

An unspoken agreement sparked between us, as did my need to tell him why I was here. "I killed King Esen."

His head shifted, and he looked up at me. "Why?"

"It doesn't matter why, just that I did." I reiterated the words he once said to me. I never killed Esen, but Alden needed someone alive to take the blame. He was willing to protect me until I turned his advances down. I would rather rot away than serve the cruel King who killed my friend.

Benji said nothing. He just pulled me in closer to him.

We finished our meal with our usual verbal spar. We continued until the guard came to the door and let us out for the afternoon. Once a week, our cell block is allowed to go outside into a courtyard.

It technically isn't outside. We are still trapped in a dome deep under the water, but it's fresh air. We get to see fish and other sea creatures swim past us. It is the only sense of normalcy we get. Most prisoners here are all from the Auk Court or have committed a crime against their court.

Upon entrance, they put us through a rigorous test, establishing our ability to use our gift. From there, they put us through an examination of our characteristics and the crimes we committed. Those of us with no trace of the gift and are deemed dangerous get sent to one of the lower cell blocks, hoping to deprive us of the world above. They intend to break us, to sculpt us into something useful for them. They do the same for those who are extraordinarily gifted. To our keepers, we are nothing more than a tool to be used. The sooner we break, the sooner we can be used.

Once I learned why I was placed in that cell block and heard Benji's story, I knew he was lying. Thieves don't get brought down that far, only the wicked and the damned.

As we stepped outside, a massive white sea serpent passed by the glass dome. Light from above the water was trickling down in small fragments. Massive mirrors surrounded the dome, reflecting the light and illuminating the otherwise dark courtyard.

Benji and I went over to our usual table that held cards. Taking our seats, we began a game, slapping the jack each time it was shown, and the winner collected the pile beneath it. Minutes passed slowly as the game progressed. Benji was winning, and with each pile, he claimed, his smile grew wider and wider.

I watched his eyes glance over my shoulder, and his grin faltered.

"What?" I asked him, not daring to look over my shoulder.

His throat bobbed. "Lion picked up a shift."

If I looked over my shoulder, the guard would take that as an invitation and approach. "Keep your head down and continue with the game," I hissed at him.

Benji gulped and did as I said. The game continued without interruption; I had one card left in my hand when he set everything down. "Come with me."

I didn't question it and followed him to the weights and punching bag. My shackles jingled with each step. He positioned himself behind the punching bag, using his shoulders to brace it.

"Punch it, Alya, he is watching. Punch it and show him you are not one to be fucked with, that you know how to fight back."

I didn't move, shaking my head. "No, if he attacks me, then won't having the element of surprise work in my favor?"

Benji rolled his eyes. "Always one step ahead of your opponent. This time, let him think he is one step ahead of you. Let him see your strength. Let him underestimate it. Let it boost his ego by seeing your weak punches. He will love the challenge. Once he attacks, then you can beat the shit out of him."

"What makes you think he will attack me and he isn't playing some sick mind game?"

He let out a sigh. "You are getting smaller every day, and I know he sees it because he left hard last time. He means to do exactly what he said he would do. Now punch the fucking bag, Alya!"

I had felt the Lion pressed against me and had hoped I was imagining it, but I knew each day I sat in the cell, I was getting smaller and smaller. The clothes they had given me now hang off me. I was becoming weak, the very thing I had promised never to become.

I ground my teeth at the thought of that, at the horrors of my past coming back to me. The fire I once was had been dwindling to embers deep within me. I had long since forgotten the promises I made to myself. The scars on my back stung, the muscles that no longer exist twitching, pleading to be used. How many promises to myself have I forgotten?

There's been so many I have lost count.

That ember roared to life, and with it came a new set of promises for myself and others. Ones that I will never break because if I do, then I will die with them.

I struck the bag.

I promise never to belittle myself again.

Punch.

I promise to defend those in need.

Punch.

I promise to avenge Lynn.

Punch.

I promise to save Benji.

Punch.

I promise to kill the gods.

Punch.

I promise to live, not just survive.

Punch.

I promise to take back what was stolen from me.

With each punch, my knuckles ran red. The skin tore more and more. Blood trickled onto my bony fingers, smearing the bag with each strike. Again and again. Over and over. My body roared through the pain of using my muscles to a full extent.

Never again will I let another define who I am. Never again will I let a man touch me without my permission. Never again will I let another use me for their gain. Never again will I let my parents fuck with me. Never again will I lose those I care about, those I love. Never again. Never again.

This is my life, not theirs. I will live it how I deem worthy. I will live a life worth telling. I will live the life I once dreamed of.

I struck the bag as hard as my body would allow. My hands were painted red, and my breaths were deep and short from exhaustion. Sweat trickled down my temple. I held my hands close to my chest, ready to defend myself.

My hair had broken free of the bun it was in and now dangled down my back. My body tingled with excitement, ready for a real fight. Ready to remind those who I am.

I am Alya Edevane, a member of the Auk Court. I am Alya Firstchild, the first angel and a fallen angel. I am Aniya, the goddess of soulmates and the seven winds. Most importantly, I am Alya Edevane, Eilam's wife.

I do not break.

Standing there breathing heavily, Benji's brown eyes peered around the bag, his teeth showing from the wicked grin he now bore. His eyes flashed over my shoulder. I followed his gaze to the Lion, who was scowling with displeasure.

I returned it with a smirk and held my hand up with a vulgar gesture. From across the courtyard, I could hear his snarl of frustration. The fire inside me burned brighter at the sound of it. Benji's warm chuckle filled my ears.

Turning back to him, he was clutching his side, which was now covered in a faint red mark that no doubt would bruise. I hadn't realized how hard I was punching the bag or that a small person was holding it on the other side. And I had struck so many times, each one was harder than the last. But he still smiled through the pain.

The Lion marked his prey and stalked over to us, ready to pick a fight. He didn't make it more than five steps when the alarms sounded. Someone was trying to escape. It was a foolish attempt; whoever they were, they would die before they made it to the tunnels that led out. They will surely perish when they reach the exit without magic. The dome is not connected to any others. Transport drivers use their gift to push water off them and the prisoners they escort. Those without the gift will drown, and if they somehow have the gift, then they will die because of the pressure change before they reach the shore.

The sirens continued to blare, prisoners frantically looking around for any sign of the escapee. Many others were already lowering themselves onto the floor with their hands over their heads. We followed suit. Watching the guards' hurried feet move about trying to secure the prisoners, I waited for one to come to collect us.

My stomach churned as the stench of him came close to me, his knee pressing into my back. I am starting to believe he is a perpetual drunk. The smell of alcohol caressed my face as he spoke down to me.

"That little display you put on for me was touching. Too bad I still don't fear you." His hands brought me up standing and pulled me in close to him.

His leather armor was damp, his stubble chin hair uneven. Nothing about this man had an ounce of attractiveness to him. He was all around a disgusting man. Lynn would call him a pig.

"You may not fear me, but there is a certain Prince who will relish in your death. You touch me or Benji, and *the* Prince of Below will torment your soul until you break, and then he will continue long after."

Lion chuckled. "I doubt he cares about some mortal girl that much. I won't waste my time worrying about him."

I smirked up at him. "If you don't fear him, you should fear the Seventh Ghost. She was there the day I killed King Esen. She owes me a life debt." Lynn was there that day, but she doesn't owe me a life debt, nor will she come to save me.

His face twitched. "I will do with you what I please. Another two weeks, and then you'll be mine for the taking."

I shrugged my shoulders and kept my face calm. "Fine, do with me what you please. It's your soul you're damning, not mine. Just don't say I didn't warn you."

He jerked me forward and pulled Benji up, who looked at me wide-eyed. The expression he wore was asking if I was insane.

I gave him a wink, and the two of us were harshly guided to the other prisoners.

The line was long, and people grumbled, asking others what had happened, who had escaped, and what was taking so long. Benji leaned into me and whispered, "Did you mean what you said?"

"Every damn word."

"How do you know the demon Prince will do that?"

"Because Prince Ove owes me a life debt as well." It was me who saved him that day on the balcony. I brought him to the fire, and I buried him in the ashes; I pulled the dagger out of his throat. His life debt is to me, and Lynn's was to Esen. He will save me when the time counts and defend me against men. I saw how he looked at Alden each time he touched me.

Ove will never admit it, but a small part of him cares about me, and if anything, I learned about him and Lynn is true. I know he will never let a man harm a woman in such a foul way.

Chapter Six

OVE

The King of Light smiled at me. "I am sure you are wondering how King Esen remained hidden. The gods crafted this isle as a gateway into the Below and a place where the Kings could gather without using their gifts. However, when they built it, they did not realize that their gifts would be allowed within. If a god has marked you, then a speck of their power flows within you, and you can use it here. I used my gift to manipulate the surrounding light, making him invisible, but your shadows absorbed the ones he made." He gestured to my hand and then to the scar on his throat. "The god who marked you was far more forgiving than mine was."

I blinked, my jaw opened. I had wanted to protect him and hide him from Alden and Dearil, but I did not give them the command. "Why did you protect him?"

"I have heard about his epic love story. How Lynnora hated him, and he fell for her at first sight. Enemies because of politics, but lovers by choice. Who am I to interfere with love?"

"You- you protected him because they love one another?"

He nodded and looked up at Adri, who gave a slight nod to him. "Adri-anna is my family, though not by blood, but she is still my family. She spoke highly of Lynnora in her youth, and then, Lynnora did the unthinkable:

she saved Adrianna's life. Consider this life debt paid."

I remember that day. Adri had killed someone in a way she wasn't supposed to, and Lynn took the blame for it. She was with the healers for a week, and Dearil said he should not have held back on her. I knew if he had punished Adri, she would have died. I never considered it a life debt; it was just Lynn being Lynn.

"Thank you," I stammered out, sounding like a fool. I looked down at my finger and the thin scar on it. How could this be the mark of a god? Which god? It was a bird that bit me, not some powerful deity. He had to be mistaken, but he wasn't. I could hear my shadows talking to me, telling me to fight and to protect.

"How did you know who Adri is, what she is?"

His smile was warm and friendly, like a summer's day. "Her father is friends with my wife's favorite handmaid. We have known about his heritage since the day they introduced him to us, and when Adrianna was a baby, he brought her to us, asking for my protection. I granted it, but the rest was up to her to get assigned to my Court. — When this war is over, I fear one throne will be lost in the rubble, and if, by some chance, it is your throne that is lost, then the Ghosts will need a home. They have crafted beautiful lies to do this unknowingly, but they will never be accepted if they live in shadows and lies. Adrianna will have a home, not just a house. I wish I could say the same for her sisters. I ask that when you become King, you protect them."

His order of protection was unnecessary. I have done my best to protect all seven of them. I have failed, but I try. Once Dearil is off the throne, then their punishments will cease. They will not have to fear the slightest bit of failure. It is something I have always known.

"King Elior — are you wanting me to stage a coup against my father?"

The King of Leevah rose from his throne and walked toward his ship. "How you claim what is yours is up to you. Seven of us have already discussed it and know you are not the tyrant that your father is. Today was not an introduction of you to us but of us to you. We all have our spies and know the man you are and the King you have yet to become. When needed, we will side with the true King and Queen of the Below."

Seven of them? Daxon will never take the side of a demon, but who is the second? With a second thought, only one king came to mind: Alden. But with him dead and Esen back on the throne, I can assure them the allegiance of eight Courts and finally end the war between demons and angels. I can end it. I can be the King who ends it all. And I will do it with Lynn by my side.

I looked down at the sleeping King. "What of Esen?"

Elior waved his hand, and two of his men lifted Esen. "I will take him with me and ensure his safety and health."

"He has three months. After that, I can not promise Lynn to him. Dearil means to make her his if we fail to conceive." I don't know why I was telling him all my secrets, but he needs to see the importance of Esen getting to Lynn. Of the promise, he made to her with his dying breath.

The King stopped next to his small boat and looked back. "I feel that once the King awakens, he will not waste a day to find the one he loves. I will pray to Aniya that he does it in time."

The goddess of soulmates will not help him if he does not wake up in time. The King and his men rowed out to sea. Adri stood beside me as we watched the boat turn into a small dot on the horizon and vanish from sight behind their ship.

She and I would be here until Dearil returns. If we return to the palace, we will be punished for not waiting. The two of us sat on a throne, her in Ellior's and me in Dearil's.

"Adri, I need a favor from you." She is the only one I can trust, and after learning more about her, I know she will keep this a secret. "I need you to find out what happened to Alya and ensure she isn't in the Auk prison."

She nodded her head in understanding but remained silent.

I can't let her be there. It is my fault if she is. If anyone so much as touches a hair on her head, I will skin them alive and force them to eat their flesh. Alya is too kind for this cruel world, too gentle for that prison. As much as I hate Alden, I'd rather her be with him. I have heard souls scream over the pains and horrors of that prison. I have seen what it does to even the strongest of souls. It is meant to break them, and I will not let her die.

***

I was wrong. I thought my father would wish for me to stay and wait for him when Esen never returned, but he wanted me to go back to the palace and screw Lynn. Thankfully, Adri was spared from punishment. She crafted her words carefully, and I let her put all the blame on me. Her words still echoed in my head as I walked to his study, where I would be dealt my punishment. *I wished to stay longer after the Prince had given up on his return.* She remained there even after we departed, claiming she would still wait for a few days if he showed up.

She didn't need to tell me, but I knew she started with what I asked her to do. And for that reason, I will gladly take whatever she was supposed to be dealt.

The twins were already waiting for us in his study, both with a whip in their hands. "Remove your shirt." I obeyed. I knew where he wanted me to stand as well. Bracing my hands on the back of the leather chair, the twins moved behind me as the King sat in his chair in front of me.

Steadying my breaths, I dove into the bottomless pit inside me, hiding in the shadows like a coward. The whip cracked and struck my bare skin. I screamed out in pain and felt the sting as the air touched the open flesh. The familiar ache of a Koya whip was not there. These were mortal whips so I could heal faster and endure more lashes.

"Where is Esen?" Dearil asked calmly, to calm.

I gritted through my teeth, "I do not know, Your Majesty." I don't. I do not know where Ellior was taking him or where they currently are. It was something Lynn taught me: pay attention to their words and only answer the question that is being asked.

Another crack of the whip struck my back, and it arched in pain. My shadows whispering to me.

Please, master, let us protect you.

No.

Let us heal you.

No.

Tell him where Esen is.

No.

Stay quiet, protect him.

Yes.

"Why is Lynn not with child yet?" Had my answer satisfied him, or did he not care about Esen?

"I don't know. It may be a side effect of the poison you have given her in the past." As the words fell from my lips, I knew my mistake was blaming him—three more lashes lit my back on fire. I will lie to protect her. I have to.

"It does not matter. Soon enough, I will break her and you. Your disobedience has gone on long enough. It is time to fully break the Seventh Ghost by killing Esen in front of her."

His words sent a rage through my body, one my shadows could not contain. The pain I felt on my raw back was nothing compared to the fury that those words caused me. I looked at the wicked King and stood straight, a fire burning in my eyes.

"You did not break her! You will never break her! Never in a million years will you have the privilege to say you broke the Seventh Ghost! There is only one person alive who could do such a thing, and that is Lynnora Knowxwood. She alone will be what breaks her, not you, not Esen, not me! How dare you think you are high and mighty because you have slaughtered thousands. That makes you nothing more than a monster, the very monster you have carefully crafted the Ghosts to be. You would be nothing without them. Without Lynn, you would not be standing where you stand! She made you into the powerful King you claim you are. She will be what breaks you, and you will never break her."

I did the worst thing I could ever do for her and me. I raised my voice against him. I stood up to the tyrant. I defied him, and I did it in his chambers. I pointed out his flaws. I reminded him of how weak he truly is.

The King's smile was cruel. "If I can not break her, as you claim, I will break you. —Tell Ava to do with him as she pleases and ensure Lynn watches. I wouldn't want her to miss out on the fun."

I lunged for him, but the twins' hands wrapped around my arm harshly, pulling me away and restraining me. I yelled out to him, "You bas—"

Darkness surrounded me, but not one born of shadows and death. It was the sweet promise of pain.

***

My body ached in ways that it had never hurt before. The taste of blood lingered in my mouth, and its stench filled my nose. The hot air wasn't stinging the wounds on my back. Aside from a pair of undershorts, my body had no touch of cloth. The cool metal embraced my wrists and ankles.

Moving my hand to rub my temple, the chains jingled and promptly stopped my movement. Slowly opening my eyes, I looked around the dark room. My arms and legs were bound, forcing me onto the stone table that was freshly stained red. A fireplace was roaring from fresh kindle just being added on to it. Beside it was a table with tools meant to cause excruciating pain. Looking over my other shoulder, I saw the thing I feared most.

Lynn was asleep, standing up, chains around her wrists, keeping her in place. Her feet bound to the ground.

"Lynn." My throat screamed in agony at the one word I said.

Her eyes lazily opened, and she winced in pain as she pulled her head up. "Ove, I-I'm so sorry. I never- I didn't think this would happen."

I forced myself to swallow. "You have nothing to apologize for. I pissed him off. This is my fault. Give it a day or two, and we will be out of here."

She shook her head, and tears flowed down her face, dripping into the stone below her. "It's been two weeks, Ove. You gain consciousness for a minute and then succumb to the pain."

I looked down at my bare body—no sign of new injuries. I saw and felt the dried blood plastered on me, as was ash. I let out an uneven breath, understanding what Ava is doing. She tortures me and then heals me, and she's doing it with mortal blades, so there is no permanent scar unless the healing does not happen in time.

Bitch.

Psychotic bitch.

"What does he want?"

Her tears continued as she answered, "He wants us to break, to be his puppets when we take the throne." Her lashes opened wide enough for me to see the fierce storm brewing in her eyes.

It was my favorite look of hers. She has a solid plan that will end in mass destruction. She will not let Dearil take anything from her. She will not let him break her. Whatever she had been going through for the past three months was over. She is the nightmare all have feared.

The tears stopped rolling down her face. She smirked and showed those deadly teeth. Gods above, please spare me. "Now break Ove."

The door to the room creaked open, and my body recoiled at the sound of it and the voice that filled the room. "Good, you're awake. We can start again." Ava stood above me, smiling. Lynn's tears were back. Were they real or a part of her plan? Once again, I do not know what she is planning, and I hate it.

I wanted to argue with Ava to get under her skin. To do something, but all my energy was gone with that small conversation with Lynn. I am exhausted, mind, body, and soul. I have no fight left in me.

My screams quickly filled the walls, masking Lynn's cries and Ava's laughs.

No. I do not care about Lynn's plans. I will not break. I refuse to be my father's puppet. I refuse. I refuse. I refuse.

Chapter Seven

ESEN

The heat was pleasant, not too warm, not too cold. It was perfect. The lightweight blanket kept my temperature whenever a cool breeze blew over me. The silkiness of it on my bare skin felt like a million tiny kisses. The pillow I clung to was plush yet firm; I felt like I was hugging someone. It was all so lovely, but not real. I will wake up in the Below any minute now, and this will have been a dream. I am dead, after all. Lynnora is dead, too.

I had killed us all in the throne room—Alya, Ove, and possibly Alden. Can Alya even die? I had committed murder because the woman I loved was dying, and I did not want to have to live a day without her.

A heavy thud pulled me from my thoughts and my dream of this blissful sleep. My eyes snapped open, and I was greeted by a sight I had not expected. I was not in a dark, gloomy field or cell in the Below. I was in a comfy four-poster bed in a brightly lit room. An entire side of the wall was missing and led out onto a balcony. Pushing the silk sheet off me, I cautiously walked onto the balcony and saw stairs leading down to the sand below. For as far as my eyes could see, it was sand. Rolling waves of sand that will make me feel dirty for walking in. Beautiful, yet disgusting. I looked at where I heard the thud and saw someone unloading bags from a camel.

I hurried back into the room, not wanting them to see me since I had no idea where I was or how I got here. If I had to guess, I would say I was in Leevah, but that does not make sense. King Ellior and I are neither allies nor enemies; we exist with one another. For me to be here with no guards outside on the balcony must mean I am in a citizen's home.

Not knowing what to do, I slid back into the bed and under the covers—listening as the footsteps approached. They were light and almost impossible to hear, but my ears had gotten good at hearing Lynnora's silent steps, which were similar. The person set something down on the table in the room and let out a chuff of air. The water turned on shortly after, and I could hear it filling a container.

"If you are going to pretend to be asleep, don't make it so obvious," A female voice said above me.

I knew I had been caught, and there was no point in pretending. I peered out of the sheet, and a woman stood above me. Her dark hair was pulled back in exquisite braids that I have seen the citizens of Leevah Court bear. Her dark skin made her blue eyes stand out. Something about her felt familiar, but I was not sure what.

"Where am I? Who are you?" I sat up in bed, ready to fight if needed.

She rolled her eyes. "I thought you were supposed to be smart. We are in a private section in the Sun Palace, and I am a friend."

The Sun Palace? King Ellior knows I am here then and has permitted me to stay unguarded. "What's your name?"

The girl grabbed the pitcher of water and filled a glass. She turned to hand it to me. "My name does not matter; all that matters is you are safe and need to get strong again."

I cautiously reached out to grab the glass from her. As my arm extended, I saw a white scar that ran the length of my forearm. I jerked my arm back and traced over it. "What happened to me? What did you do to me?" I snapped at her, holding my arm close to my chest.

She let out a soft breath. "Go look in the mirror, and I will explain everything."

I slowly rose from the bed, unsure if she would attack me with my back turned to her. I walked over to the full-body mirror and could not believe what I saw. White scars covered my body. Both my arms had long ones on the inside of my forearm. My knees had one under my kneecaps. I had one go down the entire length of my stomach. I turned around and looked at my back. Both my calves had the same scars. On my back, one went down my spine.

I spun on my heels and charged at her. "What did you do to me?" I roared at her and tried to grab her throat like Lynnora taught me. She quickly defended herself and pushed me onto the bed.

"I did nothing. As did no one of Leevah." She walked into the bathroom and came back out with a handheld mirror. She held it up to my face so I could see the damage done to it. My circular black pupils were now thin slits, and blue took over any white portion. Two of my teeth had been sharpened into deadly fangs. My tongue had been split in two. "Alden did this to you."

I looked up at her. "No. You are mistaken. He would never do this to me."

She sat on the bed beside me and grabbed my hand. I flinched at the touch but enjoyed the peace it brought me. "He did...and he took your thrown in the process."

I am not sure what surprised me more. Him taking my throne or him cutting me. He always did have a cruel sense of humor on the battlefield, but never towards me, and he never showed interest in taking my crown. "Why? Why would he harm me? Why would he take my crown if I am not dead? I am not dead, am I?"

She chuckled. "No, you are not dead, but you may wish you were. Alden cut into you for reasons I do not know yet, but I know it has something to do with you being the last Serpence demon."

I let out a nervous laugh. "A demon? You cannot possibly think I am a demon. I am the King of Arymn. I have mortal parents. You are severely mistaken, miss."

"I wish I were, but I'm not. You are a demon; how else would you explain your eyes and tongue? Or the fact that you died and came back to life?"

I died and came back to life? How is that possible? No god or goddess granted me to do so. Was reincarnation Alyas' final act? Does that mean Lynnora and Ove are alive, too?

"I must have been granted reincarnation," I blurted out before thinking of the consequences.

The girl scoffed. "The gods do not grant that anymore; they left us long ago. Sorry, Esen, but you are a demon. One that is extremely rare and extremely dangerous."

"How, though? Both my parents were mortals."

"No, they weren't. Your mom was, but your dad was the last of his kind until he had you. Your father, Wayan, was feared and respected by those who knew his name. He worked his way into power and became Dearils' advisor until his death. He was killed in his sleep and killed again before he could regain his new life. Ironically, it was your future father-in-law who killed him and took his spot as Dearil's advisor. That's going to be an awkward meeting."

I looked at her in disbelief as I processed everything she told me. This can't be happening; she has to be wrong. Was she meaning to say that Lynnora's father killed mine? Why didn't she tell me? Does she know? My mind began spinning with questions to the point the room was blurring. I leaned back into the bed and closed my eyes.

The bed shifted as the girl stood up. "Get some rest. We start training tomorrow."

"Training for what?" I grumbled, wishing this was all a dream.

"To save the world, of course."

***

I followed the unnamed girl into the courtyard that I had decided was my private one. Every day, for gods knows how long, she has been bringing me here to get stronger. We always start and end the day running in the desert. I am exhausted day after day, but I am getting stronger than I ever have been before. My muscles ache by the time I go to sleep and are screaming at me in agony when I wake. But it is all good for me. The girl will never tell me why getting stronger and faster is so important, but whatever it is, it is essential. She also refuses to tell me her name, so I call her Miss and occasionally pain in my ass. She always looks pleased when I call her that name.

The courtyard felt warmer than usual as I stepped into it. The warm sun beat down into the center, casting no shadows. No breeze could get in through the walls, and there was no mist from the fountain to cool my skin today. Miss walked over to the fountain and stood on the ledge. I looked around the area and saw it looked different than usual. Tan tiles had been replaced with red ones in a random order. Weapons lay on the dirty ground.

"We are doing something new today. You are finally strong enough to wield all the weapons I've been training you with." She was right; I have gotten proficient at using bows, scythes, war hammers, broad swords, daggers, and spears, "Today, you cannot step or touch any red tiles. If you do, you die. Your goal is to get to me and to take me down."

I shrugged my shoulders. "Sounds easy enough." She smirked and pointed towards the wall where she wanted me to start.

"Begin," she yelled at me from the fountain.

I began my race to her, avoiding stepping on the red tiles. My eyes were glued to the ground when I heard the bowstring snap. I looked up in time to see an arrow flying at me. I stepped to the side to avoid being hit.

"You're dead, snake boy!"

I threw up my hands to show I was unharmed. "You missed me!" She used the bow to point at the ground. I looked down, disappointed in myself for stepping onto a red tile.

"Start over."

I let out a growl of frustration as I walked back to the wall and took my position to start again. She nodded, and I ran again, doing my best to keep switching between looking at her and the ground, but over and over again, I stepped on a red tile, trying to avoid her arrows.

My body was covered in sweat. I wanted a minute to relax and regain composure, but she would not let me. She kept saying you do not get a break in war. You fight, or you die.

I took a deep breath, trying to center myself as I walked back to the wall for what felt like the millionth time. "Use your surroundings, Esen. Stop trying to charge at me if you know it won't work. The weapons on the ground are to simulate fallen soldiers and fallen weapons. Use them!" She sounded frustrated with me. Even I was frustrated with myself.

I leaned against the wall, seeking coolness, but found none. Looking around the courtyard, I saw the closest weapon to me: a long, skinny sword with a slight curve to it. I knew I should go for a bow to use it from a distance, but I could try to deflect her arrows with this blade. I looked at the tiles surrounding it, all red except for the one it lay on. How am I supposed to get to it if I can't touch the ground around it?

My eyes followed the tiles back to me, and I mapped a path to it. Once I get to it, I will have to figure something out.

Miss called out to me, "Ready whenever you stop daydreaming." I shook my head in annoyance and went for the sword.

With each step closer, my heart hammered against my chest, my excitement growing. I can do this; I will do this. The red tiles were right in front of me. Not knowing what to do, I did the first thing I thought of. I leaped forward, falling towards the ground with my arms outstretched. My hand wrapped around the sword's hilt as they hit the ground. My arms caught the weight of my body, and I rolled out of the dive. I stood up, ready to continue the fight towards Miss, but she just stood there looking displeased.

"That was beautiful, but you landed on a red tile."

I rolled my eyes and walked back to the wall, but I had the sword in my hand this time. The bowstring snapped before I reached the wall. The arrow flew past my head, striking the wall. I spun on my heels. "What was that for? I wasn't even ready!"

"War does not wait for you to be ready."

I stood at the wall and tried to remove the arrow from it, but it was wedged in there tightly. I finally wiggled it free and held the arrow in my hand. My heart shattered into a million pieces, my stomach turned sour, and anger flooded my veins. Facing Miss, I knew what had to be done; I had to kill her for the harm she caused.

Miss raised her bow again, aiming it at me, waiting for me to start making my way to her. I ran as fast as I could, remembering where not to step. Closer and closer. I was halfway to her when she released an arrow. I raised my sword and slashed it down, breaking it in half. I quickly dropped the sword and leaped forward. Flying through the air, I shifted into a giant, thick snake. My body shook the walls as I landed, breaking the tiles beneath me. Miss stepped into the fountain and released arrows one after another. They did nothing to my scales. The arrows bounced off me and landed on the stone with a clatter. I could see her trying not to panic as I approached her.

I reached the edge of the fountain and shrunk slightly. Just enough to wrap myself around her body and squeeze. I could feel her heart racing as I tightened my grip around her. She kept trying to wiggle out of my grasp, but it did nothing. I was too strong. This was how she was going to die. I would kill one of the Ghosts for her role in hurting Lynnora.

"Esen, let me go! You won!" She screamed out in pain as a bone snapped. "You made your point! I forfeit!" She tried again.

My anger was consuming me as her life was slowly slipping away.

"Please, Esen, she wouldn't want this," Miss whispered as her eyes fluttered shut. "She's alive," she breathed out.

My body instantly uncoiled from around her, and I shifted back. Her body fell to the ground, and I quickly kneeled beside her, trying to bring her back. "What do you mean she's alive? Where is Lynnora!" I shook her body.

Miss did not reply. I touched her neck and felt her pulse regaining its strength.

"Lynnora is where she has always been," a voice I had not heard in years spoke from the doorway.

I stood up and faced King Ellior. "Where?" I demanded.

"In the Below, King Esen. Adri will come around in a few hours; when she does, it will be time for you to save the woman you love." King Eliior turned around and left without another word.

Lynnora is alive, and I need to save her.

CHAPTER EIGHT

LYNNORA

Oves' back arched in agony, and his screams of pain filled the room. His tears spilled from his eyes, darkening the stone below him, as did the blood that was spilling from his arm and side. A new scar will encompass his left arm and torso, connecting with the old scar on his left leg.

Ava had thought that if she burned him, he would break.

But he didn't.

I have begged him time and time again to break, to let Dearil be his puppeteer, but he refuses. He refuses to partake in my plan, and he is suffering because of it.

Ava ran her finger along Oves' scared leg. "Such a beautiful injury. Does your wife know why you have it?"

Oves' breaths were heavy, his eyes tightly shut, his body twitching in pain. "Don't," he gritted out through his clenched jaw.

I looked between the two of them, searching for an answer. Ove has always said it was an accident during a punishment.

Ava tsked as her finger continued exploring Ove's bare body. "Such a shame. It is a fascinating story."

"Ava, please. Don't." Ove was begging between harsh breaths. "I-I'll do anything."

"Swear it, swear upon your mother's grave you will be forever loyal to King Dearil!" She yelled into his ear.

"I-I swear on my mother's grave I will be loyal to King Dearil."

What horrid truth could be worth that promise?

Ava smiled and began undoing the chains that bound Ove to the stone table. His body was limp from pain and exhaustion. He curled up into a ball the moment his arms were free of the shackles.

She cautiously undid mine. The moment the heavy metal fell away from my limbs, it took all my strength to rush to Ove's injured body. The fresh burns were blistering and smelled of decaying flesh.

"He needs a healer." My words were barely a whisper, and my throat tasted of blood.

Ava rolled her eyes. "Where do you think I am going?" She stood in the doorway and looked over her shoulder at us. "He took a punishment that was meant for you." She winked and left without another word.

"Bitch!" Ove hissed at her, not to be answered.

I looked down at him and saw no regret in his eyes. Making sure I didn't touch any fresh injuries, I curled up behind him and held him close to me.

"I'll make him pay for what he has done to you." I tried to whisper into his ear.

Tears were streaming down both of our faces. He shook his head. "No. I will."

***

They locked us up for a month. Each day, I watched Ava torture him and try to break him. And each day, he refused. His refusal only prolonged the punishment. No one told me why he was being punished or why I was forced to watch.

But the day she had threatened to tell me a secret of his was the day he broke. He would rather serve a monster than have me live with the guilt of knowing the reason they scarred him was because of me. I had always suspected it but never knew for sure.

The healer had done her best to fix his arm but had been commanded to leave a scar that would match his leg. And she did, but she saved his hand from the atrocity.

I understood why, and it was sickening. Dearil did not want others to know of his cruelty towards his son. Ove can wear shirts with sleeves to cover the new scar, but his hand is displayed for the world to see.

Ove lay beside me, sleeping. He only wakes to tend to his needs and then goes back to sleep. I have been wondering if he sleeps so much so he does not have to face the horrors that happened, and sleeping is his escape.

A knock on the door had me summoning my blades and covering Oves' body. The six Ghosts walked in with their uniforms on and weapons at their sides. They surrounded the bed and made the move to reach for us.

I quickly sprung into action, trying to fight them off and protect Ove, who still slept peacefully. It was futile. My body was still weak and exhausted. I have yet been able to sleep more than a few hours a night.

Adri grabbed onto my waist and pulled me off Ove. "Ove!" I screamed his name, not wanting to leave him, not ready for another punishment.

His eyes opened, and the room was covered in a darkness none had seen before. Our eyes could not see through it and make out shapes. Whispers flowed through our ears; many of them were screams of the fallen that Ove absorbed, some whispering profanities, others yelling insults.

"Thieves." A male voice called out.

"Sluts!" an old woman screamed.

"Murders!"

"Traitors!"

"Monsters!"

Their voices continued on a never-ending loop. "Silence!" Oves' voice overpowered them, and they did not dare speak another word.

The darkness remained. Adri still held me tightly, even as I tried to push her off me. Her head reached my ear. "Calm down, Lynnora, you are safe." Her voice rose to normal, "We need to leave, Ove. No harm will come to you or her on this day."

The darkness slowly faded away, revealing the others. Ove held Ava against him with a dagger already breaking her skin, blood trickling down her throat.

"Where are you taking us?"

All six Ghosts eyed one another, speaking in a silent language I knew. They were trying to figure out whether it was safe to tell us. The twins blinked twice in unison, saying it was safe.

"To the throne room, the two of you will be crowned King and Queen of the Below."

Ove looked at me to see if I knew what was happening. I shook my head no. His eyes floated to Adri behind me.

I could feel her head nod; with it, Ove's eyes watered. His body relaxed, the dagger vanished, and he left the room without another word.

I chased after him, his shadows already dressing him in a royal coronation outfit. They then floated back towards me and did my hair and dress. There were no slits up the side, no revealing bodice. The black dress had gold sparkles, and the sleeves covered my arm. I felt the weight of two sheaths attached to my legs. My daggers found their home in them.

The eight of us walked down to the throne room and paused outside the door, waiting for permission to enter. I could hear voices on the other side of it, all loud and boastful. Excitement and worry filled the air and seeped through the door into the hall we stood in.

The Ghosts arranged themselves in three rows, standing side by side in order of importance. I would typically lead them into whatever waited on the other side of the door. It feels strange to know I may never do that again and that Ava will lead them into battle and different situations.

A psychotic bitch leading the most fearsome beings.

The doors opened, showing the people who waited inside for us and Dearil, who sat on the throne with his bone crown. A smaller crown sat upon a cushion in my father's hands, who looked proud.

Ove took my left arm and wrapped it around his right. His black eyes flashed brown as he spoke only to me. "One more time."

Nodding my head, the two of us began our walk down the aisle through the crowd of demons. Many of whom we recognized as Dearils' council and their family, along with other essential demons from The Below. The crowd was silent upon our walk to the dais.

We kneeled together on the bottom step, keeping our heads down, refusing to look at the cruel King who sat on the throne.

An officiant stepped in front of us, and his voice traveled through the hall, "Do you, King Dearil, willingly renounce your claim to the throne as King of Demons and King of the Below?"

I heard the King rise from where he sat. "I do."

"Do you, Prince Ove of the Below, swear your undying loyalty to the throne and the Below? Do you swear to protect the demons within your realm and outside of it?"

I felt his body shift. "I swear to protect the demons of the Below and those outside of it."

His body moved away from mine as he rose. Allowing myself to look up at the new King of the Below, I offered him an encouraging smile. His eyes looked down at me briefly, and he gave a weak smile.

The officiant moved in front of me. "Do you, Lynn, Princess of the Below, swear your undying loyalty to the throne, to the King of Below? Do you swear to protect the demons within your realm and outside of it?"

I straightened my back and squared my shoulders. My eyes locked onto

Dearil, where he stood crown-less. "I swear to protect my King, my throne, and all demons in all realms."

Dearil's eyes hardened at my deviation from the proper words, but he could not punish his Queen so publicly.

They placed the silver crown of bones atop my head. A new type of weight surged through my body. I have known I would one day become Queen with my union to Ove, but I never suspected it would be so soon. Let alone while Dearil was still alive.

He is planning something and can not sit on the throne with whatever it is.

Ove and I turned to face our people. "Long Live King Ove, long live Queen Lynn. Long may they reign!" The officiant began a chant that swept across the hall, shaking the stone.

Over and over, they repeated the same sentences until we took our seats on the thrones. As we sat back on the two thrones made of bones, the chanting stopped, and the applause began.

The celebration continued for hours. Demons offered their congratulations and assured us of their alliance. Gifts were brought and set to the side. My father asked for my forgiveness, resulting in a harsh gesture from Ove and I. He quickly disappeared and left us.

Dearil's eyes had yet to leave us, monitoring our every move—no doubt trying to assess if he had made the right decision by passing down the crown.

Music filled the room. Demons began dancing. I had wanted to join them, but each time I tried to rise or ask Ove to join me, my body screamed with exhaustion, demanding I stay where I was.

They had brought food for us. We both slowly ate it, and with each portion of food, I set aside one bite out of habit. I know that the man who used to eat it is now dead and will never steal my food again.

My heart ached, thinking about all the lost meals I had declined him because I was trying to push myself away from him. I now wish I had taken full advantage of those days and lived them fully. Esen let me be myself with no expectations, and he seemed to enjoy who I was. Or tolerate it, at least.

Guests were slowly beginning to leave when two beings I had not seen in a long time prowled in. Sheena and Alika looked healthy and happy to see me. Both snarled at any demon in their way to get to us. As they approached, I saw Alika had a piece of parchment attached to her spiked collar.

Unrolling it, I saw my father's messy handwriting.

Lynnora,

I am sorry for any pain I have caused you and Ove. I hope one day when you have a child of your own, you will understand I did this for you to get you on that throne. I know I have a lot to atone for, and I will do what must be done to get us back to what we once were.

I hope you know I am not begging for your forgiveness because you are now a Queen but because I am your father.

My allegiance is to you and wherever you bring us. You will be an extraordinary ruler; I can not wait to see what you do.

Your mothers would be proud of you.

I love you a million.

-Trevv

I handed the letter over to Ove, who took his time to read it, and each time he did, he shook his head and huffed.

The crowd was almost all gone. Only Dearil and his council remained. I suppose it is now our council.

The warning bells rang, echoing through the entire Below, signaling an attack. The six Ghosts looked at Ove and me, awaiting their order.

"Alive," Ove said to them, sending them off on their hunt.

I glanced at Dearil, who looked angry that his prized possessions had now answered to his son and that his new king had shown mercy.

Minutes passed, or was it hours? It was hard to tell. My fingers ached, wanting to be out on the hunt with them or draw my blade against someone.

Growing bored and restless, I unsheathed a dagger and began twirling it on the throne. The tip of the blade carved a hole in the arms of the seat. Alika and Sheena had both fallen asleep waiting.

The bells stopped ringing. Whoever it was had been caught, and the Ghosts would be returning to us with them.

I blew a loose strand of hair out of my face, doing my best not to look eager and excited. It was a relief knowing someone else was about to be punished and not me or Ove. The Ghosts entered, dragging one being into the center of the room. He wore all-black leather armor, with no sign of the type of demon he was in sight.

Alika and Sheena woke up from their nap and lifted their heads, their ears raised in excitement.

Ava clutched a piece of parchment in her hands, and Ove noticed it, too. "What does it say?"

Ava held it up and read it aloud. "I never killed you that day. I hope the familiarity does not go unnoticed."

I adjusted myself and sat on the edge of my chair. My dagger stopped spinning as I looked at what was before me.

"Are you brave or stupid to try and kill the Queen of Demons?" Ove asked the hooded figure and got no response.

My curiosity won the fight, and my instincts told me to see who was under the hood before all others.

I stood over him, my finger holding onto his chin, and lifted his head to look up at me. His solid blue eyes pierced my grey ones.

"Well, aren't you a pesky little gnat? You are mine now." I smiled down at him.

The corner of his lip twitched upwards, showing the sharp fangs hidden beneath. "Hello, dearest."

The avalanche I had felt since my wedding day was of guilt, remorse, anger, and disgust. But it was all beginning to settle, leaving behind only beauty, love, compassion, and joy.

It felt like the ground under us was crumbling and shaking, threatening to open a pit to the fires below. I took his hand and smiled widely.

For King Esen had fallen in love with me for all I am, and I have fallen hopelessly in love with him for all the same reasons.

Esen moved swifter than I have ever known him to move. One second, he was kneeling before me, and the next, his sturdy chest was pressed into my back, and he held a dagger at my throat.

The Ghosts immediately circled us to close off any escape routes. He lowered his head to my ear. "I made you a promise, Lynnora, and I do not break my promises."

The edge of the blade was hovering over my throat just barely, but to those around us, it was touching my throat. The hand that held my arm behind my back was gently holding it, afraid to hurt me. *I told you I would never harm you. I am a man of my word.*

He isn't doing this to hurt me but to hurt them.

I could feel his head behind me swiveling, searching for a way out. There isn't one. He can't beat six Ghosts and Dearil.

An arrow flew past us. He stepped to the side, pulling me with him.

"Bitch! You almost hit me!" Ava screamed at Adri, who was across from her.

Adri shrugged her shoulders. "Ops."

I looked at Ove, whose shadows were fighting against Dearils and blocking him from interfering with this fight.

Alika and Sheena were protecting the King, their ears pinned to their head and snarling at Dearil. "Mal hina!" I screamed at them in demon tongue.

They obeyed and advanced on Dearil, allowing Ove to push him back. Oves' eyes landed on me. "Save her," he whispered.

His shadows engulfed us. The power of Kings had transferred to him the moment they had placed the crown upon his head. He now commands the shadows of Below and they pulled us through the realm out into the bright sun.

My feet shook as we landed on the stone floor of the Isle of Blessed.

Chapter Nine

ESEN

It was not a bad dream. Lynnora was alive and standing in front of me. The sun illuminated her tiny body, the discoloration under her eyes, the lack of life in her hair.

She is alive.

She moved over to a throne and sank into it, her eyes wildly staring at me in horror.

"You-you're alive. How?"

Moving before her, I held onto her hand and kneeled. "Turns out I am the last Serpence demon, and with that being my first death, I began the transformation."

Her eyes searched my face, looking for signs of deceit, but she only saw the truth. "I was right. I was right!" She let out a manic laugh that turned soft. "I was right! I knew it when Alya told me about your father's journals. I had suspected you were a demon the moment I saw how dark your cells were and knew only a demon would think of depriving prisoners of light. I knew it!"

"You knew I was a demon and still tried to kill me?" I pulled my hand away and stood up, towering over her.

"Oh, don't act so surprised. I have tried to kill you before, and I have saved your life several times. I didn't expect you to kill yourself. You decided to be selfish." She stood up and matched my height to the best of her ability.

Her legs shook under her. I let out a growl and helped lower her back into the chair. "Well, excuse me for wanting to live a life with you in the Below for eternity."

She rolled her eyes. "Always the romantic."

Running my hand over the side of her face, she leaned into my touch and closed her eyes. Holding it there, I let her head rest on it. "I am still mad at you for getting me killed."

Her eyes remained shut. "Good. I wouldn't expect anything less."

I huffed. "What is that supposed to mean?"

Her eyes opened with a new sense of brightness, warming my heart. "You are always mad at me for something."

"Liar."

"Thief." She rebutted. I raised my brows, asking her to explain. "A secret that you will one day learn if you hold yourself to all promises made."

"Only the ones to you." I pressed my lips into the top of her head, savoring her warmth.

We parted, and she slowly stood up with my help. She looked around the island. My eyes had yet to leave her. I do not want to lose her again, and I will cherish every second I have been granted.

"Where's the boat?" She asked harshly and gave me an apologetic smile.

"Follow me." Taking her hand, I led her to the edge of the beach. I waded into the water, and she stood on the shore looking around for something that would carry us away. "Where would you like to go, dearest?"

Her eyes surveyed me and then looked out to the north. Her body relaxed. "To the highest cliff of Ter."

Thinking of the largest snake I could, my body shifted. Water splashed as I fell into it, only the tip of my tail wholly submerged; the rest of me was barely in the water.

Lynnora let out a shriek and stumbled back. She found her voice and let out a string of curses that would make a sailor blush. Her language shifted with each curse, but I understood what they implied.

Tossing my head, I gestured for her to climb on. She violently shook her head no. I gestured again. She stood in her spot and refused to move an inch.

Slowly approaching her, I kept my head on the sand and closed my eyes. My breaths caused the sand to blow up, creating a small cloud around her feet.

I waited.

I waited for that touch. For her.

Her small hand pressed between my eyes, followed by her head. "You kill me, I kill you."

I opened my eyes and blinked in agreeance.

She slowly climbed onto my back, unsure about this. I carefully made my way into the water and swam. Her legs straddled me, her hands tightly holding onto a scale.

I headed north, not knowing how long it would take me to get there or where we would go once we got there. Two Kings wanted us. I committed treason the moment I held a blade to her throat, and Ove had let us go. The Ghosts are on their way to hunt us.

Adri said she would buy me as much time as possible but could promise nothing. Getting Lynnora to safety is solely up to me.

The bright sun overhead was slowly beginning to turn dark. Clouds were moving in, obscuring the light. I looked off in the distance of the clouds and saw the haze of rain pounding the water. Lynnora's body shifted. She pulled herself in closer to me. She saw it and braced herself for the storm coming our way, which we would have to go through.

Keeping my concentration on the snake's size, I pushed forward, tired of holding it for an hour.

The rain quickly descended on us. My vision was nonexistent. I could not see in front of me. I kept going in the direction that I knew was North.

The rain still hounded us after an hour, the waves growing harsh, pushing us around. I did my best to stay in a straight line, but not having visibility hindered it. The waves moved us to the side. I could feel it slowly turning us in the wrong direction. Correcting myself, I pushed forward.

My body screaming in agony, wanting to be back in the form of a man. I can not keep going and fighting the storm.

Please, gods, save us, protect her.

I sent the silent prayer to any god that may listen, hoping one with control of the winds or the sea will hear my plea. But none answered.

The storm raged on for several more hours. Lynnora's body shook on me. I could hear her teeth clattering. We need to rest, to find land, to get her warm. We can not keep going.

My eyelids were growing heavy from exhaustion when a weight slipped from my body, relieving some strain on me.

I spun around. Her body was gone. There was no sign of her trying to fight the waves. Nothing.

Shifting into a smaller snake meant to swim under the water, I dove. Her body was slowly sinking, her hair flowing upwards. Her eyes were closed, air bubbles were leaving her mouth and floating to the surface.

Pushing myself below the waves, I raced for her, knowing it was only a matter of time before she ran out of air. Her body landed on rocks not far below me but deep enough that the water was calm. Rushing to her side, I took one last breath and shifted.

Pulling air from above, I brought it down to where we were. Adjusting it around her mouth and nose, her chest began to rise and fall again. I grabbed her tightly, pushing off the dark rock at the bottom of the sea.

Up and up.

My head broke the surface first. Spitting out the water that was going into my mouth, I gasped for air, still focusing on keeping a constant flow of air into Lynnora and keeping water out of her mouth.

I spun around to see which way to go, but the rain still obscured any sign.

Feel, don't think.

Closing my eyes, I took a deep breath in. My instincts are designed to keep me alive. I need to listen to them to survive. If I do not, it is not just my life I am wasting. It is also Lynnora's.

Shifting into a snake, I laid her across my back and swam again in the direction I hoped was the shore.

It was not long after that I saw the cliffs of Ter. The waves pushed us forward, other waves slamming onto the rocks as they broke.

Shit. Now what?

She is still unconscious. I can not scale the cliff with her on my back. Searching for any sign of the beach, I found a hole in the cliff face instead, right above the reach of the waves.

Swimming slightly back to sea, I adjusted my positioning and rode the wave. The wave reached its peak, ready to break on the stone wall, when I leaped.

Our bodies rolled into the opening of the cliff. My body shifted back to man as we passed through the mouth of the cave. The rocks below me tore into my skin, drawing blood and leaving bruises.

Groaning as I rose, I rushed over to Lynnora's body. Her chest still rose and fell, and one eye slowly opened. "Owe," she groaned out in pain.

I let out the nervous chuckle I had been holding in and pulled her into a hug. She groaned the entirety of it, but her arms wrapped around me and embraced me as well.

"I missed you, Lynnora."

She pulled away and forced herself to stand. "Did you? Or did you miss someone challenging you?"

"Both," I smirked down at her.

She began moving her hands along the wall in search of something. "We reached the cliffs, but I am unsure where exactly."

She looked over her shoulder and smiled. "We are exactly where we need to be." She disappeared into the darkness.

"Lynnora!" I cried out to her in a panic. She did not answer.

Rushing to where she had stood, I felt the wall she was at. My hand fell into the darkness, and the rest of me followed. A small hand grabbed onto my wrist, pulling me further in.

"You sounded scared. Were you worried about me?" Her teases landed a harsher blow than she intended.

"No." Yes. I will always worry about her until the day I die and then long after that.

She let out a chuckle. "Hold on to me and follow me." I did as she said.

The rocky ground below my feet slowly raised, my calves telling me we were climbing a steep incline. I followed her, not daring to let go, afraid that if I did, I would never find her again.

Minutes had turned into hours. My legs were screaming in pain, my chest heavy in search of air that I kept replenishing the both of us with. My mouth was dry, craving water that was not laced with salt.

The ground was slowly beginning to level out. I could hear rain over us. The smell of wet soil surrounded us. She stopped suddenly. My body collided with hers, almost sending us both to the ground.

"Hold your breath, plug your nose, and stay behind me." Not questioning it, I did as she instructed.

She fumbled with something and then moved forward again. The light was seeping in through something. We walked towards the light. I still held my breath and plugged my nose. Light quickly encompassed the two of us. She turned around and began laughing.

Her hand was not on her nose, and she was not holding her breath. She continued laughing until she doubled over, holding her stomach.

"I did not need to do that, did I?"

She straightened herself, her arms draped over my shoulders. Mine wrapped around her waist. "Absolutely not. I was just curious if you would listen to a ridiculous command and what you would look like."

I leaned down, my lips grazing her neck. The tiny hairs on it stood as each breath caressed them. "I will make you pay for that."

"I look forward to it." She pulled away and opened the doors from which the light was coming.

Climbing the steps up, we walked out into a house.

A fire roared in the kitchen—a plate with half-eaten food set out on the circular table. Plates and cups were inside the sink. I remained silent, unsure when the house owner would return to finish their meal.

But Lynnora moved about as if she owned the place. She picked up a roll from the plate and tossed it to me, taking another for herself. She munched on it as she wandered around the room, her fingers tracing spices on the shelves. She nodded her head toward the opening into the rest of the house.

Cautiously following her, she led the way into a large room with many couches of different styles, all looking so comfortable to sit on. In a corner was a small pile of kids' toys and books. Lynnora moved to the fireplace and dusted off a picture frame of two ladies and two kids. She quickly tucked the picture away before I could look at it properly.

Oh gods. The toys, the picture. There are kids here.

Three doors were closed to the room, but Lynnora focused on the one next to the fireplace. She released a melodic whistle that sounded like she was saying, 'Hey, sweetie.'

Behind the door was a shuffle of feet, and an old lady spoke through. "What do you eat?"

A smile spread across Lynnora's face. Her eyes looked at me when she answered. "Gnats and other pesky little things."

The door swung open, and an old, plump lady ran out. Her hands held tightly onto a poker intended for the fire. It dropped loudly on the hardwood floors as she rushed to Lynnora.

Their arms wrapped around one another and pulled each other in close. "Hello, Mimsy."

"Hello, chickadee."

I let the two of them hug each other tightly. Moving to the mantel, I looked at the other pictures that sat atop it, and in each of them was a small version of Lynnora with a beautiful woman standing at her side.

The two of them were talking as I looked over each image, loving that a piece of her childhood had been stored here and kept safe after all these years.

"Esen, this is Mimsy. She was my nursemaid until I was six. Mimsy, this is Esen, the *rightful* King of Arymn."

Mimsy's brown eyes looked me up and down. "Pleasure to meet you, child of Wayan." I froze where I stood, not knowing what to say or how she knew who my birth father was. She turned back to Lynnora. "I am so glad you have come home at last. I have kept everything clean and running. The primary bedroom is all yours for your time here. I will go to town in the morning and collect more supplies."

She smiled at both of us and disappeared back into the kitchen. "Will they not think to look for you here first?" I did not want to ask her, but I needed to know we were safe.

Her smile faltered. "No, they won't. Dearil killed my mother here, and after that day, I swore never to come back. I have only been here one other time and had no attachment to it. They will search for us in Arymn first. And then go down the list of all the previous places I have stayed for prolonged periods."

She opened a door and walked down the hall, never once looking at the paintings of the person in them. The black-haired woman, I figured, was her mother, and the man in some must be her father.

She opened the door at the end of the hall and paused before crossing the threshold. Standing behind her, I placed my hand on her shoulder, telling her I would let her make the first step in. The choice is hers and hers alone.

She let out a shaky breath and crossed over the line. The room was simple. A bed sat on one wall, facing glass doors that looked out into the storm. A dresser had candles ready to be lit, and another fireplace was already alive. A door on one wall was open, showing a shower and a bath. She walked straight to that and undressed.

Gods, she is mesmerizing.

Whether or not she knew it, I needed to see if she had any new injuries, and we both smelled awful. It was worse than the stables a day before cleaning.

The dress left her body, and as she folded it up, I saw the raw marks on her wrists and ankles. She had been chained.

Bones were clinging to the skin, promising to break free. Her stomach was sunken in. I did not see how much weight she had lost with the dress.

She stepped into the hot water and promptly began washing her hair. Undressing, I joined her. Her back brushed against my bare skin. Reaching past her for the soap, her body went rigid.

She grabbed my arm and traced the thin scar. Spinning around, she looked over me, seeing each new marking I now bear. Her fingers traced over each one as if she knew what type of blade caused them.

As she finished examining the ones around my knees, she smirked at the sight of my dick hardening with her kneeling before me. "I thought you didn't like people kneeling."

"Shut up," I growled and brought her back to me. I held her arm carefully, looking at the red marks on her wrists. "Who did this to you?"

"Ava. Who did yours?"

"I am guessing Alden."

"I'm so sorry, Esen. I should have waited and made sure you were safe before we left."

"Do not be sorry." My eyes fell to the scar between her breasts. I pulled her chin up to look at me. "Why did you not let this heal properly?"

I had replayed that day over in my head each day since I woke up. Adri had told me Lynnora was alive, and the only possible way was if that blade was not a Koya blade.

Her words were soft, "I wanted a reminder of what I lost, of who I lost."

I lowered my mouth to hover over hers. "If I were a better man, I would not want to kiss you right now. — I suppose it is a good thing I am not a good man."

So I did.

Chapter Ten

OVE

I held in my smile, replacing it with a scowl. Esen saved Lynn. I had the strength to fight back against Dearil. Alika and Sheena came to my aid. The Ghosts did not harm Esen.

The gods blessed us today.

The moment they vanished in my shadows, I had no choice but to give the Ghosts the orders to find them and bring their Queen back alive. Esen committed treason, and it could not be ignored.

Those within the throne room had seen my aid in her rescue but couldn't punish me. I am their King. They can threaten to remove my crown, but with no heir appointed, it would be accessible to all. That is the last thing the council wants in a time of war. The crown shall remain atop my head until my death. I will not bear a child. I will not remarry. I will not take a mistress.

Lynn is my Queen, but her heart does not belong to me. That belongs to Esen, and I will not get in the way of that again. I will not fail her.

In the hours that passed, the council fell into chaos, trying to figure out what to do. None of the Ghosts saw who was beneath the hood. I only knew it was Esen because Alika and Sheena were excited to see him. Their loyalty to him was what gave it away. They never forgot his scent after all the months that had passed.

My father has yet to say anything to me. His shadows were now weaker than mine, but they floated behind him, seeking something to lash out at. Testing and poking at mine to see how they react to him. Each time, they push him back, urging him to stand down. I want to fight him and make him pay for everything, but there is a better time.

Dearil sat at the foot of the table in the seat that once was mine. He leaned onto one armrest, his other arm reaching out, holding the edge of the armrest. His ringed finger kept loudly tapping the wood, sending a chill through my bones. His black eyes stared into mine, searching for answers, seeing if I would break and confess what I know.

His sharp teeth glinted in the candlelight. "You know something, boy."

"Boy? Last I checked, I am your King, and you shall refer to me as such." All the years of punishment and his cruelty have finally paid off. I can return the favor in portions.

My shadows intensified, covering the candles and darkening the room predominantly around him.

His eyes looked over at them, assessing if they were a threat. "Please enlighten us, your majesty." Dearil spat my title out.

"No."

The room grew warm, and his shadows pushed against mine, begging to be unleashed upon me. My shadows brought him into a corner, trapping them there.

I cocked my head to the side. "Not used to being told no, Dearil?" He snarled at me. "If you want me to enlighten the council, should I tell them where I have been for the past month or what has occurred in the years that you reigned?"

"I warn you, do not make an enemy out of me, King Ove."

"I am sorry to disappoint you, Father, but you made an enemy out of me the first time you laid a hand on me." I rose from my seat and pulled up my pant leg, exposing my scar for the council to see for the first time. As I spoke, I rolled up my sleeve, showing the new scar on my arm. "You made an enemy out of me when you crippled me twice. You chose violence time and time again against me, your only son, and against the Ghosts. Against your Queens. Each time you laid a hand or shadow on them, you turned me against you! You took the same oath I took, yet you did not abide by it. I have been King for one day and have already shown more grace and humility than you have in the years you reigned!"

With my scars exposed for the council to see, I ignored the pity looks. Demons are cruel, but what Dearil did to me was something demons do not condone. They value children because they know they are carrying on their parent's legacy and wish to leave behind a good one.

Dearil rose from his seat to match me. "You were a coward, boy! I made you into something stronger! I made you into something mortals fear!"

I fell into my seat, the crown resting on my head, giving me the courage to say everything I have wished to say for years. He can't touch me without dying. I am safe.

"I made myself. After each lashing you gave me, I thought of who I wanted to be and became that man. You may see me as a coward, but I would rather be a coward loved by his people than a tyrant hated by all."

"You are a disgrace and a disappointment!" Dearil slammed his hands onto the table. The goblets rattled, and the council members looked disturbed.

I was showing them the King they used to serve. The King that only showed himself when they were not present.

"I am not aiming to please you anymore, but I am curious. What disappoints you more: the fact that I am no longer doing what you want me to do or that I am stronger than you? Because both sound like a personal problem that you must work through alone."

Dearil's hands closed into a fist, trying to contain his anger. "You may be stronger than me, but that will not always happen. That crown has not had time to adjust to your head, and the power of it is already blinding you."

I scoffed in a way that I knew would anger him. "Power is a funny thing indeed. One minute, it is yours; the next, it can be someone else's. You used your power to justify your cruelty. I am using it to stand up to a bully. You and I are nothing alike. I have made sure of that."

"I crowned you in the time of war. You will soon become what you dread. No King will respect a weak one."

"We will see about that." I told no one what King Elior had said about the Kings willing to ally with me if I were to overthrow Dearil. I hadn't had time to plan how to do it. My mind had been preoccupied with thoughts of Alya in the Auk prison, and Adri had confirmed she was. I was also being tortured for a month, which did not grant me the ability to plan a coup. I had to focus on not wetting myself and submitting to Dearil.

"Leave us," Dearil ordered the council, who obeyed after seeing this side of him.

The last man left, and the door clicked shut. We both waited until we could not hear the footsteps. "Ava broke you. She forced you to swear your loyalty to me. So you will submit to me, and I will have you rule how I see fit."

"No." I toyed with the dirt under my finger, keeping my eyes away from the scar that now encompasses my left arm. I could feel the heat growing. "She had me submit my loyalty to *King* Dearil. You are no longer King; she also had me swear upon my mother's grave. We both know there is no grave; you would not allow that. You would have her burned for what she did."

He stood hunched over the table, his hair dangling in his face as he chuckled manically. "It is a good thing that I had commanded you to kill Lynnora if you feared she would betray her King. And she did when she planned to make King Esen fall in love with her."

I continued to check my nails. "There are several issues with that. First, you *threatened* me to kill Lynnora Fenwald. She is now Lynnora Knoxwood. Second, she never betrayed *her* king. After all these years, I would think you would know to be more specific with your commands."

I knew from the moment he had given me that command that marriage was one way to get her out of it. But as time passed, and I saw her interact with Esen, I realized she was slowly switching alliances, whether or not she knew it. Her loyalty is to Esen, and it has been since she first met him.

"You insufferable-" Dearil began, but my shadows wrapped around his mouth, preventing him from talking further.

"You were saying something? Oh, right, no, you weren't. You and your tongue do not have a place in my court. You're dismissed." I waved my hand. My shadows forced him out of the room, slamming the door on his face.

Quickly covering my scars, I sank into my seat and chugged the goblet of wine set before me. My hands trembled, and my blood boiled.

"Holy shit, I did that. I did that," I whispered to myself out of amazement.

The fear and realization began to settle in. He can find other ways to punish me. He can take it out on the Ghosts, on other demons. He can still do it if he wishes to.

***

The cage looked to be shrinking, or was the bird getting larger? The lump of brown fur seemed to wither away with each night. Slowly getting smaller and smaller, death is bound to claim it soon.

Her wings could no longer extend fully, further limiting her movements. Her calls were growing increasingly desperate each night, but tonight was different.

She sat on the perch with her wings tucked in nicely. Her beautiful eyes were watching me even though her head hung low. I tried to reach out and comfort her, to break her out, but my limbs did not move.

I tried everything I knew that allowed me control over dreams, but I continuously failed each night. I failed tonight as well. The most beautiful bird I have ever seen was trapped in a cage. She did not deserve such cruelty. She should fly through the forests of Ter, over the canyons of Dahr, and under the river between Arymns islands. She deserved to see all the wonders of the world.

I watched the bird with sorrow in her eyes as they looked me over repeatedly. The faint scar on my finger hummed to life—a calming warmth radiating from it. A sense of relief passed through me and landed in my heart.

I inspected the thin line and then looked up at the bird.

"You." My words fell from my mouth, startling both her and me. I looked back at the scar, my eyes wide in realization. "You were the bird that nipped me that day. You're a goddess!"

King Elior's words floated through my head: *The god who marked you was far more forgiving than mine was.*

He had told me a god marked me, but I was blind and confused. A bird is not a god or goddess, and yet a crow is not a demon. But I am a demon who can shift into a crow. Gods and goddesses are far more powerful than me. They can easily become whatever they wish.

But what goddess marked me and why?

Legends say they only mark those they favor to grant them reincarnation. Elior will be reincarnated once, thanks to whichever god favored him. Why would one want me reincarnated?

I looked back at the bird. "I'll save you. I promise."

***

I woke up further as my knee hit the bottom of the table, and I jolted awake, sending pain through it. Letting out a groan and rubbing the sore spot. I still sat in the council room. The candles nearly extinguished. They emitted enough light for me to see the person standing in front of the door.

"Well?"

Adri nodded her head yes. Esen and Lynn made it to safety, or at least far enough away from the other Ghosts.

"Where?"

She shook her head. She doesn't know where they are. I had no idea where to bring them, so I got them out of the Below and left the rest to Lynn. She has safe houses in each Court. She will go to one of them, but it is only a matter of time before the Ghosts make their way to each of them.

I hope wherever they are, they know about Alya and her predicament. Adri had been in Leevah the past month helping Esen. She may have told him about Alya's whereabouts. With Lynn out, they can rescue her, and I can focus on killing Dearil and saving that goddess.

I am still trying to figure out where to start with that issue, but I know it must be done.

"Thank you. Let me know the instant you learn anything."

She bowed her head. "Of course, my King."

"Call them back. Orders have changed."

Adri swiftly left.

By the time I had finished replacing all the candles in the room and added more, the six Ghosts all stood before me in a line, patiently waiting for a punishment that would never come. I know my father would have given one by now, given how long it is taking them to find Lynn and Esen.

"From this day forward, you obey me and Queen Lynnora. If Dearil tries to order or punish you, you have my permission to resist and do what is necessary to come out unharmed. If that means his death, then so be it. The six of you are under my protection. No harm will come from me or your Queen. I have watched you all grow and experience death among yourselves, and I have seen your weakness. You are not one. Dearil dictated your every move and did not allow you to think for yourselves. I have seen you all obey and show no mercy except one. Adri, please step forward."

Adri took one step before the line and held her head high. She is the shortest among them and yet carries herself taller than all.

"You fought against your oppressor and showed restraint when none had. You spared Lynnora's life, allowing her to become your Queen. There are many reasons for my decision, but your refusal to kill an unarmed assailant is why I am naming you as Commander of Ghosts. All orders will be given to you, and you will coordinate everything. The line of succession is up to you. Your second and third will take your place if you fall."

Her eyes were wide with amazement, tears brimming them.

She is safe; they are all safe.

One by one, the Ghosts bowed their heads and brought their arms across their chests. "With our lives and hearts," they all said in unison.

Their actions sent a chill through my body, causing the hairs on my arms and legs to stand up. There was a time before the first Holy War when demons did such a simple act to show their utmost loyalty and to say that their hearts beat as one. If one were to falter, all would follow. To guard one's heart is to defend them all.

The act was disbanded after the war, and the demons were trapped in the Below. Many thought that since Dearil was able to force open the portal for some, he would be the first king to receive the honor of the act.

And yet here I sat, being the first King to receive it from the Ghosts.

I stood and crossed my arm across my chest. "With my life and with my heart, we shall rise."

A tremor traveled through the palace out into the darkness of the Below, seeping into the soil and water of all seven Courts, filling the air the angels breathe. A new king has been deemed worthy by the unworthy, a throne turning to dust.

Chapter Eleven

LYNNORA

Gods save me.

His lips pressed onto mine, sending warmth through my entire body, and rested between my legs. I hated myself for allowing a small moan to slip out as we kept kissing one another. It seemed to please him. His lips twitched into a smile, and he continued to kiss me.

I didn't know where to touch; I wanted to feel all of him. His solid muscles had grown since I last seen him. I wanted to trace every scar he now bore. I wanted to feel the softness of his blonde hair. I needed to feel the length of him in my hands. I didn't know where to start. I let my hands roam over his body, taking every part of him in.

He was gentle with his hands. One rested on the side of my face and the other on my hip, slowly going lower and lower. He pulled me in closer to him. I felt my breasts press against him and his length press against me, which resulted in a slight moan from him. I returned the smile he had given me earlier.

His body shifted and pushed me into the wall. The curve of the floor was becoming hard to stand on. He seemed to notice as well. He lifted one leg around himself. I pulled myself onto him, both legs wrapped around his waist. The sturdiness of him teasing me, poking at me, but never going in.

Gods, spare me.

I pushed into it, and we both moaned in unison, wanting more but doing nothing to take it further. It is his choice. I will let him make the first move.

He moved one hand up to my breasts and toyed with them as his mouth fell from mine and moved down my throat. His hand was slowly traveling the length of my stomach and then stopped as he felt the scar.

Esen pulled away and looked at it. His eyes filled with concern when he looked back up at me. "What happened?"

"Nothing."

"Liar. I have traced this scar enough times and looked at it long enough to know the one that you now bear is longer. What happened?"

My throat bobbed. "I took it out."

His head fell into mine, our brows pressing together. He pulled away to place a kiss on them and then returned to pressing our brows together. "Did you do that on your own?"

"I started to, but one of my sisters found me. She finished it for me. By the time she started closing it, I had passed out from the pain."

Adri had found me covered in blood. She first thought I had been attacked, but when she saw the blade in my hand, and the only wound was in the location of a scar she also has, she understood. She didn't ask questions as she took the blade from my hand and finished what I had started. I had seen the new scar the next day when I woke up and knew that if Ove was to look at it closely, he might notice the difference, but Dearil wouldn't.

The cruel bastard would never know that I will never sire an heir for him. I would rather be used for sex than lose Ove like my father had promised. It was the only option I could see to ensure I would still have him in my life. But Ove never once asked for sex, other than our wedding night. No, he didn't even ask then. I saw the remorse and guilt in his eyes. The sex was slow and tedious. He took his time caring for me and not fucking me. When he did, it was over before I knew it. He had made himself finish fast so it could be over. He didn't want it any more than I did, but it was necessary.

Esen pulled me in closer to him. "You cease to amaze me. Your strength is something I admire, but it will be your downfall if you are not careful. — We will clean up and then go to bed together. Deal?"

"Deal."

He carefully set me back on the ground, and we cleaned our bodies. I had yet to forget how he washes himself, and there were days I showered where I would catch myself going in the same order or muttering the same words.

Clean, clean, clean.

I let him wash my body for me, knowing he would still think I was dirty somehow. He scrubbed harder on some areas, but he was gentle where my skin clung to my bones and on my raw wrists and ankles. He took his time ensuring the cleanliness of them without causing me discomfort.

Stepping out into the bathroom, I grabbed two towels hidden in a drawer where my mom used to keep them. I held mine close to my nose and took a deep inhale. They still smelled of fresh rain on hardened soil.

It is painful being here, knowing that this place is what she had once wanted for me. Both our mothers were setting this home up for Ove and me as a sanctuary and a place for us to run to when we separated from Dearil. Ove never had the chance to see it, but I saw it once.

My mother had brought me here after being punished by Dearil for breaking an ancient vase during training. She wanted me to know there was life outside of his cruelty and that one day I would have it.

I was in the tunnels that led to the cave when I heard her arguing with someone. I wanted to help and fight off the intruder, but Mimsy had locked the cellar door, trapping me in there.

I watched through a gap in the wood and listened to them. Dearil had known about the home for some time and had planned to burn it to the ground when we made the move. But something had happened in the Below that angered him, and my mother was the subject of his punishment. I heard her screams as his shadows burned her alive, but they did not touch the house.

As she lay on the ground, she found her strength to tell the King, "The last king will fall to the untouched." His flames continued to burn her, but she resisted. "One more time, for old times' sake, Andras."

The sound of her neck snapping caused me to flinch at firewood breaking for a year after.

"Are you okay?" Esen placed a hand on my lower back to comfort me, unknowingly pulling me from my worst memory.

I nodded my head. "Just tired."

Drying off, I climbed into the bed with no clothes on. I was curious to know when the last time the ones here were washed or if they would fit me. Esen did the same. I lay my head on his chest, his arm draped over my shoulder.

My eyes continued watching the storm rage on outside. "Goodnight, dearest."

"Goodnight, gnat."

A tremor shook the house, rattling the walls.

***

The warmth of the bed and the weight of the blankets kept me asleep and wanting to stay still from now until eternity, as did the steady rise and fall of Esen's breath and his gentle fingers running through my hair.

Inching closer to him, my arms brought us as close as possible. I didn't want to let go of him.

A light lit the room up. Slowly opening my eyes, I looked outside the doors at the tree with a swing on the cliff's edge. Birds swooped in close to the house to eat the berries and nuts that Mimsy kept out for them. Esen said nothing as we watched the birds come and go with their beaks full and their stomachs satisfied.

The weight of my bladder continued to grow until it was unbearable. Peeling myself away from him, I went into the bathroom, relieved myself, and washed up.

When I returned, Esen was standing on the porch wearing clean shorts that fit him. They looked familiar. Maybe they were the ones he had on when we got here; I wasn't sure.

Grabbing a blanket, I wrapped it around myself and joined him. I tip-toed on the wet wood, careful not to step on the food for the birds and other wildlife.

Esen opened up to me, and I stood between him and the railing. His hands moved to my arms, and I began rubbing them.

"Mimsy brought us clean clothes yesterday and food. She also managed to dig up a stash of weapons for us."

Yesterday?

"How long was I asleep for?"

"Two days. You were exhausted on the trip here, and I believe you were on the brink of insanity when we showered."

I let out a chuckle. Ever since I thought I killed him, I hadn't been able to sleep for an entire night. And then Ove was tortured. During those nights, I slept maybe two hours each day. The past week, I don't know if I ever slept. I had been afraid Dearil would take me away from him or him away from me.

I had almost fallen asleep several times at the coronation. I remember falling asleep on the way here, and then I woke up when my body collided with the cave's stone floor. After that, I relied on adrenaline to keep me going and awake.

Esen rested his chin on the top of my head. "I am sorry. The other night, I should have been a better man and resisted my urges. You are the Queen of Below and married to Ove. I should have respected your relationship with him."

I turned around swiftly. He looked down at me, pained. "Don't ever feel sorry for that. I wanted it as much as you did. Ove and I have an agreement: I can take on any lover that I choose, as can he. You are who I choose, and I will repeatedly choose you every day for the rest of my life if you wish."

"I want that, Lynnora, but I will have to resist my urges until I speak to him and get his blessing."

I clicked my tongue. "Such a man of honor."

Sliding past him, I went inside and left the doors open. The blanket fell away from me as I climbed into the bed. I could feel him watching me crawl over the covers. Falling back onto the pillows, I slowly opened my legs up for him to see what was between them. He leaned against the railing with his arms folded across his chest, a smirk on his face.

I lowered one hand between my legs and began to touch the spot I desperately wanted him to touch. With my other hand, I used it to feel my breasts and move them about. My back arched as I slid a finger inside myself. As I played with myself, I kept my eyes on him, his shorts growing tighter and tighter with each movement.

Moving another finger inside me, I let out a moan, which caused his breath to falter. He wanted me as much as I wanted him. He slowly crept inside the room, his hand adjusted what hid beneath his shorts, yearning to come out.

"Mesmerizing," he whispered down to me.

"Enough for you to disregard your honor?" I moved my fingers in a circle, letting him see all of it.

He smirked. "Unfortunately not. I will watch. I am enjoying the entertainment."

I brought a leg to his chest, hoping to tease him further. He kissed my ankle with gentle, loving kisses. I stopped moving my hand when the kisses started.

His hand fell to his pants and pulled out the hardness. "I did not tell you to stop." The desire to have him watch me sent a chill down my spine and heat to the part of me he wanted to watch.

I moved my hands again, his hand touching himself. His lips kept kissing my ankle and leg, occasionally flicking his tongue.

Gods save me. This man is something new, something I have never had and never want to lose.

I felt the wetness on my fingers intensify as they worked. My body shuddered at the release that coursed through my body. My back arched as I moaned loudly, his name on my tongue, wishing it was him inside of me instead of my fingers.

I opened my eyes, and he was smiling down at me, but I could see the panic in his eyes. "Lynnora — I need you — quickly."

I knew what he needed when I saw the fear in his eyes. He was about to finish and didn't think he could handle the mess. I moved fast, my mouth replaced where his hand had been. Not a moment too soon. He finished in my mouth the moment I slid down the length of him and let out a gagging sound.

He let out a loud moan that could be heard in all rooms of the house. His hand wove through my hair, holding me there until he was completely done. His other hand grabbed onto the hand I had used to please myself and brought the fingers up to his mouth, licking them clean.

I waited until I could no longer feel his cum hitting the back of my throat and pulled away, making sure I brought back every drop that he had produced. Pulling off him, he smiled widely down at me as I swallowed every drop.

His arms wrapped around me and pulled me into a hug. "Thank you for everything."

He leaned forward, sending us both onto the bed with a thud. We lay there until the sun barely cast a shadow when our hunger told us to move.

Esen disappeared into the bathroom to shower, and I entered the kitchen with clean clothes on. Mimsy stood over the stove, cooking and smiling and humming to herself.

She smiled widely when she saw me. "I still have your old toys. I can make sure they are here in nine months."

I gave her a curt smile. "Unnecessary. All we need is food."

Sitting in the wooden chair, I poured myself a goblet of water, and Mimsy handed me a plate of food. Breads, meat, cheese, fruits of all kinds.

"Are there any peaches in that?" Esen's voice startled me.

I looked over my shoulder in time to see him pulling a shirt over his head.

"There haven't been peaches in this house since we found out."

We both gave her a polite nod, saying our thanks, and ate the food. I paused halfway through my plate and ran my hand through his soft hair. He continued eating, unaware of my stare.

"You've changed, and I do not mean just your looks."

He finished chewing the bread in his mouth and leaned back in his chair. "You noticed?" I nodded my head slightly. "It is weird. Since I awoke from the transformation, the cloud that once hung over me, dictating my life, has lessened. It is still there, but now I can breathe and think without the fear of death. Messes do not bother me like they once did. I have been able to eat food from the same plate and wait to take showers."

"How are you doing with the other changes?"

"It took a lot of adjusting, and I still am. There are times I see the scars or feel my split tongue, and I panic."

I continued running my hand through his hair. "I'm glad you are alive, and I am sorry that you had to find out about your lineage in a harsh way. I am thrilled we got those five extra minutes you desperately wanted."

His face paled, and his body grew stiff. "You heard me?"

I swirled a finger through a strand of his hair. "Every word." I heard his plea to the gods, his proclamation of love, the fear in his voice. I heard it all. "You told me I would not question your declaration, and I have not for one second, and I have not forgotten it."

I would trade anything for the woman I love. Those words followed me every day. Never once leaving me. It got me through the days I was alone in a cell. The days I saw Ove. It pushed me through Ove's screams as he was tortured.

Esen would have sacrificed the world to save me. He would have done anything to keep me alive if he knew of a way.

And yet I lied to him.

A surge of air reached into my lungs. Blinking away the painful memories, I looked at the man who loves a demon with nothing but gratuity and appreciation showing in my eyes.

I walked out of the kitchen before Esen could say anything to me. Through the hall, I could hear Mimsy's quiet voice, "Give her time. Her eyes show a new horror none have been told about. When she is ready, she will tell you and reciprocate your emotions."

"Thank you Mimsy." Esen's voice was gentle.

CHAPTER TWELVE

ALYA

It had been two days since a tremor caused the water around the domes to rattle. We had felt it inside and within our cells. Rumors quickly filled the air. A powerful angel fell, a god granted eternal reincarnation, or a demi-god was born. Those were the positive rumors, and others were harsher. A god killed another. The gods were angry at us for the war raging on land. Each rumor somehow made its way back to the gods.

With each one I heard, I knew they were all false. Whatever had happened, the gods had no control over it. This was something powerful and would alter the war.

Benji had prayed to his favorite goddess the moment he had felt it, asking for her patience. It broke my heart every time he muttered her name, my name. I have no gifts anymore, and my mother had ensured that.

To kill a god is nearly impossible due to their gifts, but you can kill a god if you can inhibit those powers. During the first Holy War, mortals had fallen susceptible to believing they could capture a god and use iron to bind them, making it easier to kill one. They were wrong.

A god can only have its powers restrained or taken away if they are tricked into it. Sometimes, a god willingly gives up their gifts to live a mortal life, but they are the weaker, unknown gods. The powerful ones with a domain to tend to or a gift to grant do not willingly give them up for a mortal life.

My mother had tricked me into giving mine up, and in doing so, I was born as an angel, later to be the first fallen angel. She had needed someone to test her ability, and I was the first being she saw. For ages, I could not control the world's winds or push one towards one's soulmate. My immortality did not leave me due to my mother's experiment. Part of it went wrong and kept my life span.

I was there the day the world split into seven land masses. I lived through the wars of angels and demons, through the one of men. I saw the Courts turn against one another and brand their kind.

But I have also seen the beauty the world has to offer. I have heard the first cries of a newborn, seen the shimmering lights over the Dahr Court, and swam in the river of Neema. I have tasted the luxury of meat from Sparan. I was there for it all and will continue being there for it all until the world ceases to support us.

***

The guards were changing for the night shift. The otherwise quiet halls were filled with a harsh murmur as guards took their positions and servants brought in food. Benji sat beside me on the far wall with his head resting on my shoulder.

"She is missing?" A guard loudly whispered to the servant who passed by our cell.

The girl nodded her head. "Not even a full day on the throne."

I shrugged my shoulders and readjusted how I sat. My rear was numb from being still for so long. Whichever Queen vanished will appear in a few days; they always do.

"Cell check!" A cold, irritating voice called out.

Benji and I rose and looked at each other, saying *who died and made the Lion the Captain?*

The horrid man waltzed into the cell, twirling his sword. He whistled a tune as he looked around, inspecting it for any sign of an escape attempt or another person. His eyes landed on me, and the whistle stopped. His smile twisted.

"Your precious Prince earned himself the title of King. Too bad his bitch of a wife wasn't able to last a day on the throne."

Ove became King?

I took a half step forward. "Who was named Queen?" Please do not say Ava, anyone but her.

The Lion looked startled at my question. "Rumor is a thin bitch named Lynn."

My fear and sorrow melted until nothing but joy and light shone brightly through me. My body radiated the warmth it had been deprived of these past four months. A wide smile bared all my teeth, my eyes illuminated with hope and love.

A laugh crept up my throat and made it past my lips. Both the men looked at me uneasily, nervous that I was having a breakdown. I wasn't.

My laughter continued to rage on until I was bending over, clutching my stomach in search of air. I persevered through the pain of the shackles on my wrists and ankles, through the hunger that has been gnawing at me.

Forcing myself to straighten my spine, I held my head high and looked down my nose at the perverted man. "Oh, you are so screwed. I am going to enjoy every moment of this."

The Lion lashed out, his hand wrapped around my throat, pinning me to the wall, his mouth open as he breathed his foul stench onto me. "I do not fear you, the Ghosts, or a weak, untried King."

My laughter continued even as he tightened his grip on my throat to silence me. "I do not care what you fear. Your death will not be peaceful. Long may King Ove reign, long live the Queen."

He threw me onto the ground. My bones groaned at the impact. Benji moved to help me but got thrown back. The Lion stood over me. "Solitary confinement should correct your misplaced loyalty. Maybe I will join you there."

I smiled up at him. "Do your worst." I spit at his feet.

He pulled me up from the ground and pulled me out of the cell when Benji cried out to us. "Wait!" He stopped pulling me and let me face my cellmate, who may never see me again. "I pray every day to Aniya because the seer said she would be the one to liberate me from my eternal torture. May she watch over you as she will watch over me."

"Your weak goddess has no place here, rat." The lion snapped at him and pulled me further out into the hall.

"You are right; she doesn't." I could hear Benjis' voice after he was gone from my view.

No guards, servants, or other prisoners questioned what was happening. I still smirked, even though his grip on my arm was painful.

Lynn is alive, and if she has not come for me yet, then that must mean she is in trouble. Her loyalty has never wavered, even when she thought I hated her. I will break out of here and save her. It is my time to save someone.

The iron cell doors came into view. He unlocked one and tossed me into the darkness. He quickly stood over me and began undoing his belt.

"Wait! I am bleeding, and I will be for about four more days at least, seven at most."

He snarled in frustration and refastened his belt. "On the eighth day, you are mine." He slammed the door shut as he left.

Seven days.

I just bought myself seven days to plan an escape, and on the eighth, I will break free with Benji at my side.

We will be free.

***

A guard brought me the slightest bit of food, no doubt on orders from The Lion—anything to keep me thin and weak. As the guard sat the food down, I could see the pity in his eyes.

"Can I ask you something?" I spoke gently, with no movements, so he would not run. He looked over his shoulder and gave me a slight nod. "What happened to the new Queen of Demons?"

Once more, he looked over his shoulder to ensure none were watching or listening. His voice was a whisper I had to strain to hear. "Rumor is she was kidnapped, and her husband did nothing to protect her."

"Thank you."

He left quickly and locked me in the darkness for the night.

Lynn is safe; otherwise, Ove would have ripped the world in two to look for her and protect her. He has made it obvious that no harm will come to her if he has a say.

I ate a few bites of my food and lay on the rotting bedroll tucked in one corner. I stared at the ceiling, thinking about my plan and how I would accomplish the impossible. I had no idea where to start. I know the rotations of the guards and servants; that is the easy part. But I don't know how to reach the surface without killing us.

All I know is that my plan of attack is to attack. Bring down every guard I can; if I manage to shatter the dome on my way out, then so be it.

Chapter Thirteen

LYNNORA

I felt the hands first trying to shake me awake. Mimsy's panicked voice swiftly followed.

"Lynn, wake up!" My eyes flew open, and I gasped for air in fear of not having any. Esen heard her plea and felt my body jolt. He quickly woke up and instantly refilled my lungs with air.

I looked at her, searching for any sign of what was wrong. She held a sword in her hand momentarily before passing it to Esen. He took it, confused.

"They found you. I saw one by the tree a minute ago. She will be here any moment now. Quickly!" She threw the covers off of us.

We both rose from the bed and dressed in our clothes from yesterday. I summoned my blades as the two of them hurried to the kitchen. Making my way to them, I saw all the curtains closed, blocking any sight of the assailant from us, but us from them, too. Mimsy remembered what to do.

They threw the door to the tunnel open. She was placing food into a bag for us to take with us.

Through the back door, I heard the familiar sound of a playful growl I had thought I would never hear again.

"Close it," I whispered to both Esen and Mimsy and gestured for her to go into it. She did not question my order. I waited for the top of her head to be fully submerged when I locked the door behind her and held my daggers up, ready to strike.

Esen took his stance, holding his sword and aiming at the back door.

I nodded at him, and he returned it with one of his own. "Come in unarmed if you wish to keep your life," I called out to the person on the other side of the door.

The handle twisted, and the door opened. In walked a short girl with two beautiful dogs at her side. "They are great trackers, but terrible hunters. I thought you would have taught them better, Lynn."

"Adri!" Esen gasped before I had time to process the casualness of her voice. He lowered his sword and hugged her. She gave a weak embrace back.

"H-how do you two know each other?" I stammered out.

They both were faintly smiling when Esen spoke. "She helped me out with my transition and training. She also gained me access to the Below to save you."

"Gods, you can't keep a secret, can you?" Adri moved away from him and began looking for food in the kitchen.

"I can! But if you think I can not, should I be the one to tell her why you—"

"Watch that tongue! You beat me once. I beat you the other fifty times."

They both made a mocking face and sneered at one another.

Unlocking the door, I let Mimsy come back up, who was clutching a stone, ready for a fight. Alika and Sheena immediately went to the closest fire and lay before it.

"How did you find us?" I finally found my voice again.

She threw open a cupboard. "Your husband lent me the girls, saying if anyone can find you, they can."

I moved over to a chair, and Mimsy sat beside me, wide-eyed with horror. Esen made himself comfortable leaning against the wall.

"Where are the others? How much time do we have until we need to leave?"

She slammed the cupboard shut and sat on the counter. "Don't worry. I sent them to their courts to listen for any rumors of your whereabouts."

"Why?" My question came out harder than I intended.

"Because she serves you and Ove, not Dearil. We all know if Ove wanted you by his side, he would have killed me the second I held the blade to your throat." Esen answered for her.

"Why?" I hate repeating myself. "Why does he not want me by his side?"

"To save Alya, of course," Adri said unnervingly casually as if we should all know what she meant.

Save her. Those were Ove's last words to me. I thought they were too Esen talking about me.

"Why, where is she?" Esen asked, pushing himself off the wall and holding tightly onto the sword.

Adri looked at all of us wide-eyed. "She is in Auk. Alden sent her to prison for Esen's death. I thought you knew that?"

"No." Esen and I both said in a breathy voice.

No. Not sweet, Alya, too good for this world. No. She can't be there. That place is meant for monsters like me. They will break her beyond repair.

"Can Ove do anything?"

She shook her head. "Not in a time of war. She isn't valuable enough to do a prisoner exchange. He wants you to get her out of there before anything worse can happen to her."

"She can not go. He can not send his Queen into enemy territory, into that prison."

I matched Adri's eyes as they told me everything I needed to know. "He's not sending his Queen in. He's sending the Seventh Ghost in."

Adri nodded her head, confirming my suspicions. "He is sending in my second, as am I."

"Your second?" Mimsy's voice startled me, causing me to flinch enough that Esen noticed it.

"King Ove has ordered the Ghosts to work as one. He appointed me their commander, and I am asking you, Lynn, to be my second should I ever fall."

My heart began to beat faster. Ghosts don't work as a group; it is always a solo mission. We are a formidable force alone but would be unstoppable together—a living nightmare.

I grabbed the fabric covering my heart to feel its rapid beats of it. "You have my blades."

"And you have my heart." Adri placed her arm across her chest.

My heart slowed, and the blood in my ears pounded as our hearts fell in sync.

We are bonded.

I looked at Esen and Adri to see if their faces showed signs of a plan forming. Esen's snake eyes were stuck on me, waiting for my decision or to hear my plan. Adri was still focused on finding food in the cupboards, with no sign of a plan.

"Adri, I know you are the leader, but can I take charge of this mission?"

"Obviously. I can't help, anyway. I need to get back to Leevah and do damage control. You, Esen, left a mess behind for me to clean up."

He threw his hands up in defeat. "I said I am sorry! I did not know I would be that big when I shifted. I will pay for the damages."

"With what money?" Adri and I asked in unison.

He pointed a finger at her. "I dislike you." The finger moved over to me. "I most definitely hate you."

I gave him a smirk that challenged him in a way I knew he would dislike. He scowled at it, causing my smirk to intensify.

"Mimsy, can you take Esen into town and get supplies, along with finding the next boat that can take us to Auk?"

She grabbed her cloak and clasped it around her neck. "I should go alone. No offense, Your Majesty, but your eyes may startle some." He and I gave her a polite nod, fully understanding the situation. She left with a small bow, and I watched her from the kitchen window until she disappeared over the horizon into the tall grass.

Adri hopped off the counter, her feet loudly landing on the wood. The sound of it resulted in a flinch from me. "Esen, join me outside for a minute."

He looked at me for my approval and then left with her.

Making my way over to a room my mother had crafted into an art room for us to draw in together, my finger traced over the table in the center of the room with two chairs on either side.

There were shelves with old paintings and drawings, racks with unfinished paintings, and supplies set about. My mother never let Mimsy clean this room. She wanted the art preserved however the gods decided it should be. If dust was to work its way into the drying paint, then so be it.

Brushing off a layer of dust from the chair meant to be mine, I sank into the wooden chair and leaned back, exhaling a sharp breath. Opening the drawer in front of me, I pulled out a large piece of parchment and laid it atop the table. My hands shook as I reached to open another drawer that contained my charcoal.

I haven't drawn since I was in Arymn, and even then, I only drew one picture. Every time I went to draw, I found myself walking to find Esen or thinking of him.

Holding the hard powder, it coated my fingers when I picked it up. I did what I knew best.

I outlined the prison from memory. All the exits and entrances, the courtyard, the halls that lead to watch towers, and the cells. I marked the few windows I saw, labeled the doors, and noted which ones required multiple keys.

My hands were covered in the black powder when Esen walked in. His chest hitched when his eyes landed on the mess. "Do you have any supplies for a letter?"

I contemplated grabbing it for him but refrained, knowing the charcoal would transfer onto whatever I touched. "There should be ink and quill on a shelf, parchment in the drawer below me." I pushed my chair away from the desk so he could reach in.

He was careful to open the drawer and avoid looking at my hands. Esen found an empty spot on the table and wrote a few words before sealing it off. He disappeared back into the hall for a second before returning empty-handed.

"What are you drawing?"

"The prison. I went there once to test its security."

"What did you find out?"

I smirked. "They heightened all the wrong spots once I left."

He smiled widely at me, his eyes shining brighter than a star on clear nights. "You drew this from memory?" I nodded my head. "Impressive, very impressive."

"Thank you. Did you... I know Ove stole an envelope from me. Did he ever give it to you?"

Esen sat in the chair opposite of me and grabbed onto his chest slightly. "He did, but I never opened it and never will. It was in the suit I wore the day I thought you died."

"You carried it with you that day?" His words surprised me beyond belief.

He nodded his head and patted his chest right above his heart. "I carried it with me every day."

My throat went dry. I could feel tears brimming in my eyes. He did that. He carried it daily and did not know what was inside it.

The door to the room opened, and Mimsy walked in, her boots leaving behind a trail of mud. Esen cringed at the mess but made no move to clean it or to scold her. She is the one who has to clean the house. She can make any mess she wants.

"I could only secure one ticket to Auk, which leaves tonight at sundown." Mimsy laid the singular ticket on the table.

I reached for it before Esen could. I can't risk bringing him with me. He is far too valuable. "Perfect. It gives me enough time to plan and pack."

"You are not going alone," Esen protested.

"I can and I will! I may be Queen of the Below, but I am a Ghost, one of the seven people properly qualified for this. It would be best if you stayed behind. You do not have proper training, and you belong on the throne. You are too valuable to send in on something like this."

"Valuable to who? You or my Court?"

"Both.—Please, Esen, I need you to stay here."

He looked me over, contemplating what I was asking of him. I can't have him go with me. If he gets caught, I can't handle seeing him chained up. It was his face I saw when Ove was getting tortured. I pleaded for him to break because I was breaking. I needed those days and nights to end so I could end. I had heard Ove's screams and gasps for air, but all I saw was the man I had fallen hopelessly in love with and killed.

Each time I see Esen's new scars, a part of me wonders if he was really in the room with me and it was never Ove.

"Fine. But let me at least pack for you."

I nodded my head, accepting that small favor. He looked over the drawing of the prison and left me to plan.

Letting out a sigh of relief, knowing I wouldn't have to bring the glass dome down if he were to get caught, I began to plan.

***

I wore a simple dress to make me appear like a commoner. My hair was pulled back out of my face. My daggers strapped to my thighs. The bag contained a change of clothing and some food; it also had a sword strapped to it. The sword was next to the bag with a note from Esen saying *I like this one the most.*

It is a beautiful sword; it is long and skinny with a gentle curve. The blade appeared to glow a faint blue each time the light hit it correctly. The hilt was ebony black, with a clear gem at the top of it.

I said goodbye to Mimsy in the kitchen and waited on the patio to say goodbye to Esen, but he never showed up. I waited as long as possible, but the sun was about to descend, and I still had to walk to town.

Letting out a disappointed sigh, I left.

***

The town was quiet, doors bolted shut, windows barricaded or broken. The smell of blood clung to the air. Weapons laid about, the soil and trees scorched—all signs of the war that was happening throughout Nevano.

I was glad the town had minimal damage and, hopefully, a few lives were lost. Stepping around a puddle of blood, the smell of it was different. Dipping a finger in it, I tried to blood.

Demon blood.

Dearil had them attack here. Had he known I would come here, and this was his way of finding me? Ove does not know of this place or most of the world. His generals and council will tell him where to strike and how. He is inexperienced, and if Dearil is still there, he can control his son.

Why did Dearil willingly step down?

The invisible chains on my wrists and ankles throbbed, the weight of the shackles pressing down and digging into my skin, reopening the closed wounds. My breaths grew heavy, and my head spun until the town blurred.

Pressing a hand onto the stone wall, I leaned onto it to steady myself, mimicking how Esen breathes when he is spiraling. Forcing my eyes to open and close until my vision came into focus.

I placed one foot in front of the other and took a small step forward. It does not matter how big of a step I take; I can take one step at a time as long as I take the steps in the right direction.

The calls of the birds quickly filled the air, as did the smell of fish and salt. A hurried murmur was traveling throughout the harbor as fleeing people climbed aboard the ship.

The ticket master stood at the edge of the dock, yelling at a man for trying to use a fake ticket to get aboard. Two guards were on their way to restrain the man or possibly arrest him, but judging by the anger and annoyance on their faces, he would spend time locked away.

Cautiously joining the line waiting to board, I kept my head low and my ticket hidden so no one would try to steal it. The line dwindled until the Ticketmaster stood in front of me.

"Ticket," he snarled, showing rotting teeth, and a foul stench poured off him.

Pulling it out of my boot, he scowled and took it, allowing me on. "Women are on the bottom deck. Try not to puke."

Nodding my understanding, I stepped onto the gangway and the ship. It was far more significant than the transporters for the Arymn Court. People were busy going to their decks, collecting belongings, or finding other people.

Slowly looking over the passengers, I noticed all had the same gaunt expression. They are refugees. All were fleeing from the war that was running rampant. Their homes were destroyed, their belongings lost, and lives taken. They have no place to call home, and the Auk Court is one of the safest because no one has successfully invaded the underwater nation. The only court that could is Arymn, and they are in an alliance.

These people are looking for a fresh start, a place to live without fear. We are the same.

I could feel every motion and every wave on the bottom deck. Hammocks spread throughout the deck, tied to posts and other stationary objects that can hold a person's weight. Women and children already occupied many. They secured their belongings to the floor below where they slept. I was careful not to step on anyone's damaged belongings or bump into them as they moved about.

There was an empty bed in the far back; very little light shone on it. Securing the bag underneath me, I brought the sword in close and laid down, hugging it. The motion of the boat was lulling me to sleep. Before falling entirely under, I thought I heard Esen saying goodnight.

Chapter Fourteen

ESEN

I might be sick. Why did I think this was a good plan? I should have listened to her and stayed behind. Lynnora was sloppy and rough when she tossed the bag around like it contained nothing important.

She does not know that I hid in the bag under her clothes. There was no way that I was going to let her go into prison alone.

I slithered out of the bag after it had remained untouched for several minutes. Staying in the shadows, I climbed to where she slept and curled into a ball resting on her shoulder. Her scent, her breaths, and the steady rocking of the ship pulled me into a sleep that I never meant to enter.

***

I stood in my throne room. People were in all different styles of dresses. There was not one theme for the ball that was being held. Some wore masquerade masks; others wore gems beaded into their suits and dresses; some wore minimal clothing. It was chaos.

My chest grew heavy, my breaths rapid, my eyes wide with horror as I tried to slow my spiral—a hand filled with calluses wrapped around my shoulder and upper arm. Jerking myself away, I looked at the man who only wore pants.

The burn scar that once ended above his hip bone continued over his side and down his arm, only stopping in a perfect line at his wrist.

Ove.

He bore a worried expression. His eyes looked at my chest. Following his gaze, I saw what he was looking at. I took in his new scar, and he also took in mine.

"Esen, please tell me you have Alya."

"Not yet, why? How are you here?" He had once told me the dream walking gift was a hoax and impossible. Yet he stood in front of me, not born of my imagination.

He ran his hands through his hair. "I don't know how to explain it, but I can feel Alya, and ever since I found out she is in prison, I can't get her off my mind. She isn't safe. I need you to hurry." He ignored my second question completely.

"Of course. Lynnora and I are on our way to her now. She says she has a plan. Alya will be out of there by the end of the week."

He let out a sigh of relief. "Thank you. Please remind Lynn to mark anyone who has harmed Alya with a K. They will be sent directly to me."

"You would punish them for harming her?"

"It is the least I can do. She is in this mess because of us."

His image began to flicker and fade. However he was here, was no longer working.

I reached my hand out for him to try and stop him from leaving. "Ove, I need to ask you something."

He braced himself on me. I could feel him turning into a solid figure, then into a wisp of air. "Esen, I do not have time right now. Please protect my Queen and Alya."

I gave him a gentle smile. "Something about them tells me they do not need our protection." Alya is a goddess. She may be disgraced, but she still is immortal. And Lynnora, well, she is Lynnora. Not a soul would survive hurting her.

Ove was gone before I could finish my sentence, leaving me with this disturbing ball.

***

Shaking my head to get the dream images out of my mind, I looked around to see if any passengers were moving. None were; all the women and children were still soundly sleeping. Looking at Lynnora, her mouth hung open slightly, and drool was dried on her cheek. She looked disgustingly beautiful.

Curling myself tighter, I closed my eyes and patiently waited for her to wake.

The sound of other women moving caused me to stir and decide to keep hiding in the bag. I do not want to see any of them naked except Lynnora. I enjoy seeing her body with and without clothes on.

I was secured in the bag when she moved. I felt myself shift in accordance with the bag being lifted. She murmured her hello's and excuse me to people she passed them, and she made her way through the crowded deck. I felt the corner of my lips try to twist up into a smile. A fearsome demon who kills for the fun of it being polite to others was heartwarming. I knew she would glare and roll her eyes if she could see my smile.

The bag grew warm as the smell of fresh air flowed through the fabric. The heat was exquisite. I wanted to stretch out and bask in it for the rest of this trip. But a snake on a ship would not be ideal, nor would a stow-away. I must remain hidden for the five days it takes us to get there.

Once Alya is back and safe, I will reclaim my throne. I never thought I would miss it, but I think of my people and what I left behind daily. The baker with his son named after a bread, the miller whose daughter sings beautifully. The farmer who tried to sell me magical beans. I miss Lar and his cooking; I miss relying on Vince to protect me.

I miss it all. Even the meetings that would put me to sleep. The arguments of the council. I got the feeling whenever I could help people out with their problems. The smiles I got in return. Fuck, I even miss when new mothers would ask for me to kiss the heads of their newborns.

I never enjoyed being called the Golden Boy, but I had earned it and let Alden take it from me. I was the youngest King and untried, yet my people seemed to love me. Those around him did not fully respect Alden. I once hated it, but now I appreciate it and hope for it.

If they still do not respect him and his claim to the throne, then I may be able to remove him from the throne with no blood loss. After everything he has done, I do not hate him. He is still my brother, if not by blood, then by choice. We grew up together, attending the same lessons, learning the same dances, and running through the halls together. We are brothers, no matter what.

The bag was set down on the wooden beams of the deck. Light filled in as Lynnora began looking for something. I curled myself into a tight ball, trying to stay out of her reach. Her clothes and the food kept getting pushed into me as she dug around.

"Where is it?" Her frustration came out in a growl. Her hands searched more aggressively.

I held in the hiss as her hands wrapped around me and squeezed hard. "There it is." She let out a sigh of relief.

I knew instantly that I was screwed no matter what I did. Accepting my fate now is better than trying to slither out of it. The sun filled my eyes as she pulled me out of the bag. She was scowling down at me, her eyes a fearsome gray. "Overprotective, persistent little gnat."

I stuck my tongue out at her for the insult I took as a compliment. She stuck her tongue back out at me.

"What are you doing here? I told you to stay behind." Her words were louder than she intended. Those closest to us looked over at the crazy lady who was scolding a snake.

She brought me in close to her chest and picked up the bag. That was when I saw the sword strapped to her waist. It looked like it belonged to her. She shielded me from the eyes of those passing by and made our way to a deck not meant for us.

Guards stood outside a door and tried to stop her from entering when she flashed her eyes and teeth at them. "If you know what is best for yourself, you will get out of my way and keep your mouths shut."

They immediately moved out of her way, not wanting trouble. She locked the door behind us and gently sat me on the table. Shifting into a human, I stayed seated on the table. Staying in that form while sleeping was more challenging than I expected and took a lot of energy out of me.

"What the fuck, Esen?"

I looked at her, amazed. "I would not let you go in there alone. My ability can come in use if needed."

"I. Do not. Care! I am not putting your life at risk for this. I need you to take back your throne. Ove can live without his Queen."

"But he can not live without his best friend." My words made her flinch and pull away from where she stood.

I took the silence as an opportunity to look around the room. Judging by the luxury, we were in the Captain's quarters.

She let out a harsh sigh. "Fine, but you will remain in that form the entire time unless you need to piss. I can't get us thrown off the boat before we reach the Auk Court."

I could hear the pain in her voice. Moving off the table, I wrapped my arms around her and pulled her into a hug. "Are you alright?"

"No," her voice cracked as she said the one word.

"What is wrong, dearest?" I began rubbing her back to try and soothe her.

I felt her chest rise and fall as she took a breath in. "I never thought about her. I had heard her when you thought I had died. I knew she was still there. But I had hoped Alden took pity on her and kept her around. I thought she was safe. I never questioned if she was taking the blame for our actions, which failed. She is there because of me."

I kissed the top of her head. "We will get her out. Alden will pay for what he did to her and you. Alya is a lot stronger than she looks. She will survive this."

She has to.

***

The remaining four days were dull. Depending on what she wore, I stayed wrapped around Lynnora's leg or wrist. She let me enjoy the warm sun as much as possible, even though I could tell she hated every second. None of the ship's crew approached her except to hand out food. During the nights, I curled up into a ball and slept above her shoulder, and if she allowed me, I slept on her chest, stretched out.

With so many people cramped in small places, people grew irritated and bored with nothing to do. Fights were breaking out among the men, arguments were happening among the women, and children were stealing toys from others. I wanted to help them, but I was not supposed to be aboard and was not their or anyone's king. I have no authority.

It has constantly reminded me of what I lost, how I lost it, and why. But it also pushed me to figure out how to regain it.

Uncurling myself, I stretched as much as possible to use my small body's many muscles. Lynnora stirred, rolling over to face me. The entire bed swayed with her movements, causing unease in my stomach. That was one thing I did not like. Any rough motion for prolonged periods made me queasy. I had almost hurled the contents of my stomach the day I hid in the bag, and I never wanted to do that again.

Her breaths danced along my body as she stilled, warming me up. Nestling in closer to her, I stuck my tongue out to give her a faint kiss. She is still Ove's, and I respect their relationship, but I am left with these small acts until he sends a letter permitting me to be with her.

One day, she will be mine, and the world will burn before I let another take her from me or lay a finger on her. I will wait a thousand years to be with her and another thousand to hear her say she loves me. She is worth the wait.

From above the deck we slept in, I heard the shouts of men from the crew. They call to ready the anchor, grab the rope, secure the sails, and more. We were getting ready to dock.

Nudging Lynnora until she woke up, she glared at me. "Wake me up again, and I will give you to the birds."

I stuck out my tongue at her and tried to roll my eyes, daring her to try. One of her fingers wiggled its way under me and picked me up. Hanging on for my life, I curled my tail around her finger and sharp nail, pulled my upper half up so I stood tall, and jerked my head to the exit.

She understood what I was motioning for. Standing up, I fell away from her and stayed in the hammock. She dug around in her bag and pulled out the armor she once wore for Dearil. The black leather was one that I had captured her in. It turns out she had orchestrated that capture, and the discovery of that left me feeling rather stupid.

Her hands were hidden in the gloves, her hair tied back in a braid. She did not pull up the hood or the mask; I understood why. She would quickly be feared, and mass chaos is unnecessary since we are still on the ship.

Her fingers traveled the length of the suit, checking for all the blades. She strapped her two Koya daggers behind her back, on the waistline. She also strapped the sword I had chosen for myself to her back at an angle for easy access.

She looked at me and whispered, "What's the Golden Boy going to wear?"

I gave her a look, conveying what I wanted to say. *You will see.*

Lynnora was satisfied with what she wore and with her weapons. Collecting the bag, she tossed it over her shoulder and scooped me up. Being mindful of all the hidden weapons, I traveled up her body until I rested around her neck and shoulders.

She climbed up the stairs through the crew's deck and, the deck meant for men. None dared bother her or even look in her direction. Those whose eyes casually wandered onto her quickly deviated away when they saw the weapons on her body. Looking down at her shoulder, I noticed she wore no patch to signify who she was fighting for.

I know she has one for each Court and one of bones for Dearil, now Ove. But the Arymn brand on her neck was enough to tell people who she belonged to. They consider her a member of Arymn, one of Aldens' people. Whomever she engages with is now a political nightmare. She is a traitor if she kills or harms anyone allied with Alden. She can only harm those who oppose him.

But the minute that hood and mask go up, she is no one. She is not aligned with any King. She takes no side in the war. She is a free agent, and that is something all should fear.

I admired her, knowing why she did not bear the mark of Ove or any other King. She does not want to be held back when she saves her friend. The sun began illuminating the top of her head, slowly traveling down her body as she climbed the last set of stairs leading onto the main deck. The chilled morning air of spring was welcoming. The air smelled faintly of lilies and fresh bread—such a peculiar smell for being on the water.

Lynnora walked over to the ship's edge, and I could see the minimal land masses of the Auk Court. We were docked at the largest island called Pondra. A small town laid out before us with rivers running through it. Boats were tied to posts at the entrances of homes, and small walkways ran along the side of each canal. Green ivy clung to the walls, and lily pads floated atop the water in bloom.

She moved to the other side of the ship, and we both peered into the water. Deep down, we could see the tops of the domes that dwelled below with the rest of the cities. Twelve domes in total, but only one held the prison. Those not native to the Auk Court do not know which dome is which for security reasons, but I have been to the capital, and Lynnora has been to the prison itself. We know which two domes are the most important. She knows where to go.

The deck was crowded with people eager to get off. We found ourselves in the middle of the hoard, all slowly making our way down the gangplank. Her feet slid in the sand that was below us. She let out a long breath of air, as did I. The first part of this rescue was complete. Now that was left was to find a way down to the prison, get inside it unnoticed, find Alya, break Alya out, escape without sounding the alarms, and finally sail back to the house in Ter. Simple would be an understatement.

Chapter Fifteen

Alya

My time was up. The week I had bought myself had passed swifter than I expected, and now I was about to pay the price for the solitude. By the end of today, Benji and I will be far away from this miserable place.

I sat on the far wall with my back pressed against the cold, damp stone. Each time a water drop fell onto my skin, it sent chills down my body. The jagged rock kept snagging at my tangled hair with each deep breath I took. I locked my eyes on the door across from me, waiting for my supposed doom to come. It will please the man who wants to break me to know that I lost more weight in the days I sat here.

I knew he was behind the limited food I was given. He wanted me small for his pleasure, and he wanted me weak so I couldn't fight back.

I may be a damsel, but I am not in distress. I will fight back no matter what. I will make him pay. I will not let him win.

Taking a deep breath, the door's unlocking sound echoed through the silent stone. Letting my body slide to the side and my limbs go weak, I continued staring at the door as the man who calls himself The Lion walked in. His boots kicked up dirt as he stepped inside, some of it onto my face, which lay on the ground.

"Took you long enough." I could hear the pleasure in his voice. If he wants weak and meek prey, I will give it to him. And when he least expects it, I will strike back.

I grimaced when his hand traced the side of my face and went down to my arms, forcing me to rise. He held tightly onto me and smiled at my weak, frail body. "I could enjoy you thoroughly in here alone, but that would not be enough to punish you for the bitch you are. Why don't we take this out to the courtyard where your precious rat of a friend can watch as I do what he no doubt wants to do to you? There may be a few other guards who will want to join in as well. You are the only bitch in your sector, after all, and we men do need to release some steam."

"You talk too much," I muttered, resulting in a blow across the face. The sting of his hit left my cheek throbbing, and the taste of blood filled my mouth. Turning my head to face him, I spit the blood out onto him.

He growled at me and pulled me along as we made our way out of the cell. My feet dragged along the stone floor, cuts and bruises forming as I tried to get a solid foot on the ground so I could walk properly. He walked too swiftly for me to catch up with him, and my desire to walk alone was causing me more pain with each faulty step. The torches on the wall lit up the otherwise dark hallway, casting shadows I had once disliked, now leaving me wondering if Ove hid in one and was here to save me.

With each passing shadow, my heart sank deeper into a pit of despair. He is not coming for me; neither is Lynn. I will have to do this on my own. And then what? Where will I go when I break us out of here? They will consider me an enemy of two powerful Courts and send someone after us. I have no home to return to. I have no family to protect me. Even with Benji, I will still be alone and constantly afraid. I suppose once Benji grows old and dies, I can shift into a bird and stay that way until generations have passed, and they will presume me dead. All I need to do is outlive my death. I can do that, but at what cost?

Who will I miss watching grow old? What food will I never taste? What music will I never hear? What Kings will I never know of, and their Queen who I will never meet? I will miss so much for the chance to survive. Is it worth that risk? Once Benji dies, then I will be alone as I was for most of my life.

The mirrors above us cast light down to the entrance of the building they had locked me in. Prisoners were scattered around doing whatever they pleased to pass the time. A few heads turned towards me and gave me a pitiful look. Do they know what is about to occur? Are they aware of the humiliation that I am about to suffer? I am not friends with a single person. I know I will have to fight The Lion on my own. None of them will come to my aid. Even if they did, it would mean a death sentence. I don't want any more bloodshed than necessary, but by the end of the hour, The Lion will die, and his soul will be in the Below.

He kept dragging me to the center of the courtyard, where Benji kneeled, tied to the ground. Oh gods, they are going to make him watch. I didn't think they would, but they are. Benji's eyes were locked on the ground, his hands tied behind his back, and his legs pinned to the ground. His knees were supporting him upright. No matter how hard he fought, he could not get up to help me. They made sure that he could not gain any momentum to rise.

A black snake with beautiful blue eyes passed over the chains that held Benji down. The snake's head looked up at me, and I could have sworn nothing but horror showed on its face. But seeing the snake raised a lot of questions in my head. The first is, how could one be here? I didn't have time to ponder all the other questions when The Lion threw me to the ground.

I watched his attention shift to the snake, and he scoffed. "Maybe the vermin will eat the rat for us." He moved to pick up the snake, but it hissed and tried to strike. To my disappointment, whether the snake struck too slow or The Lion was too fast, it had drawn no blood.

The Lion, wanting nothing further to do with the snake, prowled back to where I lay on the ground. People were watching out of curiosity to see what would happen. He stood over me and began undoing his belt. "I told you what would happen once you lost weight. I am thrilled you wanted this as bad as I do."

His belt was undone, and his pants hung open enough to show the bulge clinging to the fabric. I swallowed hard, knowing I needed him closer to strike. "Just do it already, get it over with, you bastard!"

He never liked it when I talked back to him or raised my voice. He took a step closer when the snake slithered away from Benji, hissing a threat to both of us. The snake charged at me.

Shit. This damn snake is going to ruin everything. If he bites me and it's poisonous, I will be affected to some degree, and with my body being as weak as it is, its effects will be significantly more harmful.

The Lion halted in his path. I tried to push away from the snake, but he kept coming straight for me. Then the strangest thing happened. It climbed atop my stomach and did not strike. He turned to face The Lion and reared its head, hissing at the man ready to attack me.

"A snake will not stop me from getting what I want." The Lion advanced and reached out for the snake one more time.

Somewhere behind me, a female clicked her tongue three times. "He may not stop you, but I sure as fuck will. Get the fuck away from her!" A cool female voice snapped. I contained the glee that traveled through my body. I never thought I would hear her voice again, and I definitely did not know she would rescue me after all this time.

The snake moved off me and over to the feet of the woman he worshiped. Lynnora stood there with a sword drawn, her black leather armor bearing no crest. Her grey eyes unleashed a storm of fury.

The Lion drew his sword and took a step forward, not heading Lynn's warning. "Who the fuck are you?"

It surprised me that he wasn't concerned about how she got in here and that no other guards seemed to notice her presence. All the eyes watching had turned away, not wanting to partake in the oncoming battle.

She raised the sword and aimed for The Lion. "I am someone you pissed off. I told you to get away from her, and you didn't. What happens from here on out is your fault." She took a step forward. The boots she wore now stood beside my head. The Lion moved in a direction I had not anticipated.

He sliced at the ropes and undid the bindings that held Benji down. He forced him to his feet and was using him as a shield.

"No!" I didn't mean for the words to come out, but my plea sparked something inside both the sword-wielders. A gentle breeze passed over me, and I looked in the direction it came from. The snake had changed into a man who wore armor similar to Lynn's. It had no dull gleam like hers; it shimmered in the light. Only his blue snake eyes remained visible. It was enough to tell me it wasn't Ove behind the mask.

"Take one step closer, and I kill him!" The Lion shouted as he moved the blade up to Benji's throat.

Gentle hands wrapped around my shoulder and pulled me up to my feet. My legs trembled as I put weight onto them correctly for the first time in a week. I clung to Lynn, who still held the sword up.

She whispered words down to me without breaking her and the Lion's stare. "Was he — was he going to rape you?" I nodded my head against her arm. I could feel the anger radiating off her. Her arm shook with rage. "Filthy bastard!"

She let go of me and moved towards Benji and The Lion. Horns protruded from her hood, a tail with spikes lashed around in the air. Her nails turned to claws, startling both me and the man behind me. I have never seen her nails do that, and if I were to bet on my life, the man behind me has never seen her proper form.

The Lion stumbled back, his grip still tight on Benji. The sword dug into his neck, blood as red as rubies began spilling from the cut that was forming. His eyes showed no sign of fear, only love and relief. I stumbled forward, trying to get to him and save him, but two hands grabbed around my waist, pulling me back. I kicked and screamed at the man, demanding to be let go, but he did not budge. His grip tightened around me, adjusting to each of my movements, refusing to release me.

Lynn advanced, her sword now sheathed and her daggers were in her hands. The Lion grew some sense. "Take one more step, and I kill him. I know she values his life. No friend of hers would want to get him killed."

Tears spilled down my face. What he spoke was the truth. I would never forgive her if she were the reason he died. Lynn looked over her shoulder at me and read my expression. "Very well then."

Blood sprayed across the ground in the blink of an eye, and the Lion shrieked in pain. His sword loudly clattered on the stone. His roar of pain drew the guards' attention, and alarms began to sound as they rushed to assist him. I looked around Lynn to see why he had screamed in pain. A small throwing dagger severed the nerves in his hand, prohibiting him from using it.

In his moment of terror, he released Benji, giving her enough time to rush in and pull him out. With Benji securely in Lynn's grip, I felt like I could breathe again. I stopped fighting the man behind me. Tears stopped forming in my eyes. I could feel how tired my muscles had become in the brief minutes that had passed.

I heard the arrow's release before I felt it fly past me. It was as if time had slowed down just for this horrific moment to occur. Benji stood beside Lynn, facing me. His eyes widened as they saw the arrow aiming for Lynn's heart. I caught the shine of the arrowhead, telling me it was a Koya blade. This was it. This is how Lynn is going to die, and there is nothing I can do to stop it.

His skinny legs carried his frail body effortlessly as he stepped in front of her. My screams of horror quickly overshadowed the sound of the arrow striking the man who brought me light in the darkest of places. Lynn twisted around and caught his body as it was falling to the ground. The man behind me tightened his grip and pulled me away from Benji.

I heard metal scraping against stone. The Lion had retrieved his blade with his unharmed hand and raised it above his head, ready to strike. Lynn was swift and blocked it, shielding both herself and Benji's dying body. Their blades clashed, and the battle had begun. Guards rushed in to secure the prisoners while others ran towards us to apprehend us. Each time water was thrown our way, a gust of wind knocked it off course, sending it back to the owner. One by one, the guards were grasping at their throats for something that wasn't there. Once their bodies fell to the ground, they no longer moved.

Lynn and The Lion still waged their battle. I knew she could have killed him already if she wasn't trying to protect Benji, too. Her strikes were swift and precise, but the Lion had at least ten extra years of training on her. Even with his injury, he was holding his ground.

I looked down at Benji, who was muttering something, but only blood was spilling from his mouth. My screams stopped so I could try to listen to what he was saying. "Thank you for believing in me. I always believed in you, Aniya." He smiled at me with love and devotion. "Take it all back in the name of love." He screamed as he grasped the arrow, yanking it out of his dying body and thrust it into his heart.

"Benji!" I roared his name. My scream could be heard in the land of the gods. It vibrated the glass dome above us. Water promptly spilled in from the cracks that had been created.

Summoning every ounce of strength, I had hidden inside me; I unleashed it upon the world. A wind more powerful than the storms of the ocean traveled through the prison, further shattering the glass. It rained down on us as water replaced what had once been air.

This wasn't how he was supposed to die. I was supposed to save him. I was meant to get him out of here and end his suffering.

Lynn looked back at us. "Get her out of here!" The man behind me released his grip, and a gust of wind passed. Holding in the scream that had built up, the largest snake I have ever seen was looking down on me. His tail wrapped around me, and a pocket of air was placed over my face not a moment too soon. The water was washing away the prison and all those who were there.

The last thing I heard was Lynn's voice. "Say hello to my husband for me." She slit the man's throat open, and his head fell off his body and was hidden underwater a second later. She clung to his body and carved the letter K in his chest. She let his body fall into the chaos and grabbed Benji, only to carve a letter Q into his bony chest.

The snake carried me up through the water. From below, I could see Lynn slowly swimming upwards, too. And the world around me ceased to exist any longer.

Chapter Sixteen

OVE

I heard the screams before anyone had found me. Something from above had caused a mass casualty, and the souls brought here needed judgment. They usually pass through the gates of Abyss, but there are those more foul than others who need a proper judgment and end up in my throne room awaiting a decision.

Adri opened the door to my study and bowed. "You will want to hear this."

I set down the quill and folded the parchment I had written on. Rising from my seat behind my desk, I handed her the envelope, knowing she knew who to return it to. Adri nodded her head and led the way.

The halls were still dark, but one of the first changes I made was allowing torches and fires into the Below. Our need for them is not a weakness like Dearil had made it out to be. I also hated having to strain my eyes some days to find my way around. Even though we have evolved into the darkness, we cannot see in the dark.

Screams bounced off each wall and the floor, filling the halls in every corner. What the fuck happened that would ensure this amount of chaos? I had called back as many soldiers as possible in preparations to end this war against mortals. These screams could not be from a battle.

With each step I took, the weight of the crown intensified. The double doors into the throne room came into view. The guards immediately opened the door for me, exposing what was happening within.

The room was filled with souls, all shouting and yelling. A perfect circle had formed, and in the center were two white wisps fighting.

What the fuck?

The souls parted as I walked through them and into the circle.

"Enough!"

The two souls stopped fighting. One gift of being the King of Demons is the ability to give form to the soul. Giving the two of them their previous bodies back, they both stopped fighting and looked at what I had done to them. The one with messy brown hair, skin sticking to his bones, immediately fell to his knee and bowed. The other man was larger and fuller, and his eyes were filled with disgust as he half bowed. Usually, I would be offended by the act, but my attention was on the marks they bore on their chests.

Walking past them, I sat on my throne. Adri ushered the two of them forward. The smaller one fell to his knees in a bow, and the larger one kept his head down. "Speak."

"Your—"

"Not you, the mousy one with a Q on his chest." I stopped the larger one from speaking, more curious why he bore the mark of the Queen, especially when she was not here.

He did not rise, but his head looked up, and he smiled, showing the near-perfect teeth his lips hid. "Your majesty, the goddess of the seven winds and soulmates liberated me from the prison in the Auk Court. This man beside me meant great harm to my friend, to Alya. I believe the one who rescued her and fought to protect me, to be your wife, the Queen of Below."

"Fucking shit." The large man mumbled under his breath and ran his hands through his hair.

I looked down at him in disgust. He had meant to cause harm to Alya. He may not have a physical body for me to hurt, but I will ensure I torment him for eternity. I will be the thing he fears the most. I will make him wish he had never been born.

"What were his intentions with her?"

The mousy man took a shaky breath before whispering, "He wished to defile her, Your Majesty."

Anger I have never felt before riled inside of me. I wished he were still alive so I could skin him and make him eat his flesh. Then I would make him chop off his dick, or maybe I would hold him over a fire and let it burn off. He intended to harm her in the foulest of ways. Not one punishment would be good enough for him. He deserved them all.

"Do you have anything to say for yourself?"

The vile man looked up at me. "He's a liar, your majesty. He was imprisoned because he lied and sold out his comrades. His words are not to be trusted."

"Do not insult me by lying to me!" I yelled down at him, and my anger was unleashed. "Do you know what the marks you bear on your chest mean? It is a code among the seven Ghosts and their King and Queen. Kings are expected to be cold and cruel, to serve harsh punishments to those who deserve them. While Queens are seen as soft and gentle, they offer pardons for the good. You are the only liar here. My Queen would never mismark someone." I looked over at the smaller one. "What is your name?"

"Benji, your majesty."

"Well, Benji, since my wife is not here to pardon you of your crimes, but she saw you as worthy, I suppose I will have to hold up on her end of the deal. You are hereby pardoned of all crimes you committed before your death and are granted a place in my court if you wish."

I know Lynn, and she would never mark someone with the Queen's mark unless she had a reason. Whatever the reason is, she wants him spared from eternal torture. And I have the feeling it was on behalf of Alya. The man bowed as low as he could get and said his thanks.

Looking back to the one marked for an eternity of suffering, I smiled coldly, willing my shadows to float around and taunt him. "You and I are going to have so much fun."

***

My leg shook violently as I collapsed into the bed. The warm blankets welcomed the chill in my body. I let out a moan of pleasure, feeling the comfortable bed beneath me. I hadn't been able to sleep for the past week. Each time I did, the bird was locked in a smaller, darker cage with no life left in her. She had given up, and whatever brown thing usually resided below her was gone, most likely withered away into nothing.

The knock on the door jolted me upright. "Enter." The door to my small room opened. I should have moved into the chambers meant for the King but could not bring myself to part with this room. It was always a safe place to return to, and it was where I felt happy, even in the darkest days. I did not want to leave my sanctuary just for formalities.

Adri came in, locking the door behind her, just as I have asked her to do whenever she comes in. "Ivy is in Auk consoling her King. Losing the prison took a toll on him and his Court."

"How many died?"

"We are still getting a count, but there do not look to be any survivors."

"Is she — is Alya among them?"

Adri moved over to the side of the bed and sat down. "Not that we have seen. She may have gotten out. Souls are saying a giant snake carried away two bodies. I believe it was her and the Queen. I leave in a few days to check on them and to give Esen your letter. I will return as soon as I know their outcome."

"Thank you. Where are they?"

She shook her head. "You know I can't tell you."

I hated myself for making sure she didn't tell me where Lynn and Esen were. I feared Dearil would come into my dreams, pry the information out of me, and hunt her himself. It was a shock to me he had not come to court or tried to speak to me since I threw him out. He has made no move to take back his throne or to harm me and my people. I don't trust him; I know him well enough to know he is planning something. Otherwise, he would never have given up the power he had. He loves it too much. The power he wields is a drug for him and one that he will never get rid of.

"Are you alright?" She placed a hand on my leg to comfort me.

I trust her with my life. Her concern for others is why I made her the commanding officer of the Ghosts. She is a demon who loves when all others shy away from it. She has shown I can trust her repeatedly, even before I took the throne. She has always been there in the shadows, watching over me and Lynn.

"No." I sighed. "I can't help but feel like we are all walking into our deaths and that this war will be the last of its kind. I worry none of us will survive it. And I have no idea why my father gave me the crown. That itself is terrifying."

She rubbed my leg gently. "If anyone is to know what he is planning, it is Ava. She was one of his mistresses, and with her being a Ghost, he could confide in her and command her not to speak of it. I would start there if you want to know more."

I looked at her, and she quickly looked away. "Thank you, Adri. You have been a blessing I never expected."

Her hand stilled on my leg. "Ove — I know you care deeply for Lynnora, but if you ever need company — I offer my service to you."

She still did not look at me. Gods, what she offered was wanted and needed, but I couldn't. I felt myself harden at the thought of it. It has been so long since I was inside another or even touched myself. Sitting up more, I leaned in towards her and pulled her in close to me.

"I appreciate the offer, but I can't. I know your heart does not belong to me, and mine does not belong to you. I will take only one person as my mistress, and she is currently with my wife — hopefully." I kissed the top of her head. "Stay with me tonight, Adri, to sleep, not to fuck."

Since Lynn and I got back from Arymn, I have hated sleeping alone, and after my torture, I despised it even more in fear that Ava or my father would come back to finish what they started.

Adri nodded her head and stood up, undressing into her undergarments. My shadows fell away from me. The suit I wore dissolved into nothing. The two of us crawled into bed and lay beside each other, not touching. Sleep swiftly found the both of us.

***

Her arms latched onto me like I had once done to Alya. Looking down, she held it close to her chest. Her head lay on my shoulder, and a leg draped over my leg. Pulling away from her, I left into my bathroom. The hot water poured onto my back, stinging the fresh scars on my arm. I shunned away from the sight of it and washed my body.

Adri was gone by the time I went back into the bedroom. Ensuring that the door was once more locked, I lay in bed and allowed the shadows to recreate a memory for me.

Lynn was wandering the dark streets of the Below, staying in the shadows as she was training. I flew overhead, watching her to ensure she was not being obvious with her stalking. She clung to a wall and peered around the corner, her eyes following her prey. An older girl was entering womanhood. Dearil suspected her of treason and wanted her caught in the act. He sent Lynn out to test her skills before he would initiate her. This was her last test.

So far, she was passing with no faults. I had a bad feeling about this test, knowing Dearil likes to make something unexpected happen to see how they will react. My eyes swiveled, looking for any sign of danger and any unwanted company. I would not put it past Ava to interfere and make her fail. It wasn't prohibited from tampering with another's tests; Dearil encouraged it.

Lynn was progressing down the street when a fight occurred among demons outside a tavern. She brushed past them with ease and continued trailing her target. I saw the girl disappear down an alley, no doubt trying to avoid the commotion of the brawl. I didn't see it coming, and neither did Lynn.

The girl swung a broken piece of wood at her and struck her in the stomach. I knew I had to stay back. Lynn would never forgive me for interfering. I landed on the roof and watched the two girls fight. Lynn swiftly got the upper hand and took the girl down. During the fight, the girl had lost her footing and fell. Her head smashed into a rock, shattering the bone beneath.

She died in one breath.

I landed and looked at Lynn, horrified. She had yet to kill someone, and for this to be her first kill was not what either of us had expected. Lynn stuttered as she tried to find words to explain what had happened, but nothing came out.

"It's okay. Go back to the castle. I will meet you in my room, and then we will go to your meeting with the King together." I looked down at the dead body. "I will explain what happened." Lynn promptly left, running back towards the castle.

I summoned my dagger and plunged it into the girl's heart. My shadows wrapped around her, claiming the kill as mine. They whispered into her fleeing soul a deal. She will not have to fear the demon King if she swears her loyalty to me. She swore her allegiance and was added into my shadows. Her physical body dissolved into the darkness, never to be seen again.

The scene shifted to the throne room, where no souls were wandering. The King sat on his throne, and Lynn was nowhere in sight. She had listened to me and was still waiting for me in my room.

"Prince Ove, I did not summon you." My father's cold voice still showed some love towards me.

"Apologies, my King." I fell into a bow. "I came to beg for your forgiveness."

"What did you do that would warrant such an act?"

I gulped, knowing what I was about to say. "I killed the girl you sent Lynn to retrieve alive."

There were no questions about why I did such a thing, only heat and darkness. I could barely move without feeling his heat scorching my skin. The girl was wanted to be brought back alive, and Lynn had killed her, failing the task. A life for a life is what Dearil promises, but I am his son. He will not kill me, no matter how much I anger him. He doesn't need Lynn alive. Better me injured than her dead.

"You dare interfere with the work of my Ghost!" His bellow caused me to falter. I took a step back—the first of many.

My legs carried me without my command. I was almost to the door when I felt his shadows wrap around my leg, burning the flesh to the bone and ruining the smooth skin that I once bore. I screamed out in pain as it continued to burn through me. My screams filled the chamber until there was nothing but darkness.

Lights flickered as my eyes slowly opened. The pain in my leg was unbearable, causing me to fall back under its power.

She smelled of spring on a cool morning after fresh rain. Her scent pulled me from my deep slumber. Lynn stood over my bed, holding my hand, fighting back the tears.

"You're alive," she gasped.

My throat was dry and sore. "It will take a lot more than that to kill me." I let out a chuckle. As my head turned to look around the room I was being held in, I saw the sight of my leg. I fought back the bile that had worked its way up. Quickly covering it with the blanket, I never wanted to see it again. I knew the next time the healer came in, I would kill her for not chopping it off.

Lynn let the tears fall from her eyes as she wept into my shoulder. "What happened? I waited for you, and you never showed."

I rubbed her back, and she let out a hiss. I felt the ridges of the new scars that lined her flesh. She had passed; they initiated her. Relief surged through me, knowing my efforts did not die in vain.

I let out a weak chuckle to try and comfort her. "I'm sorry. He summoned me to punish me for something that had happened earlier this week. It's a long, boring story you don't need to concern yourself with."

She continued crying and nodded her head. "You're alive. That's all that matters." She pulled away and forced a smile onto her gentle, young face. "You and I, together forever."

"Together, we will take what we want and not give a damn." I returned the smile she wore, not wanting her to know how I truly felt.

She moved over to the nightstand and poured us a small glass of chilled blood, handing one off to me. The glasses clinked together. "Here's to not giving a damn together."

My shadows dissolved back into me as the memory ended. The worst and best days of my life were those days. The day I saved her life, we made a promise that would last our entire lives.

It will always be me and her together. Neither of us giving a damn as we take what we want. I smiled at that memory, knowing it would be a promise we both uphold with our lives. No matter who we fall in love with or the horrors we endure, we will always find our way back to each other, and our love for one another will never cease to exist for as long as we live. She may not be my soul mate, but we are partners who are bonded for eternity.

Chapter Seventeen

LYNNORA

Alya didn't say anything to us on the trip back to the house. She lay there staring up at the ceiling each night on the boat. There were nights I heard her cry silently. Whatever had happened in that prison had broken her in more ways than one. Her skin was loose, her body weak. Her wrists and ankles were raw and coated in dry blood from the shackles being bound too tight.

Her hair was falling out and covered in filth. Her eyes showed no sign of the hope and love that they once had. What she once was had disappeared, and something new was replacing it. I could use it to my advantage if I were greedy and selfish. Shape her into a killer; I know she could be with the proper motivation. Force her to do what I want, convince her it is for a worthy cause. That was what Dearil did to me, did to all the Ghosts, and so many more.

I paid close attention; I learned his words and his movements. I learned everything there was to learn. I could do it, but that's not me. I am not the monster he sought to create, and I will not bring another into that life. No matter how broken one is, they do not deserve the manipulation of a greedy person.

Looking over to where Esen was curled up soundly sleeping, his horrors flooded into my mind. I know his father harmed him to *help* him. He seldom spoke of the late King, making me wonder what else he did to him to ensure an obedient Prince. He was never portrayed as a cruel king; from what I was told, his people seemed to love him. The worst he had done was have a mistress, but I don't know of a single king who hasn't had one at some point in his reign. Esen was the first and probably the last.

Studying the shimmering black scales that lined his body, they seemed to change color as the light swayed with the ship. He was soundly sleeping atop my bag. His eyes would occasionally open and search for Alya and me; then, he would go back to sleep. I wanted to talk to him, but he hadn't shifted since the prison. I wanted to know where he got that armor and where it was hidden. I had gone through all the clothes and supplies in the bag before entering the prison, and there was no sign of anything belonging to him. I knew the surge of power I felt during the final moments was not from him, either. His magic is gentle, like a breeze. That was something entirely different. It was a raw, unrelenting power born from a forgotten place. It was stronger than a king's power. It felt like a gift from the gods. I have never seen such a force that could easily shatter thick glass. I knew the moment I felt it only death and chaos would ensue. And I was right, and if it weren't for Esen, I would have been dead, as would Alya.

A scream from the top deck snapped my attention away from my two friends. Alya woke up in a panic, frantically looking around to see what was happening and to ensure she was safe. Esen jerked his head up to see what caused the commotion.

"Stay with her." I looked at him, and he nodded. Rising from where I sat, I passed by Alya, who was trying to calm herself down. I went to rub her shoulder, but she pulled away. Giving her a nod that told her everything would be alright and that she was safe, I left to find the person who screamed.

People were rushing about, trying to either run from the source or to the source. People's curiosity would be the death of them, as would mine. Climbing the last set of stairs, I saw why people were screaming. Limp bodies lay atop one another in a circle surrounding a tall man. Their chests still rose and fell. Whatever he did to them, he didn't kill them.

The sun glinted off his polished armor, the light blinding me temporarily. Moving out of its rays, I saw the tip of the triangle symbol.

Alden had sent this man.

Did he know it was Esen and I who rescued Alya? Does he know I am alive? He knows Esen is. The scars on his body are proof of it.

Being careful not to give myself away, I stuck to the crowd of women trying to console the children. Seeing and hearing the screaming children brought me back to the orphanage and that girl who found her voice when no one had. Her bravery outshone her fear. Even though her words were pure terror, she had the courage and strength to stand up to me and try to bring me down. A part of me felt guilty for terrorizing those kids, but a greater evil was among them, and I wasn't going to let him get away, just like I wouldn't let this man harm anymore.

"Get the kids out of here. Now!" I snapped at the mothers and other women. They seemed to realize the severity of the situation with my harsh tone. I helped as much as I could, ushering them down the stairs. I ascended the stairs once I knew they were well out of sight and out of harm's way.

The blades in my hand were itching to cut a throat. My stomach roared to life with hunger from not eating for a long time. The sound of grunts filled my ears as the men tried to bring down the man.

The assailant was quick and ruthless. He was ripping air out of their lungs, forcing them to their knees. Few had advanced, but none had drawn any blood from him. I have watched Esen enough to know that to use his gift properly, he has to have a full range of motion with his hand, and his fingers always eventually close. I can either keep his hand open while I deal with him or close it and not let him open his fingers. But cutting off his hands will be so much easier.

I assessed the situation and came up with a plan. Now, I need to make sure others won't interfere. After that, I can strike. My skin crawled with my thought process, knowing Dearil forced this thinking. He still controls me even from afar and is no longer the King I serve.

The men were overwhelming the assailant and able to gain some ground, but only five at most had a weapon to stop him.

"Restrain his hands! Don't let his fist close!" I shouted my order out at them. Thankfully, they had enough sense not to fight with me, and they began trying to go for his hands. One by one, the men were thrown back several feet, their bodies harshly colliding with the wood below. Some moved but were in too much pain to rise, while the others lay there. Had he been able to kill them by throwing them?

Watching this man fight reminded me why Dearil and Daxon wanted Esen and his army. You cannot kill what you cannot touch. They are a formidable force, and I have to eliminate one. Sliding through the men, I kept out of the man's view, doing my best to gain as much ground as possible. I must take him by surprise and get behind him if I can. It would be tricky with where he stood, his back to the railing, and there wasn't much distance between him and it. We could push him over if I could get enough men to charge simultaneously.

No. I know my plan. I can't change it. I can't doubt myself. I can't rely on others. I have to do this. Taking in a breath of air, I steadied myself and ran at him. His eyes widened with shock, knowing he had let someone slip past his defenses. My blade swung at his neck, but he was faster than I expected and dodged the blow that would have killed him. I tried to strike again, but my blade collided with his.

Shit.

With a sword, he can strike me from a further distance. My blades are meant for close combat. I need to fall away and reassess, but what if I don't get another chance? He knows I am here and am skilled. His defenses will be up. This is my one chance. I have to end this here and now.

We continued exchanging blows. His leg swung out and collided with my knee, sending a sharp pain through it. I screamed out in pain, my vision blinded by it. The sun above felt like it was spinning. I have broken many bones before, but my knee was new, and it was the worst pain I have experienced. The air in my lungs was ripped out as I clutched my leg and tried to pull myself away from him.

I am not stupid. I know I lost my chance, but I am useless with a leg that can't help me. His hand wrapped around my neck, pulling me to my feet. He held me against him, and his hand moved to the front of my throat, choking me further and eliminating my chance to breathe.

"I was told Lynnora Fenwald is a weak demon, but others told me not to underestimate you. The former seems to be true." His voice was cold with years of death in it.

My chest was aching, my lungs screaming for air. Forcing my eyes to stay open, I would not allow myself to faint from the pain or lack of air. If I do, he will take me to a second location. I am dead if he does. Esen won't be there to save me. The injury to my leg will be the reason I fail.

"Just kill me already."

He let out a low chuckle. "As entertaining and appealing as that sounds, he wants you alive."

I can't hold on much longer. Think Lynn, think.

Using my uninjured leg, I kicked it back, hoping to hit his leg and cause him to step back. He countered the move and swept my legs out from under me, holding them behind his own. I let out another scream of pain with the movement on my broken knee.

A shriek sounded from the stairs. I looked to see if another assailant was looking for Esen and Alya; instead, it was the Golden Boy himself. Esen wore that mesmerizing black armor that fit him perfectly. It covered his mouth and nose, only showing his eye and the thin vertical slit of black in the center.

"Only one person gets to choke my Queen, and that is not you." Esen held the sword up, pointing it at the man holding me.

The fingers around my throat twitched. "What the?" He mumbled under his breath.

Esen let out a laugh. "The goddess of the seven winds protects me. My gifts are stronger than yours." A surge of air coursed through my body. I inhaled as deeply as possible, never wanting it to leave me. "I would recommend letting her go before you piss me off further and piss off her husband. He is temperamental and the Demon King."

The man did not let me go. He raised the blade to my stomach, the edge of it breaking through my shirt and stinging my skin as he pressed it into me. Blood quickly stained my white shirt red. I held in the cry of pain.

I can survive this. I will survive this.

The sight angered Esen, and he charged at the man. His instincts kicked in, and he dropped me to defend himself. I allowed myself to scream from the impact of the wood on my knees. My eyelids were fluttering closed when two small hands wrapped around my arm, trying to tug me. Looking at who it was, I expected Alya, but it was a child with tears streaming down his face.

His dark brown hair was messy, and his green eyes pierced my soul. "Get up. Please get up." He begged me to move.

"Ove?" I said it no louder than a whisper, confused as to how this boy looked so similar to him.

He continued to try and pull me away from the two men fighting beside me. "Please, get up. You need to get up and move one more time, and then you can rest."

One more time.

Nodding my head, I held one arm across my stomach to limit the bleeding. With my free arm, I began dragging myself across the floor. My body revolted with each movement. I knew my knee was shattered, and this was making it worse. The boy continued crying and trying to help me escape the fight. Once we were at a safe distance, I positioned myself upright, my breaths short and ragged. The boy was pressing his hand to my stomach to keep my blood in me.

A shadow of a bird passed over me and began attacking the face of the man who was still fighting Esen. Its white wings were splattered red from the blood coming off him and Esen.

Oh no, Esen. To my knowledge, he has never engaged in a fight before. The blood and sweat will be too much for him, even with the change he went through. His dislike and fear of it do not disappear overnight. I need to get him out of there before it's too late.

I was trying to push myself up, but the boy was holding me down firmly when shouts of glee passed through the crowd that had not gone below. "An angel is here! We're saved!" A female cried out.

I looked to see what they were talking about, and a blonde-haired female dotted with red blood struck down the man in one blow to the heart. Esen's sword was in her hand, the hilt barely visible, the blade pushed through his entire body with the heart itself stuck on the end.

Horror and amazement passed through me. I had never seen anything like that before, and for it to have come from Alya was not what I expected. In a heartbeat, Esen's mask was off, and he was leaning over the side of the ship, spewing the contents of his stomach. Looking back at Alya, she was whispering something in his ear. Whatever she said would never be heard by anyone, not even by the man himself.

The moment they were both done, they rushed over to me and got to me simultaneously. I saw the terror on Esen's face, along with the cuts that were slowly healing without ash. None left a scar or any sign that he had been injured.

Fucking shit how badly did Alden have to hurt him to leave that many scars on his body?

"What happened?" His voice was filled with concern. I looked at Alya as she trembled. Something had shocked her.

"I underestimated his ability to fight. He wasn't letting people close, so I thought he couldn't and relied on his gift. I—"

"That is not what I mean. Why the fuck is Arymn's number one mercenary on a ship?"

"Alden." Alya and I both answered in unison. I looked at her. Her eyes were stuck on Esen, studying the features she had yet to see.

That was when I realized she did not know that Esen was alive. Oh gods, did she think we were dead the entire time she was imprisoned?

Esen rushed off to find something to set my leg with so I could walk. I looked at Alya and the delicate features that I had missed. Brushing back a strand of her hair, I said, "You're a beautiful angel."

She shook her head and pushed my hand away. "Please, don't call me that." I was confused. I have never once disliked being called a demon. Most don't, either. What is so bad about being an angel that she didn't want to be called one? I was relieved to hear her voice, knowing she still had it and was willing to use it no matter how cold it came out.

"I'm sorry we didn't come sooner. A lot was happening, and I know how shitty of an excuse that is. But I am sorry, and I know Ove is, too."

Hearing his name piqued her interest. "Where is he?"

I let out a sigh, wishing he was here as well. "He's stuck in the Below, kingly duties and all. I know he would have been here for you if he could have been."

"If he wanted to, he would have made the effort." She rose from my side and shifted into a bird flying off towards the shore that was nearing.

"Alya!" I called out to her, but she did not turn around.

Esen approached me with a splint and fabric to wrap around my stomach. "Where did Alya go?"

"She flew off. Did you know she's an angel?"

He let out a shaky breath. "It is a lot more complicated than you think. When she is ready, I am sure she will tell you."

I looked at him, impressed he had kept a secret from me. "How long have you known?"

"Since the day the Dearil ordered the Ghosts to attack you. She had no choice but to shift, exposing herself. If she had not done so, I fear you and Ove would have been dead on my balcony long before I knew you were there."

His hands worked swiftly and carefully as they secured my knee. "I thought you two were eating when we landed?" He didn't answer. "You lied to me? What else have you lied about?"

He looked at me, bewildered. "Lynnora dearest, may I remind you that you also lied to me? What I did does not change our relationship or what happened. You and Ove are alive because of her."

I knew he was right, but I was still annoyed with him for lying and not telling me the truth. "Fine. Will you tell me the truth as to what you meant when you said the goddess of seven winds protects you?"

"It is something my mother always said to me. She would tell me bedtime stories, saying that Aniya would make me stronger than my enemies as long as I had faith in her. Saying out loud that I am protected by her brings me a feeling of comfort, and it intimidates my enemy. It has been a long time since I said it before a fight; I was not sure if it would have the same effect it once did."

"Did it?"

"Yes. I could have sworn I felt her there fighting with me."

Chapter Eighteen

LYNNORA

The moment the ship reached the docks, Esen and I were thrown off for the disturbance we had caused, even though we had tried to help. I never saw where the little boy had run off to. I wanted to say my thanks, but he disappeared. It made me question if he was even there or if I had imagined it. Esen carried me on his back through the town and to the house. I searched the skies and rooftops, hoping to spot the white bird Alya could shift into, but saw no sign of her.

Every so often, I would catch Esen sticking his tongue out. When I asked him about it, he explained he was following her scent. At least she was going in the right direction of the house. The view of the one-story house came into sight, the tall grass obscuring the porch. As we neared, I saw three shapes on it. Alika and Sheena surrounded Alya. She looked to be hugging both of them.

Alya's arms wrapped around both of them, their heads resting on her shoulder. They picked up our scent and began growling at us. I was shocked. They never growl at me when they see me, and for them to protect her, something really must be wrong.

I tapped Esen's shoulder, asking to be put down, and told him to enter through the side door. Once he was out of view, I limped over to the edge of the porch. Their ears pinned back, teeth on display as they snarled at me.

"Can you tell them I mean you no harm?" I asked Alya. They are protecting her for a reason. She sniffled and whistled them away from me. Sitting down on the step, I ensured not to touch or reach out for her.

"I'm here if you want to talk. If you don't want to talk, I am still here. What you said about Ove was right. If he wanted to, he could have come for you. — I made sure they would punish the guy who tried to harm you."

"What about Benji?" She brought her legs in close to her chest.

"I sent him to the Below with a message to be spared. I'm going to write Ove and make sure he is."

She looked up at me, her eyes shining in the light as they filled with tears. "I thought you two were dead." She lunged for me and wrapped her arms around my neck, pulling me close for a hug. Wrapping my arms around her, I embraced her, not realizing how badly I needed this.

"I know, and I am so sorry for that and for everything. I should never have let you get involved. I should have made sure you were out of Arymn safely before I acted. I should have checked on you to tell you we were alive. I am so sorry, Alya. I know what happened will never be forgotten, but I hope you can forgive me one day."

"Do you forgive yourself for it?"

Her question caught me by surprise. "No." I didn't forgive myself and don't think I ever will. "Thank you for saving us today."

"That's what we do. We save each other."

Whether Alya knew it or not, she was right in many ways. From the moment I met her and Esen, I had felt myself healing and changing. Becoming someone Dearil didn't have control over, someone who didn't obey his every wish. Everything he had worked for was becoming undone, and I was becoming whole. She and Esen were healing me and saving me from myself.

"Promise me. Promise me we will make Alden pay for what he did to me." My hair that was burying her face, muffling her voice.

"I promise. Alden will pay with his life and suffer eternal torment." She pulled away from me and gave me a weak smile that was forced. "Come on, let's go inside and get you cleaned up and some food."

The two of us slowly got up. Leaning on her, we walked inside the house with the dogs behind us. Voices filled the kitchen. Mimsy was already preparing food for us.

Her eyes looked us up and down, and she clicked her tongue with disappointment. "The fireplace is alive in the primary bedroom, and the bath is warm in the guest. Clean yourselves up, and I will bring you food in a few minutes."

Not wanting to be scolded by her for not listening, we both turned around. I brought Alya to the guest room and bathroom, where she disappeared and locked the door behind her. Esen walked up to me and gave me his arm for support.

It was nice being back in our room, knowing we were safe for the night. The fire was warming the room and providing enough ash to cover my injuries. He lowered me to the ground and suffocated the fire with a flick of his wrist. We both grabbed onto the ash, smothering my injuries. I hissed in pain with the feeling of my skin tightening and sewing itself back together. I let a scream pass my lips as my bones mended together.

Esen continued to secure ash to my wounds when I looked at him. "Alden is arming them with Koya. There are mines throughout Nevano, but not even Dearil knew where they all were, so I have no idea how Alden is getting enough to supply his men and men of other armies."

"I do not know either. I did not know about Koya blades being the only ones that can harm you until you told me. Alden is clever. He must have found out through his spies, or Daxon knew about the mines."

I readjusted how I sat so my back leaned against the wall. "If I were to guess, it's the latter. Koya blades take a while to forge because of the strength of the stone. Daxon must have been mining it and forging them for years, all in preparations for the war."

Esen sat beside me and wrapped his fingers in mine. His thumb traced over the edge of my hand. "This war has gone on too long. It needs to stop before there is more bloodshed. But there will always be a war between the angels and demons, thanks to Kesa and Haedon."

"So what? We kill the gods, and this all ends?" I let out a laugh.

"I do not know, but I will fight by your side whatever you decide to do. Alya will gladly kill the gods, too."

I raised my brow, questioning what he meant by that, but he did not reveal any interest in telling me. "How can you put so much faith in me? You do so blindly and recklessly. For all we know, I will decide on something that will end us all. Would you walk into your death with the same amount of loyalty?"

He didn't hesitate to answer. "Gladly. I trust you and am loyal to you because of what I realized when we were both presumed dead. You, Lynnora dearest, are worth dying for and worth living for. You are what makes me feel whole and safe. You lighten the darkness that surrounds me. When I met you, I thought you would only lead to messing my life up, but you did the opposite. You fixed it, fixed me whether or not you meant to. That is why I will blindly follow you into my death. I have done so once before, and we survived. As long as we are together, we will survive whatever happens. I believe you are my soulmate, and if it is true or not, I will stay by your side until the darkness claims us."

I didn't know what to say or think of what he had just proclaimed, so I blurted out the first thing I thought of. "That's a lot of things to realize while dying. I would hate to be you."

He let out a laugh that lasted for a minute. He smiled down at me. "Mimsy should be ready with food. Let us go find her and see if Alya is ready."

He stood up, extending his hand for me to pull myself up with. Taking the offer, I could put some weight on my leg. It still hurt, but it was now functional. Back in the kitchen, Mimsy was plating the food for Alya, who wore a dress that did not match her in any way. Judging by the size, it was intended for Mimsy. Esen and I took our seats and began eating the food.

Alya was toying with her food when Esen cleared his throat. "Alya, you need to eat. Just one bite, please." Out of habit, I handed Esen a piece of bread from my plate and continued eating my food. Alya did not say anything or take a bite of the food. "Lynnora, did Alya ever tell you about the man she first loved?"

Alya moved fast and held a knife, pointing it at Esen. "Shut your mouth! You know nothing!"

"Then eat your fucking food, Alya. I will not baby you. You are a grown-ass adult who knows what not eating will do to you. Now sit your ass down and eat the fucking food!"

I eyed them both, amazed that Esen had raised his voice at her and that he knew something about her past she did not want to share with me.

She slowly sat down. "You are a bastard, Esen, and you know nothing."

"I know enough, Alya, and I am not going to let you waste away because men decided to abuse you. We both know you are stronger than that, and your refusal to eat is your choice."

Her cheeks turned red with anger. "My choice? No, it sure as fuck isn't! Not a single thing I went through in that prison was my choice! I did not choose to be the only female in my sector. I did not choose to be The Lion's prized toy. I did not choose to be the object he desired. I did not choose the amount of food we got, knowing each time it was less and less because The Lion wanted a skinny bitch to fuck! I didn't choose a damn thing. I am suffering now because of my lack of choices!"

"Esen, stop." I tried to plead with him, confused about why he was pushing her like this. He had told me to let her come to me, and yet he was doing this to her, forcing her to relive a nightmare. Would he do this to me if he learned the truth about what happened to Ove and me?

He ignored my request. "You had a choice, Alya. You could have left, and yet you stayed. Why?"

"I stayed for Benji! I stayed for the man who had faith in me when no others did. I stayed for the man who fought for me when none would! I stayed because I thought I had no one worth returning to!"

Tears were now forming in her eyes at the painful memories of what she endured. I know Esen would be mad at me for what I was about to do, but I am technically his Queen, and it is allowed. "Esen Thillardson, I command you to stop pestering Alya about what she went through in that prison."

He went to protest when Alika and Sheena began barking. The door opened, and Adri walked in. "Oh no. I do not like the feeling in this room. Way too tense for me." She tossed an envelope at Esen, and her eyes wandered to Alya. "So, you're the girl Ove wanted to be saved?"

I thought I heard jealousy in her voice for a split second. I watched Esen tear open the envelope and read the content within. "Mimsy, take Alya to get some clothes and make sure she eats. Adri, fuck off."

I was dumbstruck hearing this type of anger come from Esen. I have never heard him swear this much, let alone lash out at others. What is bothering him that would cause this outburst?

Adri did not seem offended by him. She bowed and gave Esen a smirk, followed by a wink before leaving. Alya was still fuming and didn't want to continue the fight, but she knew she needed proper clothes. Mimsy was already grabbing her cloak and a few coins Esen had left behind from when we went to break Alya out. She rose and impaled the table with the knife in her hand, mumbling something in a language I didn't know.

I looked at Esen, who leaned back in his chair, stretching himself out. "What the fuck were you thinking? You told me to give her time, and then you did the opposite. What is going through that pea-sized brain of yours?"

"You are right. I am sorry. I do not know what came over me. It pains me to see her like this. She used to love food. The maids would always tell me they would catch her sneaking to the kitchen in the middle of the night to get random food. Now, she will not eat. It is not like her."

I let out a sigh, understanding all too well. "Esen, she is different because of what happened to her. Things will never be the same, nor will she. Let her adjust on her own. Let her eat as much or as little as she wants. She knows what she needs. We can't force her to do something."

Esen looked at me with love in his eyes. "I will give her space." His hand wrapped around mine, and his thumb rubbed my skin.

He pulled me into a hug, kissing my neck slowly and gently. His lips slowly traveled up the side of my face and onto my lips. With each new kiss I received, it was like I was breathing for the first time, and all the times we had kissed in the past meant nothing. This would be our first kiss that lasts a thousand lives, a kiss of us claiming each other. No lies, no games, nothing but honesty and us. It's a kiss worth remembering when the world ends.

Our lips parted long enough for us to take a breath, then promptly get back to kissing one another. His fangs grazed the side of my neck, sending a chill down my spine. I felt the tips slightly break my skin. I let out a gasp as Esen bit me gently. Summoning my fangs, I returned the favor, but not so gently. Simultaneously, we pulled away, our lips painted red with each other's blood.

We licked our lips and let out a nervous laughter. I looked at where I had bitten him, and the wound was sealing itself.

I raised my brows, never seeing something heal like that before. "What?" He questioned me.

"Is my bite healing on its own?" He nodded his head just as the blood began disappearing.

What is happening?

Needing better light to look at it, I brought him to the living room, where we found Alika and Sheena in the room. I looked at the mark on Esen's throat; the wound had changed from being open to a pink scab, ending with two white scars that stood out against his skin. I have never seen anything like that before. Demons need ash to heal wounds. It should not have healed on its own.

Not knowing what to do about it, we found the largest, comfiest couch; we both curled up on it and lay there watching the fire roar. In the distance, we heard the side door to the kitchen open and close. Mimsy's voice quickly filled the house, trying to find us.

"We are in here!" I called out to her, letting her know where we were.

She came in with a broad smile, a woven basket filled with fabric. Alya walked in behind her in a beautiful dress that fit her better than the last dress.

"Look what — my gods, the mark of Aniya." Mimsy gasped as she clasped a hand to her mouth and started muttering a prayer in Ellev.

Alya halted where she was and looked at both of us, her eyes wide in horror. "Fuck," was all she said as she sank to the floor.

CHAPTER NINETEEN

ALYA

It was time. It had been since the moment they saved me. I knew it would only be a matter of time before I slipped up or Esen did. But this? I was expecting something else. Seeing my mark on their necks was not how I thought I would have to tell them who I am and what my parents are. I wanted to hold off on it for as long as possible because Lynn would be furious. I lied to her every chance I got. I hid the truth from her when I had an opportunity to tell her everything.

Lynn and Esen sat on the couch, adjusting how they sat, ready to hear what I needed to explain. Some of this Esen already knows, but the rest neither of them do. Sitting on another couch across from them, my arms rested on my knees, holding me up. A line of red filled my wrist from where the shackles had been holding me. Mimsy sat on the couch and reached for my hand to comfort me, but I pulled away. I know she will do it herself when she learns the truth. They all have.

"Lynn, I need you to know I had no choice but to lie to you for your safety and mine. I am sorry I dragged you into this and hid the truth from you for so long. Esen, you have been trying to find my truth, but books will not tell my story. My mother made sure of that. My name is Aniya, goddess of seven winds and soulmates."

"No fucking way." Esen and Lynn both gasped in shock. Mimsy began praying in Ellev. No doubt terrified by what I said, and I knew the next thing that I tell them would scare them further.

"I am also the first angel and the first fallen angel." There was no response, making me uneasy. "When Haedon and Kesa were still married, they sired me, and at the time I was born, they loved each other. That love seeped into me and gave me the gift of granting soulmates and giving me the ability to help them find one another. My aunts and uncles had claimed everything: time, war, the elements, strength, wisdom, and all the other things. But the wind was not claimed, so I took it to help people find their soul mates or mates. My family ruled peacefully, watching over the people until my father wanted more and created the demons. My mother wanted something to counter them: be stronger, faster, and better in every way possible. She experimented on me since I was immortal. Each time, my body fought it off, not allowing me to be what she wanted. It took her a hundred years to learn that it was because of my gifts and being a god. So she tried taking them from me, but I had been warned and hid parts throughout the world. She had already known about tricking gods into giving up their power. Kesa told me that if I gave her what I had, she would erase my memory of the last hundred years. She had trapped me in a cell the entire time, strapped to a table. I wanted them gone and to never feel the invisible chains that bound me. I thought I had no choice, and when she took them, she was able to change me into what she wanted. But she had lied. She had no power over my mind and left the pain with me." I gulped, nervous to continue.

"Even with all the experiments she had done to me, there were still things Kesa didn't know. One of them was that when she and Haedon created the demons and angels, their hatred had transferred into them as their love did me. The two races hated each other and started a war. I spent years as an angel doing my mother's bidding, killing who she asked, fighting for a cause I didn't believe in, all in the hopes of the pain being released. And then, one day, they were. I was in Sparan when I met a man named Eilam. I hated him with every fiber of my body, wishing for his death. We spent a lot of time together, and eventually, my hatred turned into the thing I had never thought I would find. Love. We got married, and shortly after, he got injured in the war, divulging his secret to me; he was a demon. I knew I should hate him for it and be angry about lying, but I had been too, and I told him about my past. He didn't flinch or run. He hugged me and said it would be him and me until the end of time. Always and forever." My eyes flooded with tears as I remembered everything we went through.

"I still had tiny embers of my gifts left that I had hidden from my mother after all the years, and with it, I granted him eternal reincarnation. We would always find each other each time, no matter what. Parts of my gift are still waiting for me to retrieve, some of which I had while in prison. With the war happening, it was getting complicated for us to be with one another. I had planned to meet him in Oud, and we would run away together from my parents and the war. When I got there, I saw him dying, the archangels standing over his body with a sword in their hand. They killed everyone in the town, and I was stricken with grief, unsure if my gift to him had worked or not. I unleashed the last ember of the seven winds I had obtained when I collected some of my gifts. It ripped the flesh and wings off the archangels, killing them. Pain blinded me, and I carved into their bones a promise of a lifetime to kill the gods. My mother took my wings immediately after she learned of my betrayal. I told Esen that she could live with me killing the archangels, but she couldn't live with me loving a demon, and that was the truth."

"Since then, I have searched for Eilam to see if my gift worked, and I find him in every lifetime, falling in love with him all over again only to watch him die. This time, I found him sitting in a castle room by himself. I didn't believe it at first, so I nicked his finger and tasted his blood. It was him, but it wasn't. There is something darker and foul residing within him. The only thing I could compare it to was how I feel when afraid. He tasted like true fear. I wanted to stay and see who he was, but I saw him looking at another with love, and I knew it was not him.—Lynn, why does Ove favor the form he's in?"

She looked at me, eyes wider than a deer when it was being hunted. She leaned away from Esen and placed a hand over her mouth. "It was the first kill he was forced to do. He said he felt drawn to it and wanted to see the boy grow into a man. He took the shadow and the features of the child. As he grows, it whispers to him the changes that need to be made."

My eyes lined with tears. He was just a boy when it happened. They both were.

"Oh, gods — no." Esen had put it together.

"Ove killed Eilam when he reincarnated," I confirmed what was going through their minds.

Mimsy said yet another prayer to my uncle, the god of forgiveness. He will never get it. Kesa stole his power, too.

"The mark on your neck is my mark. I created it for demons to claim their soulmate. Since demons tend to be territorial, I thought it best to mark them when they find one another so others know. Angels shed a feather, and a new one in a different color regrows in its place. Humans wed and wear rings. That marking signifies your undying love for one another. The reason it shocked Mimsy is because the marks haven't lasted more than a minute before disappearing. When I lost my magic, they vanished as well. I think when I unleashed a bit of my power in the prison, it awoke more than I realized, and it is allowing the claiming to come back."

"We're soulmates?" Lynn gasped.

"Really? That is what you choose to focus on." Esen poked her side, teasing her.

I nodded my head. "You two were destined to find each other from the dawn of time until the end of time. Your meeting would happen one way or another, no matter how hard you tried to fight it."

Esen was rubbing her back, trying to comfort her and soothing her. "You yelled at a goddess." Lynn turned her head and looked at her mate with wide eyes.

His face paled, and then he smiled. "You flirted with one."

She let out a snort. "I think yelling at one is far worse than flirting."

Their attention snapped back to me, awaiting my judgment and response. They amazed me. My past did not scare them.

"Why aren't you scared of me or mad at me?"

Lynn rose and stood over me. She lowered herself to her knees, which I knew had to be painful for her, but if it was, she showed no sign of discomfort.

Her chilled hands took my warm ones. "What do you want me to say? That you are a lying piece of shit? Because if that's what you need to hear, then that's what I will tell you." She cleared her throat. "Alya, you are a lying piece of shit, but you are my favorite lying piece of shit."

I let out a chuckle, but Esen came over to me and distracted me from what I wanted to say. He joined Lynn, where she was kneeling. "We do not hate you because you found us when we needed you most, and we found you when you needed us. If we hated you, then what does that make us? We are your friends, Alya. We can not hate you for your past. The past is the past for a reason. It is up to us to decide our future and who we become."

"Shit," Lynn let out a small gasp. "Does Ove know?"

I shook my head. "No, and I don't want him to." They both nodded their heads, agreeing not to tell him.

Falling to my knees, I wrapped my arms around them, pulling them into a hug. Tears I had been holding in all day fell from my tired eyes. They didn't hate me. They weren't mad at me. They were understanding and accepting. They welcomed me for all I was, all I am, and all I will become.

They did not shy away from the horrors I went through and the atrocities I committed. They weren't scared of me. And that was all I could ask for.

We continued hugging, not wanting this comfort to end. From behind me, I could hear Mimsy still muttering under her breath as she was trying to work through everything I had divulged.

Lynn's arms loosened their grip as she pulled out of the group hug. "We should make her some tea as she thinks this all over." We all looked at Mimsy, whose face was pale, her hands clasping her necklace. Her eyes were locked on an inanimate object across the room. Her mouth was moving so swiftly words could not be comprehended as she said her prayers.

"Lynnora, could you start some tea for her while Alya and I try to get Mimsy into a more comfortable spot?" She looked at her mate as if she was talking to him through the bond of souls. Yet another gift I had granted mates but had vanished, too.

She nodded and left into the kitchen, leaving us to move Mimsy. I stood to try and help lean her back, but Esen stopped me.

"Alya, I am sorry for what I did at lunch. I should not have snapped at you and taken my anger out on you. It was unfair to you, and I should have been more respectful of what you went through."

Moving to a couch free of another person, I sat down, and Esen sat beside me. Leaning my head on his shoulder, he wrapped his hand around mine. There was no hint of lust or desire in this act. It was simply a friend comforting another.

"You were right. I could have left the moment they tossed me in there. I could have escaped when I knew Alden turned on me, but I didn't. I chose to stay because I felt like I deserved it. If I had had my gifts, I could have saved Lynn when I thought she was dying, and we would not have been in this mess. I blamed myself for what she did and for both of your deaths. When I got to the prison, I had planned to stay there until I grieved the two of you, but I met Benji, and I couldn't leave him behind. He had endured so much, yet he had faith that he would one day be free. He wanted to protect me, and he did. I did what I could to survive, and a guard ruined it. He angered both of us to the point where we were losing faith. Each night, I heard Benji praying to a goddess who would never answer him. He was praying to me. That was when I knew I had to get him out. So I planned to use the guard who was breaking us to bring us to safety. You and Lynn stepped in when I was about to act. I had a choice each day to get myself out, but I also had the choice to save another from a cruel fate. I would rather suffer knowing another is free. I chose his freedom over mine."

"That is admirable. I am sorry for forcing my anger on you. I was angry at many things. Angry at Alden for turning on you, angry that you thought we were dead, angry at the man who stood over you. Angry knowing you suffered because of us. I was angry at myself because it was our fault for what happened to you. I was so angry when I saw that man undoing his pants that I was planning ways to make his life so miserable he wished for death, but Ove had already asked for anyone that brought you harm. I do not like seeing people not eating in response to trauma. I did it and nearly died. I never want to see you or anyone I care about get to that point."

I squeezed his hand at the bit of his past he shared with me. It warmed my heart, knowing he wanted The Lion to pay for what was done to me and that Ove had already asked for his head. The flames of the fire danced around the shadows it was casting, fighting for the space and to claim the room.

"It is hard for me to eat because of how little food I was given. I knew from experience that I had to start small and slowly work my way up to a full meal. But there is more to it as well. We called the man who hurt me The Lion. He told me he likes girls with a little bit of meat on their bones. I have always struggled with my weight and being comfortable in my skin. Hearing those words sent me into a spiral. If I gain weight, it won't happen to me, but I will dislike how I look. On the other hand, if I lose the weight, it will happen to me, but at least I will be skinny and like how I look."

"It doesn't matter what size you are. Those who want to harm you will do it no matter what, and those who love you will love you no matter how you look. The only thing that matters is that you are happy." A calm voice answered from the doorway.

My head jerked up to see the most beautiful man step out of the shadow. His arms folded against his chest, his head leaning on the frame, and his foot crossing the other.

"Ove," I gasped. Not thinking about my actions, my legs carried me swiftly to him. His arms stretched out and caught my embrace. His chilled body pressed into mine, holding me tight as he spun us in a circle until we both got dizzy.

"You came?"

"Of course I did. I heard your call."

Mimsy let out a shriek. "The King!" The three of us immediately turned to see her bowing. We all let out a little laugh. Ove walked over to her and stood above her. His shadows danced along the top of his head, and a bone crown appeared.

His hand reached down to her and grabbed onto her throat, forcing her to stand. I let out a scream of shock. Esen yelled at him, demanding that he let her go.

"What's going on—Ove?" Lynn walked in carrying a tray with tea.

Ove faced the three of us as he still held onto Mimsy. "Lynn, did you not think it strange that a certain King knew where to send his mercenary to?" His attention shifted back to the women he held. "Alden paid you a lot of gold to tell him where to send the mercenary. It's too bad gold has no power in my realm. I trade secrets for a lesser sentence. And a recent visitor was very talkative, telling me you had been playing spy."

"Lynn, please!" Mimsy shrieked, begging for her to save her.

Esen instinctively moved in front of Lynn and me, shielding us from her, but Lynn moved around him and beside her husband.

"Is this true? Did you sell us out to Alden?" She was lethally calm. It frightened me.

"You are not my Queen. I do not answer to you."

"Oh, but she is. My father was willing to share details about why you were allowed in the Below and could leave alive. You sold your soul to her. She is your master and your Queen. Her wish is your command. So answer her!" Ove yelled at her, demanding an answer.

"Fine! I sold you out, but I meant no harm. It was the only way I could spare the town from an attack.—Please, Lynn. You are my chickadee. I would never put you in harm's way."

Lynn looked back at me and then at Ove. She closed her eyes, looking pained, and when they reopened, her hand moved fast. The nails I had once seen were lodged in Mimsy's chest. A silent gasp left the maid's lips as her heart was being squeezed to death.

"I am a chickadee, and you are nothing but a pest." She ripped her hand out of her chest and walked out of the room.

The three of us stood frozen when the door slammed shut. Esen went to move and chase after her, but Ove's shadows stopped him. "Don't. I need to speak to her first." His shadows intensified, and a chill went through the air. The room smelled of something foul. I looked at where Mimsy lay dead, but her body was gone. Had Ove claimed her into his shadows?

Ove left to speak to his Queen, who is mated to another.

CHAPTER TWENTY

OVE

Lynn was already at the base of a tree when I caught up to her. She pulled herself up onto a swing and rested her head against the rope holding it up.

"How's your knee?" I didn't know how to start this conversation.

"It still hurts, but it's healed. How did you know?"

"As I said, the mercenary talked a lot. I also saw how you favored your other leg when you walked into the room."

Even though I stood behind her, I knew she rolled her eyes. Moving in front of her, I looked at her and the red that stained her hands even darker. "Why did you kill her? I was going to do it."

"Reasons," she snapped coldly.

A gentle breeze of wind passed by, moving the strand of hair covering the bite mark on her neck. "I see you and Esen had fun, and he took my advice."

She let out a huff of air. "Turns out he's my mate."

I tucked the remaining hair behind her ear. My hand stayed on the side of her face. "I know. That is another reason as to why I am here."

She pushed me away from me. "You knew, and you still fucked me. You let me marry you! How long have you known?" I stumbled back a few steps but caught myself before falling off the cliff's edge.

Letting out a sigh, I answered. "I knew the day I broke one of our rules. I saw how he looked at you and how you looked at him. I had hoped I was wrong, but when he tried to kill me, I knew I was right."

"You are a bastard Ove!" She got off the swing and started storming off to get away from me.

"Lynnora! Get your ass back here and listen to me!" I never like calling her by her first name. It felt like I was a stranger or trying to control her, but I needed her to hear me out. Just this once.

She threw up her arms where she stood and faced me. "Why? Why should I listen to you when you will probably lie to me?" She let out a laugh. "You have lied to me about so much more than I expected. I'll add this to a list of things I must forgive you for!"

"I didn't tell you so I could protect you. You are reckless even with all your plans. I didn't want you to fuck up your chance of love until we knew all the facts. I lied for you, Lynn."

The tall grass seemed to part as she stomped up to me. Her tail came out lashing, her horns and ears stuck out through her hair, and her teeth were sharp. I looked at her hands, relieved to see no sign of the claws that come out when she was beyond anger.

"My plans are reckless because people won't expect what I do. Yes, I put us in danger, but I know what we can handle. I think every possibility through and am ready for every outcome. We are the freaking seventh Ghost and the Prince of Below; our plans have to be thought out and wild. My plans work."

I blinked at her, shocked by what she had just admitted. "Did you have a plan when I was being tortured? You said you needed me to break for the plan to work."

Her throat bobbed. "No." She shook her head and shrugged. "When I saw you being tortured, all I saw was Esen's face. I wanted you to break, so I knew I could as well. With both of us broken, neither would have to feel anything that Dearil did to us. I was done fighting, done trying. I was done, Ove, and I didn't want you to try and save me like you always have."

I pulled her into a hug. Her head was buried into my shoulder, and I could feel the tears soaking into my shirt. One hand rubbed her back, and the other held her head close. "I'm sorry. I didn't know. But you are beyond lucky. The god Ver is watching over you. He always has been and always will be. You will get through this; we all will. Now, can I please tell you why I am here?"

She pulled away enough to look at me with a stone-cold glare. "I don't like how excited you sound."

I let out a laugh. "Trust me. I am not over-excited about this, but I am excited about what it means for you." She raised a brow. I pulled a handful of seeds from my pocket and showed them to her.

"No!" She tried to force my fingers closed and not let me do what needed to be done.

"Lynn, please shut up and let me do this for you?"

"Absolutely not! I may have only been Queen for several hours, but I am not letting power-hungry demons try to lay claim to that."

I let out a chuckle, which angered her. "You think I didn't consider that? I am divorcing you, Lynn, but I am not removing you from your throne. You deserve to sit beside me, but you also deserve a proper chance with Esen. I am not going to stand in your way any longer." I knew what I was doing when I saw the flowers growing in the Below one evening. I knew what to do, even though I didn't want to.

The two of us kneeled, the tall grass hiding us from the view of the world. The gentle breeze all but disappeared. She no longer smelled of spring on a cool morning; she now smelled of white sage. She smelled of her mate. Her eyes shone brighter than a star on a cloudless night, and her delicate lips were fighting the smile she was hiding.

Together, we spoke the words required for this union to be broken.

"With these seeds, we grant life to what we killed. We give back to the gods what we took in the name of love. With these seeds, we break our promise to one another." As we spoke, we dug a hole in the dirt.

I nodded at her, telling her to speak her portion, "I, Lynnora Knoxwood, part from thee. I claim none but myself. I wish for nothing but the happiness you have granted me." She poured half of the seeds into the dark soil.

"I, Ove Knoxwood, part from thee. I claim none but myself. I wish for you to take your rightful crown as Queen of Demons with the ability to love another." Filling the hole with the rest of the seeds, we both buried them.

The soil covered the seeds thoroughly, and we spoke the final words of the ceremony, "We are parted for the rest of our time. No more death will be in our name of love. What once was is no more. May the gods grant us this separation."

I held onto her hand, not wanting to let go, knowing this would be the last time we were together as husband and wife. She held firmly onto mine, our eyes watching each other. The ground shifted, and a single black flower rose from the depths. The gods have granted us what we asked for.

Our hands fell apart, and she let out a sigh. "Thank you."

"You are still the Queen of Demons, but you're free to love him. How does that feel? How does all that power you got feel?"

Her face went pale, and her mouth opened slightly. "Ove—I will never get the power that is granted to the Queen of Demons. I never received it when the crown was placed on my head."

"What do you mean? You should have. My mother is dead and no longer on the throne. That power should have transferred to you when you spoke your vows."

She licked her dry lips and sucked them in. "A part of your mom still lives. She feared Dearil was going to kill her, so she manipulated her soul and split it into several pieces. When he killed her, they scattered to predetermined locations. I only know where one went; that one is now dead."

I shook my head. "No, you have to be mistaken. She wouldn't do that. She knew better."

"I think she did it to protect the power. I believe she feared Dearil would take another who is unworthy of the throne, and that was her way to ensure the power was safe."

"How do you know this? Where are the other two pieces?"

"She spoke to me after the Ghosts attacked me. She said that she sent the pieces to those she loved most, and they are only accessible when the holder is at their weakest."

Tears left my eyes at this knowledge. I could see her again, but how weak would I have to become to do it? "Who is the third?"

Her throat bobbed, and she licked her lip again. "I'm not sure."

Lynn laid back in the grass, one hand behind her head and the other across her stomach. Moving over to her side, I mirrored her. We looked up at the sinking sky, shifting into an orange and red painting. The fluffy clouds were painted the same colors. The warm sun that was vanishing was kissing our skin as the cool night air crept onto the horizon, promising an endless night sky of twinkling lights.

I found her hand and held onto it, her thin fingers wrapped around mine, welcoming the embrace. "What name are you going to take? You are welcome to use Knoxwood still."

Her head turned to look at me, her eyes roaming over my features, and then she looked back up at the painted sky. "I'm not sure yet. I have a lot to figure out."

It was my turn to study her and the gentle slope in her nose, the long black lashes, her defined eyebrows. Each freckle splattered her cheek, her intense jawline that concealed powerful teeth. The black silky hair that seemed to have a mind of its own and would always fall in the right places when she needed it to. Her gray eyes, which I always compared to a storm, also remind me of a wolf's fur.

"They would be proud of us. Both of them."

She let out a chuckle. "No, they wouldn't. Our moms wanted us away from the court and Dearil. We escaped one monster only to walk into the den of another. They would be furious with us for going in so blindly and not fighting."

"Then why did you come here?"

She looked at me, startled that I had known about this place. "I had nowhere else to go. And during the chaotic night, one thing kept going through my mind: *when you feel lost, listen to your heart. It knows you best. It is your mind's job to convince you otherwise, so never think your way through it; feel it.* When we stood at the portal, her words guided me, and I told Esen to bring me here. It was where my heart wanted to be. "

"Your mom was always the wise one. She helped me through a lot of my emotions growing up. I will be forever grateful for her."

"I miss them both," her voice cracked with those small words that meant the world to me.

I let out an uneven breath. "I do, too. They were too kind for a world of cruelty—"

"But they never broke. They never let it change them because they knew that there was something even more beautiful for every evil thing. They did not let it knock them down. The moment they got close to it, they would readjust and do it once more until they pushed through." She rolled over and laid her head on my chest. Rubbing her arm, her body twitched at the touch of me.

We lay there until the sky had faded into blackness. The stars illuminating the sky giving those lost a way home.

"Lynn, look!" I pointed up at the sky. Her head turned just in time to see the light pierce the sky, searching for a place to land. Another one flew behind it, chasing the first. The silence returned between us, and I needed her to know the truth.

"There's something I need to tell you.—Six of the seven Kings have agreed to pull their troops from the war. They never wanted it but were pressured into it by Daxon and Dearil. They agreed to fight with you and me once we took the throne. I have been speaking with one of the Kings, and their plans changed. They will continue to back us, but Alden must die, and Esen needs to take the throne back. Once he is on the throne, they want all seven courts and the demons to go after the angels."

She did not show any sign of surprise at the information I had given her. Whether she already knew this or she excelled in hiding shock, it impressed me. "What do you want?"

Her question surprised me. No one has asked me what I want. "I want Alden dead." But they were for selfish reasons.

She let out a sigh. "Alden will die before the end of summer."

"Are—"

"Lynnora! Ove! Food is ready!" Esen called out to the field of grass. Lynnora rose and walked away. I sat up and watched her horns and tail disappear before Esen saw them.

Rising from the ground, I shoved my hands into my pockets and returned to the house. Lynn was already on the porch in Esen's arms, smiling at him when I arrived. Neither of them went inside. They turned and waited for me to join them.

*   *   *

The table was set for four, a candle in the middle, and several bottles of wine were set out. The plates had chicken, a green vegetable I hadn't had before, and mashed potatoes. We all sat at the circular table, Esen and Lynn beside one another, closer than Alya and I.

Alya kept avoiding my gaze for whatever reason. I may have pushed her too far with the hug. The most we have ever touched is when I pull her into my shadows to talk to her privately. She always fought my touch then, and we hugged longer than I expected. My shadows, thankfully, had hidden the bulge in my pants from others to see.

Our food was quickly disappearing as the conversation went on. Lynn, of course, gave Esen a bite of her food. She has done so ever since her allergic reaction. I still have no idea why it has continued for this long. Alya nudged her food around her plate, eating small bites and taking time with each one. I had heard what she confessed to Esen, and hearing such words from her mouth shattered my heart. He and I kept giving her encouraging smiles each time she looked at either of us. She looked at him more often than me, which agitated me, but I knew they had a bond that was formed through Lynn's near-death late last year.

The third bottle of wine opened, and the girls both cheered.

Oh, gods, they are already drunk. This night will not be boring.

Alya rose and held out her glass. "To us. We survived another day and will do so again."

"To us!" Our glasses clinked together. The warm wine did not touch my lips. My shadows took it in for me. I wanted to drink with them and have fun, but my mind had to be clear until I knew what Dearil was planning.

Lynn was rambling on to Alya in Vehn, both giggling about something. Esen looked dumbstruck.

"You speak Vehn fluently!" Esen half questioned, half gasped at her.

She nodded her head and let out a hiccup. I smiled at her and looked at Esen. "She speaks all seven languages fluently. She likes to lie and play games with people. I'm not sure why, but she thinks it's funny when she gets people to confess things to her when they think she doesn't know what they are saying."

He let out a gasp, "You sly demon. That was how you found out the information."

Esen's words had lost me, but Lynn knew what he meant. "I still can't believe you believed me. I thought I had slipped up, but you didn't catch it."

He shook his head. "Brat." He pulled her face close and kissed the top of her brows. Her cheeks reddened with that act.

Alya cleared her throat and stood up once more. "Since we have failed spectacularly to celebrate Year End, Lynn's birthday, and Esen's, I say we celebrate tonight and tomorrow. Tonight is the party, and tomorrow is the gift exchange for those three events." No one disagreed or protested her idea.

Lynn rose with a smirk. "Well, I suggest we start the night with a card game, and to make the rules clear, we trade in clothing, the ones we are wearing."

Oh gods, she is drunk, if that is what she suggests. I thought Esen might argue, but he was looking Lynn over with a smirk on his face. She, too, was already undressing him with her eyes.

Kesa, spare me.

CHAPTER TWENTY-ONE

LYNNORA

I have been wanting to get Esen alone and naked since Ove and I finished the separation ceremony. This will be fun, and with Alya wishing to celebrate our birthdays, I know the perfect gift for him—one of two at least. But first, I have to lose this game, as does Esen.

Ove shuffled the cards, his shoulders tense and back straight. Something was bothering him.

"What game?" He asked in demon tongue.

I shrugged my shoulder. "Dealer's choice."

Alya and Esen looked at us to translate, but we didn't.

The cards swiftly left the deck until none was left in his hand. In Ahr, he explained the game. "We will play in teams, so it goes faster. Spades trump all cards played; the highest card per round wins. The game will end, and the team with the least amount collected takes off one article of clothing each. Any questions?"

If I hadn't known how to play this game, I would not have any questions. He explained clearly how it's played.

Something is bothering him. I would have to be a blind fool not to notice the shift in his demeanor.

No one asked any questions, and we all looked at our cards. "Ove and

Lynn are on a team. Esen and I are on the other?" Alya suggested a pairing.

I had no protests, but I saw Oves' breaths falter for a second as he looked at me. "Works for me," Esen answered.

Not wanting to argue, I nodded in agreeance and watched Ove carefully. "Are you alright?" I asked him and only him.

"I'm fine," he snapped back at me. His shadows traveled through the room as if trying to figure something out for him.

The game quickly began. Cards are laid down one by one. The wine continued to flow, courtesy of Oves' shadows making sure our glasses never ran dry. Esen sat beside me, holding onto one of my hands, his thumb tracing swirls on my hand. Each time I laid down a low card, he tapped three times. When I put down a high one, he held one firm tap and then would play a card lower than mine.

Was he trying to lose, too?

The first round ended. Ove and I lost by one. He took his black shoes off. I took off the corset I had been wearing.

Laughter turned the air warm as the evening continued. My mind grew fuzzy with each sip of the wine, and with no food to snack on. Esen now had no shirt or shoes on, and each time he breathed, I caught the vein in his neck throbbing. I knew if I asked, he would take me into our room and let me have his blood, but I didn't want him to think that was why I wanted to be with him.

Alya's dress was on the floor, her corset and underwear still on. I kept my oversized shirt and undergarment on, but that was it. Ove took his socks and pants off. His shirt and undershorts still cover him.

I caught Alya glancing at his scarred leg and looking mournful. It had to be painful seeing the man she once loved being worn by a stranger and for it to be scarred severely. Ove refused to look at Alya at all during the game. He kept his eyes focused on the cards in his hand and what was laid on the table.

Ove and I lost this round by two. Standing in front of Esen, I made a show out of taking my undergarment off. He smiled the entire time, his hands helping me stand when I slid one leg out of them at a time. The small fabric hung from my finger, and I tucked it into his waistline.

Leaning into his ear, I gave him a tease. "Easy access for my King."

He grabbed them and held them close to his heart. "I will forever cherish these, dearest, and I will do anything for you." He gave me a wink.

Our lips briefly found one another, but Alya gasped and interrupted it. I looked to see what she was shocked by.

And in that moment, I knew how badly I had fucked up.

I should never have suggested we trade in clothes or purposely throw the game so I could turn Esen on. I had been selfish and didn't consider Ove and what he had been through.

His arm and side were covered in a new scar that Ava and Dearil had given him. It had taken him years to come to terms with what happened to his leg and just as long to let others see it. And I had made him show the new marred flesh in less than a month after the injury. It was still healing; it was still painful for him to feel and see.

Ove refused to look up at us, to acknowledge that we existed. "Ove, I am so sorry. I didn't think this through. We can trade in something else."

"Forget it. It's too late, anyway." He said the last four words so only I could understand the pain I had just caused him.

I didn't know what to say. How do I tell him how sorry I am for making him do this? To comfort him and tell him we all still love him the same and that we don't see him any differently.

"Some stupid demon once told me that those who love you will love you no matter how you look. And if you ask me, you are still as stunning as the night sky." Alya tried to comfort him.

"I didn't ask for your opinion, nor do I want it," his voice was harsh as he snapped at the one trying to remind him of his own words.

I tuned them out as Esen spoke to him in the language of the Kings, and whatever they were discussing was becoming a heated argument based on their body language.

Alya and I looked at each other, not wanting to be in the middle of this fight if it were to turn physical. I nodded toward the other room, and we both left without either of them noticing our departure.

The couch sunk with our weight being added to it. We both curled up into one another, hugging each other. Her legs wrapped around mine, and her head lay on my chest.

"Lynn... what happened to his arm and stomach?"

I closed my eyes, but it made the spinning sensation intensify. Opening my eyes, I knew I had to tell her. "Ove was tortured. His father wanted him to break him, and his arm was the result of one method."

"How long was he being tortured for?"

"A month." It was one month, but it felt like years upon years. I never thought it would end. I thought death would be granted to us before the chains were undone.

Her hand tightened its grip on my shirt. "Will he be alright?"

I shook my head. "I don't think so. Something in him snapped when we got out. I worry he is becoming unhinged, and with his new power, something bad may happen."

She let out a sigh. "You were with him? The entire time?"

"The entire time," I parroted her words. The memory of what he went through stung my eyes.

We both remained silent, listening to the argument in the other room. So far, there had been no sounds of any physical blows being dealt. There was the occasional scoff cluing me into an insult being given.

My eyelids grew heavy, and with each passing moment, they became too heavy for me to fight. Sleep quickly claimed me.

***

Two warm bodies were pressed into mine. Slowly opening my eyes, the morning light flowed into the room, casting golden rays across the furniture. A single beam illuminated Alya's face where she was next to me. Looking around, I saw they had moved furniture to form a giant bed. Esen lay beside me, and on the other side was Ove, holding onto Alya tightly.

I smiled, knowing he would deny it ever happened, and the moment he woke up, he would roll away from her. Alya's long blonde eyelashes opened, and she let out a painful sigh.

"Does it hurt seeing Eilam and knowing it's Ove?" I don't know why I asked that, but I had, and my stupidity was not changing.

"It is the most painful thing I have ever experienced."

"I'll ask him if he can choose another form around you. I'll make sure he doesn't know."

She shook her head. "Eilam would have wanted him to wear his skin. He was a little narcissistic. I know he would relish in the fact a King wears him."

"His shadows talk to him. I am sure Eilam does as well."

She let out a small laugh. "I hope for Ove's sake he doesn't. That idiot could talk your ear off." She sat up, pulling away from Ove. "I have someone to meet this morning. I'll be gone for an hour or two. We can go shopping after."

"Do you want me to come with you?" I don't like the idea of her walking around an unfamiliar town without one of us there. I know she can protect herself, but it makes me nervous nonetheless.

"No, I need to do this alone." She slid out from under the blanket that had been placed on us and got dressed before leaving. I watched out the window as she shifted into a white bird and flew off into the sunrise. I closed my eyes and took a deep breath, wishing she would let me in and help her.

Not knowing if she would be gone for how long, I knew I had to work fast. "Pst. Ove." I poked at him, trying to wake him up. He grumbled in annoyance. "Do you want to have sex?"

His eyes opened, and a brow raised. He looked between Esen and me before shaking his head. "No."

I rolled my eyes. "Come on. Please don't make me beg."

"Last time I fucked you with him around, I got punched, and you cut my face. I am not that stupid or horny."

"Ove, please," I drew out the words, begging him in a way I knew he liked and had difficulty saying no to. "It's a gift for him. Just this once." Maybe. Depending on how this goes, it may be the only time we do something like this, but it may also be a start to something new and exciting.

"If he gets angry, you are taking all the blame and whatever punishment that comes with."

"Fine. Now scoot closer and hold me."

I rolled over to face Esen, but I could feel Ove glaring at me as he did what I said. My back pressed into his stomach. I could feel his length already hard. Whether that had been from holding Alya or from his usual amount of horniness, I wasn't sure.

I gently kissed the side of Esen's cheek and neck until he woke up. "Good morning, dearest," his voice was deep and rough, stirring something inside me. My eyelashes fluttered at the sound, and my legs instinctively squeezed together.

"Good morning indeed." I didn't know how to tell him I asked Ove for this favor or how to start any of it. When we had people in the room with us, they were already engaging in the activity, and we slowly eased in. This is different.

Esen's hand reached for me, slowly working its way down my body, stopping abruptly at the feel of Oves' hand on my waist. His eyes flew open, and he looked at Ove, startled.

"What the—"

"Please don't be mad," I cut him off. "Ove and I talked, and he agreed to this. One time only."

Esen let out a harsh sigh. "I wish you had talked to me first about this."

Ove released his grip on me and rolled away, not wanting to be in the middle of this fight. "I'm sorry. I just wanted to make you happy and give you a gift I thought you would enjoy."

Esen gave me a warm smile. "I am not going to say no to sex. I am unsure if I want Ove to be a part of it—no offense." Ove raised his hands, indicating he didn't take any offense at what Esen had said.

Esen's hand slid to the back of my head and grabbed the hair. "Now, can you please show me what your gorgeous lips can do?" I gave him a seductive smile, his hand leading me under the blanket towards his cock. His hand briefly left my head, only to come back. The sound of a door shutting told me Ove was gone.

Sliding his cock out of his pants, I held it in my hand, slowly pumping it until it would fit into both of my hands. He let out a soft moan as I licked the length down and then back up. Taking my time teasing him with all the possibilities of what I could do, I finally let him feel it. My lips parted, allowing him into my mouth, slowly going deeper and deeper into my throat. I felt it hit the back of my mouth and then fill the tight space of my throat.

Holding back the gag that surfaced, a rush of air went in through my nose and down to my lungs, reminding me to breathe with my nose. Up and down, up and down. My spit coated his hardness with each pass, making it easier to go further into me. The sound of it hitting my throat was making him moan, resulting in me squeezing my thighs together, wanting more from him.

I could feel the dampness pooling. I had no undergarments to stop it from going onto my leg—an unfortunate mess.

The blanket covering me lifted off as the weight on the couches shifted. I tried to pull off Esen, but his hand held me on him firmly. "Be a good girl and spread your legs for him."

I opened my eyes and saw Ove inching closer with a sly smirk.

He hadn't left when I thought he did. He had stayed in the room and got completely undressed. His cock was standing tall and wanting to be used.

Oh gods. This wasn't going to be sex between two people and a third watching like I thought. It was going to be the three of us tangled with one another.

The wetness between my legs intensified.

Ove whispered something to Esen in the language of Kings too quietly for me to hear. What are they planning? Why aren't they speaking in Ahr? Something about this told me I couldn't walk for the day.

Ove was on his knees with that ridiculous grin. "Lynn, please be a good girl and spread those legs for me. I have missed tasting you on my lips."

My heart beat fast, my breaths were rapid, but my mouth was still working Esen's magnificent cock. My legs trembled in anticipation as I spread them open. Ove readjusted me onto my knees, and his head lay on the couch below me.

The tip of his tongue touched the wetness, and I moaned louder than I meant to. The warm touch of it against my coolness created more. Esen's hand continued guiding me up and down his cock. He occasionally let a moan slip from his precious lips.

Below me, Ove was feasting on my wetness, his hands working together. One was grabbing onto my thigh, holding me onto him so I don't twitch away. The other was massaging the delicate spot and would slide into me as I released another moan.

The weight of the couch shifted one more time. My mouth closed around nothing. No hands were working between my legs. There were no heavy breaths of either male. My eyes flew open in panic. I looked around the room, desperately trying to find them and see where they went.

What the fuck is happening? How did they vanish like that?

"So this is what the Demon Queen dreams about." A voice that has terrorized my life questioned from the shadows.

Dearil stood against the wall with his sharp teeth showing behind a cruel smile.

It was a dream. It was all a dream. But how much? Did Ove and I get out of the torture chamber? Did Esen save me? Did we rescue Alya? Were last night's events real? What about what Alya confessed to us?

My head spun to the point I couldn't think straight, I could barely breathe, and I desperately searched for the wisp of air Esen always gives me, only to find nothing.

Dearil chuckled as he moved forward. His hand grabbed my chin, forcing me to look up at him. "Did you think you could run from me, Lynnora? You are mine. No matter where you hide, I will always find you."

"I am not yours!" I tried to pull out of his grip, but his sharp nails jabbed into my skin, holding me there. Blood slowly began trickling down my face, dripping onto the couch below me.

Drip. Drip. Drip.

"What if I told you this was all a dream? That you are still a scared little girl hiding in a nook somewhere in the Below? All the bad things I have done to you, all the people you met and betrayed, all of it was one long, never-ending dream."

Chapter Twenty-Two

LYNNORA

No.

Please no. There was a time when I wanted to wake up from this nightmare of a life and have it all be over. But I don't anymore. I found Esen. I met Alya. I don't want that to be a part of some dream. This can't be happening to me.

All the pain I endured, all the lies I told, all the lives I stole. Had it all been done for nothing? What of the little girl in the orphanage who had a voice in the darkest of nights? I could not have dreamed that. Or Alya and her past. I can't have fabricated the way Esen makes me feel. I couldn't have created a horrible life for myself. Could I?

"I would say you are a liar and that you want something." I spat at him. I can't let him know I am second-guessing myself because if it is a dream and I wake up, he will punish me for that. I must be confident in my answer and my life.

My face was stinging from his grip. My blood is still dripping below me in a steady rhythmic drip, drip, drip.

Dearil chuckled coldly. "You know I don't appreciate that tone, darling—"

"And I don't appreciate you fucking with my mind, asshole."

His nails dug in deeper, leaving me to whimper in pain. "I thought I washed out the foulness of your words. Do you need another lesson?"

I snarled up at him. "You lay another hand on me, Dearil, and you will wish for mercy from all the gods." I ripped his hand out of my face, holding in a scream of pain. Rising to my feet, the oversize shirt I wore barely covered my ass. Rolling my shoulders back, I focused on my armor. If this is a dream, then I can gain some control over it.

My black leather armor wrapped around me, hugging and protecting me perfectly. The armor I wore as a Ghost did more than cover my identity and skin. It allowed me to become whomever I needed.

Right now, I needed the strength of all those I have faced and killed. Their blood is woven into the stitches. Their souls have touched the cold leather. They are with me, and I am never alone as long as the armor is on me.

Dearil held firmly where he stood, his hand raised to try and grab onto me again. I swiftly blocked it and smacked away his hand. His shadows moved around us in stifling heat, threatening to burn my skin.

"You can't harm me in here, Dearil. You have no power over me, the Ghosts, and Ove. You gave it all up for nothing."

He laughed. "I gave it up for power. Something I would expect you to understand."

"What do you want, Dearil?"

"I came to warn you." I raised my brows at him. I was absolutely and utterly shocked that he would come to warn me about anything. "Do not let your personal vendetta against Alden consume you. There are bigger monsters to face."

I scoffed. "Do you really expect me to believe you? You have shown no sympathy towards me in years nor shown any to Ove in his lifetime."

"I expect you to listen and consider everything as I have trained you. I warn you and only you, Lynnora, because I believe that you were meant to be mine in another lifetime. If only you had not been tainted by my failure of a son to have seen it, we could have conquered nations and ruled the realms. We could have lived until the end of time together."

I let out a high-pitched laugh. "You are delusional to think I will ever love you or have any emotion towards you other than hatred. You created us into monsters. You drew my blood for your own sick, perverted pleasure, you—"

"I am not the villain of this story, Lynn. There will be a day when you learn who it is, and it will be far too late to fix anything. I created you into what the world needs to be healthy and pure."

"You speak as if you are changing the world and ushering in a new age of peace."

He smiled, and his dangerous teeth shrank away. "Some say I am, while others don't agree." He grabbed a strand of my hair and twirled it in his fingers. "Fear is a funny thing. It can control people into doing your bidding, or it can stop people altogether. I recommend you face your fears and take control."

Smacking away his hand yet again, he let out a disappointed sigh. "Why would I do anything you recommend?"

"Because your mother's sacrifices were to get you away from your destiny. While everything I did was to ensure you had all the skills to make it there in one piece."

"You don't know my destiny."

His black eyes faded into a warm brown. Was he trying to show me his human side so I could believe him? "I also suggest you speak to Kesa before or after you kill Alden. Not everyone is who they appear to be, and it is best for all involved that you learn the truth."

"What truth would that be, exactly?"

I reached out for his shoulder as he turned to walk away. His body stiffened only to relax when he saw my small hands latching onto his shoulder.

My nails dug into his flesh, drawing black blood and ruining his suit.

"One that you do not have the power to learn yet. I know what my traitorous wife did and that she still holds the last bit of power. Why else do you think I wanted both you and Ove to break? You are two of the three pieces."

"Do you know who is the third?"

He turned to face me, and a knuckle caressed my face. Leaning away from it, he clicked his tongue. "I have my suspicions, but the moment I know with absolute certainty, I will end the bastard's life. You will one day reign as you should have from the moment you were born, dear Lynnora Knowxwood."

He walked away, his shadows trailing behind him, taking all the room's warmth. "There will be a day when you are a goddess and I by your side. Until then, Lynnora Knoxwood, I command you not to utter a word of this dream to any."

The cruel man no longer stood in the home that was once meant for safety. He no longer was holding my face or touching my hair, and he no longer controlled me.

***

Gasping for air as if I had never breathed, I frantically looked around, trying to find where I was. To see if everything I had lived through had been one long game that Dearil played on me. My chest rose and fell with each breath I clung to. My face ached from the phantom pain of where Dearil had dug his nails into me. The soft blanket covered me and my bare legs. Esen still lay beside me, clothed and asleep, Ove as well, but Alya was gone.

It was real. All of it was real, aside from the last part—I think. I must have fallen asleep right after Alya had left for her errands.

I had met them. I had found Esen. I had survived unspeakable pain. I slaughtered people. I scared children. I was a nightmare, the very same one I feared.

The golden sun rays had shifted into something darker and nastier. A storm was raging outside as if it had been for hours. How long was I asleep? How long has Alya been gone? A thundering boom echoed through the Ter Court. The sound vibrated into my bones as I let out a shriek. Esen and Ove woke up in a panic to see why I screamed. Ove's shadows cast the room into further darkness while they searched for an intruder. Esen was looking at me, concerned.

"Lynnora, what happened to you?" He pulled me into a hug.

Welcoming the warm embrace, the smell of blood filled my nose. Three drops of blood dripped onto Esen's back. Each drip haunted me—drip, drip, drip.

"I—I—" I didn't know what to say or how to say what just happened. I didn't know what was real and what was a dream. I could still be dreaming, and Dearil is punishing me for resisting him. If I expose to Ove and Esen what he told me, then I also reveal to him that I am no longer a Knoxwood, and he can no longer control me. If he finds out this is a dream, I will be punished.

Esen rubbed my back to soothe me. "No sign of anyone. Where's Alya?" Ove asked. I could hear him fighting back the panic that indeed had arisen.

Pulling out of Esen's warm embrace, I turned to face Ove, where he swore under his breath and rushed to my side. "Why aren't you healing?" I shrugged my shoulders. I had no idea why my face wasn't healing. It was a dream. He shouldn't have been able to hurt my physical body.

Was it a dream?

Yes, it had to have been. I had summoned my armor. Esen and Ove weren't there. It was a dream, so how am I injured, and why am I not healing?

The ground was beginning to shake threatening to open to the fire pits deep in the Below. My hand latched onto Esen's in fear.

Esen leaned into me, giving me the support I desperately needed. His rough morning voice whispered a loving command into my ear. "Breathe in four seconds, hold for seven seconds, and exhale for eight. Do it with me, my love."

Together, we breathed in for four seconds.

We held for seven seconds.

And together, we exhaled for eight.

Esen and I did this two more times until my breathing became normal. Until the room stopped spinning and the ground stopped shaking.

"You are here. You are safe. This is real. I have you, Lynnora." Esen's gentle words ground me further. "When you are ready, we will listen."

I breathed on my own in the way Esen had shown me. His comforting words were repeated in my head until I had them memorized. "Dearil knows where we are and that I want to kill Alden."

I can handle any punishment given to me if this is a dream, but I will not put their lives at risk over fear.

"Shit," they said in unison. Ove rose and began pacing. Esen took off his shirt, gently dabbing my skin to clean the blood off me.

The door to the front of the house swung open, letting in a gust of wind that Esen quickly blocked from extinguishing the fire. Rain pounded onto the floor below Alya as she walked into the house and quickly shut the door behind her.

Her blonde hair was plastered to her back, her dress completely soaked, as was her cloak. Her boots were covered in mud that tracked into the home. Esen stiffened at the sight of her. Ove released the breath he had been holding in.

"What happened to you three?" She removed her muddy shoes and set the wet cloak in front of the fire to dry.

"Alya, come with me," I told her before disappearing into a room.

She followed silently and shut the door behind her. "Are you alright? Who did that to your face?"

Wrapping a blanket around myself, I also handed her one so she could change out of her clothes and warm up. She took the hint, and the dress fell to the ground with a heavy thud. Her right wrist had a bandage wrapping around a small portion of it; dots of red speckled the bandage. What happened to her?

"Can you tell me if this is real? Is all that I see real or a figment of my imagination?" My voice shook with my questions.

She shook her head. "I can't. Even if I had my gifts, I couldn't tell you. I have no control over one's mind. Very few do. What's going on, Lynn?"

I let out a breath. "Dearil visited me in my dream. I don't know if I'm awake or not."

She smiled and let out a small, warm laugh. Her arms reached out to me. Walking into the embrace, my chilled body met hers, expecting to be cold, but it was as warm as the sun's rays. Each breath we took together warmed me up.

"This is very much real."

"How do you know?"

"Tell me your deepest, darkest secret."

I looked at her, stunned. But if this was a way to confirm it was real, then I will oblige. Whispering into her ear, I told her the secret I have shared with no one and will never share with another.

She smiled and let go of me. Taking my hand, we walked back out to the men, who were discussing something in hushed voices.

"Ove, Esen, please tell me what Lynn's biggest secret is?"

I wanted to scream at her. To tell them not to. I have told them both secrets I don't need the other one to know. Oh gods, was this her plan? To embarrass me?

"She makes plans that piss everyone off." Ove smirked at me.

Esen looked at him and let out a huff, doubting his words. "She is afraid of failure and disappointing those close to her."

Alya smiled at me. "See. I told you this wasn't a dream because if it were, they would have known what you told me."

A surge of relief flooded through me, knowing this was reality. "What last thing you two remember before I woke you up?"

Esen answered for them. "We made the couches into a bed and fell asleep. Why? Did something happen?"

"Nope! Nothing else happened. It was exactly as you said. We all fell asleep." All three of them eyed me cautiously, knowing I was hiding something. But there was no way I would ever tell them about my sex dream. Never in a million years.

To my relief, none seemed inclined to dig any further.

Esen moved closer to where Alya and I stood. I met him halfway, wrapping my arms around his stomach. My head buried into his chest, his defined muscles flexing each time his hand went up and down my spine. His warm lips pressed into my head, bringing me comfort.

The two of us sunk into the couch. My body curled up small, his hands and arms holding me close. We both watched as Alya and Ove stood by each other in a hallway. Their eyes do not meet each other. Ove's hand picked Alya's chin up, making her look at him. I was curious to know more, so I eavesdropped.

"Thank you for calling for me." His voice was gentler than I have ever heard it be.

"I didn't mean to call for you. I was trying to pay you back for leaving me behind."

He let out a warm laugh. "I didn't sound like that to me, little one." He brushed a wet strand of hair over her shoulder. "I am sorry I left you behind. I should have made sure you were safe."

"I'm out now. That's all that matters."

"No, it's not. I can smell the fresh blood on your wrist, and you lost so much weight. A disgusting man terrorized you, and you lost someone who you cared for. You thought we were dead."

She pushed away his hand that lingered on her shoulder. "If I need your savior complex to rescue me, I will call you. Until then, go home, Ove."

Her words startled all three of us. Esen looked down at me, asking if I knew she would say that. I looked up at him, asking the same silent question. Ove's hand fell away from her entirely and into his pocket.

His head bowed in sorrow, and he stepped away from her. He looked back up at Esen and me. "Have a good day. I will visit when I can."

The shadows in the room intensified as they collected around him. As they vanished, he was gone too.

King Ove had returned to the Below, leaving behind his Queen.

Chapter Twenty-Three

OVE

Go home, Ove.

Go home, Ove.

Her words echoed in my head as I landed in my room. She had said it as if I meant nothing to her. She had been the one who viciously killed a man. She whispered into his ear, asking me to get her, practically begging to see me again. I had already planned to see her the minute I knew they were safe, but when that man came into my throne room with no heart and screamed her name, I knew I had to see her as swiftly as I could.

So I went for her, and when I saw her leaning on Esen, I knew I wasn't needed. But her words struck a cord in my heart, knowing she would probably suffer because of one man's actions for years to come.

Go home, Ove.

I wanted to throw up hearing those words, knowing how they undid me for no reason. My leg twitched in pain.

I have been on it for far too long and have neglected rest. But how could I? There was so much to do, so many emotions to suppress, and even more plots I needed to unfold.

"How did it go?" Adri's voice made me jump. I had forgotten that she was here and that she was in my room to hold up the image that I had taken a mistress to explain my absence for the night.

I shook my head and walked to the door. Opening it, the twins stood on either side of the door in their armor. "Leave us and find me Ava." The two women walked away with a slight bow in their heads and disappeared down the dark hall.

Locking the door behind me, I stalked over to where Adri lay naked on the bed with the blanket covering her to an extent.

Fuck it. She had offered herself to me. I was no longer with Lynn; sadly, Alya clearly didn't want me.

Crawling onto the bed and over her, she smiled up at me. "What are you doing, Your Highness?"

"Whatever I want and whatever you want." I lowered my head into her neck, kissing the soft skin.

Her chest pressed against my shirt, and her breasts squished at the touch. Gods, it felt nice to be touched by another. My cock throbbed at the feeling of her body against mine. My shadows moved away from me, the fabric I wore disappearing. I felt and heard their protests. Some wanted me to lay my claim, while others screamed at me to stop. Begging me not to touch her or fuck her.

Her small hands traveled the length of my body and wrapped around my cock, and started pumping. I let out a small moan at the feeling of my dick hardening with each pass.

My tongue flicked over her mouth, her lips parting, granting me access. My hands worked their way over her body, and one landed on her thigh. Her legs wrapped around my waist, the dampness that was building between her legs pressed against my cock. It slid around, threatening to go in her.

She let out a soft moan as the tip nudged her. Her hands continued to travel over my body, but never once did they touch my scars.

She's not for you. One shadow screamed above all others.

My head hung low, and I let out a soft sigh. "I'm sorry, Adri. I can't do this."

"Can't or won't?" Her legs and hands fell off me, and she covered herself completely with the blanket.

Falling to her side, my shadows came back, wrapping me in comfortable clothes. The ones pleading for me to stop had subsided. "Both."

She scoffed at what I said. "Why not?"

"I don't need to answer you. I am the King. I answer to none."

Adri rose for the door, unlocked it, and took the blanket with her. "You sound like your father. I never thought I would live to see that day."

I growled in frustration. "Fine! Sit down, and I will tell you." She smirked and plopped down on the other side of the bed with a wide grin. I knew I didn't have to tell her, but I had no one else to talk to. My shadows never leave me completely alone, but it is nice to talk to someone alive. Someone I like. "She didn't look at me once the entire time I was there, and when she did, she gasped in horror at my scars."

She rolled her eyes at me. "Gods, you're pathetic. Stop acting like a heartbroken teenager and move on."

A scoff escaped me. "And you're a fucking bitch, Adriana."

She shrugged her shoulders and smiled at me. "I never said I wasn't. — What's so fascinating about her, anyway?"

The way she asked it made me question her motives. She almost sounded jealous. I would have said she is if I hadn't known her for years, but Adri doesn't let emotions affect her.

"Aside from being drop-dead gorgeous, something about her pulls me in." I don't know what it is, so I can't explain it. But every time I look at her, I want to fall to my knees and worship the ground she walks on. I feel like I have known her since the dawn of time and will continue to know her until the end of time. Every moment in between is precious and something I never want to lose.

Being away from her pained me every day, but I had thought she was happy with Alden and safe with him. There won't be a day that I won't regret leaving her behind.

Fuck. I should have stayed. I should have been the one to save her. I should have been the one comforting her.

I'm not jealous that it was Esen who played a hand in it all, but I am jealous that he gets to do it. I don't resent him or hate him for the freedom he has. I once had it, and I wasted it on nothing. It was my turn to be the dutiful king who protected his people.

The thought of Esen brought a tinge of regret to my heart. Had I given up the best thing I ever had to him? He makes Lynn happy. I should be happy too, right? But I'm not. I can't help but feel like I have done something wrong that I will pay for in the future. But he's done nothing wrong to Lynn. He's protected her and her secrets. He showed genuine fear when her life was on the line. He had given Alden the blade to kill her, but we had put that blade in his hand, and she had forgiven him. Esen has done nothing but love her, and the marks on their necks now show it to all.

She is a Queen claimed by another King.

"Well, whatever pulls you in, you either listen to it or don't. Either way, I saw how Esen looked at her. He worships her as much as he does Lynn. It wouldn't surprise me if he takes them both to bed soon."

Her words stung more than I wanted to admit. I have seen how Esen looks at her, but it's different from how he looks at Lynn. He shows nothing but lust and admiration for his mate. For Alya, he shows loyalty and fear.

One shadow bellowed at Adri, demanding she wash that filth from her mouth. I ignored him like I do every other time it comes to women. His loyalty to his lost love is beyond compare.

A knock sounded at the door. I gestured for Adri to get back in bed. She thankfully didn't question me. Her arms wrapped over my stomach, still being careful not to touch my marred flesh.

"Enter."

Ava walked in, trying to hold her head high but appearing submissive simultaneously. Patting the bed on the other side of Adri, I gave the psychopath an invitation.

"Sit, join us. I've gotten my fill of Adri for the day, but I didn't feel the need to satisfy her. Will you do that for me, Ava?" My skin crawled at the words I spoke and the tone I used. None have been able to resist when I try to seduce them.

It was one thing I appreciated about all the Ghosts. They take pleasure in every gender in every way possible. Few kinks are off the table to them. Dearil ensured it that way. He wanted to use them for his pleasure, and if that meant during an orgy, then so be it. They had no choice but to adjust. And I know years ago, Adri had a crush on Ava before she turned into Dearil's personal monster. Who knows, maybe my offer is giving Adri some satisfaction she still desires.

"Before you begin, I need you both to consent." I realized it as Ava undid her dress and slid into bed beside Adri.

Ava had a predatory smile. "I consent."

Adri cut me a glare, but the corners of her lips twitched upward slightly. Good, she will enjoy this. "I consent."

The two of them quickly wrapped around each other. To my surprise, Ava is taking charge. I thought she would have let Adri take control, but I was wrong. Moans quickly slipped through their lips. Their bodies bumped into mine as they moved about, trying to please each other.

A hand reached for me, and I lay on my back with my eyes closed, doing my best to ignore them. My shadows know me and what I need. One blocked the incoming hand before I had time to question it.

"I did not consent to being touched!" I snapped at both, unsure who had reached for me. But I knew it was Ava. Adri would never have made that mistake.

"Apologies, Your Highness," they both said in unison. Ava's voice was a little louder than the girl whose breast was in her mouth.

I wanted silence. To be left alone to my thoughts. To be alone in my room. But I need Ava to feel vulnerable with me, and there is no way I will willingly put myself alone in a room with her. My plan had been hasty and last minute, but I knew I could rely on Adri to help me if needed.

I ignored their moans and the bed shaking as they bumped into me. It felt like Ava was purposely grazing me as an invitation to join. My sore leg and exhaustion consumed me, allowing sleep to claim me.

***

"Daddy! Daddy, look what I found!" I ran into the empty throne room with my hands stretched out, covering the creature I had caught. No souls were being tormented, only a six-year-old Lynn sitting on the lap of her King. They both smiled at one another, telling me I had interrupted something.

Her small hand reached up to the crown of bones that sat atop his sleek black hair. He smacked her hand away as his smile turned into a scowl. She brought her hand close to her chest to nurse the pain that now encompassed it, but other than that, she showed no sign of being hurt.

I had been so excited to show him what I caught, and seeing him inflict the smallest amount of pain on her caused me to stumble. My chin harshly collided with the stone floor, the skin breaking just enough to draw the slightest bit of blood. I heard my mother's words float through my ears. *You could be his twin. It is imperative you keep your flesh unharmed in order to stay the same as the great King.*

We both shared the same narrow face, tall, lean build, pin-straight black hair. An arch in our nose and wide eyes that didn't seem to fit correctly. He had years on his face while mine was still young, but the main difference was the teeth he had turned sharp.

Fear surged through me at the thought this scratch might become a scar if I was not careful.

I stood up, ensuring I still clasped my hands around the creature, preventing its escape. My father looked down at me with a faint smile. "What did you capture, my son?"

Standing at the bottom of the dais, I opened my hands to show him the small green snake I had found. Its fangs were deep in my palm, its venom doing nothing to my body.

I smiled proudly at myself for capturing it and my plan. "I want to give it to Wayan so he finally has something to care for. I think he is lonely, not having any kids or a wife."

My father chuckled, but it was Lynn's admiring smile that I focused on. "That is a wonderful idea. You can use it to teach him a lesson as well."

She and I looked at one another, confused about how giving someone a gift could be a lesson. "How would I do that?"

"Gift him the snake and tell him to nurture it for a year. At the year's end, you will grant him one desire. But on the last day, you kill the snake, prohibiting him from his wish."

Lynn gasped and hid her head in my father's shoulder. He rubbed her back to bring her ease and comfort. "What lesson does that teach anyone?" Her voice was muffled as she spoke into him.

"It teaches him that those you care for can be ripped away from you if you do not have power. Those in power do the taking, while those with nothing do the begging."

I had heard rumors of my father's cruelty but had never seen it for myself. The worst he has ever done to Lynn and me is the occasional slap on the wrist, but nothing serious. Was this the side he hid from me and his council?

"If that's what power is, then I don't want it." I tried to peel the snake off me, but it held firmly onto me and hissed.

"Me neither." Lynn agreeing with me about something years beyond our understanding did something to me. It felt like an unspoken truce, and an alliance had just been created between us. One that meant power would never consume us like it has done to others.

"Power will always come to the two of you, just as it has me. There will be a day when the three of us rule together with the power of the gods. Death, fear, and war will be ours to command. It will be our salvation."

Lynn slid off the mighty King and approached me. Her fierce eyes looked back at the King. "I don't want power if it means a life without love."

She grabbed my snake-free hand, pulling me away from my father and out of the throne room.

Something within the King shifted that day, and my first beating was the next day.

CHAPTER TWENTY-FOUR

ALYA

The morning air was crisp and relatively calm. A gentle breeze from the ocean filled the open grass, blowing it rhythmically. The smaller tree branches groaned as they moved in the wind. It's air kissing my skin and keeping my hair over my shoulders.

The old swing I sat on moved slightly with my legs. Not too fast and not too slow. Just a calming pace that could lull me to sleep if I let it. I did the other day and paid the price. My wrist still hurts from landing on it.

My injuries from the prison were healing nicely. But without the complete abilities of being a goddess, I will always bear the marks the chains had left.

Taking a deep breath, I smelled the salty air of the sea, the spring flowers coming into bloom, and him. He always smells of rose and vanilla. He did the first day I met him, the day I thought I lost him, and the day I found him. I let out the breath, knowing Ove was walking to me, not Eilam. It was not the man I fell in love with. It is the one who murdered him and is preventing him from reincarnating.

"Hey," his voice was calm and cool. He sounded worried.

"What do you want?" I don't care how harsh it came out. I have nothing to say to him and would much rather be left alone.

"I wanted to check on you. They said you have been coming out here daily to mourn Benji."

My head jerked around to look at him. His hair was slightly messy, but he wore a suit that fit him well. "How do you know that name?"

He smiled. "I was told you liked to call him a rat, and, as you may know, rats will always have a place in my court."

"He's safe?" He is dead, but being in Ove's court is as safe as he can get.

"He is. And that bastard of a man, The Lion, is currently being mentally tortured."

I scoffed. "What is that supposed to mean?" I want to know every little detail about how he is being tortured. I want to make sure he suffers.

"He is lost in his mind, replaying one event repeatedly. I may have twisted the event slightly, and he now is forced to cut off his dick... repeatedly."

"Good."

Ove moved in front of me. His hands carefully lifted my right arm, pulling back the sleeve that covered my scars and other things. "Was this why I smelled fresh blood on you the last time I was here?"

It amazed me that day he could smell it. Lynn made no indication that she could. I looked down at what he was talking about. I had gone into town to get marked in ink. The shape was of a rat whose tail made a circle around him. It was for Benji and a reminder of the promises I made.

"That's a high possibility."

He smiled at me. "It's beautiful. I know Benji will love it. He spoke highly of you. He kept saying how you had unknowingly saved him with the help of goddess Aniya. — What is with him and that gentle goddess?"

I shrugged my shoulders. It was the last thing Benji had revealed to me. He had known who I was. He had asked me to take it all back in the name of love. But how could I when I felt none?

"Alya?" I refused to look up at him and kept my eyes focused on the ground and our feet. "Talk to me, little one. Tell me what is wrong. I can't fix anything if I don't know the problem."

The tears I had been holding in since the day I thought Lynn and Esen had died spilled down my cheek. My breaths were heavy and rapid. He wrapped his arms around me, pulling me in close to him. His warmth was everything and nothing. He is not Eilam. He can't comfort me the way he once did.

I pushed him off me and tried to walk away, but he grabbed onto me, refusing to let me run from my problems.

"Talk to me, little one."

I looked up at him in his gentle green eyes and lost it. "You left me! You fucking left me! I had no one, and you left me! I needed you, and you were gone! You fucking left me!" I choked on air, desperately trying to bring more into my lungs as I wept. He rubbed my back and pressed his brow into mine. "A real fucking friend would not have left me for the lions to find. Someone who cares for you wouldn't do some shit like that!" I beat my fists onto his chest. He took every blow with grace. "I only had you, and you left me."

I wasn't sure when my tears changed. They started as anger towards Ove but shifted to being angry at Eilam. He had left me, too. He was never supposed to get to Oud until I had established it was safe for us. They had left me utterly alone, and I hated them both for it.

"I know. There is not a day in any lifetime that I will not regret it. I am deeply sorry, Alya." He pulled me in closer, not letting me push away from him. His nose sniffled, and then I felt it. A tear dropped into my hair. "I'm so sorry, Alya," his voice broke. "I wish every day that I had stayed to make sure you were safe. I wish I had known sooner about what Alden did to you. I wish I had been there to save you, to kill everyone in that prison. I wish I had been there when you needed someone. Knowing I wasn't is something I will have to live with every day. I'm so sorry, Alya, I failed you."

My tears and snot soaked into his clean jacket. His shadows wrapped around us, making sure we were safe, and for a second, it felt like one had wiped away the tear before it fell. I could have sworn a shadow whispered into my ear—*beautiful bird, always one to trust her wings.*

Eilam. He is here. He is with me.

The world around me seemed to shift. The clouds seemed to open up, revealing a beautiful light. The wind continued to carry marvelous scents. The birds sang their songs louder. The ground felt more solid.

He is here. He is with me.

Eilam never once left me. Benji never once left me. Ove never once left me. None of them have ever left me as long as my heart still beats. They will always be with me for as long as I shall live.

Together until the end. That was what Eilam had promised me. An eternity of love, and I plan on collecting.

"You're here now. You haven't failed me yet." I muttered up at him. The shadows returned to him, and his eyes were red from his tears. A bit of snot clung to his nose as he sniffled, trying to hide the evidence.

"I won't ever leave you if you are in harm's way. I will always come for you, no matter how far away you are. I promise I will always find you, little one." His arms wrapped around my waist, and he leaned back some. "Can I tell you a secret?"

"Only if it's a good one."

"I know you can handle yourself in a fight because of the mercenary you killed. When I saw he had no heart and had a gaping hole in his back, it left me hard knowing you did that."

I pushed at him playfully. "Pervert!"

He shrugged his shoulder and smiled. "Could you blame me? Shit is hot knowing you can end a man's life so spectacularly."

I pushed away again, and he let me go this time, but his arm draped over my shoulder as we walked back to the house. "Something is wrong with you."

"There is a high possibility of that being right, but you like it."

"How arrogant and self-centered can you be?"

He chuckled, "It's confidence and a fact, not arrogance and narcissism."

"You're still a pervert nonetheless."

"I can live with that."

We reached the edge of the porch, where Lynn stood in the doorway looking uneasy.

"We need to talk. All of us."

Ove kept his arm draped over my shoulders as we followed Lynn into the house. She led us back and into a room that looked like an art studio. Paintings, drawings, sketches, and clay molds were all sitting out. A large square table with two chairs on the other side was the only place for one to sit and work. Around the table stood Esen and two others. The two bowed as their King and Queen entered.

The girls wore the all-black leather uniform of the Ghosts. Only her brilliant green eyes showed through, making her pale skin stand out. The other girl wore the same leather, but her hood and mask were off. I saw her one other time and thought she was beautiful with her darker skin and bushy brown hair that I would have thought almost impossible to style if she had not had many braids in it. Her light blue eyes looked at Ove and quickly looked away.

"What happened, Adri?" Ove asked the unmasked Ghost.

"Iris has been hearing rumors that Alden renovated his prison and is using it for experiments on behalf of Daxon."

"What kind of experiments?" Esen asked. He looked pale.

The two visitors remained silent, neither wanting to answer, but Iris did her best to speak in Arymn. "They are creating monsters with angels and demons."

"What do you mean by monsters?" Lynn looked furious.

Adri was the one who answered, "They are forcing them to breed and injecting them with a higher demon's blood for the pregnancy to be viable."

"How is that possible? There are no reports of any higher demon being taken." Ove's hand fell off me, and he stood closer to the table, his crown now sitting atop his head.

Esen took a deep breath that sounded painful. "They have my blood. Alden experimented on me while I was changing. He must have taken it then."

All the demons in the room swore the same word in their language, leaving Esen and me very confused.

It was Lynn who thought things through. "It's not possible. It has only been five months since Alden took over. That is not enough time for a woman to bring a child to term."

I stepped forward. "It is. — When Kesa created the angels, she wanted them to be faster and smarter than the demons. The only way to do that is to ensure they can breed faster. Angel pregnancies are only two months at most, but the majority have the child a little over one month in. With Esen's blood in their system, they can be with child, but it is excruciatingly painful." My hand fell to my stomach.

The memory of what Eilam and I once almost had felt like I was being stabbed by a thousand knives repeatedly. Like I was reliving the first week of the failed pregnancy. He was a lesser demon. His blood running through the unborn child was what killed it and nearly killed me.

I continued explaining how it is possible, "If they inject Esen's blood into the child before the first week is over, then the child can be carried to term, but to my knowledge, it has never been done. Excuse me."

I felt my breakfast work up my stomach and lodge in my throat. I ran out of the room as fast as possible to escape it. No matter how hard I try, I can never escape my past. It always comes back to haunt me—a curse of living for an eternity. The past will always be there waiting for me.

I clung to the porch railing, my nails digging into the wood, its splinters stabbing my soft skin. My breaths were heavy and rapid. I wanted this damn dress off so I could breathe properly. Tears dropped onto the wood, darkening it.

"Alya—"

"Go away, Lynn! I can't do this right now! I can't be in the same room as Ove, knowing he killed Eilam and knowing he will never reincarnate for as long as Ove lives. I can't fucking do it, Lynnora!"

She let out a soft breath of air. Her hands moved to my back and loosened the straps of the dress. With each one undone, a wave of air slammed into my lungs, allowing me to take a deeper breath.

"You'd be amazed at what you can do if you believed in yourself. You are stronger than anyone I have met. You have survived so much in the name of love, and you have lost so much to it as well. You have lived a thousand lives in search of the one you love. Most would have given up hope, but you didn't. You clung to it because you knew he was searching for you. You believed in him, so believe in yourself, Alya. You can do this and so much more. Come back inside so we can all find a way to stop these experiments and Alden."

I shook my head. "It won't change how I feel towards those in the room."

"Have you asked for things to change?" I didn't respond. She already knows the answer. "If you don't ask, then none will know there is a problem. Your voice is as powerful as a sword if you wield it properly."

I turned to face her. "I don't know how to approach him without feeling the need to explain my reasoning. Could you do it?"

She smiled widely at my threat. "Consider it done. A word of advice regarding him: his shadows are always there, talking to and guiding him. There are some he favors and allows to speak louder. Those are the ones he regrets killing, so he allows them once a year to speak to their family if they are still alive. All you have to do is ask."

She walked back inside and held the door open for me. Taking her hand, we joined the rest of the people, trying to figure out what to do. Lynn let go of my hand and brushed past Ove.

I heard her words hiss up to him, "I don't fucking care who you change into, but shift."

He looked down at her and then back at me. My eyes were still lined with tears and were red. His height stayed the same, but his hair turned blonde, his face rounder, and more weight was distributed throughout his body. A full beard appeared on his jaw and chin.

Seeing how effortlessly he changed startled me, but it was relieving to no longer be looking at the one I love.

Sinking into a chair, I rested my head in my hands and tuned them all out. Their conversation continued without a word for me. Paper had been drawn on, arguments had been yelled, food had been eaten, weapons had been laid out, and hours had passed before I heard my name.

"Alya, can you do it?"

I looked up at Esen, who looked angry. "Sorry, what was the question?" I blinked away the haze I had been in.

Adri looked tired and ready to leave. "Alden took a lot from all of you, and we do not believe he will willingly relinquish his claim to the throne, leaving death as the only option. They are deciding who gets the privilege to kill him. Would you like your name put in there as an option?" She was gentle as she spoke. She wasn't like Ava or Lynn. They are both cut-throat when it comes to death, but she sees it for what it is—ending one's mortal life and taking away all the possibilities it has.

I looked at the three of them. Alden had experimented on Esen, taken his throne, and pretended to be his friend and brother. He had shoved a knife into Lynn's heart to kill her. He had also plotted other attempts on her life. One of which left her without her mate and broke her heart. Alden had insulted Ove and fought against him every chance he got. He has been experimenting with his people. And then there is me. Alden had thrown me away like a piece of trash because I refused his advances. He had signed the papers that allowed me to be starved, beaten, and nearly raped. He had signed my death warrant. He had turned all the courts against me with a lie.

"Battles are unpredictable. First come, first serve."

"That settles it." Lynn rolled up a large piece of parchment. "Adri, Iris, keep the Ghosts out of this. We need to keep as few people involved as possible, and if all the Ghosts converge on one target, it will cause suspicions. Oh, and can someone please lock Ava up? She is not to be trusted, and she has a knack for knowing when shit is about to go down."

Adri smiled widely. "Gladly. Thanks to Ove, I am now the center of her attention, and she is pissing me off. We may get a new Ghost if I listen to her talk about her games again."

The three Ghosts in the room laughed loudly at that. Esen and Ove snickered as well. I know Ava was established as a psychopath by the healers, and I have seen firsthand how she likes to manipulate people. I understand their dislike of her, but laughing at her like this still felt wrong.

Ove pulled me to the side and looked down at me. "I have to get the Ghosts back to where they belong and work on things down in the Below, but you know how to get my attention should you ever need me." He placed a gentle kiss on the top of my head and pulled me into a hug.

"I won't need you."

"You're a terrible liar, but I hope it's not true. I would love for you to call for me again."

"Pervert." I pushed away from him.

He walked over to Adri and Iris, his hands gripping their elbows, and the three of them vanished as the shadows swallowed them.

Chapter Twenty-Five

LYNNORA

Esen harshly shoved clothes into a bag and searched the house for anything he needed. Whatever was going through in his head had put him in a foul mood, as did that meeting. It had left us all angry; he and Alya were most affected.

He let out a grunt of pain as he sliced his palm open on a blade he was trying to shove into his overfilled bag. Quickly moving to the fire, I grabbed some ash that had been left since it last burned.

Forcing it into his palm, he cursed at the initial pain of it. "If you were paying attention, you would know the blade wouldn't fit. What's bothering you so much?" I have never seen him this mad before and thrown off about something.

"I am furious, Lynnora, that's all."

"No shit. Alya is pissed, I am pissed, the whole fucking world will be angry once they find out what Daxon and Alden are doing. Will you please tell me why it is bothering you so much?"

He went into the bathroom and repeatedly washed the ash off his hand, muttering the same word. Clean, clean, clean.

I want to reach out to him, to hold him and comfort him, but he is spiraling, and he needs to work through it on his own.

"He is using my blood, Lynnora! He took it when I was unconscious. He experimented on me! I have no fucking clue what happened to me those three months. You at least were awake and had someone! You could do as you pleased."

I scoffed and shook my head. "Do you think I was sitting there daily drinking tea and laughing while Alya was locked up and while the world burned around us? I thought you fucking killed yourself, Esen! My heart shattered into a million pieces because I thought you were dead. Dearil made Ove and I have a proper wedding ceremony where he dressed me like a whore and eyed me like a piece of meat! I was locked away with no contact with the world aside for one day a week when Ove was supposed to fuck me. I had no one! The one time I was not alone for more than an hour was when Dearil was using Ava to torture Ove. I sat there day after day, watching him get beaten, sliced open, burned, cut into pieces, only to be healed again. But it was your fucking face I saw every day and night for a month! I would have gladly slept while being tortured if it meant I didn't have to see the man I love being broken time and time again."

His head fell between his shoulders and hung low, his hands clutching the edge of the sink. "I am sorry, I did not know."

"Of course, you didn't know. I didn't tell you, just like you didn't tell me that Alya was the first fallen angel and a goddess. Or that Adri and you spent time together in Leevah!"

He looked up at me, his eyes wide with horror. "How did you know about my time in Leevah? — Did you know I was there and decide not to come for me?"

"Don't be so self-centered, Esen. I didn't know about your time there until I saw you talk with Adri the first time, and then you all but confirmed it with the way you fight. She trained you.—Come with me." I grabbed his sword and walked outside with him following me.

Handing him the sword, I summoned my two blades. "Fight me, Esen.

We both have a lot of anger that needs to be let out before we go to Arymn, so fight me."

"I am not going to fight you, dearest."

"Fine. I will fight you, and you defend yourself." I didn't give him any time to protest. My blades were already swinging for his throat.

He blocked me as I had expected. Our blades clashed loudly, sending a ring through the field. Again and again, I attempted to strike him, only to be blocked. I have yet to determine how much time he had trained with her, but he had learned well.

I kicked at his stomach, sending him staggering back a few steps. "I know you are angry about more than just Alden and Daxon, so let me have it, or are you too cowardly to admit your feelings?" I have taunted people before to get them riled up and lash out. Esen is no different.

He didn't respond with his words, only an attack aimed at my head. My blades crossed his, blocking him, and I pushed him back.

"Weak and pathetic. You can't even beat a girl."

"You are no mere girl, Lynnora. You are the Seventh Ghost; none have been able to beat you."

"And you are the last of your kind, an unknown demon that was found. I guess you aren't worthy of being written about."

His legs swept low, trying to push me off balance. It worked, but only for a second. I rolled into the fall and got away from him before he could strike my back with his blade.

I don't feel like having to mend this shirt or deal with putting ash on my back. That is an inconvenience and one that I need help with.

"I am worthy of being written about. When I am done, there will be statues in my honor!"

I reached up with my blade and nicked the side of his arm, causing him to hiss in pain, but he did not stop his attacks.

"Wow, it's a good thing we are outside. Otherwise, I would worry your ego wouldn't fit in the room." I was well out of his reach as we circled each other. Holding my arms up casually, I continued the taunting. "So tell me, what does the Golden Boy Esen have to be angry about? Was your milk not warm enough last night?" I knew leaving out 'King' would affect him. The stripping of one's title is humiliating and painful.

He screamed and charged at me. I let him get in a swift blow to my cheek, the tip of the blade sinking deep enough that it would take several minutes and two layers of ash to heal correctly.

The sting of it took me by surprise, and I felt a poison working its way through me. I let out a shriek from the pain and dropped my blades to the ground. The pain was something I had never felt before and never wanted to feel again. I continued screaming as my knees collided with the damp soil, my hand pressing against the injury.

"Shit, shit, shit!" Esen ran to me and dropped to his knees. "I am so sorry, Lynnora."

I smacked away his hand and blinked through the unbearable pain, my tears mixing with my blood. "I don't want your apology! I want you to tell me why you are so angry."

Focus Lynnora. Focus. The pain is temporary. The poison will work its way out of your system in a few minutes. I need to focus.

My name is Lynnora, and I am the Queen of Demons. My best friend is Ove. I am in love with an annoying gnat named Esen. I am alive. I am here. I never stay down.

I am Lynnora, and I do not let the wind bend me. I do not let the ocean drown me, and I do not let the fire scorch me. Because when it does, I stare it down and say, 'One more time'.

Get up one more time.

One more time.

I opened my eyes and saw Esen shirtless. He was using the fabric to soak up the blood that was spilling from between my fingers.

Alya was standing on the porch with a fire in her eyes. She looked like she was ready to kill Esen for hurting me.

"Get her ash!" Esen yelled at the goddess, who quickly disappeared inside. He pressed his brows against mine and let out a harsh breath of air. "You undo me, Lynnora. You make me want to break all my rules. That pisses me off because it terrifies me. You want so damn much, and I want to give everything to you. I never once thought myself capable of touching another in the ways I have touched you. I am angry with you for undoing me."

"I never asked you to do those things," my voice broke with tears.

"I know, but I knew it would make you happy, and there is not a thing in this world I would not do to see you smile. I told you that I changed in numerous ways when I went through the transformation. The curse hanging over my head weakens daily, and you continue to undo me further." He kissed my forehead. "I love you, Lynnora, with every piece of my heart."

Alya fell to her knees. "What the fuck did you do to her?" She pried my hands away from the slice on my cheek.

"I thought she was going to dodge the attack. She had been holding back the entire time. I had no idea she would be this reckless."

"Reckless is putting your venom on a blade and not telling your mate, who is a trained killer."

He went to argue but saw the logical sense in my words. "How did you know?"

I glared at him, asking if he was serious about that question. "I swear you are a fucking idiot sometimes, you stupid gnat. I've seen you collect your venom each day, and now I know it would make sense for you to weaponize it because you don't have a Koya blade of your own."

"I hate you." He pushed back a strand of my hair while Alya continued packing my face with ash. The poison was slowly leaving my body, but the pain was still there, searing my face as if I had been branded once more.

"No, you don't. You just said you love me."

He smiled. "If I recall correctly, you also admitted to loving me during our screaming match."

"No, I didn't." Yes. Yes, I did, but that is a hill I will die on.

His arms wrapped around me, pulling me off the ground. "Come on, we both need to shower."

I tried to squirm out of his grip, but he didn't budge. "I don't need you carrying me like a toddler. It's my face that hurts, not my legs."

"I know. I simply do not care."

He only allowed me to walk alone once we entered the bathroom. My clothes fell off my body as he went to find more ash for me.

The warm shower heated my body, the steam filling my lungs and the water washing away the lingering blood and poison. Sinking to the ground, I brought my legs in close to my chest and let the water beat onto my scarred flesh.

The door loudly creaked open. "I found some ash. It is not a lot, but it will do — Lynnora, are you alright?"

I didn't bother looking up at Esen. I already could feel the pity seeping off him. "Leave me alone, please, Esen."

He did no such thing.

His clothes landed with a heavy thud as he undressed. His arms wrapped around me, pulling me in close. My tail, horns, ears, and teeth all came out in the blink of an eye. My tail slashed around uncontrollably, forcing space between us. He stumbled back but did not run.

I bared my teeth at him and hissed. "I said leave me alone!"

He shook his head. "I am not afraid of you, dearest. You cannot chase me away that easily."

I rose to my feet, towering over him. "Get the fuck out of here before I make you afraid of me. I am your Queen, and you will obey me." I knew as soon as I spoke those words I had messed up, but it didn't change the fact that I wanted to be left alone, and he was in my way.

He mumbled something in the language of the Kings before leaving me to myself.

The moment the door clicked shut was when I let it all come out. I screamed, and I cried; I punched the wall until it was painted red and my bones were being shown.

Again and again.

I pushed through the pain and switched hands, shattering my skin and the wall. My tail had stabbed all the soaps, spilling the liquid onto the floor and making a bubbly mess. My nails dug into my palm, slicing the muscle. My teeth bit my lips so hard that blood was all I was tasting and breathing.

Sinking to the floor, the rushing water drowned out my sobs. "I'm so sorry. I failed you, Mom. I miss you so much. There's not a day that goes by that I don't think of you and miss you. I failed you and Mother. I couldn't protect either of you when it mattered most. I never wanted any of this. I can't do this anymore. I never wanted to fight, to kill. I never wanted to plan a coup or plan a heist. I never wanted any of this. I hate it. Every part of it. All the lies, the lives I've taken, the people I've hurt, the families I ruined, I hate it. I want it all to stop, but it never does. It feels like the realms laugh in my face and say one more time. But it is always one more time and never the last." I continued to cry, thinking about how it had been four years to the day since Dearil murdered my mother.

My tears slowing and my chest steadying, I shared the last of my thoughts with a mom who would never be there to hear them. "I'm so tired, mom. You told me the hero's job will never be done until the realm is safe. But what if I am not a hero and I am a villain? Then what? Is my pain only over when the hero kills me?" I opened my eyes and looked up at the ceiling, knowing what she would say. We have had this conversation before. *The villain does not wonder if they are one. They view themselves as the hero of their cause. You are no villain because if you are, the world has failed you, not vice versa.* "But I am a villain. I have slaughtered hundreds just because I could." *To some, you are, but to others, you are Lynnora Fenwald, a demon worth fighting for, a hero who saved them from the true monsters.* "I'm no savior."

"You are to me." Alya's soft voice startled me. She stood in the doorway with her arms folded across her chest and her head leaning on the door frame. "You may not believe it, but you saved me; therefore, you are a hero."

I let out a scoff. "I am no hero. I am the villain of my life."

"If you are one, then so are Esen, Ove, and I. May we rise and fall together."

I looked at her gentle eyes and saw nothing but love in them. "We're a pathetic lot of heroes and villains, then. We can't even agree on a plan."

She shrugged her shoulders. "I have learned to expect the plans to go wrong. That's why I have never made one. I let the winds carry me where I need to be."

I rolled my eyes at her. Leave it to the goddess of the Seven Winds to rely on them to carry her.

"It's time, Lynn."

Chapter Twenty-Six

OVE

"Find me Ava." I didn't wait more than a second upon returning to snap at the two Ghosts. I need Ava to either be distracted or locked up while Lynn and the others do what must be done to get Esen back on the throne.

I should feel guilty about it all, but I don't. Dearil has used Lynn and me for as long as we can remember. Ava is the same. My skin crawled at the realization. I am doing to her what Dearil would have done.

I am not my father. I am not my father. I am not my father.

I continued repeating those words until I started to believe them. I am not him, but I do need to get things done, and if acting like him is the way to do it, then so be it. I will do what it takes to ensure their safety and the safety of my people.

The war room was brightly lit, my shadows lashing out against the flames, trying to darken them. I stood over the table, leaning on my hands with my head drooped low.

"Yes, Your Highness," Iris quietly said before swiftly departing.

Adri waited with me in silence. She waited for me to say something first, to move first. But what was I supposed to say? Where was I supposed to move to? My father never taught me what to do in situations like this. I have no advisor to guide me. There is no book or set of guidelines that helps me. I have to do this alone and do not know where to start.

What am I supposed to do if I find out that what Dearil is planning is worse than what Alden has planned? How am I supposed to choose where to send my men to? Logically, it would be to send them to the greater evil and focus on that, but what if that is Dearil? I can't leave my Queen un-maned. I can't leave my friends without aid.

I can't do this alone. I want Lynn to be here, standing by my side, giving her input. She excels in battle strategy and where to allocate resources. I should never have let Esen take her. I should have never divorced her. I need her. I need my Queen. I need the Seventh Ghost. But all I have is Adri. She is talented and fearless, but I need more than that. I need the girl who I would burn the world for. I need the girl who defied a cruel king without knowing she was doing it.

I knew there would be a day when she would leave me, but I never thought it would be so soon. I never made plans on what to do for this day.

Think, boy. You know what to do. You have all the resources you need. Just think. The shadow of a Sparan Court general whispered into my ears.

He had been growing old and sick when I stumbled across him. He wanted death, but no one would accept his challenges, and in Sparan Court, the only honorable death for a warrior is death in battle. I saw the pain in his eyes and challenged him. Two quick swipes, and he was dead. I saw it the moment the life left him. He wanted the pain to end, not his life. I took him into my shadows so he could still live and see all the world has to offer.

But think about what? What resources do I have? — I have a lot. I am a King, the King of the Below. I control all demons no matter what realm they are in. I can command those in exile to return and do my bidding. I have all the resources I need for world domination. But which resource is it that I need?

The general's words played on repeat in my head, searching for any sign of what the resource was.

Just tell me. I snapped at him, growing impatient.

You are smart, boy. Think. Listen. Feel.

I can discard you if I wish to. Maybe threatening him will help get him to tell me what to do.

You won't do that, boy. You need me just as much as I need you. You need all of us, even those who anger you. You have nothing to use against me, boy.

Think what? Listen to what? Feel what?

The voice of the first man I killed poked through. *Love is a powerful weapon if wielded correctly. Aniya would want this if it ensured the Queen's and her safety.*

Love.

Love is a powerful weapon.

Use love against someone.

Boy.

Trevv.

I need Trevv.

I felt stupid for not realizing it sooner and putting the pieces together faster, but my shadows were correct. I need Trevv.

He knows how war works. He knows the other Kings. He killed a man for this position and yet was willing to walk away from it for his daughter. He will come back if he believes it is what Lynn wants.

I looked up where Adri stood, patiently waiting for me. "Find Trevv; tell him the Queen has returned to the Below and wishes to speak to him. Find a way to throw in that she seems to be in a forgiving mood." Adri bowed and left without a word.

What did I do? He will be furious when he gets here, and she is not here and finds out Lynn never sent for him. She will probably try to kill me, too, if she finds out I used her name to get him to come. She has always known I use her against him, and each time I do it, she scowls at me but never stops me. It led me to believe she likes the attention she receives from him after. Not that I could blame her. Any positive attention from either of our fathers was a miracle we cherish while it lasts.

***

I had sat in the chair shortly after Adri left and had yet to move. My butt was going numb, my back sore, and my mind bored. How much longer do I need to wait for Trevv to show up? Where did he disappear to?

Minutes had turned into hours. Hours felt like they were turning into days, but the candles never ran out of wax, telling me a day had not passed.

The door creaked open, and Trevv stood in the doorway, bowing. "Your majesty."

Toying with my goblet, I looked at him. He still looked the same. His black hair was tied back. His horns and ears were the same. His tall, muscular build did not fade in the slightest. His dark skin was the same as Lynn's.

Gods, she is the female version of him. It's disturbing.

"Sit with me, Trevv."

He slowly rose and looked around the room for his Queen and daughter.

"Apologies for lying to you, but I did not think you would come if I sent for you."

Trevv glared at me, no doubt planning ways to murder me the first chance he gets. "I would have come if you summoned me. You are my King." I could hear the disdain in his voice. He wants me dead.

Am I making a mistake trusting him as my advisor? Will he stab me in the back or sell us out to the highest bidder? I could test him, give him a piece of information that is a lie, and see if he tells anyone, but that takes time. I don't have the time I wish I had. The war is happening whether I like it or not, and the only way to stop it is to get Esen on the throne.

Trevv sat down at the foot of the table. A servant came in behind him and poured him a glass of blood. All demons need blood to survive, but those who can shift into a mortal form need it more often.

"What can I do for you, King Ove?"

"You once said you would only respect me if I become King. Are you a man of your word?"

Trevv set his goblet down. "I am, as you very well know."

I smirked at him. "Then, as a man of your word, I want you to beg and grovel. To plead for my forgiveness. You are the reason I took so many beatings, the reason your Queen bears scares. You are the reason our late Queen is dead. So I want you to beg like the bastard you are."

He blinked as his face went pale. I still do not know why Dearil killed my mother, but it is easy to blame Trevv. He had been the one to tell Dearil that I had tried to fight him. He had a hand in my mother's death, just as I did.

She is dead because of me. I had failed her. I hadn't protected her. I live with many regrets every day. My shadows are proof of it. But she is the one regret I am not haunted by. I will never get to see her again and tell her I am sorry. I will never get to hug her one last time or hear her words of encouragement. She is gone because I had pissed Trevv off, and now I am turning to the man who aided in her death.

"King Ove, I had no intentions of ever harming you or Lynn. You are like a son to me and have been since you and she became friends. I do not take lightly my role in your mother's death. She was a Queen adored by all and a loving mother. I am deeply sorry for your loss and the pain I have caused you. I hope you can forgive me one day for all that I have done."

I turned my head to the side, studying him and each breath he took. Does he expect me to believe in this bullshit of an apology?

"I do not have the time or patience for you and your poor attempts at flattery. When you decide to mean what you say, perhaps there is a place for you back in my court." *She is here.* "Until then, you are dismissed to return to whatever hole you crawled out of. You look horrid." I couldn't bring myself to make him my advisor. I still resent him too much.

Trevv didn't say anything as he rose and bowed again before leaving.

He passed by Adri, who was walking in with Ava beside her.

Thank the gods, she had her hood and mask up. I didn't want to deal with her smile, which looked like it might kill me if I said something wrong or moved the wrong way.

Ava bowed, as did Adri. Gesturing for Ava to sit, she took the seat Trevv had occupied a moment prior. Adri moved to close the door, but my shadows intercepted her movement, preventing her from doing so. She didn't question me.

My ring tapped the edge of the gold goblet, carrying a tune through the room that lasted longer than it should have.

"Rumor is that you, Ava, were close with the late King. Is that true?"

She adjusted her shoulders back. "I was, as were all the Ghosts."

Deflection. She is wise to try to get my attention off her. It's too bad I know what I am looking for; I only need to ask the right question. But what question can I ask her to get her to reveal what I need? She enjoys these games of questions. She has mastered spinning lies around the truth. I could command her, but that will make me no better than Dearil.

"Did you share his bed and engage in sexual activity with him?"

Her eyes showed the smile she had on beneath the mask. "I did, as well as all the other Ghosts, aside from Queen Lynnora."

They all — they all had slept with him? I wanted to look at Adri to confirm this, but I knew it would give Ava the upper hand, knowing I knew less than her about my father's activities.

"Why is it that he excluded Lynn from these activities?"

Ava's eyes darkened. The smile faded away with my question. Whatever the answer was, it angered her. "Because he loves her and did not want to have her ruined before the time was right." My heart sped up. No, she can't be right. My father loved my mother. But he killed her without blinking or hesitating. "King Dearil thought they were soul mates. That was until you fell in love with her."

I didn't care if she got the upper hand. I need more information. "What do you mean?"

"Simple." She shrugged her shoulders. "Your father wanted her for himself, and when he saw your friendship with her grow, he wanted to test her and see if she would come back to him. He kept pushing her towards you to see just how far she would go, and then he would tug on the string, calling her back to him. Each time, she came back like the obedient Ghost she was; each time, he knew she was his mate. Every single beating you took was because of her, to make you realize she is not yours and she belongs to him."

No.

That's impossible.

Traitorous bitch! Mimsy screamed in my ear, startling me. *You filthy liar! Mimsy, explain to me what you know.*

Lynn is not Dearil's mate, and he knows it. His mate is the only death he will ever regret. His mate was Lynnora's mother, and he killed her because of a secret she bore. She had convinced Dearil Lynn was his daughter, and when the two of you started fucking each other, he was outraged by the act. He went to her to stop it; instead, he found her running away from him and her life. He killed her for the lies she had woven into him. He killed her for taking away the daughter he thought he had. The only reason he never claimed Lynn as his own was because it would mean admitting to his wife he loved her best friend, and even the cruel king could not speak that cruelty aloud.

How did she convince him? She looks too much like Trevv.

Kalina told Dearil it was because Lynn was the demon princess. The first demon king descended from nothing but fear. He took the form of whatever he pleased. The trait got passed on to his children and his children's children. That is why you can shift into whatever body you want. You are made of the

air around you. Lynn would have been as well if she were royalty. Kalina
tricked Dearil into believing Lynn had found a drawing of Trevv's dead sister
and morphed into her. He was not there for the first three years of Lynn's
life, so he could not argue. He had only believed her because of the power that
emanated from her. He knew she was destined for the crown, so he kept the
secret all those years, thinking she was his.

Shit.

I let out a scoff, bringing my attention fully back to Ava. "Why must a beautiful mouth like yours spill such nasty lies?"

Ava unclipped her mask to reveal she was pouting pathetically. "It was worth a shot. I was told only I and two others know the reason why Lynn was never fucked by Dearil. So what do you think you know?"

"I know the truth, Ava. And I am your king. Show me the respect I have earned and deserve. Do not waste my time playing your games. If that is what you want, may I suggest you go to a gambler's den? But need I remind you, you are a Ghost. You answer to me and Queen Lynnora. Since she is not present, you answer solely to me. Your loyalty to Dearil is no longer needed. I know you are smart enough to know when to switch allegiances. I suggest you do so soon."

She watched me, her eyes roaming my body, looking for any weakness or clue about what I wanted from her. I will give her none until she gives me what I want. I dinged my ring on the goblet again, sending another haunting call to the room.

Ava let out a sigh and rolled her eyes. "Are you going to make me do this?"

"I make you do nothing. You have free will, and I am letting you use it however you please—to an extent."

She rose and bowed. "I, Avageline Dustel, swear my loyalty to King Ove of the Demons and the Below. May I die protecting him and the throne from its enemies." She rose and took her seat. "Happy now?"

"Very much so. Avageline Dustel, tell me why Dearil stepped down from the throne."

And so she did. With each word she spoke, my heart sank into me. I had no words to express the pain I was feeling. No thoughts as to where to send my troops. I have no idea as to who to protect and who to let die. He had told me his plan when I was little. He had told me it as I grew. And yet I had been so blind.

It won't matter if we get Esen on the throne. We will all be dead.

Chapter Twenty-Seven

ESEN

We had agreed to visit the seer first. Lynnora kept insisting she was important in all that was happening. I also have a few choice words to say to her, none that will shock anyone who hears. How could she have been so wrong about my prophecy?

The Golden King will die at the hands of one who bears the marks of lightning. With his death, lies will unfold, destroying a throne.

I had technically died when I tried to kill myself to find Lynnora in the Below. Mortals do not go there and come back alive. There are those few exceptions, but they are granted a deal with the King of Demons. I have heard that the price is your soul or the soul of the one you love most. A lifetime of servitude only to once more serve upon your death.

Was that what Mimsy had paid for her ability to go to the Below? Or had she paid the ultimate price when she betrayed Lynnora? It does not matter; she is dead because of her actions, and we are still very much alive.

Looking up towards the sky, I could spot Alya flying above. She refused to come with us. Lynnora did not push her or argue. She simply nodded her head and walked away. The two of us had dawned old brown cloaks that looked on the brink of falling apart. Our hoods remained up as we maneuvered through the city. Each time we neared a guard, Lynnora walked with a fake limp, and I hunched over slightly. To them, we are just beggars, but to us, we are the Queen of Demons and the rightful King of Arymn. I knew if we got caught, there was no turning back. There is no amount of scheming to get us out of the mess. We are dead if we get caught. And I do not particularly feel like dying before I give the seer a piece of my mind and get my throne back from Alden.

We turned a corner, and the flower-shaped temple came into view. Lynnora stopped walking and looked at me. "Are you ready?" I could hear the slightest bit of fear in her voice.

What is she looking for from the seer that would make this so terrifying? Whose death does she want to learn about? What is it that Lynnora truly fears?

"I am." I nodded and tried to reach my hand toward hers, but she did not take it.

With my confirmation, she led the way through the crowded street. She approached the door and muttered, "I wish I brought the girls."

She had wanted to bring them for whatever reason but sided against it because they were too recognizable. And we need to stay hidden for as long as possible. The guards know what they look like. It would give us away too soon.

The door opened without her touching it. It did not phase her as she walked in. I could smell the heavy perfumes clinging to the fabric on the walls. Some of which had been pulled down or torn. My hand fell beneath my cloak to the hilt of my sword, ready to use it if there was an intruder. Lynnora pulled back her hood and looked around before feeling one of the ripped fabrics. Her steps slowed as she felt each rip and tear in the fabric.

A female voice I recognize called from deeper within the temple, "If you came here to destroy yet more of my belongings, you are too late, Queen Lynnora."

She breathed, and all the tension in her body disappeared. Lynnora picked her pace back to normal as she walked further down the hall. The room opened to the circular room filled with stairs leading down to the center, where the seer was sweeping up broken glass.

Every object that could be broken was. The figurines were missing heads or arms. Someone snapped the daggers in two. Gems lay shattered on the ground. Even a few gold pieces were broken. An immense amount of power is the only thing capable of this. And there is only one person I know who is strong enough to do so.

Alden.

Lynnora toed a broken figurine. "Who did you piss off for this to happen?"

"The same person you are out to kill."

"It's a shame you didn't do that for us, but you wouldn't interfere, would you, Kesa?"

Kesa? As in the all-mighty, powerful supreme deity, Alya's mother. That Kesa?

I looked at Lynnora with wide eyes, and she smirked at me. How long has she known this? How could this be possible? How could I have not known? How could I have missed this? Why did she not tell me?

My heart sank at the thought of the last question, bringing one more to my mind. What else is she hiding from me?

The seer, Kesa, glared at both of us. "If you aren't here to break my belongings, why are you here?"

Lynnora made herself comfortable on a stair and examined a broken dagger before tossing it. How is she this relaxed around a goddess? "I want to know why you lied about our prophecies?" I blurted out before Lynnora had time to answer.

Kesa looked at me and gestured for me to sit. Doing as she asked, I kept my eyes on hers. The large green eyes tracked my every breath. Once I sat down beside Lynnora, that was when Kesa decided to explain.

"I know my brat of a daughter filled you in on my ability to take one's power, so I will not lie to you about my gifts. I have all the gods and goddesses' abilities. Aside from Haedon and a few others, those you worship are now just names in the wind meant for you to think are there for you. Their eternal bodies exist without knowledge of what they once were. They live and die a mortal life like the rest of you, only to be reincarnated with no memories of anything they experienced. The same misery is upon the god of fate. I stole his gifts in his youth, and since then, he does not live past twenty-nine, an unforeseen circumstance, nor does he have his powers. I now see how all will die, but after living millions of deaths, I grew bored—"

"And I am growing bored with this conversation. Get to the part where you lied to us," Lynnora snapped at the goddess.

Kesa did not seem phased by the tone in the Queen's voice. She continued sweeping the floor. "I told people how they would die, but I also told people how they would live. That slowly turned into me telling people the day they found something worth living for, something to fight for. Unfortunately, the only way for mortals to see it was upon their deathbed. So people then began to assume what I was telling them was how they would die, not how they would survive or when they would learn the meaning of their miserable lives."

I scoffed, "And what exactly was I supposed to learn to survive with what you told me?"

She paused her sweeping and smiled at me. "What was going through your mind and heart the day you tried to kill yourself?"

My throat bobbed, not wanting to tell either of them the truth. Kesa raised an eyebrow, waiting for me to explain. Lynnora picked up a gem and held it to the light before pocketing it.

Thief.

"I was pissed that Lynnora played me for a fool and deceived me, but when I looked at her, I knew I loved her. No matter how much I hated what she did, I could not stay mad at her."

"And what did you do in response to those feelings?"

Lynnora turned to look at me. Love was shining in her eyes. "I had hoped she would kill Alden, but when he turned the knife on her, I knew I had only one way to see her again. I killed myself so I could find her and be with the woman I love." Lynnora smiled at me. I smiled back at her and mouthed the three words I never say enough.

"Did you not discover why you wished to survive? Did you not learn that love is the most powerful weapon to exist? Did you not rip the air out of the room so you could continue loving?"

I had no response. She was right. I had learned to love another and did not want to give it up. I still do not want to give it up. I had learned what I wanted in my life, and it was the woman who now sits beside me.

Lynnora pocketed yet another gem. "So then, what of mine?"

Kesa fixed the bowl that had been kicked over; the blood stained the side crimson red, along with the stone floor. I resisted the urge to go clean it.

"Ah yes, I do believe yours was quite poetic. *Good and bad will guide the living dead that is touched by nothing. A choice must be made; to live is to love, and to die is to rule.* I see you chose death, Queen Lynnora."

To live is to love, and to die is to rule.

Lynnora became Queen, knowing she would die. My heart shattered into a million pieces, like the gems surrounding me. She would rather die than love me.

"I am not the true Queen of Demons until the last is dead," Lynnora answered confidently. "Explain to me my prophecy."

Kesa turned her head to the side and looked deeply into Lynnora's eyes as if searching for lies in her words.

I was told the last Queen of Demons was dead. Had that been a lie, too?

"You are a ghost, and yet you are alive. I believe that constitutes you as living dead. Your death, however, was the death of who you once were, not the ending of your soul. When Esen killed himself, you watched the man you love die. It had broken you, killing off the last bit of you that tied you to who you were, to Dearils' favorite demon. But you were not alone in those moments. Ove and Alya were there, guiding you. They pulled you off his limp body as you screamed, trying to bring him back. They guided you on your darkest day. You may have escaped making a choice when you should have, but the day you die nears. You can not run from your destiny any more than you can run from your past. It will always catch up to you."

She had screamed for me? She had tried to bring me back to life? I never thought about what that day may have done for her; now, it consumed me like wildfire. She, too, had watched the one she loved die. Whether she will admit it or not, she does love me, and she watched me kill myself while holding me. Ove and Alya had to pull her off me to leave.

I had broken her heart, and I had done so alone. There was no cloud hanging over my head, whispering in my ear. There was no second thought to it. I had broken her the same way she broke me.

"Then I guess I don't stop running." Lynnora rose from where she was sitting and turned her back to the goddess as she ascended the stairs.

"I am not done talking to you!" Kesa yelled out at her. Her voice boomed, vibrating the walls.

Lynnora continued walking towards the exit. "I am done talking to you."

I felt the air rush past me; I had no time to warn Lynnora. She was thrown into the wall and fell loudly. Rushing to her side, she shook me off, insisting she was okay.

Lynnora pulled herself up to her feet with a scowl on her face. "What else do you want?"

"I want you to tell my daughter that her display of power was futile. She may have placed bits of her gift deep within her, but I will remain to have the rest."

I looked at where Kesa stood in the center of the room. Everything around her was destroyed, fabric about to fall from the wall and ceiling. A large cloth dangled delicately, exposing massive white wings behind it with a single feather turned black.

Alya's wings.

I know I should not interfere, but I have years' worth of anger stored up within me. "I know Alya killed your archangels and fell in love with a demon, and it hurt you. But did you not hurt her too when you experimented on her for a hundred years?" Kesa's large eyes blinked as her face remained neutral. "The least you could do is give her back her wings so she can fly again," I snapped at the goddess.

"Even if I wanted to, I cannot. Only the one who took them from her can, and he is dead."

I bit my tongue not to give away my surprise. Alya had told us Kesa took her wings. My mind began spinning once more, my chest growing heavy and hurting. I want to curl up and sleep for the rest of my life. I want the lies to stop. I want my throne back. I want this all to be over or never have happened. How many more lies will I be told and believe? How many more truths will someone else uncover and leave me feeling like a fool?

I want this to be over.

Lynnora looked at me and caught my arm as I lowered myself. "I didn't know either," she whispered loud enough for me to hear. "You need blood. You are feeling weak because you aren't eating properly."

My Queen turned to face the goddess. "I have one more question for you. After that, I will stop threatening you."

"Speak."

"What do you mean by Alya placing bits of her power within her? I thought once you took it, you take all of it."

"My daughter found a way around it. She knew I would be coming for her and hid small portions of her power within objects she cherished. I have found the three pieces and eliminated them."

"What were they?" I asked before thinking it through.

"Her favorite toy from her youth, the dove she kept as a child, and the boy Eilam. All are destroyed or dead. The magic she hid was mine for the taking."

She had transferred her magic into Eilam? No wonder she took his death so much harder. Not only did she lose him, but she lost a part of herself as well.

Lynnora was satisfied with the information she received, and I had no more questions to ask her or words to yell at her. All the ones I had wanted to use disappeared the moment I realized she could kill me before I had time even to know she was attacking.

We walked towards the exit once more when Kesa called, "There will be a day when I come to collect what is mine. I suggest you do not fight me."

"I will always fight you if it means protecting those I love," Lynnora spoke so elegantly as if she had been ruling for eons.

Chapter Twenty-Eight

ALYA

I had perched atop a roof several streets down. The rooftop was high enough for me to watch Lynn and Esen disappear into the temple. It felt weird being back on the island that my mother lives on while in Arymn Court. To know she is here while I am as well, and if she wanted, she could permanently kill me. Even worse, to know that a few months ago, I had been pulled away in my sleep by guards as I screamed, demanding to talk to Alden, insisting there was a mistake and they had the wrong person.

I spent a week in the cells below the castle before he came to speak to me, and when he did, I wished I had escaped when I had the chance.

But if I had done so, I would never have meant Benji. I would never have known Esen or Lynn were alive. I would have continued spending my days loathing my parents and what they stand for.

I bet neither of them thought I would come back and come back stronger. They both have belittled me, degraded me, thrown me in cells, allowed others to cut into my skin, and used whatever means necessary to get me to submit to them. But I won't. I faltered once, and I paid the price.

Never again. I will not yield to them or anyone. I am not their pet to keep on a leash. I am not their cadaver to experiment on. I am not their toy to use. I am Alya Edevane, and I do not break.

Taking a deep breath of the fresh air as spring was slowly turning to summer, I could feel its warmth and taste the pollen of the flowers. This is why I do not stop. I never want to give up the most minuscule things life has to offer.

Lynn and Esen had been inside for maybe ten minutes when I saw them emerge, both looking angry based on the way they were walking. The hoods of their cloaks concealed their faces, hiding any true expression they might bear.

What did they learn?

Lynn never told us why she wanted to go to Kesa, only that it was necessary. Had she gotten the information she needed, or had it been unsuccessful?

Flapping my wings, I caught a current that carried me down to them. They waited in an alleyway for me, both grumbling about something. I could hear the tone in Esen's voice, and he sounded lethal. He was out for blood.

Shifting back, I wore the same cloak as them, plus brown leather armor beneath. I know Lynn was in hers, and Esen was in whatever his armor was made of. He still has yet to tell us.

"What happened?" I asked them as they turned to face me.

They pulled off their hoods and crossed their arms across their chests. "Who *really* took your wings, Aniya?"

Lynn's eyes showed no kindness, no mercy. She was the Queen of Demons, the Seventh Ghost. My friend was nowhere to be seen. My throat bobbed at the question, and my eyes stung from the memory. "Kesa."

"Who took the blade to your skin and carved them out of your body?"

I closed my eyes and felt the tears crawl onto my lashes. "Eilam."

Lynn swore under her breath in her native tongue. Esen let out a harsh sigh. "Why lie?"

Opening my eyes, I looked into his eyes, which had changed so much.

"Kesa forced Eilam to do it. That was the final push we needed to know we had to get away from her. She then told him if she ever saw him again, she would have him killed. The archangels saw him and killed him. I swear everything else was the truth. I just didn't tell you the correct order in which it happened." I shrugged, hoping to make it seem less severe than it was.

"Once we get the throne back for Esen, you are telling Ove the truth. Your wings are inside the temple, and he may be the only one to get them back for you."

"I don't want them back," I blurted out before I had time to process what I was saying and what it meant. I knew she kept them and took them everywhere she went, but I didn't think I could ever get them back. It would require me to find Eilam, convince him to get them for me, and sew them back onto me. But do I want them? The moment they fell off my body, I felt free for the first time. I felt like the world had been lifted off my shoulders, and no one relied on me anymore. I could live the life I wanted. I could be who I wanted, with no restrictions.

I was limitless.

I have been limitless.

But is that what I still want? To not rely on others, to have none depend on me?

I looked at my two friends and found myself missing Ove. They are relying on me to take back the throne. Wings or no wings, they still need me for this. Someone will always need me for something, no matter what I look like, what my name is, or who I pretend to be. I have stayed hidden for long enough. I have let people use and abuse me. But I have also let others love me as I loved them. Ove will be rightfully pissed when he learns the truth, but he will understand. He has always been gentle with me, even when I anger him. If I want, he will get me my wings back.

"Where to next?"

Lynn and Esen opened the barrel at the end of the alleyway and pulled out the bags they had shoved in there earlier for safekeeping.

"We break into the castle." I could hear the excitement and annoyance in Lynn's voice.

***

Esen was the size of a twig in my talons. I carefully held onto him, afraid I might accidentally harm him, but he didn't flinch when I scooped him up. I had tested the strength of his scales, and they pushed back against me, but I still didn't want to find a weak spot in them and cause harm. Not when we may all die in the next day or two.

Following Lynn's instructions, I flew to the third floor and counted the windows until I found the one I was looking for. Esen slid from my grip as he jumped onto the window ledge. Landing beside him, I pried the base of the window until it opened.

Esen slithered in and shifted into a larger snake, checking the room to make sure none were in the room. Once he was satisfied, he shifted into his mortal form and locked the door.

Sending out my song, another melody answered back. Lynn was on her way. I didn't even see her leave the spot we had started at. The next thing I saw was her at the base of the wall with the three bags strapped around her. She assessed the wall and walked back towards the hedges on the other side of the path. Gaining a running start, her body slammed into the wall as she jumped up and caught a stone that was sticking out.

She made the climb up to her old room look easy, and I knew the bags she had on her were heavy. I had struggled to carry my own, yet she carried all three of ours. It made me wonder what training she underwent to become a Ghost.

Lynn pulled herself in through the window without our help. When her feet were solid on the ground, I closed the window and shut the blinds so no one could see in.

I never thought Esen would be right, but so far, he was. Alden would never expect an attack from within his castle or for his enemy to return to the most expected place. We had discussed hiding at the house Lynn purchased for a very short time when we had gone over the plan again on the transporter. But she said it was too far from the castle, and guards were crawling around the area since it was so close to the docks. They then asked where I lived while here, and I admitted I usually just found the comfiest tree or bush to sleep in at night and then used the communal baths to freshen up. Esen grimaced when I told him that. His need for cleanliness is not as dire as it once was, but it is still there.

Lynn then joked about breaking into the castle a day before the ball and hiding in the cells like she did when she first came to Arymn. That was when Esen suggested breaking into her old room and slowly making our way to Esen's old chamber. It is in one of the highest towers, with only one other room on the floor. It was not meant for the King's chamber, and Alden most likely moved to the one intended for that. We would be safe and unbothered in it.

If caught, Esen and I could get out quickly, and Lynn would need to fight her way down two flights of stairs before she could disappear into the massive castle.

It was weird being back in this room. Lynn, Ove, and I had once gotten drunk in here and all shared a bed. I had bit Ove's finger trying to confirm that he was Eilam, and I accidentally granted him reincarnation in the process, but I knew it was my husband deep within.

The room itself looked exactly like it had been left. Dresses still hung up in the wardrobe. The bed was made with the same blankets and sheets. The same soap bar sat on the sink beside the hairbrush I had seen Lynn use. The room looked frozen in time as if the past four months had never occurred.

Lynn was prying a stone up from below the carpet. She pulled out a sealed container filled with red fluid. "It's old and will probably taste disgusting, but it will work until I get time to sneak down to the kitchen and get some proper blood." She tried to pass it off to Esen, but he shook his head and lifted his hands, blocking her advance.

"I will wait," he spoke so politely I would never have thought he was still angry, but the ticking in his jaw spoke the words he didn't. He was still angry.

"The party isn't until tomorrow. I suggest we all get some rest." She disappeared into the bathroom and shut the door behind her, locking Esen and me out of it.

I began unpacking my bag when I stopped suddenly. "Is she alright?"

Esen let out a sigh. "I do not know. She is working through some things, all while trying to find herself. I think she is afraid of the world around her because of what she has done to it. And with what we learned from Kesa, I understand why."

"What did you learn?"

"Lynnora will die if she rules but lives if she chooses love."

I looked at him. "How could that be an option? You choose love. You always choose it." I may be biased with what I said, but I mean it. A crown will eventually be passed onto the next, but love is eternal. And if you truly love someone, then you are the luckiest person.

"She has never known love. She was raised to rule. That itself is utterly terrifying. To give up your only known purpose for the possibility of a thing you have never known."

"Do you think she will give it up for love and to save herself?"

He took a moment to think it through. "No. As much as I hate to admit it, she is a creature of habit, and going back to what makes her feel safe. Power does that for her, and love is a foreign concept she may never understand."

"Would you give it up for love?"

"I have."

The water turned off, and Lynn came out with a towel around her a few seconds later. "I left you both hot water."

Esen gently kissed her cheek, which she leaned into as he passed by her to shower.

Once the water was running again, I watched Lynn get dried off and dressed in a nightgown.

I started the conversation the same way I did with Esen. "Is he alright?"

She ignored me as she pulled the nightgown over her head and shimmied it down her body. The silk fabric caught on her wet skin.

"Lynn, I know you are not alright. I know I am halfway there, but is Esen alright?"

"What part of this makes you think he is alright? Was it the part where he was used for science experiments, the part where he found out he was a demon? Maybe it was the part where we had to save you from a prison you could have easily escaped if you weren't so stubborn! No, I know; it was the part where he learned that his brother betrayed him and used his blood to create things that should never exist."

Her words stung. "None of that was okay. None of what happened to Esen should have happened, but they did, and there is no changing that. We are all here to try and fix the one thing that can be fixed! We are here for him."

"No, you aren't! Esen and I are here to reclaim his throne. You are here to act out on revenge. You are here because you think you can cozy up next to me to get close to Ove. But guess what, Alya! Ove will never be Eilam. The man you love is dead, and Ove will never love you back, no matter how much you try!"

I nodded my head, fighting back the tears that lined my eyes, threatening to spill if she attacked once more. "I don't care if he never loves me. I don't care what happens between him and me! All I care about is that he lives so Eilam gets to live this one life a little longer. I know why I am here and who I am fighting for, but can you say the same? You claim you are here for Esen, but you would never have held back if you were. You are the Queen of Demons. You control thousands, yet only three of us are trying to take the throne. You are holding back because if you weren't, Esen would already have had the crown atop his head the moment you found out he was alive."

Lynn snarled at me. Her tail lashed out, slicing into the edge of the bed. "You know nothing, Alya. You pretend you are this high and mighty being who sees the good in all, but you are a scared little girl with no backbone!"

I let out a cold laugh. Her words once would have brought the tears rolling down my face, but now, after hearing them from my mother's mouth, they mean nothing. They do nothing but serve as a reminder of the promises I made.

"A scared little girl with no backbone would never have defied the gods. A scared little girl with no backbone would never have lied to a Ghost or befriended a demon. A scared little girl with no backbone would never challenge the King of Demons! I am not a scared little girl. I haven't been since I escaped my mother's grip. I am Alya Firstchild, the first angel and the first fallen angel. I am Aniya, the goddess of soulmates and the seven winds. Most importantly, I am Alya Edevane, Eilam's wife. I do not fucking get scared! How dare you insult me when you are a scared little girl!"

Lynn's lips twisted upwards into a smile. "There she is. Took you long enough to let the anger consume you."

I shook my head. "Anger is not what consumes me. It is my love for the world I desire. The love for my friends and those around me." *Take it back in the name of love.* "The love I feel for Benji, you, Esen, and Ove is what consumes me."

"Love can be a weakness. Don't let it come to that."

"Love is never a weakness; it is a motivator, it is pure, it is light. Love is not cruel and vile, nor is it cold and calculating. Love never leaves you questioning if it is real or not." Looking at my friend, I smiled. "What you fear most is not being loved by those you love. But how can you ever know if they love you back if you do not open up to it?"

Lynn plopped down on the bed as Esen walked out of the bathroom. The water droplets clinging to his muscles and new scars.

"Because I am not worthy of it," she whispered into the stale air.

Chapter Twenty-Nine

LYNNORA

I left them both asleep in the room, locking the door behind me. I know they can defend themselves, but can they do so without raising any alarms?

Sticking to the shadows and the walls, I crept through the castle I once thought might become home. Everything looked the same as if Esen had never left, but I knew how far from the truth that was. I knew that deep within the soil, the cells had been converted into labs, and angels and demons were being experimented on. How much blood did Alden take? How long has he been planning this? Was he secretly converting them while Esen was still King?

My head spun with questions as I went to the war room, hoping to find answers to anything. Pressing my ear to the door, I couldn't hear anyone on the other side. Pushing on the handle, it didn't budge.

Simple enough, the locks here are easy to pick. Doing that quickly, the door creaked open, revealing the room as I had last seen it. The only difference was there was no longer a picture of the previous king and queen. In its place sat a painting of Alden on the throne.

Narcissistic, egotistical prick.

The table in the center of the room still held a map with figurines representing each Court, ships, and soldiers, showing where the troops were advancing or falling back. Without the support of Ove; Fahir, Dahr, and Sparan were under siege. He was doing what he could to help, but he was refusing to send any demons out to protect them.

The fireplace held no ash or wood. Had Alden learned how to heal a demon and removed the wood? The plush chairs looked worn in, like someone had spent hours in them. Cabinets still looked meticulously organized and had different code names.

Pushing the button in the center of the table, the drawer opened up and was empty. I had hoped Alden would be stupid enough not to find a new location for essential documents, but he was smart. Moving over to the cabinets, I began going through them, trying to figure out how it was organized, but there was no organization. It was a jumbled mess. Esen would die if he saw this. He will see this, and his heart will stop.

Voices filled the hall leading to the war room. I looked around for another exit, but there was none. The door is my only way out and will open any second now. Everything else was too exposed for me to hide behind. Grimacing, I knew where I had to hide and how gross it would make me feel after.

Crouching down, I put my upper half into the fireplace first. One foot at a time, I put them on the walls, ensuring not to leave any footprints in the thin layer of dust. My hands pressed onto the blackened stone as I hoisted myself up, having to move fast. The door opened right as I secured myself high enough so I wouldn't be seen.

Two male voices filled the room as they entered. My skin crawled, hearing Alden's aggravating voice. How dare he stand where Esen stood and act like he is not a monster? He is no savior.

"The hybrids are coming to term. With the new race, we can eradicate the demons and find the entrance into the Below."

So that was what this was all about? Finding the Below and sealing it off?

"There is no guarantee the hybrids will have access or be able to lead us to it." A voice I recognized as Vinces answered.

"They will. Esen is a half-breed and found his way down there. Whatever instinct they have that ties them there will be strong enough in the hybrids. Their need to return to that abysmal realm will force them to act."

One of them sighed as they sat down in a chair. Footsteps sounded as they neared the fireplace. I held still, not wanting to give any sign that I was here. Silencing my breath and focusing on the ground below me, black boots covered in mud stopped at the edge of the fireplace.

"How do you think Esen found it so easily? He had been missing for a month and found it. When I last saw him, he was no more than a pile of bones," Alden inquired from Vince, his spymaster and general.

Does he still hold those titles?

"As I have told you already, sire. His breed of demon makes him hard to kill. We can only penetrate his snakes' skin when he wishes. His venom is whatever he needs it to be. His size shifts depending on his situation."

"You did not answer my question, Vince," Alden snapped, and glass shattered as it hit the wall in front of me.

Vince did not falter. "Apologies, Sire. I do not believe he had help."

"Then what is it, and do not make me ask again? If I do, that piece of glass will not be the only fragile thing shattering on that wall you're so fascinated with."

"I wonder if, during his time with his Ghost, she revealed to him where it was."

"She was stupid enough to tell him."

I wanted to drop out of the fireplace and murder the man where he sat for the insult. End it before we had time to enact our plan. I could do it and kill Vince, too, in the process. Make it look like a murder-suicide or even another intruder had done the deed, but it would raise questions when Esen comes back alive the next day to claim his throne. If I acted out on impulse, it would make everything difficult for us.

Biting my tongue, I continued to wait and listen. My muscles were growing tired and in need of change.

"I mean no disrespect, sire, but Lynnora is smarter than you give her credit for." Vince surprisingly defended me. He and I never had more than a few quick conversations in passing. I never thought he would say something positive about me. It warmed my heart that he said it, not knowing I could hear him.

Alden scoffed. "Do tell."

Looking down, I saw Vince squat down, and his hands moved into the fireplace with a small broom as he swept the dust and broken glass into a corner. He never moved in far enough for me to worry about him seeing me.

"She convinced her enemy to trust her and to love her. She took a risk coming here knowing Arymn is the strongest Court, yet she did so loudly. From the moment Esen first met her, she was scheming, and she didn't stop scheming even after we thought you killed her. She planned her death to kill Esen. She made sure you and he knew about the Koya blades being the only thing that can truly harm and kill a demon. She ensured you overheard the conversation about where she would be on her last day here. She had planned our plan out."

"It is easy to predict your enemy's next move if you know them."

"And yet she outsmarted you even when she didn't know you were her enemy. You killed those people before she made her presence known. You sent those fire-wielders after her on Fahir. You brought the boy back to kill her or Esen. It didn't matter as long as one of them died. She had anticipated everything and stopped you from furthering your plan—"

"It doesn't matter what she did to try and stop me. She ensured I took the throne."

I wanted to laugh. I had known Alden was behind all of those things, but not once did I find out why. We had tried to uncover the truth, but it had been too well hidden, and we fell for the first thing we thought it was. We thought he wanted to be King because it was his birthright, not because he wanted to experiment on angels and demons. The knowledge that we helped Alden take the throne will be a regret I will forever have to live with. To know that every life lost or destroyed at his hands is because Ove and I had thought wrong. I planned to make Esen think Alden killed me. Everything that happened after is because of my failure.

Feet scraped against the stone, and the door slammed shut. Alden had left. I could still see Vince's boots under the mouth of the fireplace.

He let out a nervous sigh and a chuckle. "I am never one to pray to gods who don't seem to listen, so I will pray that someone will this one time. I promised the King Of Arymn that my loyalty would always lie with him. I am a man of honor, and my promise still holds as long as I shall breathe. Wherever the Queen of Demons may be, I pray she knows the power that the heart of Arymn holds."

I wanted to drop out of the fireplace and wrap my arms around him, thank him for not giving me up to Alden, tell him all will be right, and that I will reward his loyalty. But I couldn't. He may have said those words to lure me into a trap. He may not have meant a single thing.

To trust is to die. That was what Dearil had always taught me, and I have survived this long because I don't trust another soul as I trust myself.

The door clicked shut once more. I held firm onto the wall until I finally knew I was alone. Vince had cleared away the dust on the floor, allowing me to land unnoticed. Pulling myself out of the fireplace, I looked around to see if they had added anything to the room. There was nothing obvious.

Water dripped down the wall above the fireplace and stained the stone a darker gray. I looked closer at the water, tracing each stone. In between two stones, water was traveling but not darkening. Pressing my ear to the stone, I gently tapped and heard the hollow echo.

My blade appeared in my hand right as I needed it. Using the tip, I poked at the bottom corner of the stone. It took a few tries, but I finally got the blade under. Moving it about, attempting to break the seal, I heard it pop, and the stone came free. I caught the stone before it fell to the ground, preventing it from giving away my presence. A small hole in the wall was covered in layers of dust and filth, and spider web strands hung from the walls of it. The hole was so small my entire hand would barely fit in if I tried. I peeked in, hoping to find something that would lead into another room or tell me what the damn heart of Arymn was. I've heard it so many times I feel like I should know what the heart is by now. Is it a physical heart somewhere within the Court? Is it a person who knows what is best for the Court? Is it something that represents Arymn? I still have no fucking clue, and yet that is all I ever am told.

My loyalty lies with the heart of Arymn. I pray she knows the power that the heart of Arymn holds.

What is the heart of Arymn?

The light of the torch flickered. As it came back onto me, it cast into the hole, illuminating a small shiny object. I quickly grabbed the torch to try and get a better look at what may be inside the hole. Holding the flame up, I strained my eyes, trying to get its light to catch on whatever was within. There was nothing. Maybe I had seen nothing.

No, I know I saw something. Without hesitating, I jammed my hand into the hole, my thumb forced under my palm to fit. I scowled at the feeling of the cobwebs on my skin and the dirt now under my nails. My fingers grazed a soft material. Readjusting them, I could pull the object out.

Shaking off the dirt and bugs, I saw a small note with a red wax seal bearing the letter 'S.' Knowing this was not what I saw, I put my hand back in, searching for whatever caught the light. I let out a groan of pain as I forced my hand in further past my thumb. I pushed it in too far.

Dislocation will be the only way to get it back out now. The tip of my middle finger brushed against a cold chain. Taking a deep breath, I focused on my nails, which extended, allowing me to grab whatever it was. I pulled my hand back out as far as possible until I needed my other hand. I held my breath as I dislocated my thumb to get my hand back out, but it was worth it.

Even covered in dirt and dust, the thin gold chain necklace I held was the most beautiful thing I have ever seen. A gold letter 'S' had gold leaves coming off it; all were filled with rubies as dark as blood. In the center of the 'S' was one circular ruby. Seven total gems, all catching the light of the flame. A shiver ran through me as I beheld it, wondering how it had been hidden. I looked at the parchment, contemplating opening it, but something told me to wait. Knowing to trust myself, I waited.

***

Esen nudged me gently, trying to wake me up. I nestled under the blanket, savoring the warmth from him and Alya. When I returned last night, they both were asleep on opposite sides of the bed. I had carefully crawled between them and fell asleep, but now I wanted to stay asleep. I wanted to hide away from the world and my responsibilities one day longer.

Alya sneezed from across the room, resulting in a bless you from Esen and a tissue to offer. Always a kind man.

My need to use the bathroom woke me up further and drove me to move. Pulling the blankets off my head, I sat up and blinked at the light that was still somehow spilling in through the window, even though it was blocked.

Esen gasped, and Alya turned to see what the commotion was. Esen's eyes were stuck on my chest, where the necklace rested between my collarbones.

"What," I growled. It is far too early for them to be harassing me about jewelry.

"Is that—" Alya began but never finished her thought.

"It is." Esen finished it for her.

"What?" I snapped, wanting to know what the fuck was wrong with them.

"Oh, this just made reclaiming my throne either a lot harder or far more easy."

Alya had a contemplating scowl as she leaned her head from side to side, thinking it over. "I think easier."

"Will someone explain before I lose my mind?"

Esen chuckled. "How does it feel being on the receiving end of not knowing?" I cut him a glare, giving him my answer. "The necklace you wear is from when the Courts first formed, from when they were one Court. It was said that the last Queen of Nevano, Queen Gila, collected seven drops of blood from each King. Gila crafted this necklace and infused the king's blood into each of the gems. She had claimed to have been a friend to the god of Fate and that he granted her one vision, the vision of a time when the Courts would once more be unified." Esen stopped talking and kept his eyes on the necklace.

"Alright, and?"

He blinked and continued. "Gila went missing shortly after she spoke of what she saw because it did not look like our world and frightened everyone. When Gila vanished, so did the necklace containing the King's blood. The King of Nevano was furious that such an heirloom could have gone missing. He asked his men to find her and the necklace, claiming that once the necklace was found, their lives could continue until the Courts were once more unified. Seven years later, a single member of every Court had been drawn to the highest peak in Dahr, Mount Tiren. There, they found her sitting in a pool of shimmering blue water with fish circling her. Her eyes had turned gold, her ears pointed, and two of her teeth were as sharp as daggers. Wings made of water cascaded down her back and into the lake. When she saw them, she smiled and gave them a message to tell their Kings."

Alya's voice was soft, "All things come in three: the necklace, the book, and the quill. In another world, the sword, the crown, and the shield. Forever intertwined, the true Queen will bear all." She breathed as she moved to the edge of the bed and sat down. "Gila was the first mortal to speak a prophecy. When she had finished it, she looked to the men and told them that whoever finds the necklace can lay claim to the court they find it in, and none can forbid it. Only then will the start of a new time begin. A time of unity, peace, and prosperity."

I ran my fingers over the stone and looked at them. Alya was clearly in disbelief, and Esen looked unsure.

"Alya, can you give us a minute?"

"Of course." She nodded her head goodbye and opened the window. One moment, she stood there, and the next, she soared into the open air.

CHAPTER THIRTY

LYNNORA

"What are you thinking?"

"Do you want to lay claim to the throne?" Esen cut straight to the point.

"It would make this easier." I don't like the plan we have. There are too many unsure factors.

He let out a scoff. "Why do you hate life so much? Why would you rather die than love and live? What is so awful about it?"

I moved to Esen's lap, trapping him where he sat. "I don't hate life. I have enjoyed every day with you and my friends. I don't want to die. I am just thinking logically. Our plan requires the council members to support you, and I saw firsthand how they spoke about demons. They know you, but those biases run deep. They will fear you. If I lay claim to the throne, I will abdicate and give it to you. I will never rule Arymn, meaning I will never die."

"And what of the Below? You are their *Queen*, you are *ruling*, you will *die*."

"I am not their Queen. A part of Ove's mother is still alive, and until that piece dies, I will not receive the power meant for the Queen of Demons. I am simply playing pretend."

He shook his head. "Does Ove know?"

"Yes."

"So you are technically not the Queen of Below because you are no longer married to him, and you do not have the magic passed down from Queen to Queen."

"I am their Queen because a crown was sat upon my head by the order of a King."

"So you will die?"

"Esen, we all will die, some just sooner than others."

He gently pushed me off him. "I am sorry. I cannot do this. I do not understand how you accept your fate when there is a way out. You have never given up on anything, yet you are on this. I refuse to accept it."

I stood before him, shocked. "Whether you accept it or not does not affect my decision. I love you, Esen, but my people need me on the throne. Dearil diminished our spirits and destroyed our livelihood. Ove is doing everything he can to repair that damage and heal the wounds that run deep in us, but they need a Ghost on the throne! They need me!"

"I need you! I do not care if it is selfish, but I fucking need you, Lynnora! You have undone me since the day I saw you. You have made me want to be a better King, a better friend, and a brother. You reminded me that there is life outside these walls and that all should be cherished. You were the one who taught me never to stay down, always to get up and fight one more time. If you go, then what the fuck am I?"

"You are a better person." My heart felt like it was ripping in two fighting with him. I took his hand and placed it on my chest. My own went to his. "Our hearts beat in sync. You are my mate, and I am yours. I will love you for as long as I can. The moment we no longer beat together, then you will know."

His arms wrapped around me, his head buried into my shoulders. "I do not want to lose you," his voice cracked.

"You will only lose me when you lose yourself."

"I love you, dearest."

"And I love you, gnat."

We held onto one another for as long as we could, neither wanting this to end. To know we love each other, to be with our mate, to comfort one another before we do what needs to be done. The feeling of love swept through the room, filling it with bright, warm energy, never to be diminished, even in the darkness.

***

The cold wall chilled my pained hands. I can do this. I need to do this. I have to do this.

I felt the invisible weight of my mother's hands pressing onto my shoulders. Their words filled my ears. *You are Lynnora Fenwald. You do not let the wind bend you, the ocean drown you, and you do not let the fire scorch you. Because when it does, you stare it down and say one more time.*

One more time. One more stupid ball. One more time, being paraded around like a whore. One more time, I was introduced by a name I do not claim. One more time making a weak man crawl before me. I can do this. I eat men for breakfast some days.

I pushed off the wall and turned around to face Alya and Esen. Alya was in a white dress with a large skirt, with glitter covering her everywhere. The bodice of the dress hugged her tightly, making her breasts look large but beautiful. Her hair was curled and resting down her back, covering her scars. She had tiny gems in her hair that I do not know how she pinned them in.

Esen wore a ceremonial blue and gold suit. His gold gloves covered his trembling hands, and a gold piece of armor sat atop his shoulders, protecting them and part of his neck. I had draped on a long cloak lined with wolf fur and had shoulder plates on it as well. This type of suit was meant to announce a war, and the sword at his side screamed to the world we were already at one.

Checking in the mirror, I ensured my paint and clothing were how I wanted it. I wore a sheer black skirt that exposed almost the entirety of my right leg. My breasts were covered by a tight black band that veered down in the center, exposing the inside of my breasts. They also attached the to same material the skirt was made out of to the back of my top, flowing down to the floor behind me. My gold paint was in neat swirls on my thigh and right shoulder. Two gold bands were on my left arm. I had painted my hands and forearms black just for the shits and giggles. They already fear me. Why not give them something else to fear more? I painted my lips red to match the blood rubies in my new necklace. I parted my hair down the center, and it fell naturally down my back. The bone crown I had been wearing when I ran away from the throne now saw atop my head.

"The guests should have all arrived thirty minutes ago. It's time," Alya said, looking uneasy. "Is Ove coming?"

"I don't think so. He said to reach out once it is over or if we need him before that; you know how to get his attention, whatever that means." Alya blushed and patted her dress, smoothing out the non-existent wrinkles.

Esen grabbed our name cards off the table before I could do it. We need to make an entrance to pull our new plan off. This is the best way. I opened the door and looked up and down the hall, ensuring no one else was nearby. Gesturing for the other two, we continued to move through the castle like this. I made sure the way was clear and signaled for them once it was.

The closer we got to the throne room, the louder the music got. I could hear the different instruments being used and the singer harmonizing with the musicians. My feet were itching to dance and to forget about the world around me. I could smell the food flowing from the kitchen, making me miss Lar's cooking.

A small chirp sounded behind me, signaling Alya found what we needed. A second later, a small serving boy came around the corner. I grabbed
onto his arm, pulling him into the alcove. His face paled when he saw the
crown on my head. He tried to bow, but my grip on him stopped him.

"Enough groveling." He hadn't even started. I didn't want to deal with
it. "I need you to deliver these to the master of ceremonies. Do not mix up
the order of the cards, or your head will be on a spike, and your blood will
be in my wineglass."

"Yes, Your Majesty," he stuttered in fear as he took the cards and ran off.

The three of us waited around the corner from the entrance to avoid
being seen by guests or the guards.

The man's voice was loud as he began speaking. "Introducing Lady Alya
of Oud."

I closed my eyes, hearing Oud, but she insisted that was where she
wanted to pretend to be a lady from.

She let go of me and walked into the room by herself. I could hear
murmurs from those who were led to believe she had been the one to kill
Esen.

"Introducing Queen Lynnora of the Below," his voice faltered but did
not stop. "The Seventh Ghost and the Heart of Arymn!" I didn't have time
to look at Esen and question if I had heard the last three words correctly.
He had already pushed me around the corner for all to see.

Holding my head high, my chin out, and my shoulders back, I strutted
in like I owned the damn place. I was about to anyway. Why not start acting
like I do now?

A collective gasp went over the crowd as I joined Alya just beyond the
entrance. The crowd fell into a deep bow. My heart raced as I looked over
at each of them. I am not their Queen; I do not deserve a bow this low, and
yet I am getting one. And I knew why. I had been introduced as Queen,
Ghost, and the Heart of Arymn. I am a perfect trifecta. I have earned each

title and the respect that comes with it.

"Introducing King Esen of Arymn!"

The crowd and musicians fell silent as Esen walked in. None fell into a bow. Esen kept his emotions in check, but it angered me. "You bowed for a Queen that is not yours. Now bow for a King that is!" My voice was lethally calm as I shouted across the hall.

Everyone did as I said and stayed there far longer than they did with me.

"Long live King Esen," Alya cheered alone.

I joined in. "Long live, King Esen!"

The room erupted with applause and cheers. "Long live, King Esen! Long live King Esen! Long live, King Esen!"

Music began playing again, this time far more upbeat and exciting than when we were in the hall. Songs were changing, and people approached us, asking what happened to him and me. We kept it simple and said everything would be explained soon enough.

There were those who saw Esen's eyes and shied away. Others saw them and kept pointing while talking in hushed whispers. Whenever I saw someone do that, I flashed them my pitch-black eyes. They would let out a small yelp before running away. As songs continued and dances happened around us, there was still a murmur in the air, talking about our presence.

The horns blared, announcing the arrival of Alden.

I looked at Esen and Alya, who both nodded. It is time. Alden always liked to make an entrance and have the crowd part for him as he made his way to the throne. Apparently, the month Alya had spent with him had been good for something. The crowd moved around me and Esen as we made our way toward the throne. It did not part, but people feared and respected us enough to move one person at a time, creating a small pocket for us.

"Introducing King Alden of Arymn!"

The crowd fell into a bow right as I sat on the throne, and Esen leaned against it. Looking over the bodies, Alden stood in the doorway with Vince and another man beside him. He was smiling at his people, and his eyes landed on me.

I waved at him with a coy smile.

"Seize her!"

Esen held up his hand. "I wouldn't do that if I were you, brother."

"Seize him," Alden said, confused about who should be seized.

"Why? So you can throw them in prison for a crime they never committed?" Alya took a step onto the dais.

The guests all rose from their bows, unsure what was happening.

"He, unfortunately, can't throw a king and queen into a prison," I informed Alya, who looked displeased.

Alden began storming over to us, the crowd parting for him. The two men followed him on his heel, Vince looking unphased while the other looked furious.

"That *thing* is not a King! He does not have Thillardson blood running through his veins. He has no claim to the throne."

"Oh, how I wish that were true. Then we could finally get a cute house in Sparan and some prairie cats." I teased Esen with a smile. My attention snapped back to Alden. "He has just as every claim to this throne as you. I, Queen Lynnora, the Seventh Ghost and Heart of Arymn, lay claim to the throne of Arymn. Do any dare challenge me for it?"

Alden drew his sword and scoffed. "I am still alive. I have not abdicated my claim, nor have I been refused it. I am the King of Arymn. You have no rights to it."

"Oh, but you see, I do. Funny little thing about fireplaces, you can find all sorts of things in them." I tapped my new necklace and rose from the throne, showing it off to the crowd, who all leaned in to get a closer look.

"It's a fake," the unknown man behind Alden said.

"Is it? Then why do I also have this?" I held up the unopened parchment still sealed with the once-royal crest.

Esen took it from my hand and cleared his throat as he broke the wax. "Surrounded by all the races, only then shall all be united, ushering all to a new age.

I, High Queen Gila Sahan of Nevano, relinquish my claims to whichever throne shall find my soul first. May the new Queen have the heart of Arymn, the strength of Fahir, the sight of Dahr, and the gentleness of Leevah. May she have the mobility of Auk, the honor of Sparan, and the patience of Ter. May the demons claim her as their own, and may she fly among angels.

A council of the nine kings and queens must occur, but none shall refute my last act as High Queen."

Esen stopped talking. Taking the parchment back into my hands, I offered it to Alden to read. The crowd was already talking and buzzing with excitement as they tried to process what had just been done.

Alden ripped it out of my hand and read the words repeatedly until they were ingrained in his memory.

"You may have a claim on the throne, but the half-breed does not!" My stomach churned hearing him speak of his brother this way. They may no longer share the same blood, but they grew up together, fought, and were brothers at some point.

"You're right, Alden," I spat out his name with as much venom as possible. "As of now, he has no claim to the throne, but come the first of next month, he will be my consort." A collective gasp traveled through the room, silencing any voices, all eager to hear what was happening.

Alden scoffed and stepped closer, looking down his nose at me. I could feel his anger radiating off him as he tried to conceal it. "Your King is Ove. He will not grant a divorce."

I let out a sweet chuckle and touched his steady chest. He hissed at my touch. "He already has, and the goddess Aniya has granted the separation.

She has also blessed me with my mate." I held up my hand for Esen to take. His warmth traveled through the gloves he had on and into my chilled fingers. I adjusted my neck so Alden could see the bite mark on my neck, and Esen pulled his shirt away enough to show the matching one on his neck.

Alden let out a curse in the language of Kings. Esen chuckled. "Scared yet, brother? I once told you never to cross me. I was reassured with your loyalty that you never would, but look at us now."

"You will achieve nothing. The other Kings will forbid it, even if it was the last order of Gila. She is dead, and no one was around at the time to confirm what the letter says."

I smelled Alya and her lightness before I saw her standing beside me with a sensual smile. "Gods cannot lie, and it was the gods who saw the meeting. We will bring a god with us to meet with the nine Kings. They will either confirm or deny what was written and the claim made. If proven accurate, you shall relinquish your claim with no fight. But should the god not show or prove us false, you may challenge Queen Lynnora for her claim to the throne."

What is Alya playing at? Gods can lie. Kesa has done so for her entire life. Alya has lied and is lying. If we bring either of them, then we are divulging a truth that has been hidden for millenniums.

Alya looked at me with a slight nod, telling me to go with her plan, to trust her. "That sounds fair unless you want to hand over the crown now." I raised a brow at Alden.

"I would rather die before I bow to you."

"That could be arranged." I flicked a piece of lint off his shoulder before stepping back toward the center of the dais. Holding my head high, I addressed the crowd, "In three days, your rightful King will sit upon his throne once more! For now, let the celebration continue."

The musicians slowly started playing their songs again, pulling the crowd back into a trance. Stepping out of the way, I let Alden take his throne before his people one last time. Esen, Alya, and I descended into the crowd, pleased with what we had accomplished.

"Summon him," I whispered over to Alya. The night was still young, and Alden was not fearful enough.

CHAPTER THIRTY-ONE

OVE

Something had to have gone wrong. Alden's pathetic soul should have been bowing before me by now. What happened up there? Why has no soul floated into my throne room with a message? My finger impatiently tapped the armrest, the white scar standing out against the room's darkness as if it were calling to something.

The door creaked open, and Adri walked in, shaking her head. No new souls worth bringing here have died. What is taking so long? Why am I so anxious about this? I don't like not being there and being a part of whatever is unfolding. I feel helpless and unsure. I knew I should have gone to make sure nothing went awry.

"I'm going to kill that fucking bitch. I knew I should have sworn off women long ago. Oh, Dal, you're so handsome; you make me laugh. Shut the fuck up, you murderess bitch," a sour voice filled the hall leading into the throne room.

I looked at Adri with my brows raised. She shrugged and opened the door for the soul to enter. I solidified his essence and saw an Arymn guard uniform—finally, someone to tell me what was happening.

The soul, Dal, stopped where he was when he realized he was no longer alone and in a hall. His eyes were wide with terror as he took in my throne room and me on the throne. "I presume you have a message for me?"

His face paled even further, and his throat bobbed as he tried to find words. "Pe-per-pervert," he bleated out.

Alya. My sweet Alya.

"How did she kill you?"

"She-she ripped my heart out. I have never seen such raw strength in someone so tiny."

I smiled at the thought of her doing something so vile. "Why you?" He didn't answer me. My anger and patience grew thinner with each passing heartbeat. "Why. Did. She. Kill. You?" I signaled for Adri. She forced him onto his knees and held onto the back of his neck tightly, forcing him to look up. He was still at a loss for words. "Find out what you can. I have a date to get to."

My shadows wrapped around me, and wind ripped through my hair and body as I was carried from one castle to the next. I had become the nothing that exists between realms.

My leg ached as I landed on it too harshly. Using the wall for support, I looked around the empty hall, trying to understand better where I ended up in the castle. From a distance, I could hear the music and smell the food. Following the sounds, I saw the double doors leading into the throne room still open, with two guards on both sides looking uneasily at the sight of me. There was no scent of blood hanging in the air, no lingering sounds of screams. Whatever they did was not according to the plan. Why would they not stick to it? Getting Esen back on the throne is essential; they both know it.

The guards saw me and raised their spears, blocking my path. "Don't bother," I said to the two of them, and my shadows pushed them back. No one bothered paying me attention as I walked in, staying close to the wall, not wanting to cause a scene until I knew what was happening.

Surveying the room, I saw Esen and Lynn dancing with themselves in the center of the room. The crowd had moved away from them, no doubt out of fear. I stayed where I was, unsure where Alya was. I know her, and I know she will be near Esen and Lynn.

A small hand wrapped around my elbow. I jerked away at the feeling of it. Looking over my shoulder, Alya stood beside me, smiling. "You came!"

"You called me a pervert. Of course, I did."

She let out a small laugh. "Dance with me, King Ove."

Little bird, little bird, why doth thou cry?

Little bird, little bird, why doth thou not smile?

Little bird, little bird, where did thou learn to fly?

Oh, little bird, will you trust thyself to carry you sky high?

Little bird, little bird, to fly is to be free, and to be free is to fly.

Little bird, little bird, will you be free with me?

A poem I had never heard echoed in my mind as a shadow whispered his love song into my ear.

I never thought I would hear those words come from her beautiful mouth. I thought she hated me and despised my existence. "Gladly." I took her hand and led her out onto the dance floor.

She looked absolutely beautiful. Her long hair curled down her back, the dress hugging every curve that had come back after being locked in the prison. Her beautiful blue eyes shone like a million stars in the night sky.

My hand hovered over her waist, fearful to touch her or to have her shy away from my touch. She moved into my hand, and my breath hitched. She wanted my warmth as much as I craved hers. My other hand held hers up gracefully and delicately. Dancers skirted away from us as they beheld the King of Demons dancing with a mortal.

"Alya." I had to slow down what I wanted to say. Never have I felt so nervous to be in the presence of a woman. She gently smiled up at me, patiently waiting for me to find the words. "There is not a goddess more beautiful than you. You, Alya, are the most beautiful thing I will ever see."

I pulled her in closer as we danced to the waltz. I felt her back stiffen at my words, but she swiftly fell at ease as I spun her. Her body pressed back into mine, and she looked up at me with nothing but love in her eyes. It felt like she was seeing me for what I truly am and was not afraid of it.

"I didn't know demons could be so romantic."

"Only when they have something worthy of their love will a demon be so sappy."

Her smile faltered, and her eyes darkened. "You wouldn't be saying that if you knew the real me. You would be running back to the Below as fast as possible."

Let her speak.

Kiss the girl.

Tell her you love her.

Shut up! I snapped at the three different voices.

"I know more about you than you may think, but I hope to continue learning more and more about you."

She leaned her head onto my shoulder as the song shifted to a slower-paced song. We continued our dance in silence, others floating around us in the music's rhythm. The two of us got lost in the sounds of the violin and the harp, both playing their mesmerizing melody. All the other songs I have danced to, all my previous dance partners, none of it mattered anymore. None of it compared to how it feels to dance with her. My heart has never ached so painfully. It has never yearned for another in their absence. Never in my life have I known something with absolute certainty. It is her. It is Alya, and it will always be her until the world ceases to exist.

"Ove," she breathed into my neck, the tiny hairs rising at the caress of her words. "I need to tell you something, and I worry you will hate me for it."

"Not now, little one, not now. I want to hear what you say, but I don't want this to end yet." I don't want to let you go. I don't want to stop dancing. I don't want her to leave.

She didn't say anything else as we continued dancing. Neither of us let the other go as the day turned to night, and the room turned black. Guests left slowly as the music dwindled. Lynn and Esen were nowhere to be seen. They must have left already. As each person passed by us to go, I expected guards or Alden to come up to me and force me to leave, but none bothered us. We did not exist to those around us. All that mattered was each other.

***

The door closed. Alya was now on the other side of it with our friends, who had told me what had happened and what needed to happen. I was relieved, knowing no blood had been shed today as planned. I didn't like the original plan of them charging in here with swords drawn and forcing Alden to abdicate his throne. It could go wrong in too many ways, but it was all we could think of on such short notice. Now, all I have to worry about is the other kings siding with Lynn and her winning a fight against Alden.

I'm not sure that's much relief, but I trust her. If she can do this, she will win. She must. She knows what is at stake should she fail, which will push her further.

I began walking down the hall, debating whether to return to the Below tonight or tomorrow. Dearil must be handled, and the Ghosts will be the quickest way to send word about the meeting. Lynn and Esen want it in three days. No messenger is that fast. It's even pushing the swiftness of her sisters.

Bastard. A shadow hissed.

I could hear the footsteps of at least five people approaching.

"King Ove," an agitating voice said from around the corner. I scowled, unable to disappear before they knew I was there.

"King Alden," I quipped as he and his guards came into view.

"You have overstayed your welcome. Leave now, or we will throw you back to the hole you crawled out of."

I snorted. "Always a pleasure being in your presence. Let me go collect the others, and we will leave." I was in no mood for a fight, but my shadows were.

He threw her into a cell. He subjected her to the Lion. Make him pay, your majesty. End his miserable, pathetic excuse of a life. End it now for revenge.

Silence, Eilam. In due time, he will face the consequences of his actions. They all will.

"No need. I permitted them to stay, but I did not extend the invitation to you, my enemy." I raised a brow at his words.

"Enemy in which sense? Political or romantic?"

Alden snarled a warning that I was hitting a sensitive spot. "If she refused to love me, she will refuse you too."

I put my hands in my pocket and shrugged my shoulders. "Then so be it. I am man enough not to be offended by the word no. I won't be a tyrant and lock her away because she hurt my ego." *Maybe one fight will be fun. It has been a while since I've allowed myself some fun.*

Alden lunged at me. His arm pushed into my throat as my body slammed into the wall behind me. His guards had all drawn their weapons.

"I recommend you do not make an enemy out of me, Ove," Alden growled.

My face remained unchanged and unafraid. My hands still rested carelessly in my pockets. "How could I when you've already made an enemy out of me?"

I unleashed my shadows upon them. Encasing us all in eternal darkness. I could not see the man before me or the arm restraining me. Voices of the dead filled the emptiness.

"Traitor." A young girl cried.

"Disgraced son and King." The old general swore.

"You betrayed your kin." A mother wept.

"May the gods curse you. May you never know love," Eilam screamed.

"Off with his head!" Mimsy's demand almost made me laugh.

Willing my voice to travel around while I remained behind, my words flowed into his men's ears. "You serve a man who takes pleasure in the pain of others. He has lied to you about what he holds in the cells below the castle. Angels and demons are forced to do his bidding. He is creating something that should never be created. Hybrids were never meant to roam this world."

"Liar! He is speaking lies. Do not listen to him," Alden yelled at his men, hoping to keep up the facade he had so carefully crafted.

"My words are the truth you fear. You, Alden, are not worthy of your title. You are not worthy of life."

"And who are you to say such a thing?"

"I was chosen by Haedon to judge your life, as were my forefathers. I know all you fear, and you fear the truth." My voice continued to float around in the darkness. Alden's grip on me tightened. My shadows pushed him off me, allowing me to become eternal darkness. "Fear is a funny thing; most run from it, but there are those who stand against it and rise. You are a coward. You will never win against me."

"I do not fear you, Ove. I never will fear a spoiled, weak, lonely demon!"

"Then why fight me? Why not join us and fight for our kind? We only want a chance to love this realm as you have done for generations."

"You spout nothing but lies. Your kind knows no beauty or love. Demons are foul, vile creatures who should never have been created."

His words were harsher than I expected. But they did not deter me from the fun I was having, inflicting doubts in his men's minds. "We know beauty and love. If not, then how can you explain our Queen? Loved and admired by her kin, sought after by mortals, even angels quake in her wake, for they wish for her beauty to be theirs."

"Your Queen's beauty is easily overshadowed by the darkness in her. She is a murderer, a widow-maker, a liar, and a thief. She is the monster we all seek to destroy."

I solidified in front of Alden, who was looking around frantically, trying to figure out where I was. His guards have long since given up that task, but they still held their swords, ready to strike should I attack.

"My Queen is the light that never dies. She is all things good and kind. Her beauty is beyond compare. My Queen is love itself. You know nothing of which you speak." Lynn is darkness. She is the evil in the world. But my words were not of her; they were of Alya. She is light, love, and beauty. She is Lynn's opposite in every way possible. That is why we both love and cherish her so much. She is all things demons aren't. She is a drop of sun on a stormy day.

Even if it is with my dying breath, I will make her my Queen.

Chapter Thirty-Two

Alya

It was time. My heart sat in the pit of my stomach as I flew to Alden's room. I had one last task to complete before we left for the Isle of Blessed. With each beat of my wings, I soared higher and higher to his bedroom window. My skin crawled with each flap, screaming at me not to go. But I had to. He had the book that I had poured my heart and soul into, and if my suspicions are correct, he also has the letter Lynn wrote Esen. Alden is a foul person, but he is sentimental and would never destroy something that means something to another, not if he can use it against them.

His window was open, revealing the large room of the King's chamber. I had thought Esen's old room was big, but this was massive. You could fit two homes in here with room to spare. In the main room sat two large couches with a table in between them. Deeper in the room was a long table with two chairs set at the head and foot of it, but only one had appeared used. A small room sat off to the right, open with a desk and shelves filled with books. There was one other door, which I presume leads into his sleeping chambers.

Shifting back into my other form, my gold dress made my pale skin stand out. The front of my hair was pulled back out of my way. Being mindful of my steps, I walked into his study, making sure my heels did not click on the stone floor. I glanced at his bookshelf, searching for the worn leather bindings holding my book together. Not finding it at first glance, I traced my finger over the spine of each book as I read the titles in hopes he had it hidden within one.

"How did you get in?" Alden's voice sounded from behind me, making me jump.

I looked over my shoulder, gave him a polite smile, and made sure my eyes shone brightly. "The guards let me in," I easily lied. I would rather die than tell him the truth. I once thought of it and wondered if I could move on from Eilam and settle down with Alden, but decades of not trusting others told me not to trust him.

He looked at me as if he could see through my careless lie, but he did not seem bothered. Alden took a step closer, and I stepped back, the books on the shelf pressing into me.

"Can we talk?" He gestured for me to sit in one seat around his desk. I looked at it and stayed where I was.

"You may talk, and I will listen, but I am not sitting down."

He sighed and sat in his plush leather seat at his desk. "It has been brought to my attention that what I did was wrong. I am sorry for blaming you for Esen's death and allowing you to be locked up. I never meant you harm."

I let out a scoff and rolled my eyes. Folding my arms across my chest, I decided I no longer wanted only to listen. I needed my voice to be heard, for my pain to be understood and acknowledged.

"You meant me no harm? How the fuck did you not mean me harm when you knew what was going to happen to me in that gods-forsaken prison? You knew what you were doing, and you did it to punish me because I did not share the same affection you had. Your anger towards Lynn and Esen was misplaced in me. You subjected me to horrors none should ever endure because when you asked for my hand in marriage, I said no. Your ego was so fragile you could not allow it to be damaged. You are weak, Alden!" He grabbed onto a glass cup filled with amber liquid, and as I spoke each word, his grip on it tightened. "No words can atone for what you forced upon me."

His hand shattered the glass, his blood dripping onto the desk below him. He didn't flinch. His eyes stayed focused on me. Anger simmering off him.

"I am not weak, Alya. I did not make the decision lightly, nor did I do it to punish you for your refusal."

"Then why did you do it? You asked for my hand; I said no, and two minutes later, I was bound in chains being led to the cells."

He threw the remaining pieces of glass that clung to his hand at the wall beside me. A shard sliced my cheek open. I let out a gasp of pain and instantly held my hand up to it. Alden stood up and rushed to my side, his hand raised with a cloth in it, ready to wipe away the evidence of what he did. I pushed him off and walked to the other side of the room, nursing the pain that now laced my face.

"I did it because someone needed to pay for what I thought was his death—"

"Did you still think him dead as you carved into his body, drew his blood, and experimented on your brother?"

He sank back into his seat and poured another glass of liquid. He threw his head back and gulped it down in one swallow. The liquid refilled his glass but emptied the decanter. "It is far more complicated than you can understand. I never wanted to harm him, but it was a necessary evil for what I needed to do. I never meant to harm either of you. When I heard what the guard planned to do to you, I wanted to pull you out, but you had already escaped and destroyed the damn prison."

I snorted. "Do you expect me to say thank you for reconsidering?"

"No, I expect you to forgive me."

"And why would I do that?"

Alden moved back over to his bookshelf and pulled on one book. A hidden compartment on the shelf opened up, revealing a singular book and a sealed envelope.

"If you want these back, you will forgive me." He pulled them out and waved them in his hand. There it was. The ultimatum, the leverage he wanted. "Forgive me and become my Queen. The book and letter will be yours, as will all Arymn offers."

His Queen? "Lynn will soon become Queen of Arymn. You cannot offer me anything. There are no riches in the world, no sights to be seen, no foods to be tasted that you can offer me. You will soon be nothing with something I want, and I do not stop until I get what I want."

Alden tossed the book and envelope onto his desk. "Guards!" His one word was the command to bring in two of his guards. They both rushed in with swords drawn, ready to fight any intruder. "Bring her to her knees."

I backed away from him and his guards, who put their swords away to bring me to my knees.

"I would recommend not touching me," I warned them sternly, hoping they wouldn't be stupid enough to try anything.

They did not heed my warning. One reached out to me. I took his arm, twisting it painfully behind his back, using him as my shield. He let out a scream of pain as his shoulder popped from me, dislocating it.

"Not another step, or I rip his arm off!" I twisted his arm more, resulting in a shriek.

"Come now, Alya. This look does not suit you. You are no killer."

I gave him a cruel smile. "I have killed more than all the Ghosts combined, and I will continue killing to protect myself. Do not think for one moment that you or your men are an exception."

Alden's eyebrows furrowed. "I know you, and you are no killer. You are small and helpless. This is due to a weak man." He gestured at me and the guard, who was still very much in pain.

"If I am so small and helpless, then how did I survive a prison meant to destroy you? How did I kill the mercenary you sent after us? How did I kill the guard who you told the truth to and stationed in the cells? I am not weak, nor am I small and helpless!" I shoved the guard at Alden, who stumbled backward, trying to catch the man.

The other three guards lunged for me. I sidestepped the first and balled my hand into a fist, striking the throat of the second. He fell to his knees, gasping for air and his hands clutching his throat. Alden drew his sword and went after me.

I quickly grabbed the sword from the gasping soldier and countered his attack. The two other soldiers surrounded me, forcing me into a corner.

Alden lowered his sword. "Give up, Alya. Marry me, and I will forgive you for your crimes."

"I'll have to pass on that terrible offer," I smirked before advancing and slicing open the throat of the closest guard—one more plus Alden. I can do this.

Thunder cleaved through the sky as clouds swiftly rolled in, bringing torrential rain. The candles in the room blew out on their own as shadows swept into the room, encasing us in darkness.

"Touch her, and you will lose more than a hand," a cold voice threatened from within the shadows.

Alden paled as he looked around, trying to find the source of the voice. "I thought I told you to leave."

I took the distraction as an opportunity to grab the final guard and hold his sword to him. A deadly chuckle answered back. "I will never leave my Queen and her friends alone."

Ove appeared next to me in a crisp, clean black suit. He flicked off an invisible piece of lint. "Hello, little one. I love the present you sent me," he purred down at me with a seductive smile.

"Pervert," I hissed up at him with a smile. I never sent the guard to him, nor did I want him to go to Ove. I just wanted him out of my way, and death was the quickest way to do so.

"Come now, Alya. You look in need of space from this monster."

The corners of my lips turned upwards and parted into a caring smile. "Of course, my king." Ove extended his hand for me. Taking it, I dropped the other guard and tucked myself close to Ove.

Shadows wrapped around us, and the air went through us as if we were nothing in the space that exists between us all. My feet solidified first and gracefully landed on an uneven surface. Catching myself, I realized we stood on the stairs.

The rest of my body quickly followed my feet, and I could see where we were. We stood on a dais in a dark throne room. I looked at the throne that was made of bones, and my stomach grew uneasy. A matching one sat beside it with a footrest at its foot—Lynn's throne.

I chuckled, knowing how much she would appreciate the footrest. She always sits with her feet on something if she can.

"Welcome to the Below." Ove extended his arms to let me take his domain in. Six beings filled the room, all with only their eyes visible below their black masks. Each of them lowered into a bow with their arm across their heart.

"Ghosts, this is Alya. Alya, meet the Ghosts." He didn't introduce them by name, but I recognized two. One was Adri because of the dark skin around her eyes, and another was Ava because her eyes were similar to Lynn's. "She is staying with us for the night. We will leave in the morning. She is not to be touched by any of you. She is under my protection, and if any of you," he looked at Ava and glared, "Try anything, I will not hesitate to kill you."

My body chilled as I thought of Eilam and that he once lived somewhere in the Below. This was his home at one point. He had friends and family, all of whom are now long since dead. But they existed. I had never thought about coming here. Angels are only allowed to do so if for diplomatic reasons. I had never considered meeting his friends or family because of it.

"You okay?" Ove placed his hand on my lower back and looked down at me, worried.

"Yeah, it's just a lot to take in."

"I will give you a proper tour once we are done with everything. Would you like to sleep in a spare room or mine? The choice is yours, and you will be protected no matter what."

I looked at him, and all I could see was the love I once had for the man he wore. The boy he killed and felt so guilty about, he made into his own. What horrid death had Eilam been inflicted that would make Ove feel this way?

My chest tightened, thinking over his question—a night alone in an unfamiliar place or beside the man who wears my husband's skin. I have shared a bed with him before, but I had been so drunk I remember little of it.

"I will join you. Do Lynn and Esen know I am here? They will worry once I don't return."

"I will send word to them." He nodded at the Ghosts and dismissed them. They all swiftly left the room.

Ove took my hand and guided me through his castle to his chambers. I had expected something grand, just like Alden's room, but his was small and quaint. Only a bed, a small table, and a wardrobe were there. The bed was pushed against the corner and neatly made. A small fireplace with lots of wood was alive beside the door.

Ove snapped his fingers, and my gold dress turned into a light pink silk nightgown. I looked down at it and scowled.

"I can't have you sleeping in the dress you were wearing."

"Thank you... for everything. I appreciate it."

He stood in front of me, his arms draping on my waist. "Of course. Oh, I almost forgot. Were these important?" He pulled out the envelope with Esen's name scribbled on it, along with the leather bindings of my book.

I let out a gasp. "How did you? When did you?" I couldn't complete an entire thought. I was in shock and awe.

"My shadows are good for stealing, not just spying." He handed them off to me.

"Thank you," I whispered, still trying to figure out when he took them and how he hid them in his suit that fit him so tightly. I ran my finger over the spine of the book and smiled. "I never thought I would get this back."

"I am glad to be of assistance. Let's go to bed. We have a long day tomorrow." I let him guide me into the bed. His clothes disappeared, showing the scars that covered half his body.

We lay there beside one another, and I rolled to face him. My fingers danced along his scars, learning them and memorizing them. He flinched at my first touch, but as I continued, his body relaxed, and his breaths deepened.

The King of Demons had fallen asleep beside me.

CHAPTER THIRTY-THREE

LYNNORA

I got Oves' message when we woke up. He had Alya with him, and Alden was a prick. I wanted to go to his room and kill him where he lay, but I knew by the end of the day, he would be dead or near death. Whether he lives or dies is up to him. But I will not be the one who is in charge of his fate today. I had decided last night when Esen and I danced together for the first time that Alden is cruel, but so am I. If he deserves to die, then so do I. And who am I to be the executioner of someone like me?

Esen held onto my hand as we stood on the island's shores. A shadow covered the surrounding sun briefly, and as it faded, Alya stood beside Ove, looking uneasy. A cut was on her cheek, still slowly healing. Esen and I both swore under our breath and raced to her to tend to the injury and her. The smell of ointment filled my nose the second I stood before her, and the light reflected off it, making the cut glisten.

"Say the word, and I will kill him before the meeting even starts."

Alya raised her hand to wave us off. "Were you able to convince Kesa to testify and say the claim is real?"

Esen scoffed, "Kesa will do no such thing to help us. She claims our company has ruined her mood and spoiled any thought to help." He looked at me nervously. "We were hoping Aniya may help us."

Ove let out a small laugh. "Aniya? No one has heard of her existence in thousands of years. How would you even begin to find her?"

Alya looked down at the sand and toed it. Her cheeks reddened. "I don't think she will be of much help, either. Like Ove said, she has not been heard from in a long time. It is best to leave it that way."

Esen placed a hand on my shoulder and squeezed it tightly. The hairs on my neck stood up, and shadows darkened around us. "Alden is here," Ove said, nearly snarling like an enraged wolf.

I looked over at my friends, memorizing their features. Alya, with her beautiful blue eyes that could hide in the sky, the tiny freckles splattered across her button-shaped nose. The oval-shaped face returned to what it once was now that she had regained a lot of the weight she lost. Ove and his perfectly straight nose, his skinny, angular face complimenting it. His tanned skin made his black eyes look normal. His short hair was tossed around like he had just woken up and not bothered with it. Esen's strong jaw was hidden beneath his short beard, which he seemed to be growing out. His blue eyes were now a vertical slit, thanks to his transformation. His soft lips did their best to hide the deadly fangs beneath, but if his lips tugged just right, I could see the tips of them.

As I looked them over, I realized not only are they my friends, but they have become the family I once wanted. They had become my court.

A goddess bound by chains to do her mother's bidding was no more. In her place was a beautiful goddess who loved even in the darkest times.

A fallen King haunted by his prophecy had turned into a powerful demon who only wanted what was best for his people.

A feared and beloved King had replaced a disgraced demon Prince who knew no love.

They are my court, and I will fight for them and what we need to unite this world again.

Standing here looking at them, I knew what must be done.

"They are all here. We should join them," Ove said wearily. Did he know what I was planning? Could he see it in my eyes and figure it out?

"Alya, will you sit beside Ove on my throne?" Alya blinked her wide eyes at me in shock.

She bowed her head. "It would be my honor, your majesty."

I looked at Ove and spoke in our native tongue, "She has been broken and rebuilt a thousand times over. Do not break her once more; that is all I ask."

"If I break her, I will willingly abdicate my throne to you."

My heart skipped a beat at his words. He would give it up in the name of love. I had been going back and forth since I heard my prophecy, trying to decide if I would do the same. Esen did, Alya did, and now Ove will, if needed. But will I? Will I find the strength and courage that they had to walk away from that sort of power?

Esen's hand fell to my lower back, gently guiding me up the beach. With each step I took, the sand shifted below me. My weight felt like it was increasing with the movement.

Kings, advisors, generals, Queens, and their handmaids filled the small pavilion, all eager for the meeting to start and to know what would happen. Ove had sent the Ghost to discreetly slip to the Kings, but they can't go up to the Kings and tell them. Servants come in handy and do the dirty work. All the Ghosts needed to do was make sure the right person overheard their conversation, and the Kings would know before the sunset that day. And based on who showed up, the Ghosts did their jobs exceptionally well.

Ove walked before me with his arm raised, holding Alya's up, escorting her to her seat. I kept my head high with my arm wrapped around Esen's as we made our way to the extra seats beside mine and Ove's throne.

All eyes tracked the four of us, and a few gasped when Alya sat in the seat intended for me. Taking my seat, I looked over the Kings and their Queens, their brands standing out against their skin. Some are pale as snow, while others are dark as chocolate. King Elior of Leevah is by far the most attractive among the other Kings, and his wife is equally stunning. Her brown, bushy hair was pulled back in braids that fell past her breasts. Her sharp, skinny face looked like it promised death, but there was something about her that screamed life. She and her husband were indeed a mesmerizing couple.

I looked over at Calder, who had a woman sitting on his lap and another with a crown atop her head sitting beside him. I wanted to rip his heart out seeing this and for his role in locking Alya up. I cut him a glare that he either ignored or did not see. I paid no attention to all the other Kings and their Queens; they have not wronged me or done something worthy of my attention.

Alden sat directly across from us with an empty throne beside him. Vince stood behind him, looking uneasy, refusing to look at me. His finger kept tapping the throne above Alden's left shoulder, but the taps made no sound.

Only one other throne sat unoccupied. I did not expect Daxon to show. We never sent word to him, but I trust his allies to have done so.

The council fell silent when my Court and I stepped on the solid stone. They were all waiting for us to begin the meeting since we were the ones who called for them. I waved my hand carelessly at Alden, telling him to start. It seemed fair that he was in charge of one last thing before being dethroned.

"I am sure you are all aware that the Queen of Demons seems convinced she is entitled to my throne because of some worthless amulet," Alden spoke in the language of the Kings so only the Kings would know it.

Ove opened his mouth to begin translating for me when I held up my hand, silencing him. "I know your King's language and all seven mortal tongues. Do not think for one second you can insult me without my knowledge. I am *the* Seventh Ghost; you have all feared me long before you saw my face. I expect that same amount of fear that I am now a Queen of not one, but two thrones." I felt bad that Alya was left out of this conversation, but she did not seem to mind. She had a slight smirk as I spoke. Does she know the language of Kings? She has lived since the beginning of time. She was alive when it was created.

Those who did not speak the language were looking between Alden and me, confused at what had just occurred. A Queen has never known the secret language.

"You are not the Queen of Arymn, and you never will be," Alden snarled and grabbed the arms of his throne. His knuckles turned white.

"We shall see about that. I have a rightful claim to the throne, and you have overextended your welcome. You have disgraced Arymn and what it stands for."

"And what makes you believe the throne is yours?" Calder's calm voice aggravated me.

Ove answered before I had the opportunity to open my mouth. "You do not get to question her, Calder. You lost that right when you threw an innocent woman into a man's prison."

Calder scowled at him and Alya. The woman on his lap rose swiftly and moved away from him. His wife flinched in response to his dislike. "You will watch what you say and the accusations you are claiming. You need my vote to get your wife on the throne."

"We are not here to vote. We are here to bring to everyone's attention the truth about this war and what it truly is about. We are here to take a cruel King off the throne and replace it with someone worthy of it," Alya snapped in the language of Kings.

Every set of eyes turned to her and blinked in unison. They were shocked that a commoner spoke their language. I could see the Kings trying to decipher if they needed to create a new language to be used among them. Elior was the only one who looked pleased about Alya speaking in the language. He looked on the verge of laughter, and he seemed to be admiring her. His wife leaned over and whispered something in his ear. He nodded at whatever she had said.

I took Alya's hand in my own and calmed her down. "Queen Gila had spoken of a time when the world would be unified. She said it would start with this necklace." I held it up and let the Kings and Queens look at it. "I had found the necklace within the castle walls of Arymn Court. The letter Queen Gila left allows me my claim."

"Alden does not need to step away from the throne. Queen Gila is long since dead. She holds no power over us. It has been hundreds of years since she disappeared," King Kaj of Ter spoke softly. His emerald green eyes were unwavering.

Ove pulled out the envelope from his pocket and cleared his throat, "Surrounded by the races, only then shall all be united, ushering all to a new age.

I, High Queen Gila Sahan of Nevano, relinquish my claims to whichever throne shall find my soul first. May the new Queen have the heart of Arymn, the strength of Fahir, the sight of Dahr, and gentleness from Leevah. May she have the mobility of Auk, the honor of Sparan, and the patience of Ter. May the demons claim her as their own, and may she fly among angels.

A council of the nine kings and queens must take place, but none shall refute my last act as High Queen."

The room roared with outrage. Too many languages were being spoken for me to translate fast enough. Kings yelled that I would never have a part of them in me. The kings also translated the letter so their people could understand the situation. Advisors were fighting with each other. Queens were panicking about their husband's anger. Generals were eyeing everyone, preparing for a battle.

"Silence," a voice cleaved through the air, eliminating all voices.

Alden was on his feet, smiling mischievously. The voice had been his. "The letter calls for all nine Kings and Queens. Daxon and his wife are not here, and I do not have a wife. The council is not complete until three others join us."

I knew then that Alden would refuse to marry anyone to spite me, to make sure I never had a complete council to lay my claim to the throne.

Esen let out a small chuckle, startling me. He had been so quiet I had forgotten he was here. "I wonder, brother, what would have happened if you did not send the one chance you had at love to a prison meant to break them?"

Love will be the undoing of the man born from hatred and deceit.

Alden's prophecy came to mind at the words Esen had said.

I looked at where Alya sat beside Ove, looking as regal as ever. She deserves to be on that throne more than any female I know. He adores her the way I do Esen. I have never seen Ove unsure about a woman in his life, never so afraid to say or do the wrong thing. She was it for Ove. Alya Edevane is his love story. One that will be told to his kids and their kids. It is a story that historians should know and plays should be written about. She is his happily ever after, yet he has no idea who she truly is and what she is capable of.

I looked back at Alden and the smug smirk on his face I so desperately wanted to wipe off. Outside, the clouds began to darken as a storm quickly approached. Thunder boomed in the distance. A chill went up my spine as I began to formulate what needed to be done.

We came here ready to kill Alden if he refused to abdicate his throne, but we never planned how. It was an unspoken agreement that if one of us saw an opening, we would take it and deal with the consequences. But to kill a king, there really needed to be a plan, and one was coming to light.

Alya would be the one to kill him. In order to do so, I had to make her want to kill him. Make her hate him to the point she despises him and wants him dead. But that would make her a killer and me a monster. Do I have it in me to manipulate my friend into killing someone? Alden doesn't deserve his title; he stole it, but that is being a royal. He was next in line for the throne, and Esen was presumed dead. Even though he killed his brother to obtain it, he still earned it. But he doesn't deserve it. He started a war among the races, creating another holy war. He is experimenting on innocent people. He has not proven worthy of his title like Esen and Ove have.

Alden continued smirking at our silence. "I presume by your silence this council of kings is over."

"No," Alya snapped. All the kings looked at her with their brows raised. "As I said earlier, we are here to make everyone aware of what is happening in not just one court but all. Alden, Calder, Kaj, and Elior have all committed war crimes against the other courts and against Nevano."

"It is King to you," Calder tried correcting her.

She scoffed and looked him over in disgust. "No, it's not. The only one among those names that deserves the title of King is Elior, who was favored by goddess Evais. The goddess of medicine and healing would not grant him eternal reincarnation if he is fated to cause harm to the innocent. I only grouped him into you delinquents because he has unknowingly aided you in your crimes."

The storm outside had finally reached us. Turning the room into a faint darkness, rain pounded onto the sand around the pavilion. Thunder echoed as lightning scattered throughout the sky.

The company all began looking uneasy and unsure about the sudden weather change. The weather did not phase Alden. "What crimes are we accused of committing?"

Alya looked at Esen and me, silently asking if he was being serious. Esen let out a displeased sigh, signaling he was being serious. Her attention snapped back to Alden. "You sentenced an innocent person to a prison meant to kill and torture. You have kidnapped innocent demons, angels, and humans to commit experiments on them that only lead to their death. There is no benefit to your experiments. It is cruel and unjust!"

Is this happening? Is Alya getting angry at Alden on her own behalf? I bit my cheek to hide a smile. Somehow, she was doing exactly what I wanted her to, without knowing the plan I was formulating. But would she have it in her to kill him?

A blinding white light flashed before us, temporarily blinding me. King Daxon sat on his throne beside his wife.

Alya grabbed my hand. "Daxon," she whispered to herself.

Chapter Thirty-Four

ALYA

Impossible. I must be hallucinating. Daxon cannot be here. He should have died centuries ago. His sister would never have allowed it. Kesa had told me she took everyone's gifts, Daxons included. I suppose he isn't Daxon; it was a person made up to keep his true identity a secret. The god of luck sat before us, acting as a mortal, but so was I.

My anger increased seeing him unaged. His silver hair was still down to his waist, and it somehow managed to never get a single knot in it, even when flying. His muscles were still hidden under the charcoal grey robes. Even sitting down, I could see just how tall he was. My hands balled into fists.

"Apologies for my interruption. May I get informed about what has been discussed?" He was so formal about the situation. I watched as his eyes wandered over everyone, assessing the threats we all held. His eyes glazed over me, instantly snapping back as he realized who sat beside the King of demons.

Thunder boomed overhead, silencing the pavilion. Everyone looked uneasy as the storm reached directly over us. This time, Alden seemed displeased with the storm. "Esen, brother, please calm down and stop this storm."

King Cahn finally spoke up. His deep voice startled me. "This is not the king's doing. This is darker and more sinister. This feels like the wrath of a god." He rose from his throne and went to the pavilion's edge, where he kneeled and began silently praying.

Goddess Aniya, I beg you to spare all the lives here on the Blessed Isle and those at sea. I offer you this.

King Cahn held up his hand and a dagger, slicing into his palm. Blood dripped into the sand below him, sizzling at the impact. A shiver traveled through my body as he made an offer to me. My mind buzzed with excitement as I accepted his offer and heard his prayer in my mind. How is that possible? Any prayer intended for me should be lost in the wind, yet I heard his and all of them.

Save us, Aniya, for we have sinned, and you are our liberator. Take us to shore as we face this storm.

Please help me, Aniya. Make them lose my scent. I can't run for much longer. Please help me. Help- the prayer went unfinished.

My heart raced with uncertainty as prayer after prayer filled my head. This shouldn't be happening. It can't be unless Kesa forfeited my gifts back to me, but I know she never would. This isn't right. What is happening to me?

The storm vibrated the pillars, dirt and dust falling onto us all. Lighting struck the damp sand, causing fulgurites to form along the shore. Collective gasps sounded from everyone as they moved closer to the pavilion's center.

"Because it is the wrath of a goddess that has been hidden for too long," Daxon said calmly. I looked at him and his gentle eyes that had always felt safe when I was little. He gave a subtle nod. "It is time for her to be remembered and to be worshipped once more."

Alden scoffed in annoyance at Daxon's religious babbling. "We are kings and queens; the gods favor us and will not harm us. Please settle down, everyone, so we can get back to Alya's ridiculous accusations so we can all leave."

"Are they accusations if they are true and have proof of your atrocities?" Esen spoke like the king he was.

His brother raised a brow, silently threatening him not to say anything. But only one person in this room can threaten him, and he will listen to her. Lynn has been unusually silent. Is she planning something or just bored and wants to leave like most of us? The sooner we stop getting interrupted and Aldens stops fighting us, the sooner we can handle business.

As I predicted, Esen did not take his brother's threat seriously. He rose from his seat and took off his shirt for everyone to see the scars that now covered his body.

"I am your proof. I am the confirmation you need to know that Alden and other kings have committed a war crime. My brother took me while I was injured and experimented on me. He sentenced an innocent to her death for no reason other than his refusal to take responsibility for his actions."

The females in the room gasped, and some turned away. A fury seemed to emanate from the kings and Vince. Had he not known what happened to his friend? Had he grieved the loss of his beloved king just to serve one who had no morals?

I felt the tension in Esen as he realized people were staring at him and ogling over his scars. He has never been one for the center of attention, but I have. I rose and gestured for Esen to sit. He did so promptly, looking relieved he didn't hold everyone's attention anymore.

"Alden must be held accountable for his crimes against his king, but also for his crimes against humanity. He stole blood and who knows what else from King Esen so he could experiment on others and try to create a race that cannot exist in this world. Humans barely tolerate demons; how do you think they will behave towards a race that has demon blood running through their veins? Alden does not belong on that throne; Esen does, and as you can all see, he is alive and well."

"He is not of the Thillardson bloodline. He never had a claim to it," Alden countered.

"And you are bastard born. Your claim to it is just as questionable as his. The only one with a legitimate and unquestionable claim to the Arymn throne is Queen Lynnora. She has found Queen Gila's necklace and the note with it, dictating what is to happen. How I see it and how you should all see it is that Arymn has no ruler, and only Lynn has a rightful claim to the throne, making her Arymns new Queen."

I surveyed every king, trying to see what they were thinking, but my rage clouded my vision, and the storm continued on. Rain was hammering down around us, thunder was booming in the sky, and lighting struck every so often.

Alden pushed himself out of the throne to stand up. "I will not be made a fool by some commoner who knows nothing! I have earned my title just as every king here has. I was trained to be king one day-"

"As was Esen!" I snapped back. My heart thumped madly against my chest. Everyone in the room disappeared from my view. All that mattered was the insufferable man who sat on the throne he did not belong in. "You stole what was already his! You believed the words of a dead man over the proof of a living one. The late King of Arymn wanted Esen to be king. Otherwise, he would have claimed him as a bastard like you. I know more than you can ever imagine, Alden! I know Vince warms your bed at night, and the only reason you tried to force me to marry you was to hide that fact because you are ashamed. I knew Lynnora was the Seventh Ghost the second I saw her walk into the tavern. I know what gods were present at the time of Gila's disappearance and her writing that letter. Do not for one second try to belittle me. I am far more dangerous and powerful than the lot of you combined."

Alden's face had gone red from either embarrassment or anger. I don't know which, nor do I care. I had proven my point. I am not some helpless girl who needs others to save her. I have played that role for too long. Now, it is my turn to save everyone, and the only way I can do that is by getting Alden off the throne. He was prophesied to die by love, and I am love itself.

"You do not know what you speak of, child! You are weak and powerless. The gods did not grant you a gift because even they know you cannot handle that power."

I let out a sadistic chuckle, and my eyes darkened. "You do not think the gods favor me. What if I told you they do more than anyone here? What if I could get the lost goddess Aniya to grant me one wish?"

"And what would that wish be? She is a harmless goddess who does nothing but love people."

"You are so wrong. She is the reason for this storm. King Cahn prayed to her because he knew her wrath when he saw it. As for my wish," I paused and opened my hand. The cool touch of leather in my hand was a warm welcome. Ove had known what I wanted without me needing to ask. He gave me his dagger. "I would wish for this blade to strike true."

I calculated how far away he was and how I needed to throw the blade before everyone had time to process my last words. The blade left my fingers, and Alden opened his mouth to protest, but it was too late. The dagger sliced through his mouth and throat, impaling him to his throne. The hilt stuck out of his mouth, prohibiting any more words from being spoken.

The false King of Arymn was dead before he could take a breath.

I gracefully walked over to where his body was and yanked the dagger free of him. His body slumped to the ground. I threw Ove his dagger back, and he caught it with ease, sending it to the place he deemed safe.

Generals and kings drew their swords, standing in front of their queens. None moved to attack; all seemed afraid.

"I just proved Aniya favors me. Do you not think she will keep me safe from your harm?"

None had time to respond. Black tendrils of shadows swirled around the room, forcing the kings back into their thrones and the general's arms to their sides. "I would put down your weapons before you make an enemy of a goddess and ghost, as well as me. Do I need to remind you I will see you at your death and can make you pay for any harm you do to Alya?" Ove's voice was terrifying, as if the god of terror had spoken himself.

Weapons clattered to the ground with a loud clang. Once everyone's weapons were dropped, Ove released his shadows from them. The only one who tried to fight them was King Cahn of Dahr, but his powers over darkness did not work there.

Daxon began slowly clapping, then sped it up until he clapped enthusiastically. "Well done. That was executed beautifully. Pun intended."

All eyes turned to him in shock and horror. "Does anyone else want to try and lay claim to the throne of Arymn?" I asked like a feral animal ready to strike again. I hadn't killed so many people in years. I forgot the rush that came with it. I once was Kesa's prized fighter and would obey her every wish. I was more than that, though. I was her messenger. I killed who she selected, never asking questions but always knowing it was punishment for my father. Once I met Eilam, I thought I could stop killing, and I did. But desperate times call for desperate measures, and the world's fate rested on me killing Alden.

No one said anything as Lynn rose from her spot beside Esen and moved over to the throne Alden's body occupied. She snapped her fingers, and two ghosts seemed to have appeared out of nowhere. They grabbed his body, carrying it to the boat that would take him home. She sat down on the throne with me standing beside her. I clasped my hands in front of me, eagerly awaiting her first order as queen.

She sat down, ignoring the blood behind her head and the streak of it down the throne. She smiled mischievously. "I suppose everyone here thinks my first act as queen will be to allow the demons into the mortal realm or for everyone to sacrifice their favorite child to me, but it's not. I may have killed and will continue killing, but I am not the monster you have all perceived me as. I was Dearil's favorite because of my ability to lead. Therefore, my first act is to call a ceasefire. Arymn is no longer participating in this war and will immediately release all prisoners, as well as vacate your lands."

A silence traveled throughout the pavilion. The rain lessened as the storm moved past us. My nerves calmed down seeing Lynn on the throne, but my hatred for Alden was still there.

A conversation slowly began as Kings negotiated among them. They talked about what was to be done about the facilities experimenting with demon blood. There was talk about shutting down the Koya mines. Conversations continued well into the next day. Advisors had returned to ships to procure food and drinks as the time slowly ticked by. Only one voice was not heard: Esens. He did not speak or eat anything. He sat in his seat, staring at the throne his mate now occupied. I knew he was trying to process the death of his brother. He still loved him even though Alden had caused him extreme harm and betrayed his trust. The two of them had grown together and learned everything together. He was a man that cared deeply, and it was causing him pain.

Conversations began ending, and people left to go back to their homes. It sounded like Navano was about to enter a time of peace, but more things still needed to be discussed. Nearly everyone had left. My friends were still in the pavilion, as well as Daxon and his wife.

The god whispered something to his wife, and she leaned over, giving him a gentle kiss on the cheek, and whispered in the language of gods, "Do whatever it takes to bring him home." He nodded his understanding, and she left.

Did he teach her our language, and does she know who I am? Thinking about those questions was unsettling, but it was not the time to dwell on them.

"Queen Lynnora, King Ove, may I have a moment alone with King Daxon?" I asked, not taking my eyes off my uncle.

I felt Lynn's eyes follow my gaze. "Of course. Do I need to fetch Alika and Sheena?"

"No need." My two words dismissed them. Ove passed by me and gently squeezed my hand before moving over to where Esen still sat.

The two of them tried lifting him, but he refused their help. "Leave me," he grunted. Lynn looked at me, and I nodded, telling her it was okay. My queen and king promptly left for the shores.

I took a breath and began the conversation I needed to have with my uncle. "So, you're alive?"

"As are you. I thought you died in Oud." I could hear the sorrow in his voice, but it meant nothing to me. He abandoned me long before I fell from my mother's grace.

"I'm sure *Kesa* wishes I did." He flinched, hearing his sister's name. "Who does she have? I know you well enough to know you would never harm anyone unless you had no choice."

He remained silent for a moment. "Our son." He produced a silver feather. "She sent this to us yesterday as a reminder of what would happen if I rebel. That was why we were late."

My heart hurt for him, but I don't know if I can trust him. He could be telling me this to make me pity him and let my guard down. "What can be done to get him back?"

Tears brimmed his eyes. "Succeed with the experiment. I don't know why, but she is determined to create this mixed race. Our son is our motivator to keep sending angels to their deaths."

"I'm sorry." I truly am sorry, but I still can't trust everything he says. "Are there any more of us that can help?"

He shook his head."Diah and Valda haven't been seen or heard from in a couple of decades, which is surprising with the war happening. Valda probably had a hand in it. Edric died...again." He rolled his eyes. It was always baffling that the god of fate could not avoid his death, but he always reincarnated. "Even if the three of them and your father turn up, they are simply a grain of sand on the beach."

I understood what he was saying, but I completely disagreed with it. "One grain may do nothing, but thousands can. Ove and Lynn have armies. They can help you get your son back and take down Kesa once and for all."

"I'm sorry, sweetheart, but your mother has grown too strong. To go against her would be your death."

I scoffed. "It's good that you would have the god of death on your side."

He rested his hand on my shoulder. "No one can guarantee he would fight alongside us."

"He would if I asked." My father owes me that much. After everything he has taken from me, the least he could do is to save us from damnation.

"It is no use."

I let out a disappointed sigh. "I wish things were different. I wish you believed in yourself and what those who care for you would do for you. I'm sorry." I struck him faster than he could deflect me. He let out a grunt, stumbling backward into his throne. He looked at me with wild eyes. I felt him using his gift to see every outcome of this fight and to ensure it ended with him as the victor. But he forgot one thing.

Esen's desire to protect those he cares for is stronger than his emotions. As I expected, Esen shot out of his seat and shifted into a giant snake. The shift caused his body to hit the pillars and the roof. Stone was tumbling down on everything. My feet carried me out fast, with Esen slithering behind me.

Without Daxon knowing, I had stolen a feather from his wing, which would warrant an insufferable amount of pain if he caught me.

CHAPTER THIRTY-FIVE

OVE

"Run," Alya screamed as she barreled down the beach at us. Her dress was splattered red.

The ground shook as the pavilion crumbled into a thousand pieces. Esen was hissing at those who survived the destruction. Only one remained: the King of Angels.

"What the fuck did you do?" I found myself saying the words instead of silently thinking about them. My shadows were cackling hysterically.

Now is not the time for that, I snapped at them. None shut up, and they continued.

"It doesn't matter! We need to leave!" Alya slid to a stop before us, kicking sand onto our feet.

"Go! I'll take care of Esen. Take her back to Arymn," Lynn demanded as she rushed off to the pavilion to do who knows what.

My hands reacted before I had time to think. I pressed Alya against me as my shadows became one with us. The loose sand fell from below us and was replaced with hard stone. The light of the castle poked through my shadows as they dissipated. Alya's chest rose rapidly against mine, her eyes wild with worry stuck staring at a white feather in her trembling hand.

"I am so dead. He's going to kill me. Oh, I am so screwed. What the *fuck* was I thinking?" she rambled on, stepping out of my grip and my shadows.

"Alya," I said her name, but she didn't hear me. She continued to panic. "Alya!" I grabbed her shoulders, trying to help slow her down. "Alya!" I tried once more, to no avail.

My hand moved to the side of her face, my thumb steadying her jaw and my pointer finger resting behind her ear. I leaned down, pulled her face to mine, and kissed her. Her lips were warm, with a hint of blood on them. Her breath stilled as she pressed into me. Her hands grabbed the hem of the shirt, holding me tightly. For one moment, all the pain and suffering I had endured was worth it because it led to this, to her.

Her hand stung my face as she slapped me, and our lips parted as swiftly as they had joined.

"Why did you hit me?" I yelled at her in disbelief.

"Why did you kiss me?" her voice matched my fury.

"Because you were spiraling and weren't listening. Why did you hit me?"

She blinked her beautiful eyes once. "Because you kissed me!"

"You—" I stopped myself from snapping at her further. I wanted to tell her she kissed me back and leaned into me. My shirt was crumpled on my waist because of how tightly she held it. And that the bulge in my pants was from her kissing me back.

Letting out a growl of anger, I pointed my finger at her. "Do not fucking move. Don't even think about moving. I need to clean up whatever mess you made and get my other two idiots out of danger."

She sucked her lips in and let out a snort. Her hand flew up to her mouth to try and cover the smile she was failing at hiding. "I did that, didn't I?"

"Did what?" Kiss me? Oh yes, she did, and I will never let her forget it either.

"Shatter one or two of Daxon's ribs and steal a feather." She held it up and twirled it in her fingers.

Growling at her once more, "You shattered his ribs?" She nodded her head and let out a small giggle. "You know what? I don't have time or patience for this right now. Don't fucking move. I'll be right back."

I didn't wait for her to respond. The beach was around me again.

What was she thinking going up against a King like that? Why did she even do it?

My questions stopped forming at the sound of two people arguing. Lynn was standing over the portal to the Below, with Esen in front of her. The pavilion and thrones were all but rubble.

"You had no empathy, Lynnora! He is — was my brother. You could have pretended to care!"

"Why should I care about the man who tortured you, who lied and deceived you? He knew the consequences of his actions!"

I stayed where I had landed, not wanting to be a part of their fight but curious about where it would lead. They both are passionate and opinionated people, and neither like to back down from something. The outcome will be fascinating no matter what.

"Fine! If that is how it will be, do not expect Ava to live if she steps foot onto any of Arymn's islands."

"She is my sister!"

"And he was my brother! I will kill her for what she did to you and Ove if she so much as dares to show her face in my Court."

Lynn's horns, ears, and tail came out as she straightened her back, making her seem taller than him, even though she was significantly shorter. "You so as much touch one hair on her, I will not hesitate to kill you. I do not care if we are mates. She is not yours to kill. She is my family, no matter what." Her voice was lethally calm. Even my own shadows coward upon hearing it.

Esen took a step away from her. "Alden wasn't yours to kill. I know you manipulated Alya into killing him," he said quietly, his voice breaking.

"He was Alya's. His prophecy was of love killing him, not me." Her eyes flashed over to me, and she nodded subtly. "Take your time returning to your palace. Your citizens need a strong King, not an angry one. I will meet you there when you are ready."

My shadows reached out to her, bringing us to our old room in the castle. My feet hadn't even touched the ground when she collapsed into the bed and sighed harshly.

"How bad is it?" I asked her, joining her at her side.

"What Alya did, or the fight between Esen and me?" I laid back on the bed and looked at her. "Not too bad. Daxon was rightfully pissed. From what I gathered, Alya attacked him when they said goodbye."

I raised a brow. "How does she know him?" I have never asked much about her past and thought Esen was the first King she met, but I may have been wrong. I could never bring myself to ask more about who she knows and her family. She has always been so closed off. I don't think Lynn knows much, either.

"You know Alya, she's very religious and knows what each god and goddess looks like. She had spent some time at Ver's temple in her youth and recognized him."

I looked at Lynn, impressed she knew this much about her. Maybe the two of them are a lot closer than I had expected. They have spent a long time together healing from the prison and Ava. It would only make sense that they talked about things they enjoyed as they worked through their trauma.

"He's Ver," I blurted out far louder than intended. I had a feeling he was a god, but I didn't know which one.

Lynn turned her head to face me and rolled her black eyes. She was still angry about her argument with Esen. "You amaze me, Ove. Alya could not take her eyes off him, and I know you have been to his temple."

"I suppose I had been a little distracted." I had been. I could barely pull my attention away from Alya sitting beside me on the throne meant for

Lynn. She had been Queen for an hour and did so spectacularly. It had taken everything in me not to kill Calder where he sat. I know he knew it was Alya who was in his prison, that he had subjected her to a terrible fate. When Adri confirmed my suspicions, it startled me that he didn't pardon her and take her as his mistress. She fits his type, but maybe the fear that she killed one King scared him away. Whatever it was, I am thankful none touched her in such a way.

Lynn smirked. "Where did you take her, by the way?"

My heart sank to my stomach as I jumped out of bed. "I'll be back!"

Swiftly running out of the room and down the halls, servants gasped and skirted away from me in fear. I slid to a stop in the hall I left Alya in and saw no sign of her.

Find her. I ordered my shadows. They quickly peeled away from me and began to search the castle.

My heart thudded against my chest with each passing moment. Where is she? Esen hasn't pardoned her yet; guards will arrest her on sight. She needs to be here; she needs to be alright.

I found her. This way to my Queen, Eilam sounded far away, yet so close. Following the sound of his voice, I wandered through the castle. Stairs led me further and further up into the tower. A spiral stair set before me went up into the darkness. I looked for a light to show the end but saw none.

Not wanting to anger my leg further, I shifted and let my wings carry me upwards. Up and upwards, I soared. My wings taking me higher up the tower. I flew into the darkness, welcoming it. Letting my senses guide me where I needed to go, Eilam kept telling me to go higher.

Why is she here? How did she climb this many stairs so swiftly? I had been gone no more than ten minutes. There's no possible way she is this fast.

Ceiling, Eilam snapped, but it was too late. My head and beak harshly collided with the end of the stairs. The impact sent me onto the stone floors below me, causing pain to lace my entire body.

Laying there for a few breaths, the pain did not ease. Forcing myself to stand, my talons scrapped on the stone, leaving claw marks. I shook my head, trying to ignore the pain, and failed.

I did warn you, my King, Eilam's voice sounded humorous.

I'm glad my pain amuses you. It's such a shame the dead can't feel pain, or I'd throw you at the wall. I growled at him.

He chuckled. Ah, *yes, the only good thing about being dead. It's too bad I have the most amazing thing in life, and you do not. It's such a shame the dead know more love than the living.*

Shut up. You know why I don't look for love.

His shadow tickled my feathers as he moved around me. *I have told you numerous times that your fear holds you back. Tell her how you feel. Who knows, she may reciprocate your emotions.*

Thanks, but I'd rather stick to not knowing.

That is your loss. Something about Alya tells me she is an amazing partner and an even better mate.

I let out a chirp that sounded like a scoff. *Mate is pushing it, but yes, she seems like a fantastic partner.*

Then get her.

I shifted back and felt for the handle to the trapdoor and found it. I paused before pushing it open. *I'm only going after her to make sure she is alright, not to seduce her.*

Eilam made a sound that told me he didn't believe my intentions. Shaking my head, I opened the door and let in the sinking sunlight. Alya was leaning against the stone edge intended to be used by archers during an attack. Her hair blew slightly in the calming breeze. Her head hung low between her shoulders.

Climbing the last few steps out, I closed the door silently, not wanting to disturb her. "I told you not to leave where I left you," I teased and stood beside her.

She looked at me, her eyes lined with tears, her cheeks red as if she had already shed some tears. Alya shrugged her shoulders. "I knew you would find me. You always do."

"Do you want to talk about what's bothering you?"

She looked back out at the island and the city below us. The sun sank low into the horizon, casting reds and pinks into the clouds. Alya didn't answer me until the sun had disappeared entirely.

"No." She let out an uneven breath. I leaned into her, trying to tell her it was okay to lean back on me and cry on my shoulder if need be. Her arm wrapped around mine, her tiny fingers intertwined with my own. My hands felt clammy against her cool, soft skin.

"There are days I want to fly away from here and leave this place behind, but things are stopping me. You, Lynn, and Esen are one."

She had included me and said me first! I am a reason she stays in a place she doesn't like.

Fuck.

I am one of the reasons she stays in a place she doesn't like or wish to be in.

"And the other things?"

"It doesn't matter now. I will never get an answer."

I turned to face her more and put her chin in my fingers. "What is it?"

She chewed the inside of her cheek. "I still don't understand why Alden did what he did. Why did he turn against his brother? Why did he use demons and angels to breed? What will their offspring do for him?" Her questions spilled quickly out of her mouth.

I gave her a small, weak smile from the corner of my mouth. "Give me one day, and I will come back with answers. He has committed war crimes. He will need my judgment. I have one other errand to do, but I will come back to you with answers."

She looked at me, and her tears disappeared. "Thank you, Ove." Alya stood on the tips of her toes and kissed my cheek warmly. My cheeks reddened at the small act of affection.

"You said you want to fly away from here, but you can't do that without wings." Focusing on just the wings of my other form, I felt them grow and increase in size to accommodate for my weight.

Alya took a step back, and her eyes widened with amazement. "How is that possible? How do you have angel wings?"

I scowled at her for the insult. "I am not an angel and do not have their wings. I can summon different parts of my bird form." I held my hand out to her. "Will you go for a flight with me?"

She took my hand and, not wanting her to back out, I pulled her in close, my hands wrapping around her tightly. My wings boomed, parting the surrounding air, and lifted us into the air. She clutched onto me and wrapped her legs around my waist. Her head buried into my shoulder.

I let out a laugh. "Do you trust me?"

She nodded her head. Preparing myself to be slapped, I dropped her ever so slightly. The weight of her body no longer being held took her by surprise, and her limbs fell off me. As her fingers slid past me, I stuck my arms back out to catch her. Her legs were now in one arm, and her back rested against my other.

"Asshole," she screamed up at me over the wind as I continued to fly.

I let out another laugh. "You can see everything now." She pinched my arm harshly. "Careful, or I might let you fall."

I flew over the city she wished to fly away from, giving her the chance to do it. The wind rushed past us, her hair turning into a whip on my neck, stinging me with every lashing. The stars shining above illuminated the night sky.

I lost track of time and flew until she shivered. At some point during the flight, her head had rested against my shoulder, her hands held loosely around my neck. A smile was on her face each time I looked down at her to check and make sure she was alright.

Her shivers told me she was cold and in need of warmth. Circling back over the tower we had left from, I landed and set her down. "I will be back in a day with your answers. Tell Lynn if you have more questions, and she will send word."

I kissed her cheek and took off with one beat of my wings.

***

Alden lay at my feet, his soul in solid form and covered in blood. Why isn't he breaking? He has nothing to lose. He is dead, and he can only get an easy torture.

The door opened, and Adri came in, also covered in blood. I lowered the knife. The blood dripped onto the stone floor. "Anything?" I asked hopefully.

"Nothing yet, your majesty. We're still hunting. I may need my second for this." She eyed Alden and was careful about her words, not wanting him to know what was happening.

We had lost Dearil after learning of his plans. The six other Ghosts are hunting for him, hoping to find and stop him from becoming the god of death. If Dearil locates Haedon and kills him, I fear what will happen. The world will shift in the chaos that will surely come with the new god.

"Don't until necessary." I want to keep Lynn out of this for as long as possible. She deserves a chance at happiness; with Esen back on the throne, she can get it. I will not bring her into this unless absolutely necessary.

"She knows the hunted the best. Her expertise will be valuable."

"Do not question me! Do not fight me on this, Adri. I will call her in if *I* deem it necessary; until then, continue hunting." My annoyance with

Alden transferred over to her. I regretted snapping at her the moment the words left my mouth, but they were needed. I am her King. If she questions me publicly and others notice, it will make me look incapable and weak.

She nodded her head and bowed. Adri said nothing as she left the small room.

"Trouble in paradise," Alden gasped out.

I looked down at him with no emotion, resisting the urge to crush his throat. If I didn't need him to talk, I would have done so by now. "I'll answer your question when you answer mine." My skin crawled, realizing I sounded like Ava and her game. My lips twitched into a smile.

"Find me the inquisitor," I ordered the guard at the door.

If Adri was back, then so was Ava. Adri refuses to let Ava have free rein anymore. I knew the guard would know who to get. They all fear her and call her that because of her skill at getting answers.

***

Ava and I were back in the small room an hour later, with Alden still crumpled on the floor. She looked at him, then at me, and raised her brow, questioning if I was serious. I held out my hand, indicating for her to do what she does best.

Ava sat on the floor and leaned back on the wall, looking at him. "I hear you want answers. I have them, but I want answers of my own. Would you like to play a game?"

Alden let out a grunt.

"I will take that as a yes. My game is simple. We each ask one question at a time. We answer it in all honesty. If one of us does not answer or lies, the other gets to cut off a limb. Since you are dead, I can't kill you, but your soul still needs your arms and legs, so those will do just fine."

Alden shot up quickly and moaned in pain from the injuries I had inflicted earlier. "I am not playing that game!"

"Oh, but you are. The other alternative is to be tortured daily and relive the day you regret most. Either you play this game and lose no limbs, play the game and lose a few, or you hate your death to the point you wish to be dead."

Alden thought it over. "Fine," he spat out.

Ava clapped her hands excitedly. "My first question is straight to the nit and gritty. Why were you trying to create half-breeds?" Alden didn't answer. He was outright refusing to even look at Ava. "May I remind you what the refusal to answer a question will lead to?"

He snarled in anger. "There is a story of a girl who is made of both. She is said to be what unites us all. For her to live, they must be created."

I scoffed. "You expect me to believe you were doing this to unite our kinds?"

He didn't answer me. He was only playing this game with Ava, not me.

"If you are desperate to unite us, why fight against Ove and his demons?"

"It was never a fight against the demons. It was against Dearil and Ove. They never would have given me what I wanted, but Trevv would have. All I had to do was get him on his throne."

Trevv never would have given up any demon to be experimented on. Lynn would not have allowed it, and he seeks her love and approval.

"What do you get out of this?" Alya continued to question him.

He sighed, and his lips twitched upwards. "I get to be called a visionaire, known for creating something beautiful. No one will dare question me or what I do. They will thank me and worship me."

I scoffed again and looked at Ava, knowing he wouldn't answer me. "The undesirable wishes to be desired. And here I thought I had a big ego."

Ava laughed at my words, but her attention snapped back to Alden. "Why did you send the Auk girl to prison for a crime she did not commit?"

I paled at her question. The topic of Alya was not one of the pre-approved questions I had told her to ask.

Alden smiled. "She was in my way. She had grown too curious, and I could see through the lies she was spinning, yet none of the answers made sense. Alya refused my advances and was no longer helpful to my goals. With her in prison, she no longer was digging around my business. It was unfortunate what happened to her. I regret it and wish someone so gentle had never been mixed into my affairs."

I glared at Ava, telling her to get back to the questions I wished to be answered. She saw it and got back on track. "Why did you turn against your brother?"

Alden looked down at the ground. Sorrow filled his face. "I had found my father's diary and learned of the Queen's betrayal. I had known what he was since we were boys, and it never affected us until they crowned him King. At his coronation, they called him a true son of Arymn. Hearing it made me angry and resent him. He is a bastard, just as I am, and yet he never experienced the cruelness of the world. After a while, I resented him, and when Daxon said he wished for angels to be held elsewhere, I took up the opportunity, and the story of the girl who is to unite us all came to mind. I knew what to do, and my anger at Esen clouded my judgment. He was not my first choice but my only choice."

Ava looked at me and nodded her head. Our questions were over, and she believed each answer to be honest. "I asked you six questions, and you were honest. In return, you may ask me six, and I will answer honestly or lose a limb."

"No need, Ava. He has served his purpose, and I am tired of his existence." My shadows lashed out, passing through him, disturbing his soul until it was gone from the world. Alden was dead, with no hope of life.

Ava opened her mouth to yell at me, but I raised my hand, silencing her. "I have another errand to run. Tell Adri not to bother her Queen. I will be back in a few days; until then, go hunt."

Chapter Thirty-Six

LYNNORA

Esen had returned after Ove disappeared. He was calm and at ease, making me nervous. What did he do to calm down so quickly? How did he get back so fast? I showered before joining him in bed, not wanting to bother him with questions. I found myself muttering clean, clean, clean as I washed myself and scraped the dry blood out from under my nails.

Esen was sitting in the bed with one arm behind his head on the headboard. He looked at me and the thin white nightgown I wore. He smirked as his eyes traveled down my body.

"If I were to apologize now, would you think it is because I want sex?"

I shrugged my shoulders. "Depends how you apologize and how much."

He chuckled and patted the bed, inviting me in. Crawling under the covers, I laid my head on his lap. His hands began running through my hair. "I am sorry. I should not have called you a heartless bitch, nor should I have threatened your sister."

"You were right as well. I was being heartless, and you have every right to threaten her for what she did to Ove and me." I paused, debating the weight of my following words. "Esen, I can never be your queen."

He looked down at me, his eyebrows pushed together. "Why? I want you by my side to rule together—" his words trailed off as he realized it.

"I love you, Esen, you annoying gnat. I choose to live and to love over to rule and to die. I want to spend the rest of our years together. I want the love Alya has for Eilam. I want us to have undying love, and if that means never to have a crown atop my head, then so be it. I will have you, and that is all I care about."

He kissed my hand. "What about your claim to the throne of the Below?"

"I will never be a true Queen of the Below until Ove breaks and is visited by his mother. I will remain Queen in name until he marries."

He pulled me upright and held me tightly. My arms wrapped around him, never wanting the hug to end. "You are my mate, my obsession, a true work of art. I love you more than words can convey, Lynnora. I hope you decide to take my name in a few months."

I read through his carefully crafted words and knew he was trying to get me to divulge what name I had chosen. But I had promised never to speak the name to anyone else. It is the last part of me that no one has met and corrupted. I want to protect it as long as possible. Never again do I want another to control me as Dearil did, as everyone in my life has.

This is my life, and I am taking it back.

"I will consider it." I got out of his grip and laid with my back to him, silently asking for him to hold me tightly. My eyes wandered over to the nightstand where a black feather had been left on top of an envelope with Esen's name scribbled in my handwriting.

"Why haven't you opened it?"

He followed my gaze. "I promised myself never to open it until the world ended."

"Have you thought of opening it?"

"Only twice. The moment you died in my arms and then again when I woke up and thought you were dead."

"How romantic," I teased him.

"I do have my moments. Get some rest. We have had a long day, and all my romance will be here in the morning." Esen kissed me one last time before we fell asleep in one another's arms.

The world and its problems disappeared around me and my mate. Whatever the outcome of today meant, we would face it tomorrow and do it together.

***

I patted the bed, searching for Esen, and found nothing besides a cold bed. Slowly opening my eyes, I blinked at the rising sun casting its lights into the room. On Esen's pillow sat a note with my name in elegant handwriting I didn't recognize.

I told you I would take what is mine. Be a good demon, and do not fight me or come looking for them.

-Kesa

My heart beat fast as I read the words over and over again, engraving them into my memory.

She took him.

She took Esen.

How did she take him without waking me up?

This can't be happening. No. Please don't let this be real.

"Esen," I screamed into the empty room without reply.

The covers were on the ground as I rushed into the other room, searching for him. Where is he? How did she take him?

No. No. No!

Them.

She said them.

My heart beat faster as my feet carried me through the castle halls to Alya's room. Her bed was neatly made, and in the center was a leather-bound book I had seen her working on once. Atop it was a gold quill dipped in red ink. My head spun, searching for a note saying where she went.

There was nothing.

They were gone.

My knees collided with the stone, sending pain vibrating up my body as I screamed out. My tears spilled down my face, the drops darkening the stone floor below me.

Esen was gone.

Alya was gone.

All that was left was Ove and I. Once more, I was afraid.

A chill went up my spine as a shadow passed through me. Mimsy's voice filled my ears, her terror blending with mine. "Ove is in danger, my Queen."

My back arched, unleashing a scream to shatter the world, wishing to cleave it in two. The ground around me trembled. Out of instinct, I reached my hand out and was greeted with nothing but air.

I was utterly alone, and no one was coming to save me from myself.

Looking into the fire, fueled with rage to kill a god, I spoke into the flame, knowing one fear would answer my prayer.

"Help me, I beg of you. I will do anything. I want them back," my voice cracked with each word.

Moments passed, and my tears did not cease. My prayer was going unheard.

Accepting my fate, I lay on my side, clutching the book, and wept.

"Hello, darling."

I looked up at him and the gentle smile he bore. I would have thought he cared if I hadn't known better, but he never has and never will.

"Will you help me get them back?" I pulled myself onto my knees, still looking up at him.

"I will help you if you help me."

I didn't care what he asked me to do. I would kill who he said to kill, and I would stalk those he wanted to be hunted. I would jump off a cliff if that was what he needed. I would kill myself if it meant saving them all.

"I will help you, Dearil."

CHAPTER THIRTY-SEVEN

OVE

My wings carried me where I needed to go. The feel of something I couldn't explain guided me over the rooftops of the middle island and straight for the temple of Kesa. Why had I been drawn here so many times? I had no idea. I just knew I had to come here, and with Esen on the throne, now felt like as good of a time as any.

The temple looked empty. No citizens flocking to get their reading from an immortal seer who probably knows very little of death. Landing behind it and shifting back, my shadows coward with each step closer to the entrance.

Cowards, I hissed at them, teasing.

None answered, not even Eilam.

The door was already open, and eucalyptus smells flowed through it. My nose cringed at the strong scent, and the heat made it worse. Going into the temple was exactly like I had expected. The hallway was filled with fabric hanging from the wall and ceiling; candles lit the way. What surprised me was the circular stairs leading down to the center, where a bowl of blood sat.

"Hello," I called out and got no answer.

I looked at the gems and items cluttering the steps and recognized where

Lynn got an absurd amount of gold from. She had come here twice, and after leaving, she always bought herself something nice. She has no gold to her name since my father paid her with food and blood. Her dad did nothing to help. The small shack she called a house on the upper island was bought with gold she stole. I knew I should have questioned how she was affording nice things after being here.

I pocketed a necklace with a blue gem in the center, thinking Alya might like it. My shadows began pulling me back towards the door. Only one kept trying to bring me forward.

If you are so afraid of a cranky old seer, then go. I snapped at them. Only Eilam stayed behind. *Cowards,* I yelled out as they vanished into nothing.

Moving to where I felt I needed to go, I saw the most beautiful set of white wings mounted on the wall as if they were a prized kill. The wings were far more exquisite than mine could ever hope of growing to, and in the center of one was a silver feather. Whoever these belonged to, they had found their mate.

Sprouting my wings, I hovered so I could examine them. My hand stretched out; the feathers were softer than anything I had ever felt. I wanted to lie in them naked and let them tickle me.

Take them, bring them back to who they belong to, Eilam whispered in my ear.

My hands worked quickly as I obeyed his command. I knew I shouldn't steal something so large and obvious, but I knew the wings of an angel were sacred and should never be mounted like this.

The clips easily undid, and the wings fell into my arms, shrinking in size at my touch. My remaining shadows took them to the one place I felt sacred. I would go back for them when I find their rightful owner.

Ove, I need you to shift into your childhood face. Do not question it; just do as I say. I have never heard Eilam sound so afraid. Landing, my wings vanished back into me, and I looked around, trying to find the threat.

Now!

I did as he said once more. My father's face morphed with mine, and I was in the skin I despised and never wanted to wear again.

Give me a voice and a body, I beg of you.

Why?

Please, just do as I ask. I am trying to save you as you have saved me.

In the distance, I heard the clicking of heels approaching. My stomach sank with each haunting sound. Eilam solidified next to me. It was strange to see the face I had worn for so long on another and to see my closest shadow friend looking relatively alive once more. His face was pale, his lower lip steady, but his finger tapping rapidly on his thigh.

He stood before me, blocking me from the view of whoever was approaching and hiding them from me. His hands moved behind him, searching for something. They stopped moving when his hand was wrapped around my wrist.

"I will never leave you, Ove," he whispered so quietly I almost didn't hear it.

"I am not doing any readings today," a calm female voice called out from wherever she was hiding.

"It's a good thing I already know how I die," Eilam answered.

The clicking of the heels stopped moving, and I felt the presence of someone else standing near us. My chest pressed into Eilam's back. He pulled me close. It is good that I am shorter and more slender than he is. Otherwise, I could not hide behind him.

I hated hiding, but if Eilam was asking this favor and sounded so afraid, I knew I should not question him.

"How are you alive?" The lady snapped coldly. Any warmth she had previously shown us was gone, and I doubted we would see it again.

"Eternal reincarnation. You should have stuck around longer to ensure a goddess did not mark me."

What is he talking about? He is dead. I killed him.

The lady seemed to understand what he meant. "She has always been a crafty pain in my ass. How is your dear wife? Still running around with those demons?"

He shrugged his shoulders. "She always said they were better company than you and your siblings. Tell her father I said hello — oh wait, he's probably too busy screwing someone else to pay you any attention."

The lady snarled at him, "I will kill you where you stand if it meant I didn't have to hunt you down to do it over again."

"I wish you luck with that. It seems a rather boring way to spend eternity."

She let out a high-pitched chuckle, the sound scraping against my ears, making them bleed.

Who is she?

"Is it okay if I call you by your name? You are my mother-in-law, Kesa," he spat her name out like it was poison on his tongue.

Kesa. The supreme goddess.

My stomach sunk lower into me. Lynn had told me how she met Kesa, and I had ignored her because I was horny. All the signs had been there, and I had been oblivious to them. How could I have been so stupid? No wonder why Lynn kept coming back here. She needed the help of the most powerful goddess.

Kesa snarled at Eilam, "You are not my family. Neither is Aniya. She lost her grace the day she fell in love with you — Where are her wings?"

Eilam chuckled. "I took them back. It was you who made them untouchable by others except the one who cut them off. Did you not think I would return for my wife's wings?"

He had cut off his own wife's wings? How old is he, and how many lives has he lived? And how — how did he manage to marry the goddess of soulmates and seven winds? Hearing him speak with Kesa explained so much about him and his love for his lost love.

"I thought you were dead. I did not need to concern myself with a pest coming back to take them. Now tell me where they are!"

"No, I'm good. See, you no longer have something over me. My wife is safe from you. She is happy, healthy, and cared for. That was what you had once promised me, but now that you can't offer me any of those things, I do not need to answer you or do your bidding. Sorry Kesa, but you lost this time."

"Love has blinded you for so long now that you could never see things for what they are. Your dear wife is not sleeping soundly in the castle above. She is, however, unconscious somewhere far away from you and her precious Seventh Ghost. But don't worry, the serpence King is with her. They should wake up any time now. Too bad it is not next to their mates."

Lynn, Esen. What does this have to do with them? Where is Esen and Eilam's wife? Who is his wife? My heart pounded against my chest at the realization. The thin scar on my finger burned in unison.

Alya.

I looked at Eilam, horrified at the realization that I had prattled on about being in love with Alya, his wife, and he had encouraged my emotions. Why did he never tell me? How the fuck have I never been told she is married and that she is a goddess?

Shit.

She did try to tell me, but I pushed her away because I wanted to savor the dance.

Do Lynn and Esen know?

"If you hurt her again, I swear no god or power will save you from the pain I will ensure you receive."

Kesa chuckled. "She is my daughter. I will do with her as I please. You, Eilam, can not save her or the others. Best you do what you do best and leave her behind."

Eilam's hand fell off my wrist as he lunged at the goddess. I didn't have time to stop him and tell him he would not harm her. He realized it as soon as she struck a hand through his chest. Eilam once more became a shadow.

Kesa was disgusting.

People have spoken about her auburn hair being the most beautiful in all the realms and how her green eyes shone brighter than emeralds. But as I looked at her, all I saw was someone disgusting. Not an ounce of beauty in her.

Her green eyes looked at me as she cocked her head to the side, her arm stretched out, and a finger pointed at me.

"Why have I never seen you before?"

I didn't know what to say. If she is the seer, then she was never in the Below when I should have gone to get my reading done. And I never came in here with Lynn because I never liked how the place felt and thought it best to stay outside to make sure no one came in.

Kesa approached me, jerked my head to the side, and examined me. "What are you?" She breathed onto me.

The world around me disappeared into blackness. My limbs grew weak as I fell into nothingness. I tried to reach out and find something to grab onto as I continued to fall, but there was nothing there.

I could only see a cage with a beautiful white bird curled up next to a black snake. Both slept, unaware of the chaos that would ensue when they awoke.

Made in the USA
Las Vegas, NV
23 July 2024